# RO'CK of Ages

*RO'CK of Ages*, a compilation of Ross O'Carroll-Kelly's most iconic and popular *Irish Times* columns since 2007, is the twenty-third book in Paul Howard's 'Ross O'Carroll-Kelly' series. Ross books have sold over one million copies, are annually nominated for the Popular Fiction prize at the Irish Book Awards – where they have won the prize an unprecedented three times – and are also critically acclaimed as satirical masterpieces. One of the series – *The Oh My God Delusion* – was chosen as Ireland's favourite book in Eason's 125th birthday poll.

T0332826

# RO'CK of Ages

*From Boom Days to Zoom Days*

# ROSS O'CARROLL-KELLY

(as told to Paul Howard)

PENGUIN BOOKS

PENGUIN BOOKS

UK | USA | Canada | Ireland | Australia
India | New Zealand | South Africa

Penguin Books is part of the Penguin Random House group of companies
whose addresses can be found at global.penguinrandomhouse.com.

First published by Sandycove 2021
Published with new material in Penguin Books 2022
001

Copyright © Paul Howard, 2021, 2022

The moral right of the author has been asserted

Typeset by Jouve (UK), Milton Keynes
Printed and bound in Great Britain by Clays Ltd, Elcograf S.p.A.

The authorized representative in the EEA is Penguin Random House Ireland,
Morrison Chambers, 32 Nassau Street, Dublin D02 YH68

A CIP catalogue record for this book is available from the British Library

ISBN: 978-0-241-99312-5

To Mary and Pat Crimin.
As owners of Kielys of Donnybrook,
you were Ross O'Carroll-Kelly's surrogate parents
and your pub was his home from home.
His Nag's Head, his Winchester Club, his Rover's Return.
But, mostly, it was his muse.
There are not enough words –
so instead all I can say is . . .

Thank you x

# 2007

The Dublin Port Tunnel is opened * Ireland crush England 43–13 on the day Croke Park opens its doors to rugby * A General Election results in a Fianna Fáil/Green Party coalition government * Apple introduces the first iPhone * Ireland are eliminated from the Rugby World Cup at the group phase following defeats to France and Argentina * The American economy goes into recession, fuelled by the subprime mortgage crisis, which triggers an eventual worldwide financial collapse * Economic commentators begin to speculate about the likely end of the period of economic growth known as the Celtic Tiger * There is an explosion of interest in a new SMS-based communications platform called Twitter *

Meanwhile . . .

'You gave them everything – including my Z4.'
*The Irish Times, 1 September 2007*

'Have you seen her yet?'

That's what he goes to me, over his shoulder, sitting on the bench in front of me.

I'm like, 'Who?' and he's there, 'Herself, Ross. Madam! No invite to the gorden party this year. Understandable,' he goes, flicking his thumb in the direction of the judge, 'in the circumstances.'

I'm there, 'I've already told you – I only go in there to pick up my expenses. And you've a lot more to worry about than gorden porties. You're looking at a five-stretch here. How the fock could you do it – as in, like, plead guilty?'

He's like, 'Because I am guilty, Ross – according to the standards by which I'm being judged.'

I go, 'I thought you'd put up a fight. What about all that stuff you said to me about the gleaming new Ireland, with infrastructure and investment and full employment, and how that was always your vision of the future, and the vision of all those others currently being pilloried before the tribunals?'

He doesn't answer.

I'm there, 'You just want to be a mortyr – for all your mates out in Portmornock. I can't believe you settled with the Revenue . . .'

'And the Criminal Assets Bureau,' he goes, not ashamed of it or anything.

I'm like, 'You gave them everything – including my Z4. Have you any idea what an actual dickhead you are?'

The judge goes, 'I'm sure we're all very interested in your Z4, whatever that might be, but if you two are quite finished, we'll proceed with the case . . .'

The end comes unbelievably quickly.

His barrister – his new barrister, who actually doesn't look that much

3

older than me – basically holds his hands up and goes, okay, my client admits basically everything, but please go easy on him and shit?

'Listen to that cloying sycophant,' Hennessy goes. He's sitting next to me in the public gallery. 'Oh, yes, he's going all the way to the top, that one – tongue up all the right holes in the Law Library . . .'

Hennessy would never have let the old man plead guilty, which is why the old man dropped him like Honours Physics.

At four o'clock on day two of the so-called trial, the judge tells the old man to stand up, which he does.

'Charles O'Carroll-Kelly,' he goes, 'whatever private beliefs you hold, the crimes of which you are guilty were not victimless crimes. As a property developer, you paid bribes in order to subvert the proper planning process and you did it in the name of greed. Most of your developments went ahead against the wishes and better advice of local authority planners, whose job it was to ensure a sensible and balanced growth for the city and county of Dublin. In doing so, you helped to create a legacy of social problems in many of the city's poorer areas . . .'

Oh my God, if they're going to blame him for Ranelagh, he's going to end up getting life here.

'Your systematic evasion of tax was part of a general culture of avoidance, which deprived the Irish economy of billions of euros per annum, starving public services such as schools and hospitals of money . . .'

It goes without saying that Ronan's loving this. He's sat beside me, roysh, turned around in his seat, telling total strangers that that's his granddad up there in the dock, and that if he'd named names he'd be sleeping in his own bed tonight, but he didn't.

'He kept that shut,' he goes, pointing to his mouth. 'First rule of the underwurdled.'

'In sentencing you,' the judge goes, 'I must give due regard to your cooperation in this matter. Once some measure of corruption was discovered, you came clean, saving the Gardaí thousands of man-hours following the complex paper trail that constituted your personal finances for the best part of your life. I note, too, that you have been an exemplary remand prisoner and the governor and staff of Mountjoy jail have been lavish in their praise of the leadership role you have assumed amongst your fellow prisoners. You have started, I understand, a prison rugby team, helping at least four long-term heroin addicts to achieve complete withdrawal from soccer.

'I hope that, upon your release, you will continue to work with those who have never enjoyed the same privileges as you and that this work will be part of your reparation to the community . . .

'However, given the scale of your dishonesty – and, in particular, your abuse of public office – I am going to impose a custodial sentence. And that sentence is two and a half years' imprisonment. You look like you have something to say, Mr O'Carroll-Kelly,' and everyone, like, suddenly sits forward in their seats.

And all the old man goes – the only words he speaks in two days sitting there – is, 'With respect, Your Honour, it would be wrong to interpret my – inverted commas – cooperation with the Criminal Assets Bureau and the Revenue Commissioners as an indicator of remorse on my part. I feel none. Thank you.'

And then it's back to the can with him.

As he's being led away, Ronan shouts, 'Don't woody about it, Charlie – we'll boorst you out of there,' and everyone in the courtroom just, like, cracks up laughing, obviously thinking it's a joke.

Outside, I notice the goys – we're talking Oisinn, JP and Fionn. Nice of them to turn up. And they're talking to someone.

A bird.

And I'd know that €2,000 Emilio Pucci kaftan anywhere.

It's Sorcha.

I tip over. It's, like, a hug from my estranged wife and high-fives from the goys.

'Result, Dude!' JP goes. 'With remission, and the time he's already served, the goy'll be out for Chrimbo.'

I'm there, 'Yeah, no, I suppose,' and then I look up to see my son being led out of court by two Gords, shouting, 'Let go of me, your doorty collaborating fooks!'


## 'Rugby has become soft porn for women.'
### *The Irish Times*, 22 September 2007

I've always been a thick and thin goy. For the past couple of weeks, roysh, when everyone else was going, 'Oh my God, this Irish team is a total disgrace, I can't *actually* believe I spent my SSIA coming to the World Cup,' I was the only one defending them.

You see, Drico, Rog, Shaggy, Dorce – those are heroes to me, because here in Kitty O'Shea's, in the hort of Paris, it's easy to see the bigger picture. It's, like, wall-to-wall scenario in here, we're talking cat-walk material everywhere you look, and it's like, how many of these birds would be in this battle cruiser tonight if we didn't have the best-looking backs in the world?

Rugby has become soft porn for women, like *Grey's Anatomy* and anything with Jonathan Rhys-what's-his-face in it.

So my eyes are everywhere. It's like, 'Look at her – Pink Juicy Couture t-shirt. Or her friend – Chanel Sunglasses. Or look at No Sunglasses . . .'

'Ross,' Fionn goes, trying to burst my bubble, 'are you part-Cherokee?'

It's like, laugh it up, Four Eyes. I'm the one who ended up bringing a total Vanessa Hudgens lookalike back to the hotel last night and – far be it from me to write my own reviews here – I was so good that the people next door lit up a cigarette afterwards.

So, like I say, the night before the France game, I'm a happy bunny – or rather I am until the moment when I get a sudden whiff of Issey Miyake and I spin around to find a piece of my past standing ten yords away, telling the borman that she asked for the Château Gaudrelle Vouvray and this is *so* not it.

I'm about to go over to her – she's still my *actual* wife – when I suddenly cop who she's with.

I'd heard the rumours that she was back seeing Cillian, that accountant tosser she went travelling with a few years ago. What I mean by travelling is that they spent twelve months in Sydney – County Bondi – seeing a lot of the local Western Union branch, where her old man would wire her enough money to keep her 10,000 miles away from Slick Mick here.

'Oh my God!' she goes when she sees me and for a minute I can't make out whether it's, like, a good oh my God or a bad one. But then she comes over and throws her orms around me and tells me it's *so* great to see me.

I'm playing it cool as a fish's fart. I'm like, 'What are *you* doing here?'

'It was a surprise from Cillian – for our fifth anniversary,' she goes, and then she corrects herself. 'Well, we *met* for the first time five years ago.' And I'm there, 'Jesus Christ, you got married and had, like, a kid with me in the meantime – it's hordly an anniversary.'

I'm looking at Cillian over her shoulder and he's, like, chatting away to Fionn and Oisinn, the traitors.

I'm there, 'Is he still working for Pricewaterhouse-whatever-the-fock?' and she doesn't answer, roysh, but she doesn't need to, because the goy's still in his Magee suit with his security ID cord attached to his belt, like the total geek that he is.

I can't even begin to tell you how much it actually bothers me that she's found someone – and it's not just because it's him.

I'll put it to you this way. About a month ago I went for a bit of physio – if I'm going to go back playing serious rugby, I've got to get my ligamentum nuchae problems sorted once and for all. So I'm in the waiting room, bored out of my tree, and, believe it or not, I stort *reading*, as in one of the magazines – *Time*, or one of those – and there's an orticle in it about Steve Wynn, billionaire casino owner and serious player – a man I can relate to, in other words.

Said in the orticle, roysh, that he rang Donald Trump up one day and went, 'Just want you to know – my wife and I are getting divorced,' and of course Donald Trump was like, 'Hey, I'm sorry to hear that,' but Steve Wynn goes, 'Don't be sorry. It's cool – we're still madly in love. We just don't want to be married any more.'

So five years later, roysh, the two goys bump into each other in Vegas and Steve Wynn's like, 'Hey, did you hear – Elaine and I are getting remarried?'

So obviously Donald Trump's there, 'Oh – what about the divorce?' and Steve Wynn goes, 'The divorce? Well, it just didn't work out.'

I thought me and Sorcha were going to be like that. Suddenly I'm not so sure.

I look over her shoulder again. Oisinn and Fionn are cracking their holes laughing at something Cillian's said, my so-called second and fourth best friends in the world.

Eventually, the dude comes over to where me and Sorcha are standing. I think about being a dick to him, but in the end I don't. Because suddenly I'm thinking about Peter Stringer, one of my all-time heroes, and the way he took the news that he was dropped for tomorrow's game.

See, people think Strings is the smallest man on the Ireland team when really he's the biggest.

So here's what I do.

I go, 'Have you got tickets for the game?'

Cillian goes, 'No, we're still looking. A friend of mine – he's with A&L Goodbody – he said he might be able to source a couple,' and while he's still bullshitting away, I reach into my back pocket and I whip out two Wilsons and hand them to Sorcha.

'Here you are,' I go, 'rare as rocking-horse shit. Six rows from the actual sideline.'

Of course, they're pretty much speechless.

'Thanks,' they both eventually go.

And I'm like, 'Hey – it's nothing.'

And, well, it literally *was* nothing. They're Fionn and Oisinn's tickets.

## 'I know a little bit of what Ronan O'Gara's going through.'
### *The Irish Times, 29 September 2007*

Miracles – it's like, when do they *ever* happen?

I mean JP would have been tracking that more than the rest of us, having spent two years in Maynooth.

I'm standing around with the goys, watching Ireland take port in an open training session in Paris.

'Four tries,' I hear myself go, 'against Orgentina – you'd have to say the World Cup is going to be over for us on Monday night.'

'Miracles happen,' someone goes.

It's Lorraine, the Limerick bird that Oisinn pulled last weekend in St Tropez. The usual fare for him. Looks like she's been hit in the face with a bag of bent euros.

'What about the miracle of Gloucester?' she goes.

I'm like, 'That'd depend on your point of view. I actually prayed that Munster *wouldn't* get that fourth try – and they did. So it was, like, no miracle for me. It was, like, the opposite and shit?'

Oisinn's looking at me as if to say, Dude, quit while you're ahead. She already hates my guts for singing 'the *three* proud provinces of Ireland' in Kitty O'Shea's last night.

'I still say you should get somebody to look at that arm,' she goes – yeah, no, typical nurse. 'You're terribly pale, Ross.'

I am feeling a bit weak actually, though I'm not going to admit that. I'm like, 'Hey, I've had *way* worse than this.'

The orm – I probably should explain why it's bandaged up.

We were on, like, a major downer after the defeat to France, roysh, so

8

me and the goys decided to hit St Tropez, where Fionn's old pair have, like, an aportment. It has to be said, roysh, it's some spot down there – we're talking sun, sea and Celia Holman Lee everywhere you look.

The only drawback, you'd have to say, is the competition – we're talking serious steroid junkies here, with bodies so brown they look like they've been swimming next to the sewage effluent. It'd take a lot to make me feel inadequate, but two hours on the beach and not a single female's given me a second George Hook.

I latched onto this total cracker – the spit of Hayden Panettiere – and I was stood over her while she was sunbathing, telling her that, as an outhalf myself, I know a little bit of what Ronan O'Gara's going through, which is why I sent him a text after the match, reminding him that form is temporary, but class is permanent, and he'll always be a hero to me and millions of others.

Turns out she's Spanish – she wouldn't know Rog if she fell over him in the bookies – but she did tell me to move because I was blocking her sun and then some dude who looked like he'd been held down and stuffed with watermelons came over and gave me a look that said, basically, beat it.

I took my red cord like a man, faced the walk of shame back to the goys and we ended up hitting this, like, seafood restaurant, right on the beachfront, to talk about the fact that, after seven or eight years out of rugby, we weren't the young gods we used to be.

Then – after four or five looseners, of course – Oisinn had an idea. The restaurant had all these dead fish, roysh, laid out on crushed ice in this, like, display case at the front – and right in the middle was this, like, baby sharpnose shark.

'What we need to do,' he went, suddenly stuffing it up his shirt, 'is create some kind of diversion. Come on.'

We followed him back down the beach and the next thing we're all at the water's edge and Oisinn's going, 'Ross, give me your orm,' and before I had a chance to go, 'Er – as in why?' he grabbed it and clamped the shark's mouth around it.

He was like, 'Quit struggling. It's dead – it can't hurt you. Look, birds love a hero – you of all people should know that.'

The goy knows what buttons to press with me.

'I'm just going to apply a little bit of pressure,' he went, 'just to leave a mark. Then you crack on you're wrestling with it. Honestly, Ross, in half an hour, you're going to be fighting the birds off with a speargun.'

'Okay,' I went, still a bit Scooby Dubious about this as he laid my orm down in, like, a foot of water. I was like, 'But just barely break the skin.'

This, like, evil smile crossed his face. He jumped, like, three feet in the air and suddenly brought eighteen stone of pure lord down on top of the shark's head.

It was, like, me who screamed first. Then I was joined by a couple of hundred others, most of them women and children, having total conniptions at the sight of me, thrashing about in the water, blood everywhere and a shark literally locked onto my orm.

It *was* hilarious, looking back on it now.

My neck is suddenly itchy and I'm scratching like a man on the Luas red line.

'Thanks for the text,' I hear a voice go. I turn around and it's Rog himself. Then he's suddenly squinting his eyes at me, going, 'Are you feeling okay, boy?'

I'm like, 'Me? Cool as a bucket of free beer,' but I'm not. I'm feeling seriously Moby here.

And then Rog disappears and I realize that I'm, like, *hallucinating*?

'Jesus, look at his neck,' I hear Lorraine go. 'Ross, you've got septi-caemia,' and that's the last thing I hear before I feel the ground reach up and hit me full in the face.

I wake up in a hospital somewhere in Paris, with the goys around the bed, struggling not to laugh in my face.

'They might be able to save the arm,' JP goes. 'If you believe in miracles, that is.'

## 'Her nayum's Blathin!'
### *The Irish Times, 6 October 2007*

One of my, I suppose, biggest problems is that I think too, like, *deeply* about shit? Like the other day, roysh, I'm in the scratcher, flicking through one of the old dear's *VIP*s, and there, all of a sudden, is a pic-ture of that Cian O'Connor with Georgina Bloomberg, the Mayor of New York's daughter, and of course my instant reaction is, there's something seriously Not Quite Right there.

I mean, it goes without saying that I'm in a different league to Cian O'Connor looks-wise, but then I'm thinking, actually maybe I picked the wrong sport all those years ago.

Okay, I do alright scenario-wise, but that horsey set – it's, like, a whole other world. We're talking looks, we're talking brains, we're talking serious wedge – plus, as anyone who's ever been to the Horse Show knows, they're banging like dodgem cors.

So I'm, like, deep in contemplation about all of this when the old Theobold rings and a little voice goes, 'Rosser – I want to arrange a meet.'

It can only be my son, Ronan.

I'm like, 'Cool – as in where?'

And he goes, 'I'm not saying it over the blower – it's a party line,' which is working class for the Gords are listening in, which, of course, they're not.

He goes, 'There's a phone buke on the hall table downstayurs, with a page turdened down – go and gerrit.'

Like a fool, I end up doing what he tells me. The page folded down is, like, pubs and restaurants and he's drawn a big black circle with morker around the name of a café on, like, Capel Street.

I'm like, 'How the fock did you get in here to do this?' but he just goes, 'Loose lips, Rosser – just be there at one.'

It's, like, hord for parents who don't have full custody of their kids, but I hope Britney Spears doesn't have to go through this shit to see hers.

He's waiting for me when I arrive, sitting at the table furthest from the door. 'One too many window-shoppers,' he goes, winking at me.

A window-shopper is, like, an undercover cop. I'm learning fast.

He's there, 'How was the rubby?'

I'm like, 'Pretty shit actually. We went out in the first round and I was the one who predicted we'd win the actual thing,' and I catch the eye of this waitress and ask for two full breakfasts.

There's, like, something different about Ronan, something I can't put my finger on, roysh, but after listening to five minutes of him babbling on about police harassment, I finally cop what it is.

He's got, like, gel in his hair and he's wearing aftershave. I know what's coming even before he says it.

'Ine arthur meeting a boord,' he goes.

I end up actually punching the air and going, 'Yes!' He really is a chip off the old block.

I'm there, 'You're a sly old dog, aren't you?' and for the first time since I first met him, roysh, he actually gets embarrassed and storts giving it. 'Ah, leave it, Rosser!'

Two breakfasts arrive. I don't know what's uglier – the waitress or what's on the plate.

'So come on,' I go, 'who is she?'

He's there, 'Her nayum's Blathin.'

And I'm like, 'Blathin?' having expected him to say, I don't know, Tracy, or Nathalie, or Shadden. 'Blathin? Where did you, like, meet her and shit?'

He's there, 'She's in Mount Anville – the junior school. We're doing *Grease* with them – modorden day, set in Mulhuddart.'

I'm like, 'Mulhuddart? Jesus!'

He goes, 'So I offered to take her out there, show her some of the sights. She's playing Santhra Dee, see. She's from out your direction – Clonskeagh.'

I'm suddenly thinking, oh my God, I know he's only ten, but is it time to have the chat – as in, *the* chat? I mean, they say it's important that kids are given the facts, so that in years to come they know what's what and they grow up with a responsible attitude towards the other thing.

I go, 'Ronan, when a goy meets a bird –' but he cuts me off, roysh, and he's like, 'Rosser, if you knew the foorst thing about the boords and the bees, then I wouldn't be here today,' which is basically true – bang out of order but basically true.

He goes, 'Look, thee teach us all that in Biodogy now – a speerm cell swims through the cervix and across the length of the uterdus and fuses with the ovum to form a zygote.'

I'm there, 'Whoah – TMI, Ronan! T-M-I! I don't know if you've noticed, but I'm actually *trying* to eat a fried egg here?'

What was wrong with the way we learned it? It's a man's occupation to stick his coculation in a woman's ventilation to increase the population of the younger generation of the world!

I'm like, 'So if it's not the big fatherly chat you're looking for, what am I actually doing here?'

'I just wanted to let you know,' he goes, 'in case you read it in the *Wurdled* on Sunday – Ine going straight . . .'

I'm like, 'Straight? As in?'

He goes, 'Ine keeping the old snout clean from now on,' and then he thinks for a minute and goes, 'Look, brace yourself, Rosser – be hodest with you, I was nebber as deep into croyum as I told you. Lot of it was just thalk. Threams, I suppose.'

I'm there going, 'No way!' because you have to humour this kid.

He nods sort of, like, sadly.

Then I ask the question that's been in the back of my mind since he mentioned Clonskeagh.

I'm there, 'So, er, have her old pair met you yet?'

'Bit eardy for that,' he goes. 'Sure we're only arthur been texting a week. Why?'

I'm there, 'No, I just wondered are they –?'

What I mean to say is – are they like *my* old pair? In the end I don't say shit, just let my voice trail off.

I look down. He hasn't touched his breakfast. I nod at it and go, 'The trick is to eat it before the fat congeals on the plate.'

'I caddent eat,' he goes.

Can't eat. Can't stop smiling. We've all been there.

# 2008

Bertie Ahern resigns as Taoiseach and is succeeded by Brian Cowen *
The Irish economy enters recession for the first time since 1983 *
€4 billion is wiped off the Irish Stock Exchange in a single day as the
world economic crisis deepens * Eddie O'Sullivan resigns as head
coach after Ireland finish fourth in the Six Nations, the team's lowest
standing since 1999 * In a referendum, Ireland votes to reject the EU's
Lisbon Treaty * Dustin the Turkey is eliminated in the group stages of
the Eurovision Song Contest in Belgrade, Serbia * Fears about the
liquidity of Ireland's banks result in long queues of people withdraw-
ing their savings * Munster beat Toulouse 16–12 in Cardiff to win their
second Heineken Cup * The Irish government announces a €400 billion guarantee to prevent the collapse of six banks due to the worldwide
economic crisis * The Large Hadron Collider is inaugurated in Swit-
zerland * Barack Obama is elected the 44th president of the United
States * Starbucks opens in Dalkey, amid protests from locals about
creeping globalization * 25,000 people take part in a so-called Grey
March in Dublin as Ireland's OAPs protest against the removal of the
automatic right to a medical card * The words 'mansplain' and 'photo-
bomb' enter *The Oxford English Dictionary* *

Meanwhile . . .

Wednesday lunchtime and I'm hanging, it has to be said. Long story, but last weekend I chatted up this Kim Kardashian lookalike who works in the VHI office on Lower Abbey Street and who turns out to be from, like, Offaly of all places.

So Tuesday night I took her for a few scoops and inevitably – if that's the word – she suggested taking it on to Copper Face Jack's.

Now, I'm not afraid to say it, I've pulled hundreds of girls in there in my time – better a country girl than an empty bed, is practically my motto. But I've never brought a girl *to* Coppers, and there ended up being a huge row at the door when I went to pay in and they tried to chorge me for corkage.

I'm in the sack remembering all of this when I suddenly hear the opening bors from 'Don't Stop Believing'. I check caller ID and it's the old man. I was going to obviously ignore it, roysh, but then I remember that my cor insurance is due.

'Sorry to disturb,' is his opening line. 'I expect you're watching the news – glued to it, I'd say.'

I'm there, 'Sorry, have we met before?'

'Gone, Kicker – can you believe it? We may never see his like again.'

I'm there, 'I need two grand. Actually, make it three.'

'Hennessy rang as soon as he heard. He's seen sense and gone, he said – and that's a direct quote. I thought he was going to go on forever, he said. Cling jealously to power despite all the allegations of corruption, while the country became an international embarrassment. It says something, Ross, that for the first twenty minutes of the conversation I thought we were talking about Robert Mugabe.'

I'm like, 'Yeah, whatever. Just ring the Sherman, will you? I want that bread this afternoon.'

'But oh, no,' he goes. 'Turns out he was talking about your friend and mine. My old jousting partner, aka Mr Bartholomew Patrick

Ahern . . . and it's the oddest thing, Ross. I'm feeling quite emotional. It's rather like that deep burgundy wallpaper I had on the wall of the study – I thought I hated it, but now that it's gone, I'm not so sure I did.'

I'm there, 'Er, sorry, all of this affects me *how* exactly?'

'Oh, he was no friend of rugby, Ross, I'll grant you that. Let's not forget the role he played in you and I having to go to bloody well Dorset Street to see Ireland play rugby. Him and that Manchester Football Club of his. I won't take back the promise I made four years ago to the voters of Dún Laoghaire-Rathdown – tough on soccer, tough on the causes of soccer.'

I'm like, 'Have you been drinking?'

'You're damn right I've been drinking!' he goes. 'Hennessy and I thought we'd mork the occasion by tucking into that crate of Château Ducru-Beaucaillou Saint-Julien we picked up when Berry Bros. & Rudd had that sale.'

'But it's, like, one o'clock in the day.'

'Well, I won't stay on the line long,' he goes. 'I expect *Six One* will be ringing, looking for my reaction. I'll tell that blasted Dobson what I think – shame on you! A good man, coursed by the bloody dogs of the press and their handlers down at Dublin Castle.'

I'm there, 'You've changed your tune. Mr Dis Dat Dees and Dohs, you used to call him.'

'Well,' he goes, 'we've a lot more in common than I would have ever dared to imagine. I don't have a monopoly on pain and humiliation, Ross. We've both suffered. Both been forced in front of these Star Chambers to answer their piffling little questions. Where did this cheque come from? Where did that cheque come from? "Excuse me, Counsel, you eat lobster thermidor for your lunch every day only because of us – me and Bertie and our kind." People who remember this country when it was a dark, TB-ridden island on the edge of the world, where it rained 366 days a year and it took six months to get a bloody phone put in. Public servants who cared enough about Ireland to want to change it, modernize it – so you show me some respect when you address me.'

I'm there, 'You need to lie down.'

'No, Ross,' he goes. 'I need to stand up. Because I've sat idly through a decade of this. A long line of great men. Dermot. Denis . . . Men of ingenuity, men of vision – men I've taken quite a lot of money from on the golf course over the years, I hope they won't mind me saying – treated like common criminals. We turned this country around. It wasn't your *Irish Times*. It wasn't your friends in the Law Library.'

In the background, I can hear Hennessy go, 'You tell the sons of bitches, Charlie Boy,' obviously just as mashed as he is.

'It was us, Ross. *We're* the economic boom. *We're* the Celtic Tiger. You think it got here by accident? Without us, the bloody Irish would still be cleaning their teeth with their own shite. I'll be saying that and a lot more when I talk to Dobbo.'

'You're forgetting,' I go, 'you're not allowed to, like, communicate with the media? Under the terms of your, like, temporary release?' That shuts him up. Not for long, though.

'Of course,' he goes, 'threaten me with incarceration lest I speak the truth. Well, Kicker, a great man once said – you can jail a man, but you can't jail an idea.'

'I think *that* was Robert Mugabe,' I hear Hennessy go.

The old man's like, 'Oh, was it? Might ask m'learned friend to strike it from the record, then.'

'It's done,' Hennessy goes.

I'm there, 'Dude, having a deranged old sot for a mother is bad enough without you going down the same road. Now I need that moolah. Are you sober enough to ring the bank?'

'Never thought I'd catch myself saying it,' is the last thing he says to me, 'but I liked Bertie. I liked him a lot,' and then I hear a loud crash as all sixteen stone of him crashes through what I presume is Hennessy's coffee table.

### 'I'm in Dalkey – protesting against the opening of the new Storbucks.'
### *The Irish Times*, 14 June 2008

You can hear Christian's excitement, even down the phone line. Lauren's only got, like, two or three days to go and the poor dude's up to ninety.

'She hasn't enjoyed being pregnant,' he goes. 'Says those nine months felt like nine years. Of hard labour.'

'Tell me about it,' I go. 'I didn't enjoy it myself. I remember telling Sorcha the day before Honor arrived, this thing better shit diamonds when it finally gets here. But it *will* be worth it – you'll see.'

Then I call him young padawan, because, well, I know he likes it, the lunatic.

'Speaking of Sorcha,' he suddenly goes, 'Lauren was talking to her yesterday. She's *not* going to Beijing now . . .'

I'm like, 'Er, no.'

'And her and Cillian are finished . . .'

'Apparently. Big-time bummer, huh?'

He's like, 'Ross, make sure she's alright, will you? Don't want to be telling tales out of school but Lauren said she sounded, I don't know, funny on the phone. You *know* what she's like.'

Which is true. She takes shit like this really badly – I know when *we* broke up, she went Hertz Van Rental. Threw herself into all sorts – trying to save dudes on death row who deserved every volt they got and animals that were focked one way or the other.

So later that day, roysh, I'm thinking about her, as I often do, and I decide to give her a quick Jonny Bell. And let's just say it's a good job I do. I knew she was capable of doing something crazy, but I wasn't quite ready for what she hits me with.

'I'm in Dalkey,' she goes, 'protesting against the opening of the new Storbucks.'

Now pretty much everyone knows how I feel about Buckys, so you can imagine me. I'm like, '*Stay* where you are. Don't even think about burning it down,' and I'm straight out to Dalkey.

I throw the beast in the church cor pork and I literally peg it up the Main Street.

There's a humungous crowd blocking the path just next to the bank, though I can pick Sorcha out from, like, fifty yords back. She's wearing the Julien Macdonald pewter Jersey tunic she stung me for last Christmas and her skinny Sevens and she's holding a placard that, when I get closer, says, 'Say No to Cappuccino Capitalism!'

I'm like, 'Jesus, look at the state of you all – it's a coffee shop, not a focking strip club.'

Without even looking at me, she goes, 'I happen to care about the world in which I live, Ross. I bet you haven't even *voted* today?'

I give her a blank look.

She's like, 'As in Lisbon?'

Oh, yeah, I heard about that on the radio.

'But that doesn't affect *me*,' I go and she shakes her head, roysh, and tells me I am – oh my God – *so* uninformed, which she means as a bad thing.

'All I know is you *love* Storbucks,' I go. 'Almost as much as I do. You've got, like, fourteen mugs from all over the world, remember?'

'This isn't *about* their coffee,' she goes, 'which I admit is amazing, especially their new Kopelani Blend. It's about globalization, Ross, threatening the fabric of our unique villages.'

I look at the other protesters. It's, like, some mix of people. All the local yummy mummies. Then a bunch of unhappy looking teenage types – the kind of weirdos who stay up all night playing games online instead of getting their bit.

'So these are your new friends?' I go. 'MILFs and soap-dodgers?'

'Don't give me that,' she goes, 'Chloe and Sophie are heavily involved too,' and it's only then I notice them – Tweedle Dumb and Tweedle Double-D. They're holding Honor and she's got, like, her own little placard, a tiny thing, that says, 'Dalkey Says No to Cultural Imperialism!'

I'm *so* not having that. My daughter was practically raised in Storbucks – went straight from breastmilk onto the decaf chai lattes.

I snatch the placard out of her hand. Sophie asks me – oh my God – *what* is my problem and it all of a sudden storts spewing out.

'This,' I go. 'It's all horseshit. I don't exactly know what capitalism is but I'm pretty sure Dalkey's not against it. There's actual *council* houses in this town selling for a million snots. *Your* old man made the *Sunday Times* Rich List, Sophie – what was it, four hundred mills? Chloe, you grew up on Coliemore focking Road.'

Then I turn to Sorcha – I'm on, like, a roll now? – and I go, 'You *worked* in Storbucks in Chicago for a summer. You said they paid really well and you'd better health insurance then someone in, like, Goldman Sachs. You're always banging on about how they give those coffee farmers a fair price – which sounds a bit wrong to me, but to each his own. Why is everyone so down on, like, Storbucks?'

Sorcha suddenly turns to me, roysh, her face full of hate.

'Just because they're not environment-damaging, Third World-exploiting corporate bullies,' she goes, 'doesn't mean we should just let them morch in here and crush our own indigenous businesses. They're the benign face of American cultural expansion – globalization with froth on top – and if you can't see that, Ross, then you've been duped by the warm, sticky feeling you get inside when you sit in one of their oversized sofas with your white chocolate mocha . . .'

It's when she mentions white chocolate mocha that I suddenly realize what this is *really* about. It's actually personal. See, I took away something she loved. Now she wants to do the same to me.

'You'll come round,' I go, 'the minute they launch the new summer frappuccino flavours.'

She's like, 'Don't count on it,' giving me the big-time evils. 'Do not count on it.'

## 'You can't knock the Rock! You can't knock the Rock!'
### *The Irish Times, 30 August 2008*

'Poor kids didn't have much of a summer,' Father McCalman goes. 'You might say it was an Iraqi summer – occasionally Sunni but mostly Shi'ite.'

His voice echoes in the humungous entrance hall and I'm, like, instantly brought back to my own first day here. The big classrooms. The teachers in their gowns. Terrified. Shitting Baileys.

I look at Ronan, standing there in his little blazer, putting on the hord-man face, ink spot under his eye. I can't believe we've come to this day already. I ask him if he's okay and he says he's moostard.

'No doubt you'll know all about the proud history of the school from your father,' McCalman goes. He's walking, like, four or five steps ahead of us, banging on. 'Four rugby internationals, five government ministers, two of Ireland's top twenty captains of industry and one Oscar nominee.'

I notice that I'm not included in the list but I'm big enough to let it go.

I'm there, 'Lot of big hitters, in other words. The important thing is not to be, like, intimidated?'

Ronan's like, 'Intimidated? I wouldn't know how to spell the bleaten woord.'

Neither would I. Literally. I hope they do a better job educating him than they did me.

We turn into the corridor that leads to, like, the main assembly hall and end up running straight into Fionn.

He's there, 'Hey, Ross,' glasses on him, the usual. 'Father. Ronan. Hey, Ro, I've got you for History and English.'

'Ah, nice one,' Ronan goes, not knowing Fionn like I do.

'Hey, Ross,' Fionn goes, 'remember when this was us? Our orientation day? Top dogs in the junior school, then we came here . . .'

I'm there, 'Yeah, no, when you're that age, everyone who's older than you seems like an actual grown-up, don't they? That can be, like, pretty frightening.'

'Boys,' Ronan goes, 'I was there in Albufeira when Fat Johnny Mitchum put six fooken caps in Gull Burden. I helped Winker and Nudger caddy him to the hospitoddle. Lost three pints of claret. Most of it, I ended up weerding.

'I was in The Jolly Hangman in Finglas the night thee sprayed the place, looking to get Nudger's brutter. Bullet split me Selma Blair – me Ma had to turden it into a side-parting.

'I was there in the back of the car when it all kicked off after Whitney Houston at the Point. On the M50, minding usser own business, when the Westies start squirting metal our way.'

I look at Father McCalman, who's obviously thinking, what the fock is happening to this school?

'Buckets of Blood took four slugs,' Ronan goes, 'lost conthrol of the wheel. We ended up getting thrun off the motorway into a field. Had to pop me own shoulder back in that night – fook-all to kill the pain except a mouthful of brake fluid.'

I make a sign to McCalman to say, basically, don't worry, it's all in his head.

'So if you think Ine godda be skeered of a bunch of Tristans and fooken Tiernans.'

'Come on, then,' Fionn goes. 'Mr McGahy's about to start the orientation address.'

We stort walking again, the four of us, towards the double doors at the end of the corridor. You can already hear, like, the clamour inside.

'I was there the day Nudger did a runner from the Fowur Courts,' Ronan goes. 'Brief said he was looking at a five-stretch – a five-stretch? For a fooken jump-over? Fedda said he couldn't do any more boord. Two weeks he lived in our coalshed – middle of bleaten winthor. Law found him. Big fooken muckers. Took eight of them to take us down – with thruncheons . . .'

I look at the photographs lining the walls. Black-and-white pictures of pretty much every school team going back to the 1920s. My old man's up there somewhere. And me and the goys.

'I was there in Dublin Tattoo Solutions,' Ronan goes, 'the day Andy Cahill got fooken shanked. He was getting a dotted line put across his billy goat. Mad, cos Dosser Raymond comes in – the doorty-looken doort boord – puts a blade up again it. Phut! Andy's head's flapping around like a fooken windsock.'

From inside the assembly hall, we can hear the clamour building. They're, like, chanting something.

'I've seen things'd make your teeth itch,' Ronan goes. 'I was there the day they pulled Jemmer O'Toole out of the canal. What was left of him. Reckon he was alive when they thrun him in, thrussed up like a bleaten Christmas toorkey. The fish had eaten he's eyelids, so he's lying there on the bank, just staring up at me. Staring, man. Buckets put his hand on me shoulder and says he, "No one retires from this game, Ro – this game retires you."'

I can hear what it is they're chanting now – that old refrain: 'You can't knock the Rock! You can't knock the Rock!'

'Saw Jody Ormonde one time,' Ronan goes, 'Liffey Vaddey car park – Samurai sword stuck in he's leg. In he's leg! Hit him so hard with the thing, they couldn't get it out. Had to leave it there – two grand's worth of a sword. And Jody walking to the hospital, not a bother on him.'

Fionn opens the double doors and it's like he's just opened an oven. The heat of the place.

The chanting stops and every single head turns our way. A hundred and fifty kids, like Ronan, storting out on a new road, kacking themselves but not wanting anyone to know.

I watch his shoulders drop. I watch his face go pale. I watch him bite his bottom lip.

There's a roar.

'Attention!'

It's McGahy.

I tell Ro that I'll wait outside in the cor for him. And I will – even if it ends up being hours.

'Whatever makes you happy,' he goes, but he's nodding – nodding like the Churchill dog. And I think, who'd be twelve again?

> 'This bloody recession! My old man said
> it wouldn't affect me!'
> *The Irish Times*, 13 September 2008

Fionn wakes me up, roysh, first thing Wednesday morning. I ask him what time it is and he says it's eight o'clock. I'm like, 'Dude, the world better be about to end,' and he goes, 'Well, if you believe certain scarists in the media, Ross, it is.'

Usually, roysh, I'd turn over and go back to sleep, but the thing about sharing an aportment with a goy who won *Blackboard Jungle* three years in a row is that you can end up learning loads of shit, even if most of it is pretty much useless.

So I end up following him out to the kitchen slash living room, and there, sitting in front of the Liza Minnelli with a full fry, is not only Fionn but Oisinn and JP as well.

'We're having an Armageddon breakfast,' Oisinn goes. 'Get some guilt-free, saturated fat in your orteries – you're not going to need them where you're going.'

Fionn must see the look of, like, confusion on my boat because he explains. 'It's the biggest physics experiment ever undertaken. They're using a Large Hadron Collider to re-create the moment when the universe came into existence.'

I shrug my shoulders and go, 'Why bother?' which gets a humungous cheer from the goys, as in, that's pure Ross – total legend.

Fionn – typical teacher – goes, 'Ross, you might as well ask, why did we send a man to the moon?'

We sent a man to the moon? I stare at him for a few seconds, not knowing whether he's ripping the piss or not. I pull one of my *comme ci, comme ça* faces, then burst my fried egg open onto my plate.

'What if this was it?' JP goes. 'I know some of us believe in another life beyond the temporal, and some don't. But what if, when they press that button, there's a blinding flash and Eamonn Holmes's face there storts to melt. And we all know we've got, like, five minutes left on this Earth. Who's your first phone call to?'

'Let's Eat In in Sandyford,' Oisinn goes. 'Get wings delivered,' and that gets a huge laugh.

JP and Fionn both choose their old pairs but I'm torn between, like, Ronan and Sorcha.

I'm like, 'Ro's one of those kids, you know, he'd probably survive the world blowing up – one of his famous schemes – so I'd say it'd be Sorcha. She'd probably still be in a snot with me about something, though – our last five minutes on Earth, we'd be on the phone, as usual, neither of us saying a thing.'

The TV screen is suddenly filled with men in white coats, pulling levers, sending sporks flying.

JP's like, 'What about your family, Ross? Your mum and dad?' and I don't know, roysh, it must be all this talk of, I don't know, death and blahdy blahdy blah, but I suddenly find myself thinking, I suppose, kind thoughts about the two stupid tossers.

I'm suddenly there, 'I'll say this for my old man, I really admire the way he's making a go of things since he got out of prison. Laundering his offshore millions so he can finally go straight.

'And my old dear and her *FO'CK Cooking* programme on TV – yeah, no, it makes me want to spew when I see her licking her lips while handling raw chicken on national television, but it's not the worst thing on RTÉ, is it?'

I hate hearing myself talk like this.

Oisinn's there, 'Okay, big one, goys – if you could have your time on Earth all over again, what would you do differently?'

Fionn goes, 'I'd probably do Physics instead of Orts in UCD. When I won the Young Scientist of the Year award, it should have been a sign that that was the route I was supposed to take. It sounds crazy, but right now I should be a mile under the ground on the French–Swiss border.'

'That doesn't sound crazy,' I go. 'We all wish you were too.'

In fairness, everyone laughs.

JP's there, 'I wouldn't do anything differently, not even turning my back on the priesthood. See, it's our experiences, good and bad, that make up the person that each of us is today. And I'm very happy with who I am today.'

JP will have to be watched – sounds to me like the Krishnas have got to him now.

'If I could change one thing,' Oisinn goes, 'it'd be my final game of online poker. Folding my hand with three 1os and 50k in the pot – what was I thinking?'

I'm suddenly having one of my world famous, I suppose, philosophical moments.

I'm like, 'No offence, goys, but I wouldn't be sitting here with you lot. I'd have my own gaff, probably in LA, sharing with two or three Heidi Montag lookalikes. And everything works by remote control . . .'

Fionn suddenly shushes me. He's like, 'Here we go,' and suddenly we all sit forward in our seats, as a dude in a white coat gets ready to push the button. We hold, like, our breath. He pushes the button.

We wait . . .

And wait . . .

And then suddenly . . .

Fock-all happens.

'Looks like I'm going to work today after all,' Fionn goes, standing up.

I'm like, 'That's it? You got me up in the middle of the night for that?'

He's there, 'Well, not just that, as it turns out. Remember what you were saying there about, you know, having your own gaff? Well, there's probably never going to be a better time for me to bring this up. Ross, I need to rent out your room.'

I'm there, 'Wait a second, that was just like a game we were playing – ultimate fantasies and shit.'

'Look,' he goes, 'I said you could sleep here for a few nights after your old dear kicked you out. But times are hard, Ross. I need to find a proper, paying tenant.'

'This bloody recession!' I go, thumping the actual coffee table. 'My old man said it wouldn't affect me!'

He's like, 'I'll give you a month to find somewhere else.'

Then Oisinn has to chime in.

'Cheer up, Ross,' he goes. 'It's not the end of the world.'


'It said on the news that the banks were going bust!'
*The Irish Times*, 18 October 2008

Sorcha's famous damsel in distress act gets an outing whenever she decides that she might like to, I don't know, be *with* me again? Usually, she'll ring me to come and rescue her from some date that's taken a disastrous turn, where the goy has maybe expressed the view that Whole Foods is a profit-driven corporation that trades on a perceived public morality or that Nelson Mandela beats his dog.

Or, classically, she'll let the petrol in her cor run right down – or, since she got her old man's old Merc converted, the rapeseed oil – then ring me and ask me to come and get her from Dundrum.

So you could say, roysh, that Thursday's call came as no actual surprise? I'm sitting in the gaff with Ro, watching *The Wire*, with him helpfully translating all the street slang for me, when all of a sudden the *Hawaii Five-O* theme tune fills the room.

'Looks like you got a two-way,' Ronan goes.

It's Sorcha on the other end, bawling her basic eyes out.

It turns out, roysh – and it's not funny – that her granny's gaff has been turned over. Basically burgled – and they've, like, *trashed* the place? Sorcha's old pair were in Puerto Banús and she didn't know who else to ring.

So me and Ro, roysh, tear around there. Sorcha meets us at the front door. The place is a mess. The granny, who I've got a hell of a lot of time for, even though she hates my actual guts, is sitting on the sofa in the middle of what looks like a war zone, with a blanket around her shoulders, holding a sherry large enough to wash her hair in.

Obviously shock.

Sorcha goes, 'I was at yogalates when she rang,' and for some reason I'm thinking that yogalates is one of those things you're going to hear less and less about now that the country's financially focked again. Sun-bruised tomatoes, as well. And, I'd imagine, cors that run on rapeseed oil.

She sits down beside her granny and puts her orm around her.

Ronan asks if they took anything and Sorcha says no. Then he walks over to the broken living-room window and mutters something about doorty low-life – doorty fooken low-life, at that.

'It's this new one per cent income tax levy,' Sorcha goes. 'People out there are getting desperate. There's going to be a lot more of this kind of thing.'

We all just nod, I suppose, sadly.

I ring the Feds and it's the usual crack – they'll send a cor around when one is available, contact your insurance company, maybe throw out your old toothbrush.

Then I stort cleaning up. Ronan's suddenly looking majorly shifty.

'I, er, might head off,' he goes, 'if the Filth are coming round.'

I'm there, 'Ro, you were with me – you've got, like, a cast-iron alibi,' but he goes, 'Thee might steert asking questions about why Ine not at school.'

Some father I am – I never asked that question myself. Although I suppose, given where he comes from, watching *The Wire* is kind of school.

He slips out the back way, roysh, and just when I think he's gone, I hear this laughter coming from the conservatory – or, as they call it in this port of Foxrock, the orangerie.

When I go out, he's pointing at this humungous plant – must be, like, six feet tall – in the window.

'Rosser,' he goes, 'what the fook's she doing with a cannabis plant?'

I'm like, 'Cannabis? Are you sure?' which is a ridiculous question, of course.

He's smoked more of it than I've had hot models.

I peg it back into the living room. I look at Sorcha's granny and I'm like, 'You've got a literally cannabis plant out there! The Feds are on their way! What? The fock?'

Sorcha goes, 'Ross, stop shouting – can't you see she's in shock?'

I'm there, 'She's going to have a focking screw screaming in her face every morning if the old Coq Hardi come here and see that thing.'

'You bought it for me,' the granny suddenly goes. 'For Christmas one year.'

'Did I?'

Actually, I think I actually did – as, like, a joke? Didn't think she'd still have it.

I'm there, 'We've got to get rid of it.'

They follow me out to the orangerie and the four of us end up just, like, staring at it.

'It's supposed to be good for glaucoma,' Sorcha goes. 'We could tell the Gords she has glaucoma.'

'Glaucoma?' I go. 'There's enough there to keep Ronan's entire estate peaceful for a month.'

'Now you're singing my tune,' Ro goes, helping me lift the thing. 'This is the answer to all me Christmas present woodies.'

I'm there, 'You're never watching that programme again. Now, help me get this thing outside. We'll stick it in the shed slash utility room.'

'It's locked,' the granny goes and suddenly she's the one looking a bit, I suppose, shady.

Sorcha's there, 'Okay – you have the key, don't you?' and after five minutes of basically faffing around, with our backs pretty much breaking trying to hold the plant, she hands Sorcha the key and we all go outside to the utility room.

Sorcha turns the key and opens the door. In front of us, roysh, are maybe fifteen or twenty milk churns. Sorcha turns around and goes, 'Gran, what are all these?'

She doesn't answer. We put the plant down. Ronan goes over, opens one and looks inside.

'Moy Jaysus!' he goes. 'They're stuffed with bleaten muddy, so thee are.'

Me and Sorcha are both like, 'Money?'

Ro's there, 'Hee-or – you're not a dealer, are you?' obviously delighted at the idea.

'No,' Sorcha's granny goes, 'I took it out of the bank a couple of weeks ago. Well, it said on the news that the banks were going bust, so I wasn't going to trust them with it.'

'Oh my God, this is what the burglars were after,' Sorcha goes. 'Gran, did you tell anyone about this?'

'Just my friends from the Active Retirement,' she goes. 'And one or two I met in the post office. And a girl I know to see on the 46A . . .'

Sorcha's there, 'Ross, get the cor storted. We need to get this money to a bank.'

> 'Now, these shams here, with the crowns on
> their heads – they're the three Seánies.
> Dunne, Quinn and FitzPatrick.'
> *The Irish Times*, 13 December 2008

Sorcha invites myself and Ro over to put up the deckies and it's nice, just the three of us, plus Honor, doing it as a kind of – I suppose – *family*?

The baubles – bought from local craft shops and made from fully sustainable materials – have been hung on the Earth-friendly, agrichemical-free tree, which Sorcha had imported from Norway, paying money to some reforestation crowd in Peru for the carbon offset.

So the world's happy.

I certainly am. I'm actually thinking, this is what Christmas is really about – family. And mulled wine. And Quality Street. And a Bond on RTÉ2.

Ronan takes Honor by the hand and tells us they're going into the living room to set up, like, the *Nativity* scene? Sorcha pulls a face at me and goes, 'I was thinking of having, like, a secular Christmas this year? It's just that, oh my God, Shiloh and Poet – as in, Honor's little friends? – they're coming around for a playdate on Christmas Eve. They're not Christians, Ross. I so don't want to, like, cause offence?'

But then the two of us suddenly stop and listen to Ronan's voice coming from the next room. 'Reet – this is Meerdy. And this is Joseph. They're not maddied – but Meerdy's pregnant. Don't ask how – you're getting into a whole wurdled of trouble there.

'Thee have to go from Nazerdut to Bethleheddem for a thing called a ceddensus. Nowadays, the fowurm comes around – think you can even do it online. But remember, reet, there's no Interdet. There's no cars, no Danny Day Luas, no nuttin – just a doddenkey. That's reet, Hodor – this fella here. Good girdle.

'So Meerdy's up on he's back and they're nearly in Bethleheddem. They're in, say, Lucan – heading in . . .'

Me and Sorcha are both just listening with our mouths open.

'Meerdy gets a payun,' he goes. 'Says she, "Hee-or, Joseph, this fedda's cubben tonight, so he is." Says he, "Are ye shewer?" Says she, "You bettah believe Ine shewer – he's kicking like Mossy bleaten Quinn hee-or."

'There's no Hoddes Street, of course. There's no even Mount Keermil, Hodor. So Joseph spies this inn – say it's the Spawell, for argument's sake . . .'

'Hey,' I'm suddenly whispering to Sorcha, 'we should be, like, recording this. It's like those poor kids from the inner city. Shocking holy saint. *They* made a focking fortune.'

She's like, 'Ross, I don't think even you would stoop so low as to try to make money off your son's back.'

'So Joseph,' Ronan goes, 'he sidles up to the doe-her. Says he, "Addy chaddence of getting one of yisser rooms and that?" Sham who runs the place says, "Ah, you're ourra luck, me auld flower. We're buked out sodid, so we are. It's all redundancy peerties and that. You know yisser selves – the ecodomy and that."

'Ine putting a modorden spin on this now, Hodor. So Joseph looks at this sham and says he, "Is there addy rooms in this towun?" and the fella says, "Is there wha'? There's nuttin *but* rooms in this town. See them apeertments over there?"

'Joseph says, "The ones with the scaffolding still up? Yeah, what's the Johnny McGory?"

'Says he, "Builder caddent fiddish them – banks won't gib him addy mower muddy. He'd let you put yisser heads down there – a hundrit a week, I'd say, no referdences, nuttin. He's desperdut, so he is."

'Next thing, they're in! A property with huge potential in an up-and-cubben area, convenient to all local thransport links. And it's there that Meerdy has the babby – a little babby boy, reet. Thee wrap him in swoddelin, whatever that is, and thee call him Jesus.

'That's it, Hodor, you put him in there – the little bitty baby, born in

Bethleheddem. Now, these feddas hee-or – yeah, thee look like shep-herds, doatunt thee? But they're not. They're pig feermers. And they're arthur losing their livelihoods, reet, because the pigs is infected with all sorts. No one wants their sausages and their rashers addy mower. So now they're on the sthreets, reet, and they're looking for somewayer. So Joseph says, "Come on in, feddas." Gibs them a roowum. Dudn't even sublet it. Gibs it to them.

'Now, these shams here, with the crowns on their heads – they're the three Seánies. Dunne, Quinn and FitzPatrick. We used to think they were wise men, but we doatunt addy mower.

'That's it, put them in there. Because they're arthur losing evoddy thing as weddle. And now thee've nowhere to stay thumselves, so Joseph says, "Mon in hee-or, feddas, loads of roowum – you'll be moostard."

'And the reason they're moostard is because of this little one hee-or looking over them. And you know what we're godda call her? We're godda call her Hodor – because what she is, see, is a little angel.'

I turn and look at Sorcha. We've both got, like, tears streaming down our faces.

'This stordee,' he goes, 'you can tell it loads of diffordent ways, Hodor, but it all stacks up the sayum. Me ma says this is what Christ-mas is about, see. It's not about the presents. Except only a little bit. It's about us all lubbing one anutter.

'And that, me little segosha, is the stordee of Christmas.'

# 2009

Barack Obama is sworn in as the 44th President of the United States * An outbreak of Swine Flu is declared a global pandemic * Starbucks closes its doors in Dalkey after only thirteen months as locals boycott it in favour of local coffee shops * Anglo Irish Bank, one of the great success stories of Ireland's Celtic Tiger period, is nationalized * In a second referendrum, Ireland votes to accept the Lisbon Treaty * *Avatar* is released and becomes the highest grossing movie of all time * Anglo Irish Bank's hidden loans scandal is revealed * Ireland's unemployment rate doubles to more than 400,000 in the space of a year, with an average of 1,500 people losing their jobs daily * Ronan O'Gara scores a seventy-eighth-minute drop goal to give Ireland victory over Wales in Cardiff and secure the country's first Grand Slam in sixty-one years. Declan Kidney is named IRB International Coach of the Year, the first Irish coach to win the award * RTÉ Economics Editor George Lee wins a Dáil seat for Fine Gael in the Dublin-South by-election * The National Asset Management Agency (NAMA) is founded, to take over land and development loans from Ireland's banks * The Progressive Democrats Party is officially dissolved * An estimated 120,000 people march in Dublin in protest at the government's handling of the economic crisis * Gardaí raid the headquarters of Anglo Irish Bank in St Stephen's Green, Dublin * Ryan Tubridy replaces Pat Kenny as the host of *The Late Late Show* * The dublinbikes scheme is launched * France beat Ireland in a football World Cup qualifier thanks to a handball by Thierry Henry * A Brian O'Driscoll intercept try helps Leinster overcome Munster in the Heineken Cup semi-final at Croke Park, a match billed as rugby's All Ireland final. Leinster go on to win the Heineken Cup by beating Leicester in a close final *

Meanwhile . . .

> 'I think I'm beginning to see the funny
> side of this whole recession thing.'
> *The Irish Times, 7 February 2009*

So One F rings me. Says some friend of his from the *PAYE Daily Worker* – or whatever rag it is – is ringing various RTÉ celebrities, trying to embarrass them into saying they'll take a pay cut. Wants the old dear's number.

I'm there, 'Dude, my old dear's number is, like, a state secret. You've no idea how seriously she takes that whole privacy thing. It's 087-223 –' and I end up just giving him the thing.

What can I say? He's a mate.

Then I have to tip downstairs, of course, to wait for the call to come.

Waiting for me, at the kitchen table, is the most hilarious sight I've ever seen. Every morning, bear in mind, for as long as I've been alive, the old dear has had a nine o'clock hair appointment for – at the very least – a blow-dry. So you can imagine the laugh I have when I cop her, sitting in the kitchen, with a towel around her neck and latex gloves on – doing her own hair.

I shit you not.

The pen is only Padraig, of course, because there's bleach and all sorts of other shit involved. I pick up the box and sort of, like, snigger. I'm like, 'What the fock are you doing?'

'Bloody paparazzi!' she goes. 'They're outside Foxrock Hair Design! They're outside Pamela Scott! They're outside the Lord Mayor's Lounge! Waiting – just *waiting* – to get a shot of me, living it up on the licence-payers' money!'

I laugh.

'Reduced to this,' I go, 'I think I'm beginning to see the funny side of this whole recession thing.'

She doesn't get a chance to answer, because her phone rings. The tune is, like, Michael Bublé's 'I Just Haven't Met You Yet'.

'Hello?' she goes.

Whatever's said, roysh, she's immediately not a happy camper about it?

'How! *Dare* you!' she goes and I honestly haven't seen her this angry since some kid mistook her for Twink coming down the steps of the Westbury two Christmas Eves ago. 'What RTÉ pay me for my cookery show is my business and nobody else's!'

Of course, I can only hear her side of the conversation. But I can, like, guess the kind of shit that's being said on the other end.

'Well, I didn't bloody cause it . . . No, I am not prepared to take a pay cut . . . I don't care *what* Miriam is doing . . . *Or* Marian . . . Well, if that's what they've decided, then more power to them. They do their thing, I do mine . . .'

Her voice is all high-pitched and she's got liquigel and developing crème dripping down her face.

'I mean, why am *I* getting this call?' she's going. 'Why not Rachel Allen?'

This is one of those things that's actually too funny? I whip out my phone and stort filming it. It's, like, this *has* to go on YouTube!

And not a moment too soon either because it's at that exact point that she suddenly loses it – and we're talking in a big-time way.

'Share the pain?' she goes. 'Share the pain? Let me tell you something about pain. Yesterday, I did something I've never before lowered myself to do. I bought – oh, I can hardly bring myself to say the words – a permanent hair-colour kit. The girl on the checkout was a fan of my books – have you any idea how demeaning that was for me? I had to tell her it was a birthday present for my maid.

'And you talk to me about sharing the nation's pain? I'm sitting here, rubbing this awful . . . *concoction* into my hair. I happen to have a sensitive scalp and, let me tell you, it's burning – *burning* – my head. And you sit there, whatever tabloid it is you're from, and you talk to me about pain?'

I'm laughing so much, I can hordly keep the camera steady.

'I happen to be one of the country's most celebrated cooks,' she goes. 'Avoca Handweavers have taken four – four! – of my recipes and Jenny Bristow has referred to me as her guru. Her words – read your *RTÉ Guide*, dear.

'So you can take your bloody sackcloth austerity and you can stick it up your . . . well, I wouldn't like to say the word in a family newspaper – whatever kind of families it is you're pandering to.'

I don't know what the bird on the other end says then, but the old dear ends up having another eppo.

'Greed?' she goes. 'You say the word like there's something wrong with it. Do you think you look down on me or something? There's nothing wrong with greed! Let me tell you something – you and who-ever reads you – if it wasn't for the greed of people like me and my estranged husband, there would never have been a Celtic Tiger. You lot would still be breathing through your mouths and eating cauliflower morning, noon and night. Yes, that's *on* the record!'

I nearly have an actual hort attack I'm laughing that hord. This is going to be 2009's Zip Up Your Mickey moment, I can guarantee you that.

I get, like, a long, lingering shot of her boat, guck still dribbling down it, steam practically coming out of her ears, then I aim the lens at the box from her permanent hair-colour kit.

And the closing shot turns out to be the punchline, because the camera's picking up what she clearly doesn't know yet but will in, like, an hour's time when she gets out the hairdryer. I put the camera right up to it, making sure to get in the two words on, like, the front of the box.

It says Radiant Ruby.

### 'I'm told this was Seán FitzPatrick's very chair!'
*The Irish Times, 28 February 2009*

The old man rings me – says him and Hennessy have got, like, some-thing to *show* me?

Three o'clock in the day and already half mashed.

He says he's sending his driver. Ten minutes later, as good as his word, the Merc rolls up outside the gaff.

'What's all this about?' I go.

But all Radoslaw will say is, 'He haff soorprise for you.'

Croke Pork, I have to say, doesn't hold the same horror for me that it once did. I'm actually walking across the exact spot where Shaggy scored his try against England when I hear the old man roaring at, like, the top of his voice.

'Kicker!' he's going. 'Kicker! Up here!'

I look up and there they are, between the two stands, underneath the Supermac's sign and above the one for Silvermints – him and Hennessy, raising their brandy glasses to me.

'What the fock are you doing up there?' I automatically go.

'This is the Anglo Irish Bank corporate box,' the old man shouts. 'Or should I say *was* – we've only gone and bloody *bought* it!'

Of course I'm up those stairs two at a time.

It's an unbelievable room – humungous, roysh, and bang on overlooking the *actual* halfway line.

The old man's sitting in this massive leather recliner.

'I'm told this was Seán FitzPatrick's very chair,' he goes, trying to, like, adjust the leg-rest. 'It's an ill wind that doesn't blow for someone, eh, old chap?'

Hennessy just laughs.

I'm there, 'God, you're like a couple of vultures,' but at the same time – I have to admit – I'm picturing me and the goys in here for the England match.

'No,' the old man goes, standing up, 'like two great entrepreneurs, we simply got in first – to coin a phrase. Of course it's set all sorts of tongues wagging. Newspapers and so forth – *including* Messers Collins and Beesley of your own parish – ringing up to know were we part of this famous Maple Ten that everyone's talking about. "No comment," I said. "All I'll say is you know me as a man who's always put the national interest first."'

He walks over to the window. Being honest, if there wasn't a sheet of glass in front of him and a witness in the room, I'd probably push him over the edge of the stand.

'I don't know whether it's being up so high, or England tomorrow, or maybe that bottle of XO that Seánie left behind, but I'm feeling rather patriotic this afternoon. Puts me in mind of the day I took you to see your first rugby international, Ross. God, now you're taking me back. Nineteen hundred and eighty-two.

'You won't remember it, of course, hadn't even had your second birthday, but naturally I wanted to immerse you in the game from as early an age as possible. Wales – that was the first game you ever saw. Lansdowne Road. Still have the ticket stubs to this very day . . .'

He doesn't, by the way. I let someone use them for roach material at a porty in the gaff years ago.

'Of course the build-up was all about Campbell and Ward. Oh, Hennessy, you and I had some famous rows, didn't we, over who was

Ireland's rightful number ten? Sometimes to the point of very near fisti-cuffs. In fact, the previous year, when poor Ollie was switched to centre, I said that was it. I was never going again – the IRFU would have to plan for a future without my support.

'Well, you say those things, don't you? "The West Stand won't be the same," Hennessy said, "without that big voice of yours booming out. I'm sure the players will miss it." Damn your eyes, Old Scout, you knew how to get to me – and you knew I'd be back.

'The good news was that Ollie was in at number ten for the Wales match. When people ask me about you, Ross, and the extraordinary things you did on the rugby field, I always take them back to that day. Because you were there, you *saw* it – for my money one of Ollie Camp-bell's greatest ever performances in the green jersey.

'He set up – I think I'm correct in saying – two tries for Moss Finn. The second was an absolute dream – dummy, sidestep, dummy, pass. I looked at your little face, Ross – I was holding you, like so – and there you were, with your eyes wide open. Read into that what you will, but *I will* remind you that you would later make that particular move your own.

'The next game, we didn't take you because, well, it was in Twick-enham. Tomorrow's opponents – i.e., the incorrectly spelt *auld* enemy. Hennessy and I were in the exact corner where Ginger McLoughlin scored. Oh yes, you can see us in all the photographs.

'And, of course, the famous conversion that followed. From the sideline. Bloody gale blowing. You know, I think that was the closest you ever came, Hennessy, to admitting that Campbell was at least as good as Ward – certainly technically superior.

'I remember ringing home, from the bar in Jurys in Kensington. I said, "Fionnuala, put Ross on." "Charles," she said, "he's only a baby." "All the better to remember this," comes my famous reply. So she held the receiver up to your ear and I must have recounted the entire match to you, while Hennessy there fed coins into the slot.'

'So you were a knob then as well?' I go, just letting him know that buying a corporate box doesn't mean we're suddenly going to become all palsy-walsy.

'I remember saying to you on the phone, "England, put to the pro-verbial sword. Rest easy, Little One. Rest easy now." Then next up, as everyone remembers, was Scotland. Twenty-one points to twelve, with the Triple Crown – capital T, capital C – not to mention the cham-pionship, secured. Campbell kicking all the points.

'And you know what I remember most about that day? I had you on my lap, Ross – just here – and every time the chap stepped up to take a kick, I would do this – just gently swing your right foot in what you might call a kicking action. Second half, I forgot all about it – the excitement of the match and so forth – but Campbell's about to slot over yet another penalty when your godfather here turns to me and says, "Charlie – look!" He's staring at your little feet – or more particularly your right foot, which was swinging, like this. Like you were about to take the kick . . .

'I remember saying – because it was a terribly clever thing to say – that the present was obviously in good hands, but so too was the future.

'Nineteen hundred and eighty-two. Country was on its bloody well knees – just like it is today. But those chaps – oh, those chaps – had us dreaming all sorts of crazy dreams.'

## 'You, in the camel-hair coat and the hat – sit the fock down!'
### *The Irish Times*, 23 March 2009

He's talking to Jack Kyle. The dude's sitting, like, seven or eight rows behind us but the old man is still talking to him.

'History calling,' he's going, loud enough for half of Cordiff to hear.

'A date with destiny, full point, new par,' and you can see Jack Kyle thinking, 'Er, whatever?'

'Oh, I was there in '48,' the old man makes sure to tell him, 'when we beat this same shower. Make no mistake about that. I was still a babe-in-arms, of course, but my father took me, just as I took this chap here in '82,' and he tries to get me to stand up then?

I just shake my arm free and tell him to stop making a tit of himself.

You can see practically half the crowd looking at him, thinking, who is this tosser?

'Bears your name, I'm proud to report! Ross Kyle Gibson McBride O'Carroll-Kelly! Described by no less a judge than Tony Ward as the best number ten never to play for Ireland!'

He *actually* described me as the greatest waste of natural talent he's seen in half a century of watching rugby, but that's a whole other *scéal*.

'And that little chap beside him there is his own boy – you might say the *future* of Irish rugby!'

Someone eventually shouts, 'You, in the camel-hair coat and the hat – sit the fock down!' which, thankfully, he does. He asks me what he's missed and I tell him practically the entire first half.

He's there, 'Oh, you know what I'm like when I stort discussing the greats of the game, Ross!'

'Who was I named after?' Ronan goes and I know exactly what he's thinking, because I follow his line of vision to you-know-who, shaping up to take a penalty on the Welsh ten-metre line.

Of course, the easiest thing to do is to tell him what he wants to hear.

Except it's, like, complicated between Rog and me? See, a lot of people would be of the opinion that I was the better tactical kicker, the better place-kicker, the better basically all-round player. I just liked the life too much and he ended up getting all the breaks.

He steps up and pulls his kick wide of the post.

'You were named after Ronan Keating,' I go, which *is* actually *true*? 'Your mother loved that song, "Isn't It a Wonder",' and I look at his little face and, being honest, he's totally crushed.

But you can't lie to your kids.

Anyway, where all of this is going is that half-time – you know the script by now – we're six points down and the old man is telling anyone who's prepared to listen – as well as quite a few who aren't – that what Ireland lack is a kicker of the calibre of Stephen Jones and the great crime, for which the IRFU must stand indicted here today, is that they have one – except he's sitting here in the bloody well stand!

The match restorts. Two quick tries and he's suddenly changed his tune.

'The dream is on!' he's going.

I'm telling Ro how Tommy Bowe has been, for me, the revelation of the Six Nations, if that's an actual word. But he's in, like, total awe of the green ten.

He's there, 'Did you see Rog's chip over the top, Rosser?'

I pull a face like I'm not that impressed?

'That's actually not as difficult as it looks,' I go, and I feel instantly guilty, because if there's anyone in this stadium who knows what a moment of complete and utter genius that was, it's me.

So you know what happens next. We let Wales back into it and the old man's saying that now is the time for certain individuals to stand up and be counted.

The minutes are disappearing fast. It's, like, ruck after ruck and I'm thinking, now would be a good time for Rog to drop back into the pocket.

But I look and of course he's already there. Then the ball is in his hands. And then he's suddenly splitting the posts.

I didn't see Stephen Jones's penalty. Ro and the old man didn't either – they had their hands over their eyes. But me, I was just staring at *him*.

See, there are those who say it could and should have been me down there today, but those people are wrong.

I could never do what he does and that's a hard thing to admit when you're pushing thirty and someone else is living your dream.

When Jones misses, all hell breaks loose. Literally. In all the excitement, I even end up hugging my old man, if you can believe that.

He turns around to say something to Jack Kyle but he's gone, and you wouldn't focking blame him either.

So we end up just sitting there – three generations of us, you could say – staring into space, just emotionally spent.

And I turn to Ro and I go, 'You know I was only yanking your chain earlier?'

He takes the rollie out of his mouth and looks at me, his little eyes wide.

I'm there, 'You weren't named after Ronan Keating. You were named after Ronan O'Gara.'

It turns out that I *can* lie to my kid. But this smile – worth a Grand Slam and two Heineken Cups in anyone's money – just explodes across his face.


'But today we can all forget about the
current economic blahdy blah.'
*The Irish Times, 23 May 2009*


I'm looking around me. See, we get a bad rap – and by *we* I mean, like, *Leinster* fans? But, despite what people say, we really do come in all shapes and sizes. There's goys here with Aviator shades on their heads, goys with Oakleys on their heads, goys with Ray-Bans on their heads.

I think Oisinn sums it up best when he describes it as a real cultural melting pot.

'I've just realized,' Fionn suddenly goes, 'I don't even know what it looks like – as in, the *actual* Heineken Cup?'

JP's there, 'We know where it's been for the past twelve months.

We'll probably know it when we smell it,' which has everyone in the entire queue laughing.

I mention the story I heard, that when Wasps won it the year after Munster, they couldn't bring the focking thing indoors for six months for the hum of Beamish, swede mash and red diesel. I swear to God, roysh, you can't hear the flight announcements for the sound of high-fiving.

We move a few steps forwards. I'm looking at JP, Fionn and Oisinn, these three friends of mine who've followed this team, through thick and thin, for pretty much three years, on and off. And there's a real sense that it's all been, like, leading towards this day? Even for, like, eighty minutes, we can forget about all the other shit that's happening in our lives.

For instance, Oisinn, it has to be said, looks ten years older than his actual age. It's no secret that all the moo he made from *Eau d'Affluence – Scent of Tiger* is gone.

JP's orm is in a cast. He broke three fingers trying to put his hand through the window of an X5 that him and his old man were trying to repossess. I think if they X-rayed his hort, they'd discover that that's broken too.

And, as for Fionn, for the last two months, all anyone's heard him talk about is, like, the pension levy? And *he's* a teacher, the poor focker – that's a vow of poverty in itself.

But today we can all forget about the current economic blahdy blah.

No one even minded paying the four-hundred-and-fifty snots for the flights – as long as it keeps people from the likes of Carlow and Louth away from Murrayfield. It might be true that, economically, we're heading back to the 1970s, but the last thing any of us wants is a bunch of O'Reilly the Builder types showing up and trying to associate themselves with the Leinster brand.

One or two of Dorce's mates stop by to say basically hi. Even though they're Clongowes, they'd still have, like, a *begrudging* respect for us? One of them goes, 'This time last year, huh?' then he sort of, like, laughs.

He's obviously heard the story. One of my greatest ever moments – and that's saying something with the life *I've* led.

Yeah, no, it was, like, Munster versus Toulouse. To cut a long story short, we ended up watching it in Sinnotts, of all places – a seething hogpen of sweating Munster fans, with me and the three goys sitting smack bang in the middle of them, listening to them sing 'The Fields of Athenry' and whatever else.

Up my sleeve, roysh, I had my secret weapon – a universal TV remote, which I picked up in Argos in the Stephen's Green Shopping Centre for something like fifteen snots. In the first half, roysh, about five seconds before Denis Leamy got over for Munster's try, I hit a random button through the canvas of my sailing jacket and suddenly everyone was left staring at the *Hollyoaks* omnibus, screaming blue focking murder.

Of course, me and the goys were cracking on to be *as* pissed off as everyone else. I was looking around going, 'Who *did* that?' laying it on like peanut butter. 'This is bang out of order – and we're *talking* bang?'

The borman found the *actual* remote and stuck the rugby back on. So everyone copped that Munster had scored and the place went literally ballistic – you know what their fans are like when they're winning.

The next thing, roysh, Rog is stepping up to add the points. He does his whole routine and, just as he's coming out of his golfer's stance, it was like, *flick* – and I switched over to an old episode of *Columbo*.

The place went absolutely chicken oriental.

I was there, 'This is no longer funny – if it even *ever* was?' while Oisinn and JP demanded that the borman find out what the fock was going on.

Anyway, we managed to get away with it until Toulouse brought the game level in the second half and – story of my life – I storted to get a bit cocky. I managed to find the volume button and actually highered up the sound. That's when somebody copped what was happening and I quickly disappeared under a landslide of angry red jerseys.

I tell Dorce's two mates, 'If I'd known then that, in twelve months' time, we'd be the ones playing in a Ken Cup final, I'd have been laughing all the way to A&E!' and they just shake their heads in, like, total admiration, as if to say, what a legend.

## 'Brian Lenihan! As I live and breathe!'
### *The Irish Times, 7 November 2009*

'Of course,' the old man goes, loud enough for the entire Horseshoe Bor to hear, 'what you've been reading over the last few days is only half the story! There's a lot more to it than that – oh, that famous night of 17 September, the year of Our Lord, two thousand and eight! A lot more! But you can torture me! You can electrocute me. You can – what's this these CIA chaps do – watersports? You can give me the full treatment and still my lips will remain sealed – for Charles O'Carroll-Kelly is a man of his word!'

People go back to their drinks and their conversations, which kills him, of course. He hates not being the centre of attention.

'There was a knock on the front door,' he goes – again, he's up in the Fred Elliott decibel range. 'The time was one a.m. At first, I thought it was Ross here – thought he'd met another nice girl in one of these, quote-unquote, nightclubs that he likes to go to and was looking for a bed for the night, as was often his wont.

'Imagine my surprise, though, when I opened the door to see Brian Lenihan standing there! Brian Lenihan! As I live and breathe! Like Banquo's bloody well ghost!

'I had met the Minister many times and I knew he respected my views on all matters financial. Of course, he remembered me from when I was a member of the Leggs of Lower Leeson Street School of Economics, which Hennessy and I set up as a bulwark against the influence of the Doheny & Nesbitt's crowd.

'Brian was one of several young bucks who listened, with rapt attention and no little awe, as my solicitor and long-suffering golf portner and I held forth on the great issues of the day!

'Now, he told me in a hushed tone, he needed my help! I took him down to the kitchen. I noticed that he was nervous and fidgety. His suit looked like he'd slept in it. He had bags under his eyes and his tie was undone.

'He also stank of garlic, for which he apologized. He said he'd just come from McWilliams's place, where he'd been given a cup of – can you believe it? – instant coffee! The garlic was to take the taste out of his mouth!

'"I told McWilliams some old guff about it giving me strength and keeping me healthy and alert,' he said, 'so as not to hurt his feelings."

'Then his eyes took on a sad, distant look. "You know," he said, "I thought freeze-dried coffee crystals had become a Third World thing. I suppose it's another sign of how much trouble the country is in."

'Of course, I could understand the chap acting like he was – the financial world was collapsing around his ears. The Irish banks were running out of money fast!

'We sat at the kitchen table, and he leaned in close to me. In a hoarse voice, almost whispering, he said: "What would you do?"

'Well, I had troubles of my own, of course. Given the perilous state of the nation's finances, I was having to seriously rethink my plans to repatriate the €48 million that I hid in Andorra during the boom years, through a series of business fronts, including my cheesemongers in the Merrion Shopping Centre.

'But if there's one thing that Charles O'Carroll-Kelly is famous for, it's putting the national interest first. So I took a piece of kitchen roll and, on the back, I began to, very patriotically, sketch out a plan to save Ireland's economy.

'The important thing, I said, was to avoid the kind of panic that would lead to a bank run. Most of our senior bank management, they're great guys, really terrific – I should know, I played rugby with enough of them – but you wouldn't trust them to hold your ice-cream cone while you tied your shoelace.

'It's vital, I told him – I'd even say mandatory – that the public never finds out that these chaps were essentially taking depositors' money and putting it on the City's equivalent of a dead cert in the 3.30 at Punchestown – so keep emphasizing the international dimension to this crisis . . .

'It was almost three a.m. when there was another knock on the front door. Who could that be? I thought. When I opened it, there, stood in front of me, was Mary Coughlan, whom I knew well from the famous tent in Galway. "Hello,"' says she. I've airbrushed out the expletives – this is a public bar, after all.

'She said she needed my help. She, too, had bags under her eyes. She also, I noticed, had bags at her feet – two black bin-liners, which were stuffed with €50 notes. Her life savings, as it turns out, which she'd withdrawn from the bank that very afternoon. "Do you still have that walk-in safe?" she asked.

'I said yes – but it was no thanks to those Criminal Assets chaps. They wanted to dynamite it, even though I gave them the combination. One, nine, eight, two – year of the famous Triple Crown. Ollie and Slats and what-not.

'"Yeah, whatever," she says, pushing past me into the hallway. "Look, this is only for a short while. I wouldn't trust them fooken banks to find their arse in the bath." I told her to fire away. She stopped midway up the stairs.

46

'"Is that Lenihan's car outside?" she asked. I said it was. "Don't tell him I'm here," she said. I told her my lips were sealed.

'I went back to the kitchen. Brian asked me who it was and I told him it was Mary Coughlan. He said he hoped I didn't tell her that he was here. I told him my word was my bond.

'Then I returned to my ministrations with the pen and the kitchen roll. Oh, the feeling of power. I was suddenly transported back to that basement wine bar, back in the day, as I sketched out a remedy for a country hovering over the, inverted commas, precipice. Except this time it would become policy.

'Within an hour, I had drawn up what would soon be unveiled as the bank guarantee scheme. Then I made a pot of plunger coffee. "None of that NASA stuff you get around at McWilliams's place," Brian commented, rather acerbically, I thought – as we sat and watched the sun come up.

'It was shortly before seven a.m. when there was a third knock on the door. I went outside and opened it again. Who was it? Brian Cowen. As true as I'm still – barely – standing here. Another member of the Cabinet!

'Of course, by now, I was running out of rooms in which to put them. The Taoiseach leaned in and, in a voice barely audible, said, "I need your help . . ."'

# 2010

Heavy snow brings Ireland to a standstill at the start and end of the year * George Lee resigns from Fine Gael and Dáil Éireann after just nine months, complaining that he had 'virtually no influence or input' on government economic policy * Volcanic ash from the eruption of Eyjafjallajökull in Iceland grounds air traffic in northern and western Europe for weeks * In a landmark legal ruling, pubs in Limerick are permitted to open on Good Friday to accommodate fans of Munster and Leinster, who are playing in a Celtic League match in Thomond Park * Fine Gael leader Enda Kenny survives a leadership bid by Richard Bruton * Terminal 2 opens at Dublin Airport * Mary Byrne, a Tesco checkout worker from Ballyfermot, becomes a household name after her performances on UK talent show *The X Factor* * The International Monetary Fund arrive in Dublin, despite official government denials that Ireland was involved in discussions about an economic bailout * Eurozone countries agree on a rescue package for Ireland in response to the country's financial crisis * Brian O'Driscoll marries Amy Huberman * Seán FitzPatrick, former chairman of Anglo Irish Bank, is declared bankrupt *

Meanwhile . . .

'I don't think we'll be seeing many 10 registrations
on the road this year.'
*The Irish Times, 23 January 2010*

'Whoa, nice car!' he goes.

See, I've never been one to count my chickens before they *hatch*? But when the tester says something like that to you – what? – thirty seconds into your driving test, you immediately know he's cool, certainly not the kind who's going to fail you just because you're a thirty-year-old Trustafarian sitting in a brand-new Five-Serious.

'Actually, thanks,' I go. 'It was, like, a birthday present to myself. The big three-oh and blah, blah, blah,' and I watch him rub his hand along the leather interior – real, by the way.

He's there, 'I don't think we'll be seeing many 10 registrations on the road this year, the way things are going,' and I'm like, 'Yeah, it's supposed to be pretty bad out there,' because I want to come across like I care.

'Indicate,' he goes.

See, that's me trying to drive and think about world affairs at the same time. I indicate, then take the turn out of the test centre and on to Orwell Road.

Some dude behind me ends up blasting me with his horn.

'There was actually plenty of room for me to pull out,' I try to go. The tester dude gives the rear-view mirror a twist to check out the goy, who has attached himself, practically, to my bomper.

He goes, 'Put your foot down,' and at first, roysh, I presume I've, like, *misheard* him?

I'm there, 'Dude, I'm already, like, ten Ks over the speed limit here – and that's habit more than anything.'

'Come on,' he goes, egging me on, 'he's driving a shitty little Golf – and he's beeping at you? Show him what this car can do.'

So I end up shrugging, then just giving it some Dubarry leather and, ten seconds later, the Golf's just a speck in my rear-view.

The tester just cracks his hole laughing, obviously seriously impressed.

'That'll show him – little prick,' he goes. 'That was a nice piece of driving, my friend. We'll take a right just up ahead. Again, indicate.'

See, I keep forgetting in all the excitement.

'So this is, what, your first time sitting the test?' he goes.

Suddenly, it's, like, *my* turn to laugh. I'm there, 'It's actually, like, my twelfth?'

He's like, 'What?' and he's genuinely surprised.

'Well, fourteenth,' I go, 'if you count the two times I went down the country to sit it.'

'Fourteenth?'

'That's the thing – I can't believe you don't know me. See, I've become a bit of a celebrity around the various testing centres. The last time I sat it, for instance, the dude stuck a Padre Pio medal on the dashboard.'

He laughs. I'm getting an unbelievably good vibe from him.

He's like, 'Look, it'd be ridiculous for me to expect you to drive like a robot. Because you know and I know that the second you've passed your test, you're never going to drive like that again. No, what I look for, first and foremost, is confidence.'

Of course that's muesli to my ears.

I'm there, 'Confidence happens to be one of the things I'm big on. You could even say it's my thing.'

Uh-oh, I'm suddenly thinking, that traffic light's been orange for a long time. Except it's definitely too late to stop.

'Ah, fang it,' the dude just goes, like it's not a big deal. 'I saw nothing,' so I do what he says and I end up driving straight through it.

I'm there, 'Loads of people say that it's about who your tester is rather than how you actually drive?'

He's like, 'Just between ourselves, there's a lot of truth in that.'

'See, a few times I sat it, I got the impression that I'd failed before the examiner even sat in the cor?'

'They have to fail a certain percentage, you see.'

'Well, with me it was always small stuff – as an example, not leaving sufficient distance between my cor and the cor in front.'

'It's any little thing.'

'Yeah, see, my attitude, especially when it comes to motorways – which I know I shouldn't technically be on, by the way – is that the outside lane is for me and the inside lane is for everyone else. That's what my wife says about me. Even though we're actually separated.'

'I'm sorry to hear that.'

'Hey, ain't no thing but a Chandler Bing. We were probably always better as mates.'

'What else have you failed on?'

'Well, one of the times I failed it down the country, I was on this really narrow country road. See, they tell you it's easier to pass it in Wicklow, but that's actually horseshit. So this woman's coming towards me and she's driving an Acura MDX – thing's built like a focking petrol bowser. But she won't pull on to the grass verge to let me past – afraid of getting her tyres dirty. So I wound down the window and I was like, "Er, there's a focking reason it's called an off-roader, you know?"'

'And you were failed for *that*?'

'Lack of courtesy, was the official reason . . . Well, I also killed a pony.'

He scribbles something in his clipboard, then goes, 'Okay, you can return to the test centre now.'

I'm like, 'Really?'

He's there, 'I've seen all I need to see. I'm happy to tell you – you've passed your driving test!'

I punch the air, then instinctively go to text Sorcha.

'Oh,' I suddenly remember, 'I shouldn't technically be doing this, should I?'

'Text away,' he goes. 'You've passed after fourteen attempts – you deserve it.'

I'm there, 'Well, just so you know, I'm actually mentioning you – I'm telling her that you're the soundest tester I've ever had.'

I take the right turn back into the testing centre and it's then that I realize that something is wrong. You could say it's, like, a fifth sense I have? There's, like, a crowd of people outside in the cor pork and they're all staring straight at my cor. When I get closer to them, I realize that three or four of them are, like, Gords.

'Oh, shit,' the dude goes.

And then it suddenly hits me.

I'm there, 'You're not even a driving tester, are you?'

He doesn't get the chance to even answer. Suddenly, roysh, two men in white coats step from the little huddle of people and approach the passenger side of the cor.

'Come on, Tommy,' one of them goes, 'you know that's not your job any more.'

Some other dude – presumably my real tester – taps on the window and tells me to wind it down, which I do.

He goes, 'Sorry about that. He got into the car before I could stop him. You're going to have reschedule the test.'

I'm like, 'I'm not focking rescheduling. I've just driven the perfect test!'

'Is that right?' the dude goes. 'Do you know you don't have your seatbelt on?'


## 'We're crank-calling George Lee!'
### *The Irish Times*, 13 February 2010

They're sitting in their usual corner of the Horseshoe Bor, giggling like a teenage disco – and as drunk as one as well.

This is, like, four o'clock on a Wednesday afternoon we're *talking*? Hennessy's still celebrating getting his driving licence back, though I'm not sure what the old man's excuse is, just that he's got a brandy in front of him the size of a focking sheep-dip.

'Ssshhh!' he has the cheek to go when he sees me, his finger to his lips, like I'm six years old again.

I'm there, 'What's the Jack?' because Hennessy, I notice, has the old Wolfe Tone clamped to his ear.

'We're crank-calling George Lee,' the old man whispers – the hum off his breath could strip wallpaper. 'Oh, we've been at it since lunchtime.'

I'm like, 'Yeah, no, so it would seem.'

'Yes, a couple of chaps I know in Fine Gael – they're very unhappy with him walking out on them, Ross – and, well, they were only too happy to pass on his details. Oh, we've been having great sport!'

I look over at Hennessy. He's putting on this sort of, like, high-pitched voice, like a crazy old woman, going, 'Now, I didn't vote for you myself, but you were elected to represent me, for better or worse, and I'm told you're a man who gets things done. Now, Mrs Callery three doors down – she's a martyr to her rheumatism but she offers up her suffering for the people of Zambia where her sister's worked in the missions this thirty year – she has a little dog that keeps doing its business on the pavement outside my house. Now, whatever she's feeding him, it's clearly not agreeing with him . . .'

Hennessy's suddenly silent for a few seconds, then he goes, 'Resigned? No, I didn't hear. Oh! Never mind. I'll call Olivia Mitchell so.'

He hangs up, then he and the old man collapse in pretty much hysterics.

'The poor guy's right on the edge,' Hennessy goes. 'I think three or four more calls will do it.'

I'm looking around me.

I'm there, 'Would you not leave the dude alone?'

The old man dries his eyes.

He's there, 'We're just hammering the message home, Ross, that public representation isn't easy.'

Hennessy goes, 'Although you made it *look* easy, Charlie.'

'Er, no he didn't,' I go. 'He ended up in prison for taking bribes,' which suddenly softens both their coughs. 'Hang on, are you telling me you rang me, got me out of bed, then got me to drive all the way into town – to watch you two punk George Lee?'

'No,' the old man goes, 'we called you here to tell you the news – that I, Ross, am about to re-enter the very world from whence our friend, George, has fled.'

I'm like, 'English, please.'

'Well, if you're asking me for the exact moment when I realized that I was being – inverted commas – *called*, it was while I was driving along the south quays on Monday night, minding my own business, listening to that Harry Connick Jr CD that your mother left in the car when we separated, thinking about the wisdom in his lyrics – "It will be spring again!" – and how they could be applied to the challenge facing Ireland's economy. I like to stay positive, as you know.

'The next thing is, I'm being pulled over by a couple of these *lady* Gordaí. This is a fine how-do-you-do, thinks I. What's all this about? One of these – like I said – *ladies* approaches the driver's side, tells me I was doing forty kilometres per hour. Was I indeed? says I. Thanks for the information! Now we can all get on with our lives! Then she hits me with it! Out of the blue! The new City Centre speed limit, if you don't mind! *Thirty* kilometres per hour!

'Naturally, I figured it was some kind of joke. Honestly, Hennessy, for a moment I thought you'd sent me another of these famous stripograms of yours – I mean they were very attractive.

'Anyway, various comments were passed, back and forth, until eventually I accepted that they were who they said they were and that this folly of theirs was real.

'"Thirty kilometres, says I! If I got out and pushed the bloody thing,

55

I'd cover more than thirty kilometres in an hour. Anyway, as I sat at the next lights, totting up my penalty points in my head, the old Vice-Chairman of the Board was singing 'There is Always One More Time' and that's when I had it, Ross – my eureka moment. We've forgotten what it was that made this country great for eleven and a little bit years – what we need now, more than ever, is strong leadership!'

I'm there, 'Are you saying you're going to stand for George Lee's seat?

'No,' he goes, 'I'm going to stand to become Dublin's first directly elected Lord Mayor – and by directly elected, I mean by the people!'

I end up having to laugh?

I'm there, 'I suppose it'd be handy to have a place on Dawson Street to crash every time you fall out of this place.'

He doesn't even acknowledge it. It's, like, so difficult to hurt the focker sometimes.

'This was once a great city,' he goes, suddenly all misty-eyed. 'But look around you, Ross. Look at the degeneration. The Berkeley Court, gone. Restaurants – *fine* restaurants – doing grill menus and early birds, attracting all sorts. We used to be the Singapore of Western Europe, for heaven's sakes. What happened? All I see when I look around this city I love – the southern part, at least – are the signs of defeat, of surrender!'

Hennessy throws his drunken tuppennies in then.

'This city needs to start believing in itself again. Charlie, tell him about the poster we thought up.'

'Yes, my election poster,' the old man goes. 'It's going to be one of these split-screen affairs. On one side, a picture of Grafton Street, as it is now, the full horror – the head shops, the tattoo parlours, the fifty per cent off signs. On the other side – your correspondent here, wearing the chains of office, with a yonderly look in my eye, as if spotting the happier times on the horizon. And underneath – this is the master-stroke, Ross – the slogan. A Total Mare . . . A Total Mayor!'

Hennessy goes, 'You're giving me goosebumps, Charlie. No, you're giving me goosebumps *on* my goosebumps.'

That's enough for the old man.

'Give me the phone,' he just goes. He takes it, then hits redial. He's like, 'Hello,' putting on a squeaky voice too. 'Is that George Lee? Yes, my wife and I are trying to find out are we entitled to a medical card . . .'

'Whatever happened to this self-centred, cut-throat
people we're supposed to have become
during the Celtic Tiger?'
*The Irish Times, 27 March 2010*

They're porked the full length of Brighton and Torquay roads, causing
absolute mayhem. We're talking Volvo S60s and Ford Explorers. We're
talking Mercedes S Classes, Volkswagen Touaregs and Porsche Box-
ters. We're talking Audi TTs and Jaguar XKs. There's even a Maserati
Quattroporte.

They've come from literally the four corners. Glenageary. Milltown.
Ballsbridge. Rathgor.

Solicitors. Estate agents. Architects. Quantity surveyors. On and on,
they just keep coming, the queue 200, maybe 300 yords long, some collecting food porcels, some bringing them.

The village has never seen anything like it – the first night of the
Foxrock Food Bank.

The old dear, Helen, Fionn and JP are stood behind this long table
at the entrance to the racecourse, literally surrounded by food. It's
everywhere.

In plastic boxes, glass bowls, steel terrines, earthenware dishes. It's
wrapped in tinfoil, cling-film, greaseproof paper.

Vichyssoise soup. Apricot and smoked bream paella. Venison sausages and Oileán mash. Shrimp bisque flambé. Enough to feed an actual
ormy.

The old dear's in her absolute element, of course.

'Deeva Newton,' she's going, 'did one of her fab guinea fowl fricas-
sees. Alice Roos took it – poor Alice – said it'll do her for the week,' and
then she's like, 'Next!'

They're listening to people's stories as well.

'How awful!' I hear Helen go. 'Thirty years paying into a pension
fund, then to find that out! How about a hunter's pie with Madeira and
redcurrant?'

It'd nearly put you in good form just to stand there watching.

Fionn asks me what I think and I tell him I'd have to say, in all honesty, fair focks.

'Yeah,' he goes, 'we just can't believe how people have responded.
We've had as many givers as takers, Ross.'

57

'I ask you again,' JP goes, all smug with himself, 'whatever happened to this self-centred, cut-throat people we're supposed to have become during the Celtic Tiger?'

To be honest, roysh, I'm only, like, *half* paying attention? Honor's in training, you see, for the Little Roedean's Montessori Sports Day at the end of April and I have her running laps, back and forth, between the post office and the Gables, just to build up her stamina for the 50m sprint.

I always said, roysh, that I'd never end up being one of these, I suppose, *pushy* parents? But, at the same time, I do want my daughter to be competitive. See, it's suddenly a tough world out there. Make eye contact with someone these days and the next thing you know they're asking you to validate their porking.

I suppose it's all about finding a happy medium.

I click the stopwatch as she comes toddling over to me, all out of breath.

'That's a personal best for you,' I go, because athletes need constant positive feedback – I know I did.

'Again, Daddy!' she goes. 'Again! Again! Again!' Her face is suddenly lit up like a Polish church. It's possibly the endorphins.

But, at the same time, I'm thinking, if only I'd had her appetite for training, Declan Kidney wouldn't have been talking about my rugby career last weekend in terms of what might have been for Ireland.

'Okay,' I go, 'just two or three more,' but then I end up having to physically stop her, because Sorcha suddenly arrives on the scene – she doesn't exactly agree with me training our daughter – followed by my old man.

He has, like, a brown paper bag in his hand?

'We've brought some fish and chips for the workers,' he goes, except he says *fish and chips* like it's some foreign food he's only just heard about.

'*Fish and chips?*' the old dear gives it. 'How fun!'

He puts his orm around Sorcha's shoulder.

'Well,' he goes, 'I'm going to have get used to it, it seems. My election strategist here tells me that junk food – inverted commas – is all these chaps live on during campaign time.'

He really believes he's going to be the first directly elected Lord Mayor of Dublin.

Sorcha's there, 'Even though I'd recommend a healthy, balanced diet, fast food is good for, like, short-term energy bursts?'

I go, 'Maybe we'll take Honor to Abrakebabra for brekky before the big race, then!'

Sorcha gathers her up in her orms.

'Oh my God!' she goes, with the big-time dramatics. 'She's burning up, Ross! Have you had her running?'

'Hey,' I go, 'I can't stop her. It's in the genes. It'd be like John Oxx telling *Sea the Stors* not to run. Do you think the horse would listen? Er, I don't *think* so?'

The old dear changes the subject then.

'Oh,' she goes, as she hands out the last of the ballotine of Anjou pigeon, 'how's the speechwriting coming along?'

This is Sorcha's new job, by the way, since her boutique in Powerscourt Townhouse Centre went tits up.

'Wonderful!' the old man goes. 'Sorcha's just been showing me some of her early drafts. Oh, it's all suitably inspiring stuff. Hope, I think, is going to be our leitmotif, if you'll pardon the French.'

Sorcha goes, 'We want to, like, emphasize to people – like President Obama did? – that even though we're facing difficult times, we can, all of us, still be inspired and stuff? Despite everything, Dublin is still an amazing place to live.'

'Well, south of Leeson Street Bridge,' the old man makes sure to go, 'and east of the M50 . . . Portmornock and Malahide can be pleasant – they just built them in the wrong bloody place, that's all.'

A cork suddenly pops and we all automatically cheer. Helen has opened a bottle of champagne. She pours it into plastic cups and we all sort of, like, stand around, waiting for someone to make a toast.

'To the Foxrock Food Bank,' the old man goes, 'and your wonderful success here tonight. And to the future. Happier transports to be!'


## 'Drico has drawn a line in the sand.'
### *The Irish Times*, 3 July 2010


Yeah, no, I wondered would I get the call? Then I finally did – pretty late in the day as well. Might have known he'd make me sweat it. But Monday morning the invitation finally dropped through the letterbox and I was stood in the hallway giving it the old left to right, thinking how you'd *have* to say fair focks – bygones be bygones and blah, blah, blah.

See, me and Drico *have* had our differences down through the years, most of them rugby-related. I happen to know it drives him mad that, whenever we meet each other, I always make a point of wearing my Leinster Schools Senior Cup medal *outside* my shirt?

But then, in my defence, when Tana Umaga did what he did a few years back, who was the one who stood outside Kielys and told RTÉ's Colm Murray that a *true* Maori warrior would never do something shitty like that?

That's right – it was me.

So it's fair to say there's, like, a mutual respect there. *He*'s on the record somewhere as saying that I *could* have played at number ten for Ireland had I not pissed my talent up against the wall – which was an amazing thing for me to hear, because I don't *always* get the recognition?

Straight away, I rang JP with the news.

'Guess where I'm going to be on Friday?' I went. 'A certain county called . . . er, Leitrim? That's not a misprint, is it?'

He was like, 'No, it exists, Ross. I sold a fair few houses there back in the day. The Commuter Belt Just Went Out a Couple More Notches – front page headline in the *Irish Times* property section. God, will we ever see days like that again?'

I was there, 'Sorry, can we just bring the conversation back to me for a minute? This is, like, a major deal, Dude. You know what this invitation says?'

'That you've been forgiven for getting mullered and telling Amy that you were in love with her in Krystle on Paddy's Night?'

'No – well, yeah. But also that Drico has drawn a line in the sand. He's saying, you know, "We're both in our thirties now. School was a long time ago. I've achieved all I've achieved and you've – in all fairness to you – achieved all you've achieved . . ."'

'Fock all,' JP went – but I was big enough to let it go.

I'm there, 'I like to think he's also saying, in his own way, thanks. A lot of the things he does on the rugby field he pretty much copied from me.'

JP went, 'So, who are you going to bring?' and I looked down at the invitation again.

I have a plus-one!

I storted running through, like, a mental Rolodex of all my exes, trying to come up with one who would take my call without immediately hanging up on me.

'What about my cousin?' it was JP who went. 'Erin Ferris?'

I was there, 'Erin Go Braless?' which is what we call her for reasons I *could* explain except I know that a lot of children read this column.

He was like, 'Yeah, you went out with her before. Did you know she once knocked back Dorce one night in Club 92?'

Which I didn't know. Of course, for me, that was immediately it. I was thinking, can you imagine Dorce's boat when I walk through the doors of the church with *her* on my orm?

I was like, 'What's she up to these days?' because the last I heard she was in, like, recruitment.

'She's doing, like, spray-on tans. Well, you know how things are on the job front. But that's the honest beauty of it, Ross – she could give you, like, a colour for the day? Meaning you'll really stand out. The rest of the goys, remember, have just spent a month in the New Zealand and Australian winter.'

Literally ten seconds later, I was on the Wolfe to Erin, going, 'Hey, Babes, it's Ross, don't hang up! You'll never guess what I've got here in my hand!'

'Ten o'clock in the morning is a bit early for a booty call,' she went, 'even by your standards.'

I explained to her that it wasn't that at all – not this time – it was actually an invitation to *the* event of the year and I wanted her to be my basically plus-one.

Judging from the 'oh my God' count, she was seriously impressed.

I was there, 'We'll drive up to this so-called Leitrim on Thursday afternoon. But you get over here a couple of hours beforehand and sort me out with a serious Jackie Chan.'

She's like, 'Yeah, no, cool.'

So Thursday morning – good as her word – Erin arrives at Rosa Parks, the oportment complex where I'm living, with all her gear. I don't know how many of you are familiar with the – let's just call it – *process*, but basically Erin pitched this pretty much tent in my bathroom. I lashed on a hairnet and some paper jockeys, then stepped into it, while she stood outside with this thing that looked like the gun from a petrol pump and literally spray-painted me, like poor people do to their cors.

Of course, while this was all happening, I was still babbling away, going, 'Yeah, no, with me and Drico, it's a real *Sliding Doors* thing? As in, back in the late nineties, we were both stors of our school teams, me in Castlerock, him in – and I'm going to have to say the word – Blackrock. Then *obviously* our careers took off in different directions . . . Hey, does that tan not look a bit dork to you?'

She was there, 'No, it'll lighten up when it dries. Continue – what you're saying is really, really interesting.'

'Oh, well, it's just that, you know, *he* obviously went on to captain

Ireland and the Lions. Grand Slam. Heineken Cup. Record try scorer. Marrying . . . well, *she* knows how I feel about her. Whereas, I . . . Well, I went the scenic route and I . . . Well, I . . . Do you know what, I wish *I'd* focking speartackled him now when I had the actual chance!'

'Finished,' she suddenly went.

I was like, 'Great. Can't wait to see this.'

I stepped out of the tent and checked myself out in the full-length mirror. There was no preparing me for the shock. Erin was smiling like a monkey eating shit out of a hairbrush. I was literally blacker than a bailiff's hort.

'What the fock have you done?' I went. 'I can't go to the wedding looking like this!'

She was like, 'Ross, you're not going to the wedding.'

And that's when I heard the sniggering from outside the bathroom door. It was JP. And it was suddenly obvious to me. *He* printed up the invitation. His idea of a joke.

You know, I'm so slow sometimes they could put deckchairs on me and sail me round the Caribbean.

### 'He talks some amount of shite that McWilliams dude, doesn't he?' *The Irish Times*, 6 November 2010

David McWilliams is on the radio saying that *the* most important person in Ireland right now – in terms of the country's potential for economic recovery *in* the short term – isn't Brian Cowen. And isn't even Brian Lenihan. It's actually *X Factor* finalist Meerdy Burden.

'If Meerdy succeeds in capturing votes,' he says, 'in the same way that she's captured the horts of a frankly ravaged nation, there's no doubt that she'll be the ultimate winner of *X Factor* 2010, thus generating a sense of elation among Irish people in the days immediately after the delivery of what promises to be *the* most difficult Budget in the history of the state.

'This – let's just call it – feel-good factor,' he says, 'will guarantee an increase in national confidence of the kind not seen since we were routinely winning Eurovision Song Contests in the early – let's remember – embryonic years of the Celtic Tiger. And this confidence, in turn, *will* precipitate a return to consumer spending in the weeks leading up to Christmas.

'In that sense,' he goes, 'Meerdy Burden – a checkout lady, remember, from Ballyfermot, who first entered our consciousness singing, 'I Who Have Nothing' – is very much Ireland's Eva Perón. Or at least the Eva Perón of the Irish retail sector.'

I laugh.

I'm like, 'He talks some amount of shite that McWilliams dude, doesn't he? Blackrock College, of course – I'm tempted to say it.'

Except the old man has that, I don't know, *distant* look in his eyes?

'Reminds me of the kind of conversations that Hennessy and I used to have back in the day,' he goes. 'I think I've told you about the old Leggs of Lower Leeson Street School of Economics, which we called ourselves to distinguish us from Colm McCarthy and his Doheny's crowd. Oh, happy times!'

This is us, by the way, sitting in the Shred Focking Everything van on Mespil Road. It's my old man's latest venture and – yeah, no – we've got a pick-up in, like, fifteen minutes.

'You've probably noticed,' he goes, 'that your *old dad* is a little more chipper than usual this morning.'

I'm just like, 'No,' because it doesn't pay to let him get too palsy-walsy with you.

'Well, I am! You see, I rather think we've turned the corner, Ross, in terms of this current economic what's-it.'

'Er, *what* are you basing that on?'

'Just a sense I get – being in business and so forth.'

'*Being* in business? We're shredding documents. Evidence, in other words. You said it yourself. People aren't ready to hear what it was that made this country great for eleven and a little bit years. All we're doing is making sure that no one finds out.'

'Exactly,' he goes, whipping out a Cohiba that'd give a focking stud horse a complex. 'But look how many others have moved into our line of work since we set up Shred Focking Everything. There's Get Rid Quick, Slash & Byrne . . .'

'So?'

'*So?* Don't you appreciate the work we're doing, Ross?'

'What, shredding things to stop certain people – mainly *your* friends – being sent to jail?'

'Well, not just that. In a metaphorical sense, I like to think that we're burning the field to make the soil fertile for new growth. Preparing the ground, if you will, for the next, inverted commas, boom.'

'Yeah, whatever.'

'You mork my words, Kicker, we've already seen the worst of this famous current economic business. What's this the song says? The only way is upwards!'

We're sat there suddenly listening to the theme tune from *The Fast and the Furious*. It's my phone ringing. I check the little screen and it's from, like, a *blocked* number? I take a chance and answer it anyway.

I'm like, 'Ross O'Carroll-Kelly. Since 1980,' which is basically a *thing* I've storted doing.

'Oh, hello,' she goes.

She has a voice that for some reason has me immediately picturing Candice Swanepoel.

She's like, 'This is Nadia Calderwood from, like, Ephesus Property Management?' and I actually laugh. Ephesus are the crowd that are supposedly *managing* the Rosa Parks estate these days.

I'm there, 'Sorry, go on.'

'Well,' she goes, 'we're just ringing around to inform all our residents – we'll be doing it formally by letter as well – that demolition work is about to begin on the three unfinished blocks.'

I'm literally like, 'Er, demolition work?'

'Yes, they're actually going to do it by controlled explosion. That's why we're asking people to keep their obviously windows closed. There's bound to be a lot of dust.'

I'm there, 'Whoa, horsey! I'm still back at demolition here. What are you even talking about?'

'The unfinished blocks. The builder has decided to tear them down. The place is going to be a bit of a moonscape for a while.'

I'm there, 'Sorry, do you mind me asking why this is happening?'

She actually laughs at that. 'Have you just woken from a two-year coma or something?'

'Excuse me?'

'Well, I presume you've watched the news at least once since September 2008.'

'Continue.'

'I'm talking about the collapse of the country's economy.'

'In other words, the recession – yeah, I know all about it. But hello? Those blocks are, like, nearly finished.'

'But the builder doesn't have the money to complete the work. He's as good as bankrupt,' she goes, and then she does this funny little laugh. 'Just like the country.'

I'm there, 'There must be someone who'd be prepared to finish them. They're actually amazing aportments. And you goys said it yourselves on that huge banner you hung from one of the blocks – fifteen per cent already occupied!'

She finds this, for some reason, hilarious as well. 'That's called trying to see the glass as being half full,' she goes. 'Or fifteen per cent full, in this case.'

I'm there, 'Can I just say, this isn't the dream we were sold when we bought our gaffs there. What would the *actual* Rosa Parks say about this if she was alive today? Has the builder even thought about that?'

'I doubt it. He lives in Portugal now. Anyway, like I said, there's also a letter on its way to you. The demolition is happening on Thursday, the eighteenth of November. There'll be noise. And don't forget, the windows.'

Then she just hangs up.

I turn to the old man. Er, *what* was that he said about us having already seen the worst of this thing?

I'm there, 'I'd love to know how Meerdy Burden is going to make *this* better.'

# 2011

Taoiseach Brian Cowen resigns as leader of Fianna Fáil and is succeeded by Micheál Martin * A General Election sees the two government parties, Fianna Fáil and the Green Party, decimated. Fine Gael and Labour form a coalition government, with Enda Kenny as Taoiseach * Queen Elizabeth II visits Ireland, the first reigning British monarch to do so since Ireland gained its Independence * Leinster stage a remarkable second-half comeback to beat Northampton 33–22 and win their second Heineken Cup * Osama bin Laden is shot dead during a military operation in Pakistan * Prince William marries Catherine Middleton * Singer Amy Winehouse dies * US President Barack Obama pays an official visit to Ireland, including his ancestral village of Moneygall, County Offaly * An Occupy Wall Street protest is staged in New York, sparking a new form of demonstration. It is followed by an Occupy Dame Street protest as government austerity measures cause hardship for millions of Irish people * Goalkeeper Stephen Cluxton converts an injury-time free-kick as Dublin beat Kerry to win their first All Ireland football title in sixteen years * In a special televised address, Taoiseach Enda Kenny tells the Irish people that the economic crisis is not their fault but warns of difficult days ahead * Apple CEO and co-founder Steve Jobs dies * Ireland pull off a major shock by beating Australia at the Rugby World Cup, but are defeated by Wales in the quarter-finals * Seán Gallagher, a businessman and reality TV personality, becomes the front-runner in the Irish presidential election, until an erroneous Tweet, read out during a TV debate, changes the course of the contest. Michael D. Higgins is elected the ninth President of Ireland *

Meanwhile . . .

'Happy to see the back of the Greens, with their
mealy mouths and their rental bikes.'
*The Irish Times, 22 January 2011*

'So Brian Cowen's wife says, "What are you doing home? I thought
you were playing golf with Seán FitzPatrick today." And Brian Cowen
says, "Huh! Would you play golf with a man who's forever trying to
sneak his way out of the rough, who's constantly asking for Mulligans
and who can't be trusted to do simple arithmetic?" His wife says,
"Probably not, no." And Brian Cowen says, "Well, neither will he!"'

It's possibly the first joke I've heard Hennessy tell that doesn't
involve a man who hasn't had sex for thirty years and a genie who
grants him three wishes. Of course, the old man laughs like it's the
funniest thing he's ever heard.

It's eleven o'clock on a Thursday morning and the two of them are
already half-cut. I have to pretend to clear my throat for them to even
notice me standing at the door of the old man's study. You could disin-
fect Beaumont with the brandy fumes in here.

'Kicker!' he goes. 'I didn't hear you come in.'

I'm like, 'Yeah, that much is obvious.'

'Your godfather and I were just discussing politics. The intrigue
and so forth. I think I speak for both of us when I say we'll be happy
to see the back of the Greens, with their mealy mouths and their
rental bikes. Tell him, Hennessy. Tell him that terrifying statistic you
told me.'

Hennessy's there, 'In a lifetime, the average worker will hand over
€200,000 in taxes to pay for initiatives that began with the words, "In
Scandinavia, what they do is . . ."'

'Terrifying,' the old man goes, 'isn't it? Wait a minute, Ross, is that a
frown I see? Don't tell me this current economic business is finally getting you down.'

I'm there, 'I told you before, it's not affecting me. I can't believe you have to even ask me what's wrong.' Except he just stares back at me, roysh, blankly.

'Okay,' I go, 'so there I am, a few weeks back – it was during the snow – and I'm walking over Ranelagh bridge one night. There's a woman in a cor and she's stuck – as in, she can't get over the bridge because her wheels keep spinning on, like, the ice? So I tip over and go, "Can I be of any assistance?" giving it the big-time gentleman act.

'So I end up giving her a shove over the bridge. She says thanks and tells me that it's nice to see that, despite everything I've got going for me, I'm still a nice, down-to-earth goy. That's when I should have suspected. But I didn't. I just gave her a wink and, well, obviously the guns, and she went on her way.'

'This story sounds mightily familiar,' it's, like, Hennessy who goes.

I'm there, 'Yeah! The reason being that the next day she rang Newstalk and told them that Brian O'Driscoll had rescued her from the snow the night before.'

They both act upset for me, in fairness to them.

'You?' the old man even goes. 'You were the famous knight in shining ormour?'

'Exactly. And I wouldn't mind, but I've only done maybe three good deeds in my entire life. And of all people, *he* ends up getting the credit.'

The old man – I think it's a word that's used – grimaces? 'I could have Hennessy here send him one of his world-famous solicitor's letters. Cease and desist and what-not. I'll leave the wording to you, old scout.'

I'm like, 'No, because that'd come across as, like, sour grapes? Yeah, no, people will say it's, like, pure jealousy. And especially because it's him? I mean, I already feel like he's living the life that was actually meant for me. It's literally like something out of a science-fiction movie.'

The old man gives me his best sympathetic look.

'By the way,' I go, 'do you still have that franking machine?'

'Franking machine? I have to confess, Ross, you have me intrigued now. I was going to ask you when you walked through the door what that was under your orm.'

It's a stack of, like, brown A4 envelopes.

He goes, 'Wondered were they CVs . . . Worried I was about to lose your services to a rival document-disposal company. Get Rid Quick. Or even Slash & Byrne.'

'They're just spring-break brochures.'

'Spring-break brochures?'

'Yeah, I'm sending them to Rog and Strings and the rest of the Munster goys. I mean, they're going to have fock-all else to do come April.'

He and Hennessy laugh, in all fairness. 'Oh,' the old man goes, 'speaking of unsolicited mail, you won't credit what arrived with the morning post. A bill from those wretched electronic-toll people for – get this – using the M50 toll! Oh, I gave them a piece of my mind. Said I hadn't been north of Sussex Street for at least six months. It's obviously one of these mistakes they're famous for.'

The thing is, roysh, it's actually not? See, I actually borrowed his wheels over Christmas. Had a couple of nights of non-committal fun with a little scrump-nugget from Malahide.

'It was me,' I end up going. 'I borrowed your car.'

'Oh, Ross, I wish you'd told me. These bloody fines, they increase . . . what was that word you used, Hennessy?'

'Logarithmically,' Hennessy goes.

'That's the one. It started out as €3 per journey. Seems now I owe them €100,000. Did you know that if you don't pay after ten weeks they can take your house and sell your children for vivisection? I mean, how did they get these powers? I shall be making it a central plank in my campaign for mayoral office.'

'It's a pity,' I go, really just thinking out loud, 'that no one's ever invented, like, a wobbly licence plate?'

'A what?' they both, at the same time, go.

'As in, you press a little button and your licence plate sort of, like, wobbles from side to side? So basically the camera can't get a reading on your actual reg.'

The two of them look at each other with what can only be described as pretty much awe.

'Charlie,' Hennessy goes, 'it's like listening to you thirty years ago.'

The old man lays his hand on my shoulder. He looks prouder than he did the day I brought home my Leinster Schools Senior Cup medal.

'This family has already made one fortune during a recession by, well, let's just say, operating on the fringes of legality. Seems it's true what they say. The apple doesn't fall far from the tree. Hennessy, call the patents office.'

## 'This isn't doing 120 Ks on the Rock Road, Ross. It's serious.'
### *The Irish Times, 5 February 2011*

Oisinn says he can't believe the ad he heard on the radio this morning. There's a supermorket chain offering an entire family meal – we're talking meat, we're talking veg, we're talking potatoes – for €7. He says he can't believe it's the same country that he left two years ago, when he porked his cor in the short-term cor pork at Dublin Airport, left the keys on the front passenger seat and pretty much disappeared.

He's right in a way. I mean, *seven* yoyos? Two or three years ago you'd have dropped that in the bucket of whatever GAA club was packing your shopping. But I still feel instantly bad, being the one who persuaded him to come back and face the muesli – specifically the 70-something million he owes the banks.

'Hey,' he suddenly goes, 'you can take that look off your face right now.'

I'm like, 'What look?' but we've been mates too long for me to even think about trying to bullshit him? 'Okay, cords on the table. I'm worried that you're going to realize what a dump this country suddenly is and do another pork and hide. And that this time I might not be able to find you?'

He laughs, then he gets suddenly serious. He's wearing a humungous black Afro wig, red-tinted shades and zebra-skin suit. I should have possibly mentioned that I've thrown him a belated thirtieth birthday porty in Krystle and the theme is, like, pimps and hos.

'I'm not going anywhere,' he just goes. 'This is where I belong, Ross.'

I'm there, 'That sounds very much like fighting talk to me.' We're both having to shout to be heard over the sound of Katy Perry.

'I don't know about fighting talk. I'm prepared to face it, though – whatever it is.'

'Well, the word on the grapevine is you've got Hennessy Coghlan-O'Hara on your case. End of discussion.'

'Well, not quite. All he's done is set up a meeting between me and my creditors.'

I'm like, 'Er, how many penalty points has he managed to get – I don't know – expunged for us down through the years?'

'This isn't doing 120 Ks on the Rock Road, Ross. It's serious.'

'Well, I for one have faith in him. He's as dodgy as they come. But either way, happy birthday, Dude.'

I look – it has to be said – amazing, and I think even my critics would admit it. I'm wearing, like, a purple silk shirt, open to the navel obviously – any opportunity to show off the old squeezebox abs – ridiculously tight trousers, shades, a white Stetson and – the Crème de la Mer of the entire outfit – the old dear's white genuine seal-fur coat.

I let my eyes do a drunken sweep of the club. All of the girls are here – we're talking Chloe, Sophie, Amie with an ie – all of them dressed the same: in other words denim minis, pink boob tubes and the old PVC slag wellies. I can tell from her body language that Sophie is going all out to try to be with Oisinn tonight. She's just, like, staring at him, her little mouth working like a trout about to take a fly.

Fionn arrives with Erika. He gets his round in – I'll say that straight away in his defence. He says they drove past one of these famous ghost estates this afternoon. It was in, like, Mullinavat, a name that immediately brings me back to my days as an estate agent and the job I had – even when the Celtic Tiger was still going – of persuading people that it was a commutable distance from Dublin.

He's like, 'What did that sign say again, Erika?'

'Oh, yes,' she goes, 'it said twenty per cent already occupied.'

'Twenty per cent,' Fionn goes, 'with an exclamation mark at the end – like it was an actual selling point that one out of every five houses had somebody living in it!' He pushes his glasses up on his nose. I still can't believe he's, like, marrying my half-sister. Of course it might end up never happening, with a bit of luck.

It's me who ends up asking the obvious question. 'What were you even doing in Mullinavat?'

He's there, 'Looking at a site. It's my new business idea,' and he's, like, full of himself.

I actually laugh. I'm like, 'Business idea? Yeah, can I just remind you that you're supposed to be, like, a schoolteacher?'

He goes, 'Yeah, that's actually where the idea came from. Battle re-enactments!'

'Battle re-enactments?'

'Exactly. For students studying History for the Junior and Leaving Certificates. Eight or ten Saturdays of the year, they can gather in a field and actually participate in historically correct re-creations of the major battles they're learning about in school – everything from the Siege of Leningrad to the Battle of Clontarf to the massacre at Scullabogue. It's a way of gaining a better understanding of the main military flashpoints they're learning about but doing it in a way that's engaging and, dare I say it, fun.'

I just pull a face. I mean, it's an incredible idea, but I'm not going to let him know that.

Erika takes a sip of Sancerre, then goes, 'One thing that's certainly not in short supply in this country at the moment is fields. There's a lot of developers out there who paid ridiculous money for land that's never going to be built on. A lot of them are happy to rent it out. Well, they're obviously desperate to get something back.'

I go, 'You two seem to have really thought this through.' Fionn takes it as a compliment.

'Well, yeah, Erika's done up a whole business plan,' he goes, the two of them suddenly lost in each other's eyes. 'I mean, she's spoken to all the main schools, and there's genuine enthusiasm for the idea. We think we could have as many as 2,000 people for the first one.'

I'm like, 'Two *thousand*? Paying how much each?' Of course he's too cool to even tell me. He just turns to Oisinn.

'We'd love to take you on,' he goes, 'as a sort of business adviser.'

Oisinn laughs. 'Dude, I'm hardly in a position to advise anyone on business.'

'I disagree,' Fionn goes. 'You and Erika ran that divorce fair at the RDS a few years back – it was a huge success, from what everyone remembers.'

Oisinn just shakes his head. He's only back a few weeks and he's already landed a job. And, from the way Sophie's looking at him, she'll be going at him later like a mush dog.

He goes, 'It's great to be home,' and he genuinely means it.

> 'This is something I'm famous for,
> of course – thinking too deeply.'
> *The Irish Times*, 12 February 2011

I had, like, a significant birthday recently? We're talking the big three-one. And while knocking back a few celebratory pints of Responsibly in Kielys of Donnybrook Town, I have to admit, I found myself – I think the phrase is – taking stock? As in, thinking about the years and how quickly they go by.

It's, like, one day, you're young, good-looking and loaded and you're working your way through the female population of South Dublin like a bad rumour. The next, you're staring down the barrel of your forties and an age where pulling an all-nighter means getting a good night's sleep without having to get up for a piss.

This is something I'm famous for, of course – thinking too deeply. But whenever the likes of Johnny Sexton and Luke Fitzgerald ring me for advice, the one thing I make sure to tell them is to enjoy it. Because today you're listening to the adulation of the crowd. Tomorrow you'll be listening to . . .

'Oh my God, what are you driving?'

That's Honor, by the way – my five-year-old daughter, who I'm supposed to be bringing to Montessori. 'It's Seán FitzPatrick's old Beamer,' I go. 'The old man bought it for me at, like, an auction?'

She sort of, like, screws her face up, like she's caught the whiff of bad plumbing. 'Who's Seán FitzPatrick?'

I laugh. Can't help it. It's the same dilemma that a lot parents are facing – as in, what do we tell our children?

'Seán FitzPatrick was a very clever man,' I go. 'He actually played golf with your granddad.'

'Why does it say wanker on the side?'

'Honor, you shouldn't even know that word. But it's because a lot of people are very angry with him at the moment.'

'Well,' she goes, giving me the elevator eyes, 'you should be one of them – if he sold you this piece of crap. It's from, like, '92?'

'Yeah, no,' I go, helping her into the back seat, 'like I said, he didn't sell it to me? It was, like, repossessed and the old man stuck in a bid for it.'

She's like, 'Yeah, whatevs!'

She insists on sitting in the back – I don't know if I mentioned – because she likes the feeling of being basically chauffeured.

I get in the front and stort the engine, while she whips out her phone and storts immediately texting someone.

I'm there, 'See, the thing is, Honor, it's not so much the cor as what it, like, symbolizes?'

I watch her in the rear-view basically shrug. 'Which is what exactly?'

'I suppose you could call them the olden days.'

She shakes her head. 'Oh my God,' she goes, looking back down at her phone, 'you are so lame.'

This is possibly me again showing my age, but I remember a time when kids only spoke to adults like that on *The Late Late Toy Show*.

Remember you'd watch some little kid getting snippy with Pat Kenny, and the entire audience would laugh, and you'd laugh at home, and everyone you met for the next week would be laughing about it as well – but at the same time you were secretly thinking, if she was mine, I'd dangle her by the focking ankles from the top of the Stephen's Green Shopping Centre until she apologized.

Nowadays, as far as I can see, all kids talk to their parents like that – like they think adults are pretty much stupid? There's nothing we can do about it, of course. All we can do is accept it. I just don't know where it comes from. TV possibly.

My phone all of a sudden rings. It's the old dear. I stick her on speaker. There's no hello, how are you, or anything. She just goes, 'Did you hear the wonderful news?'

I'm like, 'Ireland has agreed an extradition treaty with Bolivia and the plastic surgeon who did that to your face might finally be brought to justice?'

She doesn't respond to that. Wouldn't give me the pleasure, see. Instead, she goes, 'No, Ross, they're turning my book into a movie.'

The book she's talking about, of course, is her recession-era misery-lit novel, *Mom, They Said They'd Never Heard of Sundried Tomatoes*, which people are actually buying, proving that this country isn't as hord-up for money as McWilliams and all that crowd claim.

'It's been optioned by Warner Brothers,' she goes. 'They said that the story of little Zara Mesbur and a country's struggle – told through a child's eyes – to come to terms with the current economic paradigm is a modern classic that recalls the works of Charles Dickens.'

I'm like, 'Yeah, whatevs!'

'And it's a story that I hope will give people heart, Ross. Because there are terrible things happening out there. Did I tell you what they're selling now in Marks & Spencer?'

'I don't know – reusable teabags?'

'Worse. Bread and jam sandwiches, Ross. Bread and bloody jam. Oh, it's like something from *Oliver Twist*. Anyway, you and I must go out to dinner to celebrate.'

'I'd rather eat roadkill off a bus tyre than have a meal with you.'

She goes, 'Okay, I'll book somewhere,' and then she just hangs up.

Honor's still texting away merrily, by the way. I look in the rear-view and go, 'Who are you texting there?'

Except she doesn't answer.

I'm like, 'Who are you texting, Honor?'

She looks up again, madder than the Old Testament. 'I said my friend Malorie. Are you deaf or something?'

'Sorry, Babes, I mustn't have heard you.'

'Er, try cleaning your ears out, then? And park on the opposite side of Merrion Square. I don't want anyone in Little Roedeans seeing me arriving in this piece of, like, junk.'


## 'A Charles O'Carroll-Kelly presidency is just what the country needs.'
### *The Irish Times*, 11 June 2011

How's Seán FitzPatrick's old cor running, the old man wants to know.

I'm like, 'Fine,' because it's quicker all round just to give him an answer.

'Because he still asks after it, you know. Just the other day, in fact, on the difficult fifth hole in Delgany. "How's that old cor of mine running?" says our friend.'

'I already told you it was running fine. I mean, yeah, I end up taking a fair bit of abuse for it. People shouting shit at me in the street. Wanker, traitor, blahdy blah. I pulled up at the lights outside the dole office in Dún Laoghaire last week and someone tried to drag me out on to the road through the window on the passenger side.'

'Good Lord!'

'Hey, it's no worse than what I had to put up with when I was, like, captaining Castlerock back in the day. I actually don't mind being a bit, I don't know, notorious?'

This is us standing over the shredder, by the way, feeding documents into it. We're coining it in. We've done nine, like, pick-ups already today and we're wiping the floor with Slash & Byrne, Des Troy Evidence and the rest of the opposition.

'Oh, it's well I remember,' he goes, 'what you went through to win that senior cup medal. Do you remember a couple of nights before the final, you and the chaps were accused of wrapping the Newbridge College coach's cor in – what's this they call it – cling-film?'

I laugh.

'I had to get Hennessy to send one of his world-famous solicitor's letters,' he goes, 'to stop the school making in public the same accusations they'd made on the telephone to me.'

I'm like, 'Well, it's probably only fair that I tell you, then – it was actually me.'

'What?'

'Me and Oisinn. We did it to, like, fock with their heads. Destroy them mentally before they even went out on to the field.'

This is all news to him, of course, and I can see that he's, like, struggling with it.

'But why did you deny it at the time? You said you were in your room the whole time, cramming – for your Irish oral, wasn't it?'

'That's because I knew you'd buy it – and I knew you'd defend me, like the sap you are.'

'Oh, well,' he just goes. It's very difficult to actually hurt my old man, much as I try. 'I suppose the point I was trying to make still stands. You have to be prepared to suffer the brickbats and the whatnots if you want to lead . . .'

He's shaping up to tell me something. I just know it. He's grinning like a focking axe-killer.

'Go on,' I go, 'spit it out.'

He's like, 'Well, do you remember a few months back, all that talk of your old dad here running to become Dublin's first directly elected Lord Mayor?'

'Not really. A lot of the time when you think I'm listening to you, I'm actually just nodding while focusing on a point in the distance. I've become a pretty much yoga master at ignoring you over the years.'

'Well, Kicker, it turns out that I have a confession of my own to make. The Lord Mayor business was nothing more than a smoke-screen. No, the real prize I'm after is something far greater. Ross, I put out a press release yesterday to the effect that Charles O'Carroll-Kelly intends seeking a nomination to run for the presidency!'

That gets my instant attention. 'The presidency?' I go. 'The presidency of what?'

He looks at me like the answer should be somehow obvious. 'The presidency of Ireland, of course.'

I laugh so hord, I end up nearly herniating myself. 'I thought you were going to say the presidency of the golf club! The presidency of Ireland? You want to be the President of basically Ireland?'

'It might surprise you, Ross, but quite a number of people – your god-father included – are of the view that a Charles O'Carroll-Kelly presidency is just what the country needs at this, well, uncertain juncture in our history.'

'Er, what are you even talking about?'

'Well, positivity, Ross. Its spirits lifted. That's what I'm all about, isn't it? You saw me on *The Frontline* a few weeks ago, telling Pat Kenny to stop referring to the current economic crisis and stort calling it what it really is – the current economic challenge!'

'You were booed. Didn't someone try to throw a dig at you?'

'Oh, I'll win people around, don't you worry about that, with my message of hope. Yes, we're in something of an – inverted commas – bind. But look on the bright side. We've got the IMF in, giving us a dig-out, plus we've got NAMA, looking after some of the poor unfortunates out there who've lost almost everything through no fault of their own. No, it's time Ireland stopped focusing on the negative and put its best face forward.'

'And you're our best face? Jesus, I've seen better faces in the fish cabinet in Cavistons.'

'I hear the note of caution you're sounding, Ross, and it's respectfully noted. Oh, I know what you're thinking. You're worried that my deciding to run for public office is going to mean it's open season on your old dad. The papers will be picking through my past life, looking for something, anything, to use as a stick with which to beat me . . .'

'Er, you did *how* many years in the clink for bribing county councillors? They won't have to dig too deep.'

'But I've got broad shoulders, Ross. I can take it.' It's at that exact point that his phone rings. It's Hennessy – I can just tell by the way his face lights up when he answers. 'Ah, my election agent! I'm just in the process, old scout, of winning over a key voter here!' and that's when I watch his face turn suddenly serious.

He listens for a bit, then he storts, like, shaking his head, giving it, 'No! No, they can't! Surely even our press would never stoop so low! But that was years ago!'

I'm straight away laughing, even though I don't know what it is yet. Maybe he was right – he's already succeeded in lifting my spirits.

Anyway, this continues for the next five minutes or so, then he hangs up, looking, it has to be said, as sick as I've ever seen him.

'Go on,' I go, 'this should be hilarious.'

'You remember when I was elected to Dún Laoghaire-Rathdown County Council?' he goes. 'Well, I did an interview during the campaign. It was, I should add, an academic, hypothetical and intellectual discussion, during which I just so happened to mention that I thought the unemployed should be allowed to have only one child, like in China. And now several newspapers seem determined to twist my words completely out of context.'

'I bought two aportments, remember,
in a place called Bulgaria.'
*The Irish Times, 9 July 2011*

I don't know why he insists on putting himself through it. Putting me through it as well? The plan was to go to Kielys for a few Sunday lunch-time scoops. Except when I picked him up from his old pair's, he said he wanted to come here, presumably to see this instead. Although I don't bother arguing. It's Oisinn, after all.

'Here,' I go, squinting my eyes, 'that's that painting you bought that time. What was the dude called who did it?'

He's like, 'John Kingerlee,' except he doesn't say it in, like, a defensive way?

I end up just shaking my head. 'I'm going to be one hundred per cent honest with you, Ois, I never knew what it was actually of?'

'What?'

'Well, obviously a painting's got to be of something. Either a cow or a house or a – I don't know – waterfall? Especially one that costs – how much was it again?'

'Fifty Ks.'

'I mean, fifty focking Ks. I used to stare at it sometimes – you know, when you used to throw your famous porties – and I'd think, maybe those white blobs there are actual clouds. Or sheep even. But that was with, like, six or seven cans of Responsibly inside me.'

Oisinn just cracks his hole laughing, which is nice to see. He goes, 'It's a grid composition, Ross,' as if that's any excuse.

I'm like, 'Dude, no offence, but when you first showed it to me, that was the first time I wondered whether the whole Celtic Tiger thing had maybe gone a little bit too far. Pictures that aren't actually of anything – here, I might even throw McWilliams that line next time I see the focker in Finnegan's.'

This is us, by the way, staring through the railings of his old gaff on Shrewsbury Road, while a team of, I suppose, removers strips the place basically bare.

'Do you want to know the hilarious thing?' he goes. 'I bought it without even seeing it.'

He doesn't seem half as upset as I expected him to be. In a funny way, bankruptcy actually suits him?

'I wouldn't beat yourself up over that,' I go. 'That's just was the way it was back then. I bought two aportments, remember, in a place called Bulgaria, which I couldn't even pick off a map at the time. Still couldn't. That's if it's even still there.'

I watch two men carry out a nineteenth-century mourning bed, then just fock it down, like it came from Horvey focking Norman. I watch Oisinn's face for a reaction, except there's none.

'So,' I go, 'what's going to, like, happen to all this shit?'

'It'll be auctioned off,' he goes, easy breezy, 'and the proceeds divided among my creditors.'

'This focking recession!' I go, actually kicking the railing – I don't know why? Possibly just to offer him a few words of support. 'If I ever run into Brian Cowen . . .'

'It's fine, Ross.'

'. . . he'll be decked – and that's a promise.'

He laughs, then just puts his orm around my shoulder. 'Ross, I'm telling you, I'm okay with this.'

'What, with everything you own in the world being sold to . . . Jesus, who even knows who?'

He looks back at the gaff. 'I'm telling you the truth. I don't actually care.'

I'm like, 'Er, you must do? I mean, why else are we here?'

He shakes his head. 'I just wanted to see would I feel something – you know, if I saw it happening with my own eyes.'

'And you're saying you don't?'

'I actually don't.'

'Even though that's an actual Comtoise longcase they're just focking in the back of that van there?'

'But I have no attachment to it, Ross. I've no attachment to any of this stuff. Most of it I didn't even buy myself. I focking hired somebody to buy it for me. I mean, I won't miss any of it.'

'What, even that writing bureau? Like, that was from, I don't know, some other century – literally ages ago.'

'I couldn't even tell you what room it was in, Ross.'

'It was in the vestibule.'

'The vestibule,' he goes, suddenly turning his back on me. 'Whatever.'

He stares up the road, like he's taking it in for the last time. I suppose in a way he is.

'Hord to believe,' I go, 'that this was, like, the most expensive road in the world to buy a house.'

He's there, 'It was actually the sixth most expensive,' trying to put a positive spin on things.

'Even so,' I go, 'they used to complain around here that the billionaires were pushing out the millionaires. Now, it might end up being like one of those actual ghost estates. Who would have ever seen that coming?'

He turns and storts walking back to the cor. He climbs into the front passenger seat and I get in beside him.

I'm like, 'Let's hit the battle cruiser, will we?' Except he pulls a face. He's there, 'I, er, might just go home. Well, back to Mum and Dad's.'

Yeah, back living with his old pair. I could literally weep for him.

'Dude,' I go, 'there's some kind of Gaelic match on today. I heard it on the radio. Kerry against someone. Could be Cork. Why don't we hit Bellamy's. It'll be full of muckers.'

'I don't know.'

'Here,' I go, 'open the old glove box and see what's in there.'

He does exactly that and I watch this smile suddenly erupt across his face. He recognizes my old universal TV remote.

'I'll stick it up my sleeve,' I go, 'just like the old days. Every time it looks like it's about to get interesting, I'll switch the actual channel.'

He laughs. He actually cracks his hole laughing? I genuinely think I'm one of the main reasons he's coping so well with the shit-storm that's blowing through his life right now.

It's called, like, friendship.

'Okay,' he just goes, 'let's do it.'

'He's in surprisingly good form for a man who's just
had his gaff on Shrewsbury Road repossessed.'
*The Irish Times, 30 July 2011*

I see Oisinn wandering along Appian Way with a dog. And I'm talking about an actual dog? It's unfortunate, but given the dude's dating history, it's necessary to point out that detail. I pull over – I'm in the old Shred Focking Everything van – and I go, 'Dude, what the fock?' and even he laughs at the, I suppose, madness of it. I'm like, 'What kind of dog even is it?'

He goes, 'It's a chow chow. It's my old dear's.'

He looks well, it has to be said. It's like the weight of the world has been lifted from his shoulders.

I'm like, 'I don't get it. What's the angle here?' because he's always got something up his sleeve.

He's there, 'There's no angle, Ross. I'm bringing my old dear's dog for a walk.'

'Oh,' I go. 'By the way, I take it you've heard Christian's home from the States. Sacked.'

Oisinn shrugs. 'He was let go with a generous severance package, Ross. That's how the corporate world works. He's supposed to have over-spent on that casino project by $400 million. He can't be too surprised.'

I look at the chow chow sniffing my tyres.

I'm there, 'I suppose you're right. It's all a bit depressing, though, isn't it? Superquinn up for grabs. Leinster training in Tallaght. Drico with his credit union account and McWilliams advertising cider. There's a lot going on in the world right now that you'd have to say is wrong.'

'He doesn't actually drink it, Ross. It's only TV.'

'I know he doesn't drink it. I mean, I know one or two heads in Dalkey, don't forget. When all the other kids were knocking back flagons at the back of the quarry, he'd roll up with a bottle of Pimm's No. 1 Cup. Every-one knows that story. I'd be more worried about – I don't know – the message it sends out. I'm not in any way a fan of my old dear, but she reckons that keeping down with the Joneses is the new thing.'

Oisinn knows me well enough to know that when I stort getting deep and – I suppose – philosophical, you'd better stort running for cover.

He just nods and goes, 'She could have a point.'

I'll say it again, he's in surprisingly good form for a man who's just had his gaff on Shrewsbury Road repossessed.

'I wonder who'll end up living in your old place. Some focking vul-ture, no doubt.'

He gives me a look, like I'm off my meds. He's there, 'You don't know?'

I obviously don't? I'm like, 'Know what?'

You can imagine my reaction when he goes, 'Ross, your old dear bought it.'

My mouth is suddenly slung open like something that's just been pulled off a fishhook. 'My . . .'

'She's moving in next week apparently.'

Well, you can guess what I do next. I put the beast into Drive and I take off with a screech of rubber loud enough to melt the wax in a chow chow's ears. I point the van in the direction of the Four Seasons, where, I might have mentioned, the old dear has been living for the past year, like the focking Major from *Fawlty Towers* – if you can picture the Major wrapped in seal fur and with two pounds of his own arse fat injected into his face.

I don't even need to go up to her room. She's sitting in the lobby café, feeding scones into the giant black hole in the middle of her face. Of course, when she sees me, she tries to act like nothing's happened? She's all, 'Oh, hello, Ross! Well, your daughter is a natural, I'm sure you've heard. The camera loves her!'

She has enough make-up on her face to paint a focking cruise-liner.

I'm there, 'Is it true you've bought Oisinn's gaff?'

She goes, 'I beg your pardon!'

'It's a basic enough question. Are you the vulture who bought Oisinn's old place?'

'Ross, it was for sale.'

'Yeah – because the bank, like, repossessed it?'

'Yes – and put it on the morket. I'm as entitled as anyone to . . .'

Her phone storts, like, vibrating on the table. This is how rude she is – she actually answers it, leaving me just standing there.

'God, you've a face like a ploughed field,' I go, except she just flicks her hand at me, telling me to go away.

It's just as I'm noticing the second teacup on the table that I hear Sorcha's voice. I turn around. She must have been in the old Josh Ritter.

'Oh, this is very cosy,' I make sure to go. 'Did you know she bought Oisinn's gaff?'

She smells great, by the way – if that's not too weird a thing to say about your STBX.

'Ross, don't even try to bring me down,' she goes. 'I'm in amazing, amazing form at the moment.'

'Oh, has your old man come up with a new way of bleeding more maintenance out of me?'

'No, if you must know, I've got a job.'

'What? Where?'

'My friend Claire and her husband Garret are opening an ethical vegetarian restaurant called Eat, Bray, Love. They want me on board for my retail experience.'

'Bit of a comedown, isn't it? Going from owning your own boutique in the Powerscourt Townhouse Centre to working for someone from – you said the word yourself – Bray?'

'Well, we're all having to adjust to the new economic paradigm, Ross.'

The old dear suddenly gets off the phone and goes, 'No, it's not going to be as simple as I thought, Sorcha?'

Sorcha's like, 'But you own it, don't you?'

'Yes, but it seems planning permission would be required. And, as Charles will tell you, it's not as easy to get as it was in the good old days.'

'Oh my God, that's so unfair!'

I end up having to ask, of course. 'What's this about?'

You're not going to believe what comes out of the old dear's mouth. 'I've also bought the first house that Charles and I lived in after we were married.'

I'm there, 'The one in the 'Noggin?'

'It was technically Glenageary, Ross.'

'The one you always describe as your Dachau? Er, why, can I ask?'

'I'm having it pulled down,' she goes, like it's the most normal thing in the world to say, 'and rebuilt in the garden of Shrewsbury Road.'

'Why?'

'To remind myself of how far I've come, of course.'

Sorcha goes, 'A lot of stars in America do it, Ross,' actually defending her?

I'm there, 'Yeah, I've seen *Cribs*, Sorcha,' and then I just stare at the old dear, as she sips her Oolong, and go, 'You're pure evil – like a focking James Bond villain or something.'

'Let me guess. You got into another fight in
Shanahan's, defending Michael Fingleton?'
*The Irish Times*, 13 August 2011

When the old man rang me and said he was in Crumlin Gorda Station, I have to admit that my first thought was for myself. Sometimes the work we do here at Shred Focking Everything would have to be described as, like, borderline illegal? A dude from a company you'd all know had given me eighteen bags of documents an hour earlier and, I swear to God, he was sweating like a petting zoo – kept asking me about some technology that the FBI supposedly has that allows them to put shredded documents back together. He asked me did the Gords have it.

I actually laughed, because I remembered seeing a Gord that morning, sitting at traffic lights on the Stillorgan dualler – on a focking mountain bike!

'I wouldn't worry yourself,' I went. 'It's backwards those goys are going.'

But when Dick Features rang and said he'd just been questioned for, like, sixteen hours, my first instinct – I have to admit – was that I was far too good-looking to go to jail. The company has a protocol that we're supposed to follow if the Gords ever come calling – it's written on the side of the van in red capitals. But I had, like, an alternative plan. I was going to sing like a focking treeful of swallows. I was going to tell them that the old man is the actual criminal mastermind and I'm just his idiot son.

The truth, in other words.

'No, no,' he went, 'it's nothing to do with the business, Ross,' and then he broke off and storted roaring. 'Give me my bloody shoelaces, so I can get out of this confounded place!'

I laughed. 'So, what happened?' I went. 'Let me guess. You got into another fight in Shanahan's, defending Michael Fingleton?' I have to admit, there was no preparing me for what he said next.

'If only it were just that again. No, I was arrested – if you can believe this, Kicker – on suspicion of attempted kidnapping!'

I laughed. 'Er, kidnapping?' I told him I was on my way.

I had to hear it. Even if it meant going to Crumlin.

When I got there, I noticed he had a black eye and a split lip, and he was having a major borney with, like, the desk sergeant? He was there, 'Oh, you'll be hearing from my solicitor. Make no mistake about that!' and then, after a few seconds, 'What station did you bring him to, by the way?'

'Store Street,' the desk sergeant went. 'They released him an hour ago.'

I was like, 'Come on, I've got the van porked outside.'

He got in and just, like, shook his head. 'Sixteen hours to establish my innocence,' he went.

It wasn't until we were back in single-digit postcode territory that he could bring himself to tell me the story of what had happened.

'Well, Hennessy and I had just enjoyed eighteen at the K Club. Oh, your godfather was on fire, Ross – not just with the sticks either, but with the banter and the badinage – to say nothing of the friendly raillery. For instance, I made a complete mess of the famous seventh. Won't even tell what I corded, Ross. I said to our friend, "How would you have played that hole if you were me, old chap?" You know what he says? "Under an assumed name!" I mean, have you ever heard the likes of it, Ross?

'Well, it got worse on the back nine. Says I to your godfather, "You know what, I feel like bloody well drowning myself in the lake." And says he, "Charlie, I don't think you could keep your head down for that long!" And that's just a flavour of it, Ross – on and on it went! Hennessy! Oh, he'd humour a dying man!'

I was there, 'Is there any danger of you finishing this story before I need to focking shave again?' because it never pays to be too nice to him.

'Oh, yes, of course,' he went. 'Well, we were driving home and Hennessy had, well, one or two matters to attend to in Walkinstown.'

'Walkinstown? Jesus.'

'Well, he has one or two properties out there. Office buildings. Half finished, of course. Or half storted. Depends on what way you think this bloody economy's going. Anyway, as we're going along in Hennessy's cor – the famous Bentley, naturally – I notice what looks very much to me like a kink in the shaft of my driver.'

I laughed. 'There's no focking mystery there. He obviously did it while you were in the clubhouse having a hit and miss.'

'Well, that's always been the rumour about Old Hen, of course.'

'So, what, you wrapped the club around his head for cheating, he decked you and then you both ended up getting lifted?'

'No, no – nothing like that. No, I just happened to look up from my ministrations with Big Bertha when I spotted a woman – late twenties, early thirties – walking along the road in her pyjamas and slippers. Her pyjamas and slippers, Ross! At two o'clock in the afternoon, if you don't mind!'

I just, like, shrugged. 'Everyone out there does that. Why do you think they call it Sleepwalkinstown?'

'Well,' he went, 'I wish I'd known then what I know now. See, I figured she must have walked out of some hospital or other. And there she was, wandering up and down the Walkinstown Road in the middle of the day, dazed and bewildered. So I said to Hennessy, "Pull over here, old scout. Charles O'Carroll-Kelly is about to do his famous Good Samaritan act." So I jumped out, walked over to her and said, "In the cor! You're coming with us!"'

'Whoa, whoa, whoa,' I went, 'did you have the golf club in your hand at the time?'

'Unfortunately, yes.'

My jaw just dropped.

He just shook his head – I think it's a word – but ruefully?

'Turns out she'd only popped out for a box of twenty cigarettes,' he went. 'And she thought this was an abduction attempt.'

'So who did that to your face?'

'Well, she did. I wouldn't mind, she was only a slip of a thing. It was as if I'd been hit by the South African pack, then Peter Clohessy had been told he could have whatever was left.'

I just cracked up laughing. 'And did Hennessy not get out of the cor to help you?'

'Afraid not. No, in fact, he centrally locked the doors. Well, he's got an important pro-am coming up in Portmornock this weekend. I expect he didn't want to aggravate that troublesome shoulder of his.'

My old man. Utter knob though he is, you'd have to say, there's never a dull moment.

> 'Ro, please don't tell me the tickets are for
> Hill 16, 17 – whatever the fock it is.'
> *The Irish Times, 24 September 2011*

I'm turning the beast into a little side street in Ballybough and I'm already remembering why I hate Croke Pork – even when we had to play our games there? There's a dude and I'm presuming his daughter, both wearing fluorescent yellow bibs, and they're – get this – directing me into a porking space that I was perfectly capable of finding myself.

And I immediately know why, of course. By the time I get the door open, they're practically on top of me.

'Be a tough ould game today,' the dude goes. He's built like a focking petrol truck – he looks like the kind of bouncer who would have thrown me out of Renords head-first back in the day.

'Let's get one thing straight,' I go. 'I've no even interest in this game. I'm only here because my son – for whatever reason – is into it. And I'm not giving you a focking cent, by the way.'

He's like, 'Soddy?'

I'm there, 'Soddy, nothing. This is a public street. I don't have to pay you or anyone else protection money for the privilege of sticking the jammer here. End of message.'

She gets in on the act then – as in, the daughter?

'It mightn't be here when you come back,' she goes. Then she calls me one or two names as well – most of which I've heard before. She has a mouth on her like a sewage pipe.

I whip out the old iPhone and – you'll love this – I take a photograph of the two of them, standing there with their mouths slung open like dolphins at feeding time.

'There ends up being a mork on that cor,' I go, 'and I'm giving your mugshots to the Feds.'

Ronan is waiting for me outside the Clonliffe House.

'People in bibs demanding extortion money for letting you pork,' I go, just shaking my head. 'Doesn't happen at the Aviva, can I just say?'

Ronan laughs. ''Mon in here,' he goes. 'We'll get a pint and a short – couple of looseners for the day that's in it, wha'?'

I'm like, 'Er, we won't, Ro.'

'Why not?'

'Because you're thirteen years old.'

He laughs again. 'Always woort a try,' he goes. 'You'll be distracted one day and you'll say, "Fear enough."'

'I doubt it, Ro. Come on, let's just go in and find our seats.'

That's when he says it. 'Seats?'

Thus sudden feeling of basic dread comes over me. 'Ro, please don't tell me the tickets are for Hill 16, 17 – whatever the fock it is?'

He rolls his eyes and tells me – his father, remember – not to be a 'fooken oul' one', then he heads off in the direction of the ground, with me trotting after him.

The Hill – as they call it – turns out to be every bit the horror show I expected. Why does everyone from that side of the city want to be a character? It's like they're all auditioning to be the next Brendan Grace. They end up having great fun with me, of course.

'Look at this fedda,' I hear one goy go. 'He's arthur taking a wrong turden on he's way up to the corporate boxes.'

Which, of course, everyone finds hilarious. Then another goy cops my Henri Lloyd, and possibly my Dubes, and goes, 'Hee-er – where'd ye park the yacht?' Except obviously the T is silent on this side of the city. The point is, I've never actually sailed – which means the joke is technically on them.

'Just take your fooken medicine,' Ro tells me out of the corner of his mouth. 'Steer straight ahead, Rosser, and don't make eye contact with anyone, reet?'

I'm like, 'I've no intention of it, Ro.'

The teams run out. It turns out that Dublin are playing against Kerry. The place basically erupts. Ro storts giving it loads.

'Go on, Burden It. Today's the day, Burden It.'

Burden It Brogan is his new hero. Five years ago, it was The Monk. As a parent, I suppose I should be relieved. Although there'll always be that little port of me that wishes it was Drico or Dorce or even Rob Kearney that he idolized. Of course, I can't resist bringing up yesterday's events.

'They should have sent Cian Healy and Paul O'Connell in to talk to the IMF,' I go. 'They'd have gone, "Here's, like, 300 billion – give it back to us whenever. Or even never." God, Ireland were awesome yesterday.'

'Will you shut the fook up about the rubby,' a voice behind me goes. 'He's talking about the rubby, lads. You're not at the fooken rubby now.'

Ro shoots me a disappointed look. I just hold my hands up to say, 'Okay, I've made my point. I happen to think we're in with a very good chance of reaching the World Cup final. But I'll say no more about it.'

The game storts. I have to admit, roysh, I only end up half watching it? Mostly, I'm watching Ro. The confident way he holds himself. He's becoming a young man. He must have shot up twelve inches in the last year. And a couple of weeks ago, his voice broke. Happened overnight. And all I could think about was how it seemed like only yesterday that we were going to see my old man in Mountjoy and Ronan's little squeaky voice was echoing around the visiting room: 'Doorty screw bastards.'

Now look at him. Like I said, he's not a kid any more. He even has a girlfriend, called Shadden Tuite, and it seems to be going well – certainly if the hickeys on his neck are anything to go by. He looks like he's been shot with rubber bullets.

The point I'm trying to make is that I'm really, really proud of myself. As a father, I'd have my definite critics, but I don't think I did too badly.

The match? I'm going to shock you now by telling you that it ends up being not nearly as bad as I thought it was going to be. The halves are actually shorter than they are in rugby, which is a bonus. And of course the entire thing – like the famous Leinster Schools Senior Cup final of 1999 – ended up being decided by an injury-time kick from distance. Father Fehily used to say that Gaelic football would eventually become rugby – it just happened to be going through a particularly ugly stage of its evolution.

'Three steps backwards,' I go, 'four to the left. That's how I'd take it if I was –'

'Stephen Cluxton,' Ronan goes. 'Here, Rosser, you were a kicker – is he gonna put it over?'

It feels amazing to have my son ask me that. I check out the dude's body language.

'Nothing surer,' I just go.

And obviously I'm right.

When it's over, we wander back to the cor, which of course ends up being up on blocks. I mean literally up on blocks – wheels, gone. I spot the dude from earlier and his daughter, leaning against the gable wall of a house, both sniggering away at me.

'You better get the wheels back on that thing,' I go, 'with the speed of a focking F1 pit crew.'

And you could knock me over with an actual feather when Ronan turns around and goes, 'Rosser, this is Shadden – me girlfriend.'

## 'Guess which bank they bought shares in, everyone?'
### *The Irish Times*, 29 October 2011

Sorcha's old man hates me like I hate Thomond Pork. The happiest day of his life – he's on the record as saying – was the day his daughter storted divorce proceedings against me. So you can probably picture his face last weekend when I breezed into the old gaff on Newtownpork Avenue while he was trying to chair, like, a family conference?

They were all sat around the Escana dining table that I remember shelling out two Ks for back in the day – and that's not me being bitter about my marriage. There was, like, Sorcha, her old man, her old dear and her sister – Hafnium or Arnica or whatever the fock she goes by.

'What the hell is he doing here?' the dude went. See, he's never appreciated my whole routine.

I was like, 'Saturday is one of my court-appointed unsupervised access days. I'm here to bring my daughter to Dundrum Town Centre – if that's okay with you.'

That's when I noticed that Sorcha and the sister had both been crying. Sorcha was actually still in tears? Her make-up was all over the shop, like she slapped it on pissed.

I was like, 'What's going on?'

Straight away, Sorcha went, 'Mom and Dad are selling the house.'

I presumed she was talking about the family gaff in Killiney – and I presumed right.

The old man was there, 'I'd prefer not to talk about this in front of outside parties,' meaning me. That explained why he was so hostile when I let myself in, singing a Rihanna song at the top of my voice.

The sister was like, 'I still don't understand why you're selling it.' I couldn't be a hundred per cent sure her name isn't Polonious or something like that.

'I told you,' he went, 'I will not discuss it in front of him.'

But Sorcha's old dear ended up saying it anyway. 'We have some financial troubles – like a lot of others.'

Sorcha piped up then. 'They borrowed money to buy bank shares.'

The sister was never the brightest crayon in the box, yet even she seemed to instantly know what this actually meant, because her jaw just dropped.

'They borrowed money,' Sorcha went, like she was still trying to get her own head around it. 'Basically remortgaged the house. To buy bank shares. And guess which bank they bought shares in, everyone?'

No one answered and the question just hung there in the air for about twenty seconds. Her old man reached across the table to touch Sorcha's orm. She just pulled away. 'Don't touch me!' she just went. She loved that gaff, you see. 'How could you have been so stupid?'

'Look,' he tried to go, 'I was planning to retire early. Wanted to make it as comfortable as I could for your mother and I. Those shares went through the roof, you know.'

'I can't believe you've known about this – how long, two and a half years? And you've kept it to yourself. That's the house I grew up in!'

'We thought we could trade our way out of it. We were sure the villa in Quinta do Lago would hold its value.'

'And you were wrong.'

'Yes, we were wrong. If you want to hear me say it, I'll say it. But we can't just bury our heads in the sand, Sorcha. We have to deal with it and that's what we're attempting to do.'

Sorcha just shook her head. 'All of my childhood memories,' she went, 'the happiest moments of my actual life, are wrapped up in that house . . .'

'But you'll always have those memories.'

'You told me I'd always have the house! You said it'd always be a refuge for me. On the morning of my wedding day – do you remember that? – you said that when things inevitably went wrong with Ross, that my old bedroom would always be there for me.'

Like I said – hates me.

The sister – who is still living at home – was only storting to get her head around what the whole thing was going to mean for her.

'Oh my God,' she went, 'have you even thought about where I'm going to live?'

'We're looking at apartments,' the old dear went. 'Another few years and that garden was going to be too much work for us anyway. A lot of people out there are downsizing.'

'So, what, I'm going to be living in, like, an apartment with you?'

The old man then ended up having a – literally – freak attack with her. 'You're twenty-five years of age!' he went. 'Do you not think it's time you stood on your own two feet?'

The sister was like, 'Excuse me?' the same way Sorcha does when she's riled.

'How many courses have we paid for you to do?'

'Edmund,' the old dear went, trying to calm him.

'And you haven't worked a bloody day since you left school.'

'Er, I've done Smirnoff promotions?'

'And meanwhile,' he went, 'it was your mother and I who paid for you to go gallivanting around Australia,' and he nodded at her top tens. She had them – as they say in these ports – augmented while she was in Adelaide.

He turned on Sorcha then. This is a father and daughter, bear in mind, who've never exchanged an angry word in their lives. She's the apple of his actual eye?

'And how much money did I put into that shop of yours?' he went.

She was like, 'It was actually a boutique,' feeling the sudden need to defend herself.

'How many years was I writing cheques to cover your losses? I must have given you half a million euro to keep that place open – even during the good times. You ungrateful little . . .'

The next thing I heard was the sound of, like, chair legs scraping off the floor. Sorcha stood up, stared at her old man and went, 'I want you to leave – now!'

I honestly hadn't seen her that upset since the Iraq War kicked off. Or certainly since the time she stepped into a puddle of oily water outside Wilde & Green and destroyed a brand-new pair of chestnut Uggs.

It was a definite first, though. I've always been the least popular person in the room at Lalor family get-togethers. Now he knew how it suddenly felt.

There's a word you often hear used to describe these times in which we're living – and that word is, like, unpresidented.

'He told me it wasn't 2002 any more. He said
we were all going to have to learn to stand
on our own two feet.'
*The Irish Times, 5 November 2011*

Sorcha told me she needed four hundred snots for a new clutch. So I shelled out. We said we were going to handle this divorce in, like, an amicable way and she needs that cor of hers to ferry Honor around. Anyway, now she's standing in the living room in Newtownpork Avenue showing me the clutch she bought and she's asking me if I think it goes with her black Yves Saint Laurent sequined dress or whether she should have got something possibly more muted?

Men and women – we will never, ever understand each other. That's just a fact of life.

I bite my tongue, though, because she's down at the moment. She has been all week.

'Have you spoken to your old man,' I go, 'you know – since?'

She's like, 'No,' and she says it in, like, a super-defensive way. 'Oh my god, you think I'm being hord on him.'

I'm like, 'Possibly.'

'Ross, you heard the way he spoke to me. He's never raised his voice to me in my actual life.'

'Which shows you how much pressure he must be under. Look, I know he's never been my number-one fan. He blames me for ruining your life. Which is fair enough. But he also chooses to ignore some of my more amazing, amazing qualities. So I'm the last one in the world who should be defending him.'

'And yet you are?'

'All I'm saying is you're the apple of his actual eye, Sorcha. I just think, all the shit he's already going through – him and your old dear. Losing their life savings. Having to sell their gaff. And now you're giving them the big silent treatment – how long is it now, a week?'

'He told me it wasn't 2002 any more. He said we were all going to have to learn to stand on our own two feet.'

'He mightn't have meant it literally.'

'He did mean it literally.'

'Jesus. No one's saying that's right.'

'He actually shouted at me.'

'No one's saying that's right either. But what are you most upset about – that, or the fact that he's having to sell the home you grew up in?'

She stares into the distance for a good sixty seconds. In fact, I wonder is she going to even answer. Then she goes, 'I guess I'm just coming to the realization, later than a lot of girls, that my dad isn't Superman.'

I laugh. 'Superman had his enemies. He didn't have every focker in the street telling him to stick his money in bank shares. Or telling him to buy investment properties in – where was it again?'

'Quinta do Lago.'

'Quinta do Lago! It's hord to even say it now without smiling. The point I'm trying to make is that, yeah, your old pair focked up. They focked up in a major way. A lot of people did.'

She reacts to that as if she's been stung. 'Oh, no you don't, Ross. Don't you dare give me that "We all portied" line. Yeah, no, we're all paying the price – but some of us actually didn't lose the run of ourselves?'

I'm remembering the time she paid some Tibetan dude in Crumlin nine hundred snots to have her spirit recentred while his wife burned eucalyptus candles and played 'Bridge Over Troubled Water' on the pan pipes.

Again, I say nothing.

'Look, Sorcha,' I go, 'you know as well as anyone that there's very little going on between my ears. My head is like a focking snow globe. Who am I to be dishing out advice? But Father Fehily used to say this thing – perfection is something we're forever seeking in everyone else, yet never in ourselves.'

She looks away. 'That is an amazing quote.'

'See, I wrote a lot of them down. The only writing I ever did do in school. Can I tell you something else, Sorcha?'

'What?'

'I was always jealous of your relationship with your parents. I mean, I honestly would have liked a bit of what you always had. And I'm telling you this for nothing – you do not want to end up the way I am with my old pair.'

'You're getting on well with Chorles these days.'

'It's better than it was – there's no denying that. It's still not great, though.'

'And Fionnuala really loves you, too, Ross.'

'That woman's not capable of love. All she's interested in is collagen, Bombay gin and doing evil. But seriously, Sorcha, give your old man a break.'

I obviously manage to get through to her, roysh, because she suddenly gets up and says she's going to ring him – maybe ask him over to the house so she can, like, apologize properly. She goes out to the kitchen.

I stare at the TV for a little while, then she comes back and says he's coming over. She's as giddy as a kid on Skittles.

'Oh my god, I've literally nothing in. Ross, where are you going to go when he comes?' See, he hates even being in the same room as me.

I'm like, 'Sorcha, calm down. I'll hit the bricks the second the dude gets here.'

She throws her orms around me and tells me I'm the most incredible person she's ever met in her life and that it – oh my god – hurts her that some people can't see the actual good in me?

An hour later, there's, like, a ring on the doorbell. I go out and answer it. Sorcha's old man looks at me like I'm a tampon he's just found floating in his hot tub.

'Come in,' is all I go.

He's there, 'I don't need an invitation from you to enter my daughter's home,' and then – because he never can resist it – he goes, 'You know, when I look at you, I think of all the things that Sorcha could have been in life had she not suffered the misfortune of meeting you. Her mother and I rue the day it happened.'

There's a great smell coming from the kitchen. Sorcha's obviously baking.

'She's in there,' I go, nodding in the general postcode of the kitchen.

He looks me up and down and goes, 'Huh.'

I get in my cor and drive home.

## 'She's wearing her good Alexander McQueen trouser suit.'
### *The Irish Times, 12 November 2011*

I call into Sorcha's gaff during the week and I end up hearing one of the weirdest conversations I've *ever* heard? Ronan is in the kitchen, interviewing Sorcha for a job. At least, that's what it sounds like.

'Can you think of a perroblem,' he goes, 'that you've encounthered in the past at woork and tell me perhaps how you dealt with that perroblem?'

'Well, firstly,' *she goes*, 'I'm really glad you asked me that. My previous job, as I told you, was as the owner, manager and chief buyer for Sorcha Circa, a boutique specializing in both contemporary and vintage lines. I've always believed that the best way of dealing with any challenge is to, like, meet it head on? So, just as an example, a couple of years ago I was supposed to be the first shop in Ireland to stock this – oh my God – amazing, sassy, red lace skater frock that went really well even with just gold gladiators.

'Anyway, I'd told everyone – including *Image* magazine – that no one else in Ireland was going to be, like, stocking it. The next thing I heard, there was a shop in, like, Ashford that was supposedly going to have them as well. I thought, Oh! My God! They're going to make, like, a total liar out of me? So I rang up the supplier and I said, "Okay, I'll double the size of my initial order if you promise not to give them to that other shop." And that's exactly what ended up happening – I got them exclusively.'

I push the kitchen door. They're both sitting at the table, one opposite the other. She's wearing her good Alexander McQueen trouser suit. And he's just having a flick through her CV, nodding, you'd have to say, thoughtfully.

I'm just like, 'What! The fock?'

Sorcha just flicks her hand at me, as if to say, Not now, Ross!

'Very good,' he goes. 'One mower question. Do you have any weaknesses, do you think?'

She smiles at him. 'That's a very good question and thank you for asking it. I can be a bit of a perfectionist? If I do something – oh my God – it has to be done right. And I tend to expect the same standard of care and attention to detail from everyone I work with? Also, sometimes I can be, like, impatient? If I'm given a deadline by which to have a task or project completed, I tend to work flat-out to try to get it finished ahead of time?'

'Okay,' I go, 'I'll refer you to my earlier question, which still stands, by the way. What the fock?'

'I have a job interview,' Sorcha goes. 'Ronan is just helping me to prepare.'

'Hey, that's great,' I go. Then I turn to Ronan. '*Hang* on – it's not with Buckets of Blood, is it?' Buckets of Blood is his mate, the debt collector.

Ronan rolls his eyes. 'No,' he goes, 'it's not with Buckets of Blood.'

'I'm not saying who it's with,' Sorcha goes, 'because I don't want to, like, jinx it? But I'm very excited.'

I'm there, 'I can hear it in your voice.'

She wanders over to the fireplace and checks her lippy in the mirror. She looks well, it has to be said.

'I had an – oh my God – amazing chat with my dad, Ross. Okay, I'm still upset about them selling the house. Of course I am. I mean, there's, like, a tyre swing in the gorden that's been there since I was, like, a little girl? I mean, I can't even bear the *thought* of someone else's daddy pushing them on it. But my dad is right when he says we can't just bury our heads in the sand and pretend it's still 2002.'

I'm there, 'You're possibly right.'

'Okay,' she goes. 'Wish me luck.'

And me and Ronan, at the same time, go, 'Good luck.'

We stay sitting at the kitchen table. Ro comes here sometimes to do his homework, see. I can't believe he's sitting his Junior Cert next year. Where do the years go? *He* has, like, his books spread out and he's, like, scribbling away furiously.

'What's that?' I happen to go – just showing an interest.

He's like, 'Maths. Ine trying to woork out the coordinate geometry formula for this triangle here.'

I just nod and pull a face as if to say, Hey, we've all been there – which I focking haven't, of course.

'Then I've to prove anutter theorem using congruent triangles. Don't woody, Rosser, Ine not gonna ast you to help me.'

We both crack our holes laughing at that one. I have to admit, though – I do suddenly breathe easier.

Anyway, an hour later, we're still sitting there when the house phone suddenly rings. It ends up being Sorcha.

'Ross,' she goes, 'do you know is there any champagne in the house?'

I'm there, 'I *doubt* it, Sorcha. I don't think I've tasted the stuff since 2008.'

'Can you pop out to O'Brien's and pick up a bottle? Tonight, we're celebrating.'

I'm there, 'Yeah, no probs. What are we supposedly celebrating, by the way? I'm just wondering would prosecco do the same job?'

'I got it, Ross!'

'Okay, what are you talking about?

'The job I went for.'

'That's great,' I go. I'm actually genuinely happy for her? 'Although you still haven't told me what the actual job is.'

'Ross,' she goes – and this without any hint of laughter at all – 'you are now talking to the manager of the new Euro Hero discount store in the Powerscourt Townhouse Centre.'

> 'An increasing number of people are turning to discount stores, as the recession continues to bite.'
> *The Irish Times, 19 November 2011*

Vodka chocolates. Silly string. Some movie that Angelina Jolie did when she was, like, twenty and has probably never bothered her hole even watching herself. Forty copies of it. On VHS. Grease remover tablets. Packs of sixty-four clothes pegs in the colours of the Ireland flag. Twenty-metre scart to 2-RCA phono leads. Fingerless gloves, 95 per cent acrylic, one size fits all. Bottles of bath and shower gel with characters on them that look like *Star Wars* characters but aren't? Fruit jellies that taste of literally nothing. Bottles of hand sanitizer in wild berry. A movie about snooker with a young Bob Geldof in it.

I try not to let Sorcha see what I'm thinking. Except she does, of course. She can read me like *The John Deere Coffee Table Book of Big Tractors* – eighty copies of which are piled up on a table, waiting to be shifted.

'You can take that look off your face,' she goes.

I'm like, 'What look?'

'Er, the one of, like, disgust?'

'I wouldn't describe it as disgust. It'd be more deep shock. I just had no idea that people lived like this.'

It's her first day as manager of the Euro Hero discount store in the Powerscourt Townhouse Centre – in the actual unit where Sorcha Circa used to be. I'm there to offer supposedly moral support.

'Ross,' she goes, 'an increasing number of people are turning to discount stores, as the recession continues to bite.'

'It doesn't make it right, though.'

'Well, right or not, they're a pretty much fact of life now? My boss – as in, like, Mr Whittle – he says we're providing an actual social service . . .'

'We?' Only one day in the place and she's already a company woman.

She's there, 'My gran, just as an example – Oh! My God! – loves these shops? She said in her day they used to call them huckster shops. And you could buy literally anything in them, from a needle to an anchor.'

I'm like, 'What about a framed photograph of a waterfall with moving lights inside it that makes tropical bird noises when you walk past?'

She takes it out of my hands. 'If you've only come in to mock me, Ross . . .'

I end up feeling instantly bad then, so I go, 'Hey, I want to take that.'

'What?'

'I want to buy it.'

'Ross, I've had a long day . . .'

'I'm serious, Babes. I've decided to support you. So I'm going to take it.'

In a weird way, I actually admire what she's doing, even though – at the same time – it kind of disgusts me?

'Do you have cash?' she goes.

I'm like, 'No, I'll stick it on the old Visa cord.'

'I'm afraid we can't process credit card transactions for purchases of less than €10.'

'What?'

'It's only a fiver, Ross. Mr Whittle said it wouldn't be worth the cost of, like, processing it?'

'Okay, I'll take this, er, bicycle puncture repair kit as well.'

'Okay, that brings it up to eight.'

'And what about this set of six plastic coat hangers?'

'Still only nine.'

'And the pet lint roller. I'll take the pet lint roller.'

She takes all of the shit from me, rings it through and sticks it into a bag. As she's handing me my receipt and purchases, I end up asking the question that's possibly on both of our minds?

'What do you think Honor's going to say?'

I look at her little face, trying to be brave. 'Well,' she goes, 'we'll know soon enough. Linh is bringing her in straight from school.'

Linh is Honor's nanny. Nothing to look at, in case you're wondering. No one can say that Sorcha didn't learn from experience.

I'm there, 'And you're saying that Honor doesn't know what your new job even is yet?'

'Don't make such a big deal of it, Ross. It's like my dad was saying – Honor is going to have to adjust to the new economic paradigm, just like I've had to and millions of others like me.'

The kid is going to shit an organ. I know it and she knows it – but she insists on putting a brave face on things.

'There's, like, seventy-five boxes of diabetic chocolate gingers left over from Mother's Day in the storeroom,' she goes. 'Do you think people would buy them for Christmas?'

That's when Honor arrives. It's actually Linh's voice that I hear first. She goes, 'This is the place, Honor,' and I turn around to see my daughter walking into Euro Hero with her nose, as usual, stuck in her mobile phone.

She's sort of, like, chuckling to herself. 'Oh my God,' she's going, 'LMFAO! Deena Cortese looks like a bowling ball in Uggs,' no idea at all that she's walking into a discount store. There's an argument to say that that's why these kind of shops shouldn't even be on this side of the city. 'Er, hashtag – who is your stylist?'

'Hi, Honor,' Sorcha goes. 'Welcome to Mommy's new place of work.'

Honor's head goes up. She doesn't say anything for literally twenty seconds. She just looks around her, taking it all in. The 2011 calendars with a picture of an Airedale terrier for every month of the year. The mechanical pencil set with the rip-off *Littlest Mermaid* pictures on the packaging. The soap that doesn't even have a name – it just says 'SOAP' on the outside and smells of Loughlinstown Hospital. The faux-bronze ashtrays with the little man standing on the side having a slash.

She takes it all in with her mouth open, then she looks at Sorcha, closes her eyes and let's the loudest horror movie scream out of her that I've possibly ever heard. It's like, 'Aaarrrggghhh!!!'

'Well, you're just going to have to accept it!' Sorcha's going.

'Aaarrrggghhh!!!'

'You can scream all you like, Honor. It's like you always hear them say – we are where we are. And, like it or not, this is where we are.'

'Aaarrrggghhh!!!'

'We're all doing what we have to do to get by.'

'Aaarrrggghhh!!!'

I get suddenly worried about her, though. I'm like, 'Sorcha, I think she's hyperventilating.'

Sorcha's there, 'She's not hyperventilating. She's being a spoiled little . . . madam.'

She is hyperventilating, though. For once, she's not play-acting. She has genuinely lost it.

'Breathe!' I'm telling Honor. 'Breathe!'

She can't actually catch her breath, though. She's turning literally white.

'Sorcha,' I go, 'quick – get me a bag.'

But she still doesn't believe it's for real. 'They're fifteen cent each, Ross.'

'Sorcha,' I end up having to shout at her, 'just get me a bag!'


### 'This is just what I'm doing now. I'm honestly happy.'
### *The Irish Times, 3 December 2011*


I ask Sorcha if she's heard from Erika – since the girl split on her supposed wedding day, that is – but she doesn't even look at me, just goes, 'I don't want to talk about her,' as in the girl she used to describe as her best friend forever.

She's been listening to a lot of Sufjan Stevens this week and talking about the – if this is a word – impermanence of things? I think she feels even more betrayed than Fionn by Erika's last-minute flit.

Typical of my soon-to-be-ex-wife, though, she's throwing herself into her work – managing the Euro Hero discount store that now stands where her Sorcha Circa fashion boutique once stood.

I'm looking around the shop at the magnetic can openers (€2) and the Australia-to-US plug adaptors (€1) and the grey crimplene under-bed storage bags (€3) and the leftover plastic Hallowe'en masks (50c) and I'm thinking, it's hord to believe that this is still the Powerscourt Townhouse Centre.

Honor hasn't taken the news of Sorcha's new job well – she is terrified, of course, that someone from school is going to find out about it. She's hiding in a corner of the shop behind a pair of oversized aviators and the breathing mask that her mother bought during the SARS scare of 2003.

Sorcha even says it to her. 'Take off that silly mask, Honor.'

'Er, no,' Honor goes. 'I don't want to catch something.'

I don't say it to Sorcha, of course, but the kid has a point – the shop smells of dust, wrongly spelt eau de colone and desperation.

Sorcha is suddenly talking over my left hammer to a group of English girls who are giggling at the hen's night accessories. 'There's fifty per cent off the iron-on faux-diamanté transfers (€1),' she goes, giving them the sales pitch. 'And the Last Night Out sashes (€2) and the L-plate deely boppers (€2) are Buy One, Get One Free. Oh, and with every €5 spent, there's a free Hottie Whistle!'

All the birds are there, 'What?'

One of them is alright looking – the rest are focking lagoon creatures.

'A Hottie Whistle,' Sorcha goes, suddenly producing one from a little bowl on the counter. 'When you're all out in, like, Busker's and one of you sees a goy who's, like, totally hot, you do this . . .'

She puts the whistle in her mouth and gives us three or four serious blasts on it.

All the girls laugh. Whereas I could focking cry. A year ago, she was standing in the exact same spot telling people that – I don't know – a playful hot pink bow adds a much needed pop of colour to an Oscar de la Renta sequined gown. Or that the best summer layering advice any-one can give you is to steer clear of matchy-matchy and keep your colour palette soft.

And now she's reduced to this – pushing pink Stetsons (€3), shot glasses on a neck chain (€2), lollipops shaped like penises (€1) and Hot-tie Whistles (50c, or free with every purchase of €5 or more) to packs of focking hounds.

The girls – and I'm using that term loosely – say they'll have a think about it and they might come back, then they drift out of the shop, still giggling like dopes.

Honor looks at me and goes, 'Did she tell you that Rosanna Davison called in? And that she – OMG – burst into tears when she saw what Mom had been reduced to. Er, awks much?'

'She did not burst into tears,' Sorcha goes. 'She was in shock. Ross, you know how much Rosanna loved my boutique . . .'

I'm there, 'She was never out of the focking place.'

'Well, she hadn't actually heard that it was closed down. She came in earlier to see could I order her this – oh my God – amazing violet Marchesa mini that Diane Kruger wore to the premiere of *Pieds nus sur les limaces* . . .'

'And here you are,' I go, 'flogging seven-piece screwdriver sets (€3) and magic brush and matching shoe horn gift packs (€2). Jesus, no wonder she burst into tears.'

Sorcha's like, 'She didn't burst into tears, Ross. She was concerned about me, that's all. I was like, "Rosanna, it's okay. This is just what I'm doing now. I'm honestly happy. And I'm really well – especially within myself?"'

I'm like, 'Poor Rosanna, though. I must text her.'

It's as I'm saying this that a customer suddenly arrives at the counter. It's a woman. Nice as well. I don't think she's that unlike Adrianne Palicki? Sorcha switches back to sales-assistant mode.

'How are you finding everything?' she goes.

See, she's still got the clothes shop patter.

'I have a complaint,' the woman goes.

Sorcha's like, 'Oh?'

'This shampoo,' she goes, then slaps this, like, two-litre bottle (€1) down on the counter. Whatever is inside it is the actual colour of French mustard.

'Did it not do what it says on the bottle?'

'I don't know. Because I have no idea what it says on the bottle. The only word I recognize is shampoo. Everything else is in, I don't know, Indian.'

'I think it's actually Farsi,' Sorcha goes. 'I recognize some of the script. A really good friend of mine represented Iran in the Model UN at school.'

'It made my scalp bleed,' the woman goes.

'What?'

'My scalp bled – when I tried to wash my hair with it.'

My instant reaction would be, what the fock do you expect for a euro? Honestly, it's the size of a lorge bottle of Coke. Except Sorcha is unbelievably professional.

'I am so, so sorry,' she goes. 'Okay, the first thing I'm going to do is give you your money back.'

'The money isn't the issue . . .'

'No, I insist. Okay, there's your euro. Now, I'm going to promise you that I'm going to investigate this thing fully.'

'I already made an effort. There's a telephone number on the back of the bottle there – presumably for the manufacturer. I dialled it, but the number isn't valid. The country code doesn't even exist.'

'Oh! My God!'

'You really shouldn't be selling it, though. It couldn't have passed any kind of safety checks. I was washing my hair and there was actual blood on my palms. I just thought I'd say it to you.'

'Well, thank you – and for being so understanding as well.'

'I just wouldn't like to think of it happening to anyone else. Especially someone old.'

Off she goes with her euro – the focking busybody. Honestly, I'd have run her – I don't care what she looks like.

Honor sniggers behind her little mask. She's like, 'Er, toats embarrassing?'

Sorcha just ignores her and tells me she's going to ring Mr Whittle, the owner.

She goes, 'Ross, will you do me a favour? Get those bottles of shampoo off those shelves – quick.'

# 2012

A controversial Household Charge of €100 is introduced * The France v Ireland Six Nations match in Paris is cancelled just minutes before kick-off due to a frozen Stade de France pitch, leaving thousands of Ireland fans who travelled disappointed * Seán Quinn, once Ireland's richest man, is declared bankrupt by the High Court * A group of housing rights activists, including Joan Collins TD, successfully prevent an attempted eviction in Mountrath, County Laois, in scenes that are described as 'reminiscent of the Land Wars of the nineteenth century' * Less than half of the country's households have paid the new Property Tax by the deadline * Novelist Maeve Binchy dies * The Irish government pays €1.25 billion to bondholders of the former Anglo Irish Bank in the face of considerable public opposition * Gardaí destroy the Occupy Dame Street Camp in an overnight raid * Barack Obama is re-elected President of the United States * Nike lands itself in the centre of a major controversy after naming its new, St Patrick's Day-themed runner 'The Black and Tan' * Boxer Katie Taylor wins a gold medal in the lightweight division at the London Olympics * Environment Minister Phil Hogan seeks refuge in a Carlow Cathedral to escape Property Tax protesters * Leinster beat Ulster at Twickenham to win their third Heineken Cup * 'Get Lucky' by French electronic music duo Daft Punk is the hit song of the summer * Clerys, one of Ireland's best-known department stores, is put into receivership * Facing expulsion, former Taosieach Bertie Ahern resigns from Fianna Fáil * Gardaí use pepper spray to hold back anti-austerity protesters outside the Labour Party conference in Galway * Irish Water is established * Vladimir Putin is elected President of Russia * Taoiseach Enda Kenny tells the World Economic Forum in Davos that the Irish people 'went mad borrowing' during the years of the Celtic Tiger *

Meanwhile . . .

The old man has a *Romeo y Julieta* the size of a focking courgette clamped between his Yasmine Bleeth. I think about saying something to him – as in, 'Er, what would your cordiologist think?' – but I let it go because it's, like, New Year's Eve and the dude is on a serious roll.

'I see Nicolas Sarkozy is urging all of us to remain stoical,' he goes.

I'm like, 'Who the fock is Nicolas Sarkozy?' and I actually mean it *genuinely*?

He ends up nearly coughing up a lung. 'Exactly!' he goes. 'Who indeed! Oh, I should know better than to try to draw you into a debate about the international sovereign debt crisis – you and your acerbic wit, Kicker!'

Four o'clock in the afternoon, by the way, and he's already half-twisted.

'So,' he goes, 'where are you going to be ringing in 2012? I expect it'll be with your wonderful daughter.'

I'm like, 'Er, probably not. Her mother's in a bit of a strop with me at the moment.'

His face suddenly lights up. 'Oh, yes!' he goes. 'Yes, I met Sorcha's dad – poor old Edmund – coming out of the famous Terroirs on Christmas Eve. He said the Christmas tree you picked up for Sorcha was infested with something.'

I'm like, 'Yeah, basically *weevils*?'

'Weevils! Good Lord! I thought they went out with Tuberculosis and sending children down mines. That's the recession, I suppose.'

'Well, either way, her gaff is, like, *infested* with them? She's had to move out while the place is being pretty much fumigated.'

The old man pulls a face. 'Bad luck, old scout. Still, I've got a bit of news that might succeed in returning a smile to that famous face of yours.'

I'm there, 'What kind of news are we talking?'

'I'm talking about work, Ross.'

'Work? Why the fock do you think that would put a smile on my face? Even the mention of it makes me want to get under the sheets and hide.'

'Work's not a dirty word any more, Ross. In fact, our friend Sarkozy makes a valid point. We should all be putting our best face forward. Which is exactly what I'm about to do.'

'What are you talking about?'

'The government is planning to send out something in the order of two million leaflets, Ross, informing people of this new hundred-euro household charge that's coming into effect. Well, under European law, our friend Enda is required to put the job of distributing those leaflets out to tender. And I'm planning to put in an offer that's going to wipe the bloody floor with An Post.'

'You've changed your tune,' I go. 'I thought the household chorge was a desperate measure by a government bankrupt of ideas and the fore-runner to a property tax designed to penalize entrepreneurs like you. At least, that's what you said on *The Frontline*.'

He shrugs. 'That's before I realized how much bloody money I could make from this thing.'

'By delivering leaflets?'

'Exactly. Be a wonderful complement to the shredding business, don't you think?'

I'm like, 'Whatever,' and that's when my phone all of a sudden rings. I can see from caller ID that it's, like, Sorcha – she always ends up forgiving me, it has to be said. I answer by going, 'I hope you're ringing to apologize for overreacting.'

Except I can hear straight away that she's upset. 'Ross,' she goes, 'where are you?'

I'm there, 'I'm shooting the shit with Knob Head here. What's up, Babes?'

That's when she tells me. She's in, like, work. She's managing the Euro Hero discount store in the Powerscourt Townhouse Centre – you may or may not have heard. A few weeks back, she took this shampoo off the shelves because some bird – a busybody, if you ask me – came in complaining that it made her scalp bleed. Anyway, according to Sorcha, Mr Whittle, the owner, was not a happy rabbit when she told him on the phone. He's on his way into the shop and Sorcha wants me to be there – that's how actually scared of him she is.

So I leave the old man to his cigor and his dreams and I point the old three-serious in the direction of town.

I can hear, like, raised voices coming from the shop, even from the little newsagents at the top of the stairs. So I quicken the pace. Mr Whittle turns out to be a big, sweaty dude – only in his mid-twenties, I'd say – and he's already giving out yords to my soon-to-be-ex-wife. He's practically jabbing his finger in her face and going, 'Who facking told ya to do it?' because he's, like, *English* from the sounds of him? 'Who facking told ya, eh?'

Poor Sorcha's on the verge of actual tears. 'I tried to ring you,' she goes, 'but you were in Cyprus.'

'So you took va decision – va facking unilateral facking liberty – to just go ahead and facking do it?'

I just step in between them. I know in the past I possibly haven't treated Sorcha the way she deserved to be treated, but I'd do time to protect the girl – and I'd do it happily.

He's there, 'Who the fack are you?'

I square up to him – wouldn't take much to deck him. I'm the man who Frankie Sheehan once described as one of the five toughest-tackling backs he's ever played against – a second cousin of Oisinn's overheard him say that in Flannery's in Limerick one night.

I end up just staring the dude down. 'No one speak likes that,' I go, 'to my still technically wife.'

Sorcha probably didn't expect this to turn into an actual confrontation – certainly not so soon.

'Ross, please!' she goes, obviously having second thoughts about ringing me. 'I *need* this job.'

This dude has the town halls to actually sneer at me – he's one of those, I don't know, cockney wide boys, like you see in *EastEnders*?

'Listen to the gell,' he tries to go. 'She's tawking sense.'

Sorcha shoulders me out of the way then and goes, 'Just to tell you, Mr Whittle, I tried to contact the manufacturer.'

'You what?'

'I rang the number on the bottle,' Sorcha goes. 'But it's no longer active.'

'*I'm* in contact wiv va manufacturer.'

'And what's he saying? I presume he shares our concerns?'

'Va stuff has been tested – not vat it's any of your facking business.'

'Well, can he provide us with certification to that effect?'

'Eh?'

'This woman's scalp was actually bleeding.'

'Look, vare's naffing to warry abaht – va shampoo's awight. It were a rogue one, vats awl.'

I go, 'One rogue recognizes another, I suppose,' which is unbelievably clever for me.

He knows he can't beat me physically, roysh, so instead he goes, 'Do you want *er* to be still working ear tomorrah?'

I don't even answer him – wouldn't give him the pleasure.

He turns back to Sorcha then and he goes, 'Be a smart gell – get vem facking bottles back on vem facking shelves. Uverwise, you're facking sacked.'

### 'It's the lower middle classes and their creeping aspirationalism.'
*The Irish Times*, 21 January 2012

So I'm driving along Shrewsbury Road last Saturday night and there's, like, fifty or sixty cors porked the entire length of it, which straight away struck me as somehow *unusual*? It definitely wasn't Funderland traffic, I knew, because they would have all been towed by now. And anyway, the cors were too good to belong to what the locals call 'bloody Funfairians' – we're talking Ford Explorers, we're talking Mercedes S Classes, we're talking Volvo S60s.

It was only when I copped Delma's Volkswagen Touareg – as in, Delma who was chairperson of Just One Day (the Ban Poor People from the National Gallery on Tuesdays pressure group) – that I realized there was a porty in full swing in the old dear's gaff.

I *say* the old dear's gaff, of course, but it'll always be Oisinn's in *my* mind? Yeah, no, she just swooped in like a vulture when the poor dude lost everything in the whole current economic thing.

Obviously, I've no interest whatsoever in what the old dear gets up to – Brooklyn Decker could play her in the movie of her life and I still wouldn't watch the focking thing – but, at the same time, I have to admit, I was a bit hurt at not being invited.

She's my mother and I'm her son. She should have at least asked me – even if it was just so I could turn around and go, 'No, thanks, I'd rather sit at home all night repeatedly shooting myself in the face with a focking nail gun.'

Anyway, like I said, I was hurt, so I threw my cor in behind Angela's Audi TT and decided to find out what the deal was.

Oh, it was a porty alright. There must have been, like, a hundred people in the house, all friends of the old dear's and the old man's, all knocking back cocktails.

Bublé was on – isn't he focking always? – there were plates of the old dear's gruyere and shiitake mushroom canapes being passed around and everyone seemed to be talking about Fallon & Byrne and how they hoped it could make it through its current difficulties.

'It's needed,' I heard at least three people say. 'I definitely do believe that.'

The old dear was holding court in the living room, a Martini in her hand, at least another pound of cellulite transferred from her orse to her face since I saw her last.

I stood at the door. All her friends from The Gables were sitting around, listening to her going, '*We* can't take them. We simply can't. I realize there's terrible suffering there. We've all seen the horrific images on the news. But we simply can't take these people in without it adversely affecting *our* quality of life.'

I wondered at first was she talking about refugees from some, I don't know, famine, or even tsunami. Then I realized she wasn't. She was talking about the people of Terenure.

'I'm not an iceberg,' she went. 'I'm capable of looking at people who are suffering and saying, "How awful for them!" And I know I don't need to remind anyone *here* about my famous charity work. Hurricanes, fires, nuclear catastrophes – I've arranged tray bake sales for them all. Earthquakes? Anything above seven on the Richter scale and I had the flour and the Salter Brecknell out immediately – baking, baking, baking. Delma, you know that.'

Delma nodded. They were all half mashed, by the way. 'It is possible to feel sorry for people who find themselves in a situation,' she went, 'but, at the same time, to say, "I'm sorry – there's nothing we can do." And, anyway, I think we all know what the agenda here is, Fionnuala. They don't want to be part of the Dublin South-East constituency. They want to be part of Dublin 4. It's the lower middle classes and their creeping aspirationalism.'

Delma was always a D4 hordliner. She was the one who storted the campaign to have Irishtown and Ringsend redesignated Dublin 4e.

'Quite right,' the old dear went. 'As Charles said to Michael McDowell one night in Shanahan's, "If the people of Terenure want to live in Dublin 4, why don't they simply buy houses in Dublin 4? A damn liberty expecting Dublin 4 to come to them.""

'Charles has a wonderful way of putting things,' it was Angela who went. 'Some of his letters to the *Times*, you'd nearly want to cut them out and keep them.'

Delma was like, 'The question is what are we going to *do* about it? God knows, the value of our homes has taken enough of a hit without the people of Terenure being given – what was this my husband called it? – oh, yes, *parity of esteem* with the residents of Dublin 4.'

'Lovely phrase,' my old dear went. 'Lovely, lovely phrase.'

She grabbed the voddy and topped up everyone's drinks.

Delma was there, 'While feeling sorry for them – which we all obviously do – this campaign of theirs must be stopped, Fionnuala. Otherwise, we're going to end up living cheek-by-jowl with Dolphin's Barn and Crumlin and wherever else there is.'

Angela was like, 'Let's occupy something. That's what all these young people are doing nowadays. Occupy this. Occupy that. You know Gwuiny – Gwuiny who runs the Sandymount Wine Guild trip to Provence every year? – well, her son is occupying Dame Street!'

The old dear was like, 'How fun!'

'Yes, he's taken a year off from his architecture degree and that's what he's decided to do.'

Delma went, 'Well, what are *we* going to occupy? You're not suggesting something *in* Terenure, are you?'

'Perhaps.'

'Jesus! Well, what's *there* to occupy? I mean, do they have a Luas station or something?'

'I have no idea. I've only ever driven through.'

The old dear went, 'I'll investigate it. I think you're right, though, Delma – this really does need to be nipped in the bud.'

The next thing I felt was a sudden *hand* on my shoulder? Then I heard the old man go, 'Look who's here, everyone! It's Kicker!'

That's when the old dear looked up and noticed me for the first time.

I was like, 'Yeah, thanks for inviting me to your porty, by the way.'

She went, 'I didn't want any of your unpleasantness, Ross, and I don't wany any of it now.'

I had to laugh at that. 'What's this porty even for?' I went. 'What are you actually celebrating?'

The old man was like, 'Did you not hear, Ross? Your mother and I – our divorce came through yesterday!'

And they just smiled at each other across the room, genuinely happier than I've ever seen them. How focked up is that? They don't even have it in them to hate each other's guts like normal divorced couples.

And it was something I never thought I'd ever hear myself think, but in that moment what went through my mind was that Terenure would be actually better off staying where it is.

## 'This team has brought me more happiness than pretty much anything else in my life.'
### *The Irish Times*, 19 May 2012

Something I've possibly never told you before. When Johnny Sexton was, like, seventeen years of age, I sat down with him one day in McDonald's in Stillorgan and gave him some advice on how to handle the pressure of being potentially *the* greatest out-half this country has ever produced.

I'm happy to say that he ignored every single word I said to him and, this weekend, at still only, like, twenty-six, he could win a third European Cup to go with the Leinster Schools Senior Cup he won with – I hate to say it – but Mary's.

This is me being philosophical in the deportures lounge of Dublin Airport. It's, like, Friday night and we're sitting at the gate, waiting to board – we're talking me, Sorcha and our six-year-old daughter, having decided to make a pretty much *weekend* of it?

Tonight, we're hitting some supposedly amazing sushi place in Covent Gorden, then tomorrow Sorcha is going to take Honor around London to see all the famous sights – we're talking Harrods, we're talking Alexander McQueen, we're talking the big Stella McCortney store in Mayfair – while I head for Twickenham with the goys, who are all flying over tomorrow morning.

I'm sitting there, roysh, just watching old YouTube clips on my iPhone – Rob Kearney's two tries against Cordiff, Cian Healy's against Clermont Auvergne – and everything feels suddenly right with the world.

I even go, 'Can I just say something here? This team has brought me more happiness than pretty much anything else in my life.'

Honor looks up from her own iPhone and goes, 'And you're telling us this *why* exactly?'

I'm there, 'I'm just making the point, Honor, that I could be bitter. Had the cords fallen differently, I might have been actually *playing* tomorrow? It didn't work out for me. But I still love this team like a basic family.'

Honor just, like, rolls her eyes and goes, 'Er, hashtag, *lame* much?'

I don't say anything. She's just going through one of those really bitchy phases that girls on our side of the city call . . . well, life.

Sorcha just, like, sad-smiles me. She looks well, it has to be said. She's had her roots done and I know she's been on the Weight Watchers for the last three weeks. She's still got it, is what I'm saying.

So they make the pre-boarding announcement – anyone with infants or anyone requiring special assistance and all the usual blahdy blah.

Honor jumps up and storts walking towards the air-hostess who's, like, checking the boarding passes, with me and Sorcha trailing after her, carrying her three pieces of cabin baggage like we're her – I don't know – *valets* or some shit?

By the time we make it over, the woman is telling Honor that she'll have to wait until her actual seat row is called, which Honor isn't happy about, given the way she's, like, *glowering* at her?

I'm like, 'Okay, what seems to be the issue here?' ever the diplomat.

The woman goes, 'Parents with infants are entitled to pre-board. This girl isn't an infant.'

I'm prepared to accept that, roysh, but Honor obviously isn't. Under her breath, she goes, 'Yeah, fock you.'

I do what a lot of these parenting experts tell you and decide not to make an issue of it – as does the air-hostess, in fairness – but then I catch Sorcha staring at me and I realize that she wants me to say something, I suppose as the girl's father.

So I end up going, 'Er, possibly don't talk to people like that, Honor – blah, blah, blah.'

Except the kid comes straight back with, 'Yeah, it's actually a song? Er, CeeLo Green?'

I turn around to Sorcha and I'm like, 'It is an actual song. She has us there, Babes.'

You can imagine how that goes down.

Sorcha goes, 'What?' because she's always said that I indulge the kid too much.

'I'm just saying, it's a definite song. I think it's the album version. It's hord to know what we can do – that's the point I'm trying to make.'

'What you can do,' Sorcha goes, out of the side of her mouth, 'is discipline your daughter.'

I just keep staring straight ahead, though. There's, like, a lot of other passengers listening and I'm thinking, Okay, let's all just chillax here. We're about to have a cracking weekend away. But that's when it all storts to suddenly unravel.

The air-hostess isn't happy with where we're standing.

'I have to keep this area clear,' she goes. 'You're blocking people who are trying to board the aircraft.'

Honor just looks at her and goes, 'Oh, no! Sad emoji!' and then, under her breath, she's like, 'What a stupid bitch!'

The air-hostess looks at her and goes, 'I *beg* your pardon?' and I'm suddenly thinking, Oh, no, please, no.

And that's when Honor says it.

She's like, 'Do you do your own make-up – or does someone shoot it onto your face with a focking paintball gun?'

There are literally gasps from the other passengers. It's actually a line she stole from me, in fairness, but I end up just rolling my eyes in a sort of kids-say-the-dornedest-things kind of way.

It's a good ten seconds before the air-hostess gets it together to say something. And then she goes, 'Okay, *you're* not getting on this plane.'

Sorcha's like, 'Excuse me?'

'This girl is not getting onto this plane. She's being rude and abusive.'

'But –'

'Please move away from the gate before I have to call security.'

Which is what we end up having to do.

'Come on, Ross,' Sorcha goes, with literally, like, tears in her eyes. I feel like shedding a few myself. I'm the one who's going to miss the focking Heineken Cup final.

I'm there, 'I can't believe this is actually happening.'

It's like it's a dream or something. But a few minutes later, we're walking back through Duty Free when it suddenly storts to dawn on us that it's actually happening.

Sorcha all of a sudden stops, turns around to Honor and goes, 'Who told you it was okay to speak to another human being like that?'

Except Honor just goes, 'Whatever!' and keeps on walking.

I'm there, 'Sorcha, I actually think it was the air-hostess who was bang out of order. I thought she didn't exactly help the situation. Do you know what? I'm going to go back and have a word with her.'

Sorcha's like, 'Ross, please don't.'

'No, I'm going to do it, Sorcha. I'm going to give her a piece of my actual mind.'

'You're actually right – she did inflame the situation.'

'You walk on. I'll catch up with you.'

A few minutes later, I arrive back at the gate. I'm just, like, staring at the woman, who's all smiles again, not a care in the actual world. I'm thinking, How focking dare you try to keep me from supporting the team that I've followed through thick and sometimes thin.

I morch straight over to where she's standing. Then I put my head down and hand her my boarding cord. Luckily, she doesn't recognize me.

'Have a nice flight,' she goes.

Sixty seconds later, I'm buckling myself into my seat. Maybe, in time, Sorcha will understand why I did what I did. Maybe she won't. But this I have to say in my defence. I love Leinster. And, unlike my wife and daughter, they've never, ever let me down.

## 'Then she hands me *Pretty Woman* . . . the skeleton key of romcoms.'
### *The Irish Times*, 8 December 2012

So I'm sitting in the other night, rewatching the 2012 Ken Cup final – *as one does* – when there's suddenly a familiar whiff in my nostrils that I recognize almost instantly as *Love, Chloé*, a perfume that has always done it for me and which Sorcha sometimes throws on when she wants something.

I look over my shoulder and – roysh enough – she's standing in the doorway with a slightly embarrassed smile on her face and enough perfume on her to anaesthetize a humpback whale ahead of major surgery.

She goes, 'Is this an important match?' which I know from my years of exposure to women is Passive Aggressive for, 'Can you turn the rugby off, please?'

'All rugby matches are important,' I go, because it's a point that should be made. 'What's up?'

She goes, 'Nothing. I was just wondering did you fancy an early night?'

My jaw is suddenly on the floor.

Just to fill you in on a little bit of backstory here, Sorcha and I have been back *living* together for a few *months* now? But she's been, let's just say, withholding certain privileges from me until I can prove to her that I'm capable of being faithful. I've got a set of nuts on me here like Jupiter and Neptune. But it sounds very much to me like I'm being propositioned now.

'What do you mean by an early night?' I go. 'As in, what specifically is being put on the table?' because I don't want to spend the rest of the night looking at her with her nose stuck in a book, gasping every fifteen seconds and telling me she actually feels *sorry* for people who've never read Jonathan Franzen?

She smiles and goes, 'Do I have to spell it out for you, Ross?' and suddenly she's walking up the stairs with me trotting stupidly behind her like Simba after Mufasa.

I'm already unbuttoning my chinos when she reaches the top of the stairs and goes, 'Although there *is* something I want you to do for me first,' and, like probably most males, I'm thinking, Shit, that sounds suspiciously like foreplay to me.

But I follow her into the bedroom anyway and that's when I see the cordboard box on the bed. A cordboard box I recognize. The one that holds my entire collection of romantic comedy DVDs.

I'm like, 'Okay, what's going on?'

Sorcha hands me a black bin bag and goes, 'I want you to throw all of these movies out.'

I'm there, 'What the fock?' which, I think, is a natural enough reaction.

She goes, 'I know why you have them, Ross. They were part of your seduction routine.'

I'm there, 'You don't know what you're talking about, Babes.'

She's like, 'Ross, I've heard you refer to this as your toolbox.'

She knows exactly what she's talking about, by the way. You don't become Ireland's leading philanderer without having the right equipment – and the contents of this box have been as vital to me in bedding literally thousands of women as my stock of incredible, incredible chat-up lines.

'If you're serious about being faithful to me,' she goes, 'then you're not going to need these any more. I want you to leave them out for the bin men tomorrow – as a demonstration of your commitment to me.'

I'm like, 'Could we not just stick them in the attic, Babes?'

Except she doesn't answer. She just pulls *Ghost* out of the box and hands it to me. I stare at the cover and a lot of memories come suddenly flooding back to me. You make your move when the ghost of Swayzee tells Demi Moore that he loves her and Moore goes, 'Ditto.'

I drop it into the bag with the sadness of someone saying goodbye to a lifelong friend.

Then she hands me *Pretty Woman*. *Pretty* focking *Woman*! The skeleton key of romcoms. There's not a lock it's ever failed to pick for me. Roberts and Gere on the fire exit stairs. Roberts – looking a bit cross-eyed – goes, 'She rescues him right back,' and she throws the lips on him. And that's *your* cue to do the same. Get in!

'In the bag,' Sorcha suddenly goes. I do as I'm told.

I pull the next one out myself. It's *You've Got Mail*. Jesus Christ! What a movie! The *Sleepless in Seattle* of the Internet age, with Hanks and Ryan at the top of their game. Catnip for women. I have a sudden memory of Suzanne Dardis – who was doing International Commerce with Mandarin in UCD – with her hands all over me like a focking spider monkey.

'Ross,' Sorcha goes, 'you're just making it horder for yourself.'

She's actually *right*? I suddenly ask her to hold the bag open for me. Then I take the box and I tip its entire contents – we're talking *Maid in Manhattan*, we're talking *Only You*, we're talking *The Notebook* (Jesus!) – into it.

Then I bring it downstairs, outside and – like the final scene in my own romcom – I drop it into the black, general refuse bin.

Father Fehily used to say, 'Never be afraid of change. Some things come to an end so better things can come to a beginning.'

And up there in that bedroom, waiting for me now, is a woman who loves me for all my faults and all my amazing qualities. And I'm going to try to be a good husband to her.

And sure if it doesn't work out, those movies are all available now on download.

# 2013

Music retailer HMV closes its Irish outlets as CDs and DVDs become increasingly obsolete * The year is designated the International Year of Quinoa * The Irish Bank Resolution Corporation (IBRC), which assumed the debts of the former Anglo Irish Bank, is liquidated by the government * Benedict XVI resigns as Pope, the first pontiff to do so in almost 600 years. He is replaced by Pope Francis * A plan is unveiled to link the Luas Red and Green lines, work on which will last several years and result in significant traffic disruption in Dublin City Centre * Tens of thousands of people march against the bank debt burden in protests in Dublin, Cork, Limerick, Galway, Waterford and Sligo * Whistleblowers allege widespread corruption in the driving penalty points system * Former British Prime Minister Margaret Thatcher dies * Former South African President Nelson Mandela dies * President Michael D. Higgins criticizes austerity politics in an interview with the *Financial Times* * The word 'bingeable' enters the language as a way to describe a TV show that's conducive to being watched for a long period of time in a single sitting * Ireland is declared a 'tax haven' during a US Senate hearing * Irish out-half Ronan O'Gara retires from rugby * The *Irish Independent* releases the Anglo Tapes, recordings of senior Anglo Irish Bank staff laughing about persuading the state to give them billions of euro in rescue money * Anti-home-repossession protesters force the cancellation of a property auction in the Shelbourne Hotel in Dublin * In a referendum, the electorate rejects a government proposal to abolish the Senate *

Meanwhile . . .

> 'Link the two lines, Ross! Connecting the people from
> *here* to the people from . . . out *there*.'
> *The Irish Times*, 20 June 2013

I'm short of moo and my cor tax is due, so I call out to the old dear's gaff hoping that (a) she's out and (b) the code to the safe is still 1, 9, 6, 2, the year she *claims* to have been born, denying at least a decade and a half of her existence.

She *is* home, though. I find her in the kitchen – eight fingers into a bottle of Bombay Sapphire at, like, twelve o'clock in the day.

'I suppose you saw it as well,' she goes, literally shaking, 'on the television last night.'

I'm like, 'Okay, unless you're talking about Sorcha's *Nell McAndrew Front Room Fit Camp* DVD, the answer is no. I need eight hundred snots, by the way.'

She knocks back a mouthful of gin. Her blood must be about seventy per cent proof. I must remember not to cremate her when she's gone. They'd have to drop sand from helicopters to put her out.

She goes, 'I'm talking about the programme on RTÉ about this public tramway thing.'

She means the documentary about the Luas. She has, like, no day-to-day exposure to the kind of people who use public transport and she feels there should have been some kind of warning beforehand that people from Dublin 4 and Dublin 18 might find some of the following scenes disturbing.

'It was dis, dat, dees and dohs,' she goes. 'I thought prosperity was a tide that was going to lift all boats. Clearly not, from the way some of these tram people spoke and dressed. For the first ten minutes, I thought I was watching a rerun of *Strumpet City*.'

I'm like, 'Why didn't you just switch over the channel?'

'Well, I'm very glad I didn't. Because had I switched over, I wouldn't have found out about this plan that's afoot . . . to link the two lines.'

'What?'

'Link the two lines, Ross! Connecting the people from *here* to the people from . . . out *there*. Do I have to spell it out for you, Ross?'

'Maybe you do.'

'As your father said, it's like grafting a human ear onto a mouse. It's both pointless. And unnatural. And it probably gives an unfair advantage to the mouse.'

'You'd want to lay off the giggle juice. You're mullered, woman.'

'I'm not mullered, Ross, I'm furious. I'm furious with the government. And I'm furious with Fionnuala O'Carroll-Kelly. Because I've taken my eye off the ball. Oh, I've been too caught up in my highly successful writing career – book *and* film – and neglected my role as an advocate for the most morginalized and discriminated-against people in our society. I'm talking about the urban middle classes.'

'Anyway, like I said, I need eight hundred snots. Is the safe combination still the alleged year you were born? Here, I must check if the fifteen years missing from your life are in there as well! You focking scarecrow.'

'How dare they!' she suddenly shouts.

It's definitely how dare *they* and not how dare *you*. That's how upset she is.

I'm there, 'Look, what do you care if they link the Red and Green lines? You don't even live anywhere near the Luas any more.'

'I have friends in Foxrock and I'm still very much port of the community out there.'

It's true. The Gables have named a breakfast special after her. The Holy FO'CK. It's basically eggs Benedict with a side order of bitterness and sexual frustration.

I'm like, 'You've wasted so much of your life getting worked up about shit like this. And where has it ever got you?'

'Well, we stopped the council from putting that wretched halting site on Westminster Road – where it would have been inappropriate.'

'Yeah, but you failed to get Funderland moved to the Northside.'

'We got that awful Molly Malone statue removed from Grafton Street. And that was after years and years of campaigning.'

'Yeah, but you couldn't stop them allowing charity shops to open on the same street.'

She laughs – a really, like, *bitter* laugh? 'Have you seen some of the so-called *sales* they're having in the shops? Oh, they're all charity shops on Grafton Street these days.'

She stands up. I'm pretty impressed that she still can.

'No,' she goes, 'I will not stand idly by while this *assault* is carried out on an area that I love – and where I *am* loved.'

I haven't seen her this up for a scrap since she copped Jackie Lavin with a full basket in the Five Items or Less queue in Donnybrook Fair three Christmas Eves ago.

'I am going to fight this!' she goes. 'Watch this space!'

## 'A recording. Of a phone conversation. Between me and a certain David Drumm in the autumn of 2008.' *The Irish Times, 6 July 2013*

It's been a mad two weeks. The whole Anglo Irish tapes thing has been bad news, I know, for Ireland. But for the country's third-fastest-growing confidential document disposal service, it's been, like, a *godsend*?

As my old man says, there's nothing like a business scandal to stir a country's corporate conscience and, for the past ten days, I've been busier than a cat burying shit on a hordwood floor.

Six o'clock on Wednesday night, roysh, I've just done my last job of the day, when my mobile suddenly rings and I answer with the usual, 'Shred Focking Everything – secure, reliable and environmentally questionable. How may I direct your call?'

It ends up *being* him – as in, like, my old man? – and he sounds in a seriously agitated slash mullered state.

'Can you, em, pop in to see me?' he goes.

Fifteen minutes later, I'm sitting in his study, listening to him muttering madly to himself, while he pours himself a glass of brandy big enough to strip the paint from the Sydney Harbour Bridge.

'You'd have to worry about the message it sends out internationally,' he goes. 'What will it do to Ireland's reputation as a banana republic if conversations like this can just leak into the public domain? There's a lot of people won't want to do business here.'

I'm like, 'Sorry, you invited me out here to listen to this?'

He pushes a Dictaphone across the desk to me.

'No,' he goes, 'I invited you out here to listen to this.'

'What is it?'

'A recording. Of a phone conversation. Between me and a certain

David Drumm in the autumn of 2008. It has the potential to be very embarrassing if it ever gets out.'

'Er, you record your phone conversations *why* exactly?'

'Just in case somebody says something compromising that I can use against them at a later date. It was a piece of advice that Hennessy gave me when I storted out in business. But this time it's *me* who's been bloody well compromised.'

He presses play and I listen to the conversation. I'll give it to you, like, word for word.

COCK: 'Pip pip and what ho!'

I probably should point out that COCK is Charles O'Carroll-Kelly, not David Drumm.

DD: 'Hello? Who is this?'

COCK: 'Drummer, it's Charles.'

DD: 'Who?'

COCK: 'It's the famous Charles, old bean!'

DD: 'Charles O'Carroll-Kelly?'

COCK: 'Right and correct.'

DD: 'Charles, what do you want? Sorry, I'm kind of busy at the moment.'

COCK: 'I expect you are! That's why I'm ringing. Just to offer you my support – moral, obviously, rather than financial – at what I'm sure is a very difficult time for you and all the chaps at my favourite bank. And to say, you'll come through this. Trust me, in five years' time, you'll be looking back on this time and laughing.'

DD: 'I, er, hope so.'

COCK: 'The government are going to do something, I presume?'

DD: 'At the moment, we don't know.'

COCK: 'Well, they have to! What's the alternative?'

DD: 'We're trying not to think about that.'

COCK: 'You've got to be tough with them, old chap.'

DD: 'We're not really holding a lot of cards.'

COCK [chuckles]: 'I'm laughing here because I'm thinking of my son, Ross, whom you might remember from the famous Castlerock College Dream Team of '99. When he wants money for something, he comes to me and says, "Gimme the moolah!"'

DD: 'Gimme the moolah?'

COCK: 'You could almost say it's a catchphrase of his.'

DD: 'Gimme the moolah!'

COCK: 'That's it. Quote-unquote. Or "Gimme the focking moolah!" if it's a particularly lorge sum he's looking for.'

DD [laughs]: 'Okay. And does that approach tend to work?'

COCK: 'Well, it's probably not much of a reflection on my parenting skills, but, yes, I have to say it does. Actually, I played nine holes with one of your chaps recently and I was telling him a story about the self-same Ross. He came to me once and he said, "I need seven grand. My cor insurance is due." As I was writing him the cheque, I said, "Is that how much cor insurance costs these days?" And he snapped the cheque out of my hand and said, "No, I just pulled it out of my arse." Seventeen years of age! I thought to myself, Oh, dear, what kind of a monster have I raised?!'

DD: 'I've got to go. I've another call coming through.'

COCK: 'Well, best of luck, old sport. And remember what I said!!'

DD: 'Gimme the moolah!'

COCK [laughs]: 'That's the style!'

The call ends.

*I* laugh then? I can't help it. I'm like, 'I can't believe you put all that stuff in their heads.'

'Well,' he goes, 'you can see now why I don't want this getting out. I have my political ambitions to consider. What would it do to the future of New Republic?'

'Why don't you just smash the tape with, like, a hammer? Or throw it in the fire?'

'Because I'm worried it won't destroy it sufficiently. That someone might still be able to, I don't know, *retrieve* the information by some means or other. That's how paranoid I am. I haven't slept in days, Ross. But then I thought, wait a minute – why not call in a professional to do the job?'

Meaning, presumably, *me*? I take the little cassette out of the machine. I'm like, 'Consider it disposed of.'

He breathes a sudden sigh of relief. He's there, 'I can't even begin to tell you what this means to me, Kicker.'

'But it's going to cost you,' I go.

He's like, 'Of course,' already dialling the number into the safe.

I'm there, 'Ten grand.'

'Ten grand?' he goes. 'Where did you get ten grand?'

And I'm like, 'Don't force me to use the line.'

### 'I'm engaged in a campaign of civil disobedience.'
### *The Irish Times, 10 August 2013*

The old man rings me at eleven o'clock in the morning and – get this – asks me where I am.

'I'm in bed,' I go. 'What do you think I am, a fisherman?'

'Ross,' he goes, 'it's your mother,' and that's when I cop the tone in his voice. It's serious. It kind of reminds me of the time she grabbed Miriam O'Callaghan in a headlock on Morehampton Road when she failed to get a People of the Year Award nomination and a fire crew had to break three of her fingers to get her to release her grip.

I'm there, 'What's she done now, the mad old crone?'

And he tells me. Except I don't believe it until I drive into town and see it with my own eyes.

The old dear, plus a group of maybe two hundred women just like her, have decided to protest the planned link-up of the two Luas lines by lying down on the tracks, bringing the entire service between Horcourt Street and Stephen's Green to a literally *halt*?

It's a pretty astonishing sight, I have to admit, this long line of well-preserved, middle-aged women, lying widthwise across the tram tracks for the guts of a kilometre, smelling of Chanel and Estée Lauder and singing 'Something Inside So Strong', the anthem of the old dear's previous campaigns to have the *Fair City* set moved to Kilbarrack and get a Donnybrook Fair for Foxrock Village.

I end up walking from Little Caesar's to TGI Friday's, studying this horizontal identity parade of South Dublin women with perfect hair and expensive orthodontics, trying to pick out my old dear. Eventually, I find her, lying on the section of track opposite Dandelion, her eyes gently closed as she murders every note of the song.

'They could drive one of those trams over your face,' I go, just by way of a greeting, 'and still not crack the first layer of foundation.'

There's something about my mother that brings out the best in me.

She opens her eyes to find me staring down at her. 'I don't have time for any of *your* unpleasantness,' she goes. 'I'm engaged in a campaign of civil disobedience . . .'

I'm there, 'You're engaged in a campaign to make a focking show of yourself. *And* me. *And* the old man.'

'Your embarrassment,' she goes, 'does not figure anywhere on my list of priorities. What they're proposing to do, Ross, is inhuman.'

'What, connecting the Red line to the Green line?'

'Connecting Ranelagh to Drimnagh. Milltown to Tallaght. Leopardstown to Fetter-bloody-cairn. And Fortunestown! There's a place out there called Fortunestown! It's like something from a cowboy movie!'

I'm there, 'What do *you* care anyway? The last time you used public transport, there was a focking horse pulling the thing.'

'*Our* world and *their* world shouldn't even be on nodding terms with each other. I mean, that's why our economy is in the state it's in.'

'I think all the muck you've had injected into your forehead and lips over the years has storted to leak into your brain.'

'The crash was caused by People Like Them being encouraged to think they could live in the manner of People Like Us, then borrowing accordingly. If it was up to me, it's a wall they'd be building, not a rail extension.'

I turn around. There's a Lady Gorda standing a few feet away. She's a looker as well. A lot of them are lately.

I'm like, 'If you're going to pull out the truncheons at some stage, stort with this woman here. But aim for the orms and legs. The rest of her is just rubber.'

The Lady Gorda goes, 'Can you step back, please, Sir?' and that's when I know that something is about to go down.

Suddenly, Gords stort closing in from both directions. They've obviously had enough and decided to put an end to it. I end up being pushed backwards until my back is against the railings of Stephen's Green and I offer some last-minute advice slash encouragement.

'Remember,' I go, 'you're wasting your time if you go for the face. Your batons will just bounce off it.'

And that's when *the* most incredible thing happens. The Lady Gorda steps forward – she's not *unlike* Caggie Dunlop, except obviously from Roscommon, or Kerry, or one of those – and she whips out, not a truncheon to beat some sense into my old dear, but a loudhailer.

'Sydney Vard,' she goes, 'has just launched its winter collection of new and vintage furs. Why not pop in and view their beautiful hand-picked collection of coats, jackets, reversibles, gilets, capes and headbands, in both up-to-the-minute *and* timeless classic styles?'

The old dear is like, 'Hold the line, Girls! Hold the line!'

The Lady Gorda goes, 'The special in Carluccio's of Dawson Street this lunchtime is a ravioli with truffled mushrooms and Grana Trentino D.O.P. fonduta.'

'Be strong!' the old dear goes. 'Just think of the words.'

Except women are already storting to stand up and drift away. It's, like, a slow trickle at first, but the Lady Gorda keeps up the pressure.

'After lunch,' she goes, 'why not visit Pamela Scott and view their range of exciting labels, such as Sophie B, Twist, Olsen, Gerry Weber, Bianca and Betty Barclay, as well as their stunning eveningwear brands from around the world? But make sure to set at least two hours aside for a visit to Brown Thomas . . .'

It's the most incredible piece of crowd management I've ever seen. I mean, I'd still prefer to see them cracking heads. But within fifteen minutes, everyone has cleared off and my old dear is the only one still lying across the tramline.

'Put this one in the van,' the Lady Gorda goes. 'She can spend the night in Pearse Street.'

### 'Spoiler alert!'
*The Irish Times, 5 October 2013*

JP says he finally got around to watching the last ever episode of *Breaking Bad* last night and then he laughs in a way that would have to be described as, like, *knowing*?

I'm there, 'Am I the only one who was actually, like, disappointed with the ending?'

And JP, Oisinn and Christian all suddenly roar at me, like I'm a wet dog at a white wedding. They're like, 'NO!!!'

I go, 'What?'

JP's there, 'Spoiler alert!'

'What do you mean?'

'Christian hasn't seen it yet!'

'Yeah, no,' Christian goes, 'thanks for ruining the focking ending for me, Ross.'

I'm there, 'I didn't even say what happened. I just said I was disappointed.'

'Which means I'm going to be watching it with the knowledge that I'm possibly going to be underwhelmed by the ending.'

'Well, how far into it are you?'

'I actually haven't storted it yet. I'm watching *Deadwood* at the moment. I'm three epsiodes into Season Two. Actually, no, I'm two episodes into Season Three.'

'So it could, be, like, six months before we're actually allowed to discuss *Breaking Bad* in public?'

'Might even be longer. I promised Lauren we'd go back and watch the last two seasons of *The Good Wife* before we do the whole *Breaking Bad* thing. I've heard good things, though.'

I just roll my eyes. Whose even round is it? Mine. I order four pints of the good stuff.

JP asks Christian what he thinks of *Deadwood*.

Christian smiles and nods and goes, 'It's definitely not what I expected. Especially that thing.'

'What thing?'

'*That* thing?'

'Oh, *that* thing!'

'I didn't give it away, did I – by saying there was a thing?'

'You sort of did.'

'Sorry.'

'It's fine. I've already seen it. Although don't say any more because I know Oisinn hasn't seen it yet.'

'Can I borrow it from you,' Oisinn goes, 'when you're finished? I need something because I've actually just finished *Homeland*.'

Christian's like, 'I keep meaning to get around to *Homeland*. Is it any good? Although don't answer that question.'

'I won't.'

'Yeah, no, definitely don't, because it's on our list. But *is* it good? Again, don't say.'

'I'm not going to say.'

'Good. Because I'm looking forward to it even more now.'

JP's like, 'Is anyone watching *The Newsroom*, by the way?'

I'm like, 'No,' because whatever I'm watching, it always seems to be the wrong focking thing.

'Er, why aren't you and Sorcha watching *The Newsroom*?'

'Because you told us to watch *Breaking Bad*. It was while we were three episodes into Series Four of *The Wire*. You said, "I can't believe you're still watching *The Wire* and you're not watching *Breaking Bad*!" So I switched to *Breaking Bad* and now you're saying you can't believe that we're not watching *The Newsroom*. And the very minute we stort watching *The Newsroom*, you'll say you can't believe we're not watching some other focking thing.'

Oisinn goes, 'But you saw *Homeland*, didn't you?'

I'm like, 'Yeah, we saw *Homeland*.'

Oisinn goes, 'And what did you think of the end of Season One – again, without actually saying, because JP obviously hasn't seen it.'

'I thought it was a complete waste of . . .'

'Whoa, whoa, whoa,' JP goes, 'you're creating an expectation again, Ross.'

'I'll tell you what you all *have* to watch,' Christian goes.

Oisinn's there, 'Go on. You always know the good ones.'

'*Battlestor Galactica*.'

'*Battlestor Galactica*? Is that, like, a space thing?'

'I'm not going to say because I don't want to give away any spoilers. But it's one you should definitely watch, if you haven't already.'

JP nods. 'I haven't seen it, but I've heard good things.'

Christian's like, 'Good things? Nothing specific, I hope.'

'God, no.'

'Try not to hear anything specific. Because it *would* actually spoil it for you. The same thing nearly happened to me with *House of Cards*.'

'What?'

'Yeah, no, my cousin nearly let slip what happens at the end of Season Two.'

'Did he, though?'

'No, thank God.'

'I actually saw *House of Cards* myself.'

'What did you think of it?'

'I'm not saying a word.'

'Nor am I.'

'Good.'

Fionn arrives then and catches the tail end of the conversation.

He's like, 'What are you talking about? It wasn't *Breaking Bad*, was it?'

Oisinn's there, 'No, but we were earlier.'

'What did everyone think of the ending? Although don't say.'

'We won't.'

'Because I haven't seen it. I'm going to get around to it. But do you know what I've just started rewatching?'

'What?'

'*The Sopranos*!'

We all smile. Because *everyone* has seen *The Sopranos*, which means we can actually *talk* about it?

I'm there, 'So is it still as good the second time around?'

JP goes, 'Spoiler alert.'

I'm like, 'How is it a spoiler alert? We've all seen it.'

Oisinn's like, 'Because I'm thinking of rewatching it myself – after I've finished watching this other boxset I've storted watching. By the way, you all *have* to watch it!'

Fionn's like, 'What's it called?'

'I don't even want to tell you the name in case it spoils it for you.'

'It sounds good.'

'I'm not saying if it's good or not. I'm just saying you'll have to watch it.'

I'm there, 'It's not *Six Feet Under*, is it?'

'Fock's sake!' Oisinn goes. 'Spoiler alert!'

# 2014

An estimated 130,000 people take part in a march in Dublin against the government's plan to introduce water charges * Ireland secure the Six Nations Championship on the day that Brian O'Driscoll retires from international rugby * The age of eligibility to receive the state pension is raised to sixty-six years * Superstorm Christine, the most destructive and prolonged storm to hit Ireland in twenty years, causes an estimated €300 million worth of damage across the country * The Ice Bucket Challenge becomes a social media phenomenon * American property magnate Donald Trump buys Doonbeg Golf and Hotel complex in County Clare * Scotland votes against independence from the United Kingdom * Michael D. Higgins addresses both Houses of Parliament while paying the first official state visit by an Irish President to the United Kingdom * A series of five sellout concerts by US country singer Garth Brooks at Dublin's Croke Park is cancelled after promoters fail to obtain a licence * The Rosie Hackett Bridge opens across the River Liffey in Dublin City Centre * Former President Mary Robinson is appointed the United Nations Special Envoy for Climate Change * The word 'manspreading' enters *The Oxford English Dictionary* as a means of describing an open-legged sitting position adopted by a man that encroaches on an adjacent seat or seats in a public place * Sky Sports broadcasts a hurling match for the first time, the Leinster Championship match between Kilkenny and Offaly * Mount Carmel Hospital, birthplace of Ross O'Carroll-Kelly's wife, Sorcha, goes into liquidation *

Meanwhile . . .

'There's nothing wrong with crying, Honor,
especially when it's the end of an era.'
*The Irish Times, 7 June 2014*

I'm sitting outside L'Officina in Dundrum with a hangover that's genuinely trying to kill me. Sorcha knocks back the last of her cappuccino
and asks me if I'm okay.

I'm there, 'Yeah, no, it'd probably help if I *borfed* at some stage?' and
she nods like she understands.

Honor, I should mention, is banging a teaspoon off the table at, like,
five-second intervals, while just staring at me. Every time the spoon
hits the table, it's like someone is flicking my brain.

I'm like, 'Honor, can you possibly stop doing that?'

And she goes, 'Yeah, that's the third time you've asked me that question and my answer is *still* the same? Why should I have to change my
behaviour just because you had too much to drink last night? Hashtag,
it's not all about you,' and she continues hitting the table with the spoon.

I notice two or three people outside the restaurant looking over in
our direction with their mouths wide open, quietly thanking God that
she's not their daughter. I'm convinced you could tackle the world's
birthrate problem by showing everyone in China a sixty-second You-
Tube clip of Honor even on a good day.

Sorcha stands up and goes, 'Okay, I just have to go to Fran & Jane
and Molton Brown and possibly BT2. I won't be long.'

I'm there, 'Sorcha, take her with you. I'm begging you.'

Except Honor doesn't move. She's like, 'I think I'll stay here, if it's
all the same to you. I have text messages to catch up on.'

And all Sorcha can say is, 'Try to go easy on your father, Honor. Yesterday was a very emotional day for him. It's all still a bit raw for him,'
and off she flounces, leaving me alone with the bill and an eight-year-
old girl possessed by the spirit of Chucky.

The second her mother is out of sight, she goes, 'He was only a
rugby player.'

I tell myself not to get involved. She's only looking for a reaction. I just stare at a point in the mid-distance and I try to block her voice out using the same technique I used to block out the haters back in my playing days. Except this morning, like I said, I'm hungover to fock and Honor can smell weakness like a shork can smell a paper cut.

'I heard you crying when you came in last night,' she goes. 'Oh my God, *you're* supposed to be the adult.'

I go, 'I wasn't crying. I had a couple of sticks of Heinemite and I spent a couple of hours watching old footage on the laptop.'

'And crying. Like an actual baby.'

'Okay, there may have been a few tears. There's nothing wrong with crying, Honor, especially when it's the end of an era. It'd be like if . . .'

I try to think of something that Honor likes – a band, a TV programme, a designer label – that might upset her if it suddenly came to an end. But I can't think of a single thing that she cares about. Honor came out of the womb bored and her mood hasn't changed noticeably since then.

She laughs in, like, a *cruel* way? 'You can't think of anything, can you?'

I'm like, 'Not offhand, no.'

The two birds at the next table are talking to each other out of the corners of their mouths – obviously about us.

Honor goes, 'It's a miracle that I'm as emotionally stable as I am. Crying over a rugby player.'

I was actually crying over *two* rugby players, but I'm not going to give her that ammunition.

I'm there, 'Keep your voice down, Honor. He could be shopping up here. And he wasn't *just* a rugby player. He was the greatest rugby player of all time – and that's me calling it. He did things on the pitch that you'd nearly need to watch them seven or eight times on the Internet afterwards to persuade yourself that they actually happened. And he didn't just do it against the weaker teams, like Italy and – okay, I'm getting a dig in here – Munster. He did it against Australia, England, New Zealand. It was a case of the bigger the opposition, the bigger the performance – very, very similar to me in an exact-opposite kind of way.'

She picks up her phone, already fed up with the conversation. I'm on a serious roll, though.

'The talk in Kielys last night was that they should retire the number thirteen jersey,' I go. 'I didn't think that was enough. I said they should retire the entire sport of rugby. Look, I was pretty blitzed when I said it, but I'm having moments this morning when I think I might have had an actual point. It comes in waves. Actually, I might still *be* blitzed.

'I suppose the other reason I'm sad is that, for a lot of people, there was always an element of "that could just as easily have been Ross O'Carroll-Kelly out there" whenever he played. Don't forget, we were schools cup players together. Both went on scholarship to UCD. One just happened to go in one direction while the other went in the other. It's kind of like that movie *Sliding Doors*, except Gwyneth Paltrow *missed* a train and I didn't bother my *hole* to train. I suppose seeing him finally retiring is a reminder to me that it's possibly never going to happen for me.'

Without looking up from her phone, Honor goes, 'You mean the fact that you're three stone overweight and you haven't played rugby since before I was born isn't reminder enough?'

And in that moment, I snap. I reach across the table, suddenly remembering the one thing in the world that my daughter actually does care about, and I grab her phone out of her hand. In the same movement, I throw it, like Rory Best feeding a lineout, and it sails through the air and lands, with a little plop, in the middle of the fountain.

Honor looks at me in, like, total shock. One or two people actually clap and say fair focks – this dude could actually write the book on how to parent a South Dublin child. And that's when Honor turns around to me, her face twisted into a sneer and goes, 'You know that was actually *your* phone I had in my hand?'

'She's trying to get me to do the Ice Bucket Challenge,
except I'm having literally *none* of it?'
*The Irish Times*, 7 September 2014

Honor calls me a chicken and I end up just laughing.

She's like, 'You are a chicken. You're, like, a totally gutless excuse for a human being.'

And to think, the parents of other kids my daughter's age are writing down their children's quotes so they can chuckle about them together when they get older. I don't write down anything Honor says for fear of it falling into the hands of a social worker.

'You're a spineless weasel,' she goes, 'and I can't look at you for more than three seconds without feeling the need to spew.'

This isn't just gratuitous abuse, by the way. She's trying to get me to do the Ice Bucket Challenge, except I'm having literally *none* of it?

See, one thing I'm not is an attention junkie.

I'm like, 'Honor, you're not going to get me to do it by calling me names. Can I just remind you that I faced down entire stadiums full of haters back in my rugby-playing days? I never let a hostile crowd affect me. I just pulled up my jersey, gave them a look at The Six, then went back to taking care of business.'

I smile at the memory. God, I really was great.

Honor is silent for a few seconds. Then she recycles and decides to change the angle of approach.

'I'm just trying to remember,' she goes, 'which Irish rugby player it was who said you were one of the ten toughest opponents he's ever faced.'

I'm like, 'It was Gordon D'Arcy – and he actually said top five.'

'Top five. Oh my God, I remember that interview. You cut it out and stuck it in the back of your Sad Book.'

'It's called a Rugby Tactics Book, Honor.'

'Whatever. He said you weren't frightened of anything. He said you were a true warrior, who'd rather be carried from the battlefield on his shield than back out of a challenge. But I suppose that was a long time ago.'

Now it's my turn to be suddenly quiet. She definitely knows what buttons to press with me.

'Go and get the bucket,' I hear myself suddenly go. 'I'm not going to have anyone saying that I'm not the unbelievable competitor I was back in the day.'

Honor skips down to the kitchen and I tip outside to the back gorden, where Sorcha – as it happens – is deadheading flowers.

I'm there, 'I suppose you better get ready to film this,' and she ends up just laughing.

She goes, 'I thought you said you'd never do it. She got inside your head, didn't she?'

'Look, if it got back to Dorce that I backed away from this, I think it'd genuinely crush him.'

She laughs, then shakes her head and whips out her iPhone, just as Honor emerges from the kitchen, wobbling from side to side with the weight of the bucket. I sit down on the little pork bench next to the back door. And then, as she walks up to me, holding the bucket in both hands, I instinctively do something that I straight away regret.

I reach out, and, with the palm of my hand, I touch the side of the bucket.

Why do I do it? If I'm being totally honest, it's to check that it's actually ice-cold water in there and not boiling hot water from the kettle.

But Honor sees me do it and I watch her expression of excitement suddenly change to one of sadness. I try to cover my tracks by going, 'I was just making sure that it was definitely cold enough,' except she's too clever to fall for that.

'You thought I was going to throw boiling water over you!' she goes. Then she puts the bucket down and runs back into the house.

Sorcha's like, 'Go after her, Ross,' which is what I end up having to do. She's sitting at the kitchen table, looking all upset.

'Honor,' I try to go, 'I was just double-checking. It'd be an easy mistake for anyone to make.'

'Am I really that horrible?' she goes. 'Do you really think I'd be capable of doing something like that?'

'Of course I don't.'

I say it with possibly less conviction than I intended.

'Nobody likes me,' she goes.

I'm there, 'Honor, that's not true.'

'It *is* true. Parents tell their children to stay away from me because I'm a bitch.'

'You're not a bitch, Honor. I genuinely like to think that.'

'I'm horrible.'

'You're not horrible. And will I tell you how I know you're not horrible? Because you gave me a massive, massive boost to my confidence a few minutes ago by reminding me about that famous Gordon D'Arcy interview. I'd actually nearly forgotten what I meant to the dude. And by bringing me to my senses, well, you've actually made my day.'

'Really?'

'You make my day every day, Honor. And those parents who tell their kids to stay away from you – you know something? I pity them. I genuinely pity them, because they're never going to know just how lovely you can sometimes be.'

Oh, that does the trick. She straight away brightens up.

'Come on,' I go. 'Let's go and prove your old man's critics wrong!'

We step out to the gorden again, me holding her hand. Sorcha smiles at me and I can tell what she's thinking is that being a good father is just another of life's challenges that I've managed to nail.

I take my seat on the bench again and Sorcha storts filming. I close my eyes as Honor hoists the bucket up with all her strength, then goes, 'This is going to be hillair!' and she tips the contents over my head.

I brace myself for the cold feeling, except it's not the temperature that hits me. It's the smell.

'Okay,' I go, afraid to even open my eyes, 'what *was* that?'

Honor's like, 'The run-off from the dishwasher. I emptied the hoover bag into it and some fish-heads. And then some pink dye, which is going take about a week to wash off your skin.'

I open my eyes in time to see her disappearing back into the house. 'Mom,' she goes, 'email that video to me. I want to see can I make it go viral.'

### 'There's so much about selling gaffs that I thought I'd forgotten.'
#### *The Irish Times*, 4 October 2014

There used to be a standard test to discover whether or not you lived in a good area. First you rang the Gords to tell them that a man with a balaclava and a crowbar was climbing in your living-room window. Then you rang Domino's to order a twelve-inch pizza with everything on it. If the Gords arrived *before* the pizza, you could describe the area in which you lived as 'desirable'. If the Gords arrived *after* the pizza, well, you could rest assured that your gaff was never going to be the subject of an 800-word piece in the property supplement of, say, *this* newspaper?

They were simpler times, of course. But then people like JP's old man discovered something. There would be far more money for estate agents if we all just pretended that *everywhere* was a desirable area. It was this discovery, during the good old days of the Celtic Tiger, that led to Sean McDermott Street being described as 'Dublin's Notting Hill' and Bray being called 'Wicklow's very own Hamptons', both, as it happens, by JP's old man, my new employer and former mentor – Barry Conroy of Hook, Lyon and Sinker.

There's so much about selling gaffs that I thought I'd forgotten, but, after a week back in the office, it's all suddenly tripping off my tongue again. 'A fully-fitted kitchen' means a kitchen. 'Within commutable distance of Dublin' means it's not on an island in the Atlantic. And 'deceptively spacious' means that they counted the space in the cavity walls and the width of the building bricks when they measured up.

'Neoclassical', 'ort deco' and 'well-appointed' mean literally nothing, but prospective buyers seem more comfortable when they're mentioned than when they're not.

Yes, you'd be surprised at how quickly it's come back to me – but then I know I'm not alone in that.

JP's old man is convinced that the coming boom is going to be even bigger than the last one, which is why he wants to make sure that everyone at Hook, Lyon and Sinker is on top of their game. Monday mornings are given over to, like, staff training – or staff reconditioning, as the man himself calls it. Most of us have been out of the game for the past five years. We're all a bit rusty. That's why we're here.

'Okay,' he goes, 'we're going to play a little game called Accentuating the Positive.'

He's standing at the top of the room like an actual teacher and there's, like, fourteen of us sitting behind our desks, listening to this morning's lesson. It's literally like being back at school, except obviously I can't use the fact that I play rugby as an excuse for refusing to answer questions. I'm living in the real world now.

A photograph of a gaff fills the projector screen behind him.

'This dilapidated grief hole is on the North Circular Road,' he goes. 'Frankly, I wouldn't let my mother-in-law live in it – and I really dislike my mother-in-law. I'm going to give you the bad news about this house and I want you to spin it as good news. You ready?'

We all nod. I seriously love this.

'Firstly, it's in shite order,' he goes. 'The roof won't survive one more bad winter. It's fifty yards from Mountjoy Jail and if you want to take a dump, you have to do it outdoors. I'm a prospective buyer. Sell me this house.'

One or two dudes jump in straight away, keen to impress.

'It's, em, a good fixer-upper,' one of them goes, 'with plenty of potential.'

JP's old man remains stony-faced – not impressed.

Some other dude has a crack at it then. He's like, 'An exciting opportunity has arisen in an increasingly popular area.'

JP's old man just shakes his head. 'Come on,' he goes, 'you're just giving me the old spiel. Give me something new. Excite me.'

That's when I hear my voice automatically go, 'Early viewing is recommended for this exceptional period residence, situated in the hort of one of Dublin's most vibrant urban communities.'

A smile erupts across his face. 'Okay,' he goes, 'you've got my attention. But the place is falling down.'

I'm there, 'It's a mature property with a strong history, whose character is only enhanced by its gentle state of decline.'

'There's ivy growing on the inside walls of two of the bedrooms.'

'It has an authentic rustic feel.'

'There's no natural light in the place.'

'Privacy and seclusion are amongst its myriad chorms.'

'The walls are so thin, you'll be finishing your neighbour's sentences.'

'A strong sense of community is just one of its unique selling points.'

'No indoor toilet.'

'Adding to the personality of this property is its strong Georgian Dublin feel.'

'The bedrooms. Jesus, you'd have more space if you lived in The Joy.'

'The rooms are sensibly proportioned to offer ease of maintenance.'

'And there's a hideous lean-to at the back of the house with a corrugated plastic roof.'

'One of the property's stand-out features is an atrium that serves as an exciting entertainment space.'

'I've been trying to shift this eyesore since 2007.'

'This superbly presented property has retained its value through the recession. We would recommend availing early of the opportunity to view. And can I randomly throw in the word Bauhaus and possibly even rococo?'

'Yes, you can,' he goes. 'And then you can stand up.'

Which is what I end up just doing, while the rest of the staff burst into a spontaneous round of applause.

'Because that,' he goes, 'was an absolute master class in how to sell houses.'

'Wendy Wagoner is in PR . . . she's in the
process of PR-ing me!'
*The Irish Times*, 18 October 2014

If you stuck a potbellied pig in a pantsuit and gave it a bag of make-up to play with, it would end up bearing an uncanny resemblance to the woman who calls herself my mother. I mention this to her as well, as she's stepping out of the Westbury Hotel, dressed like a woman who thinks she's twenty years younger and thirty pounds lighter than she actually is.

She ignores the insult and goes, 'You're probably wondering with *whom* I've been lunching.'

I'm not even sure that's proper English, but I don't bother pulling her up on it. Instead, I go, 'Judging from the hum coming off you, I'd say your old friends, Gordon's and Hendrick's.'

I always lift my game when I'm around her, in fairness to me.

She's there, 'I was *lunching* with Wendy Wagoner,' and she lifts her eyebrows like this should actually *mean* something to me?

I'm like, 'Who's Wendy Wagoner?' allowing myself to become sucked into the conversation. I'm too nice for my own good sometimes. 'Is this yet another donor you're using to farm fat for your forehead?'

'Wendy Wagoner is in PR,' she goes. 'She PRs people. And, right now, she's in the process of PR-ing me!'

I'm there, 'Why are you being PR-ed?' already regretting asking.

'*That's* the exciting news,' she goes. 'I've set my sights on winning a Rehab People of the Year Award this year.'

'You set your sights on winning a Rehab People of the Year Award every year. And yet you never win one. And there's a very obvious reason for that. They don't give them out for evil.'

She goes, 'That's why Wendy is helping me to improve my public image,' and then something weird suddenly storts happening to her expression. It's as if the thousands of pulleys and levers underneath the layers of silicon and orse gristle that make up her face suddenly kick into life. I can see her top and bottom teeth. It's like staring into the back of a bin lorry. That's when I realize that the woman is trying to smile.

I'm there, 'You're going to give yourself an aneurysm.'

'Well, Wendy thinks I should show off my caring side a bit more,' she goes. 'It seems to be what people want, especially in this day and age, when things are apparently difficult for a great many people.'

It's at that precise moment that this woman, Wendy – like she said – Wagoner, comes through the revolving door of the hotel, wearing a Bluetooth earpiece and clutching an A4 Filofax in the crook of her orm. She's, like, blonde, mid-forties, with loads of make-up and a slight underbite.

I think what I'm trying to say is that I probably *would* if it came up in conversation?

'Who's this?' she goes, looking me up and down.

I'm like, 'Yeah, no, I'm her *son*? The name's Ross.'

Wendy's like, 'Her *son*? Fionnuala, you never told me you had a son!'

I can't tell you how much that hurts.

'Well,' the old dear tries to go, 'it never occurred to me that having a son was important, especially in the context of all my other achievements.'

'That's what she said to the midwife,' I go, 'five minutes after she delivered me.'

'Delivered me,' Wendy goes. 'Hmmm.'

That's the other thing I have to tell you about this woman. She's got this really irritating habit of saying the last two or three words of every sentence as *you're* saying them? It's like she's too busy to wait for *you* to finish what you're saying – she has to do it for you.

It's incredibly annoying.

I'm there, 'The reason she wanted to keep me a secret from you is that I've got the goods on her.'

'Goods on her – hmmm.'

'For instance, I know that all of her so-called charity work was actually a racket.'

'Racket – yes.'

'I know she ripped off the ideas for all of her books and I know she's got more rubber in that face than a focking bus tyre.'

'Bus tyre.'

'She didn't tell you about me because I know where all the bodies are buried – and by the way I'm not even using that as a figure of speech.'

'Of speech, okay. I'm looking at him, Fionnuala, and I'm thinking where do we place him? As in, how does he fit into the paradigm we're constructing for you?'

She cocks her head to one side and she looks me up and down for about thirty seconds, puckering her lips and sort of, like, moving them from side to side.

She goes, 'I suppose he's handsome in a rugby idiot kind of way. A lot of girls like that kind of thing. I suppose if we could get him to go to some of these charity events I've been telling you about, as a kind of chaperone to you. Fionnuala O'Carroll-Kelly, loving mother – it's the kind of thing that might play well, especially if we can get pictures into some of the social pages.'

'You're actually dreaming,' I go, 'if you think I would be seen in public with that bet-down horse-beast.'

'Horse-beast, yes. I think it's something we should definitely consider, Fionnuala.'

I'm like, 'Yeah, dream on,' and I go to walk away.

That's when the old dear all of a sudden goes, 'Did you borrow my car, by the way?'

I'm like, 'Yeah, I borrowed your cor. So-called. It was to drive out to Ronan's gaff. I wouldn't bring my own out there. I value it too much.'

'Well, I got a notice in the post yesterday to say that I had *four* penalty points.'

'Yeah, no, there were speed cameras everywhere that day. Suck it up would be my advice.'

'But they're not *my* points, Ross.'

'Well, you're going to have to take them. My licence is nearly full.'

Wendy Wagoner smiles. She goes, 'This is what we in the PR business call *leverage*.'

I'm like, 'Oh, fock.'

'I'll send you a schedule,' the woman goes, 'of the various events you'll be attending with your mother over the coming weeks.'

I'm like, 'This is basic blackmail.'

And she goes, 'Blackmail, hmmm.'


# 'There's a lot to be said for complete and utter ignorance.'
## *The Irish Times*, 15 November 2014

The most exciting day of the school year for a lot of Mount Anville moms and dads is the day of the parent-teacher meeting.

They arrive at the school in a convoy of all-terrain vehicles, dressed for a night at the National Concert Hall, giddy at the thought of hearing that little Siofra or Mathilde has a genuine gift for poetry, or languages, or maths, or debating.

Me, I'm happy if I can get through the afternoon without hearing that my daughter has scalped a teacher or blinded a fellow student in an acid attack.

It's a day that literally terrifies me and I know that Sorcha feels the same way, judging from the number of outfit changes she went through before we left the house. It was like being backstage at a Kylie gig.

In the end, she went for a cape and trilby combo that's apparently a very popular look for A/W14 and Honor sat on the stairs humming the theme tune to *The Good, the Bad and the Ugly* as we were going out the door.

Anyway, we've been at the school for almost an hour and so far we've seen Ms Taite, who teaches her Ancient Arabic, as well as Speech and Deportment, and Ms Brock – the famous Foxy Brocksy – who has her for Upholstery and Self-Esteem.

Neither of them, in fairness, had any stories to tell us about atrocities committed by our daughter since the stort of the school year. No fires, no floods and everyone has the same number of knees they had at the end of August. I couldn't be more proud of her. Sorcha doesn't share my happiness, though. She can't just accept that, as far as Honor is concerned, no news is excellent news.

She goes, 'Did Ms Taite seem, I don't know, *frightened* to you?'

I actually laugh. This is while we're sitting in the corridor, waiting to see *Bean Uí Dhálaigh*, her year head, who takes her for everything else.

I'm like, 'Frightened? What are you talking about?'

'I just thought she seemed a little, I don't know, *reticent*?' she goes. 'Like she was holding something *back*?'

'If you don't hear about a problem, Sorcha, then the problem doesn't exist. That's always been my approach to life. There's a lot to be said for complete and utter ignorance.'

'I mean, I asked her straight out – you heard me, Ross – was Honor being cheeky and disruptive this year. And she totally fudged it: "Those definitions can sometimes come down to the way we interpret behaviour."'

'That's good enough for me, Sorcha. The message I took from that was, "Keep doing whatever it is you're doing as parents, because, from where I'm sitting, you goys are nailing it and I think I'm going to have to say fair focks to you."'

'That's not the message I got at all.'

'Well, that's because I think you're being possibly paranoid.'

'And Ms Knox – why did she keep looking over my shoulder when she was talking to me?'

'I think she has a bit of a honky eye. I actually like it. I think it's cute on her.'

'And what did she say when we were going out the door? "If Honor asks you what I said about her, what are you going to tell her?" Does that not seem, I don't know, sinister to you?'

'I don't think so. I genuinely don't think so'

It's at that point that Bean Uí Dhálaigh steps out of the classroom into the corridor. Looks-wise, she wouldn't be the best. I know that's not strictly relevant to the story, but I like to give you a bit of colour.

Her greeting, it has to be said, takes us both by *surprise*?

'Hello!' she goes, her orms stretched wide, then she air-kisses Sorcha on both cheeks and gives me a proper, like, full-on hug.

I'm thinking she's possibly mistaken us for someone else, except then she goes, 'Honor's mom and dad! How are you both?'

Sorcha's there, 'Er, we're good,' feeling obviously as confused as I am. 'Thanks for asking, Bean Uí Dhálaigh.'

'Oh, please,' the woman goes, 'call me Una. Sit down there. Why do you look so worried?'

I end up just laughing.

'To be honest,' I go, 'smiles are one thing we don't expect to see when we come to the school. This is the first parent-teacher meeting in three years where we haven't been advised to have a solicitor present.'

She goes, 'All I will say in response to that is that the job of teaching brings with it a great many challenges. Our main job, as educators, is to get the best out of young people. If we fail to do that, then it's the fault of the teacher, not the pupil.'

Someone else is taking the rap for the way my daughter has turned out. Not surprisingly, I'm on it like an Easter bonnet.

'This is music to my ears,' I go. 'I love your attitude and I really mean that.'

Sorcha's face is lit up like I don't know what.

She goes, 'Are you saying that Honor's behaviour has improved this year?'

'Oh, no,' the woman goes, still grinning like a donkey trying to shit a house brick. 'She's the most appalling child I've ever had the misfortune to teach.'

I'm like, 'Why are you smiling when you're saying that?'

'Because,' she goes, 'I'm leaving!'

'Leaving? Leaving the school?'

'Leaving the school! Leaving teaching! Leaving everything!'

'Oh my God!'

'That's right! For as long as I can remember, I've wanted to teach children – to fill their hearts with a love of learning and their minds with a passion for inquiry! I've been doing it for ten years and I've loved it! But after ten weeks in the company of your daughter, I've realized that it's not what I want to do any more!'

'Well,' I go, 'at least she's done some good,' always trying to see the positive as a parent.

But Sorcha's in literally shock.

She's like, 'You're saying our daughter has put you off teaching forever?'

'Not just teaching,' she goes. 'She's put me off children. I told my fiancée three weeks ago that I'd changed my mind about wanting kids and now he's ended it.'

'That's like, Oh! My God!'

'It *is*! Now I'm jobless *and* single.'

There won't be many takers for her and I'm not saying that to be a dick.

Sorcha's like, 'You poor thing.'

'No, it's wonderful,' the woman goes, 'because look at me! I'm smiling! There are six weeks to go until the Christmas holidays and then I won't have to see your daughter any more!'

Again, trying to see the good in Honor, I go, 'You're actually the third teacher we've seen today and you're the first who's had any complaints about her.'

She laughs.

'Are you talking about Nuala Taite and Fay Brock?' she goes.

Sorcha's like, 'Yes, we've seen both of them, although I got the distinct impression that there was a lot they weren't saying.'

'Of course there's a lot they weren't saying. They're terrified.'

I'm like, 'Why would they be terrified?'

'Because,' she goes, 'one of them is going to become her full-time teacher after Christmas.'


### 'The children are missing!'
*The Irish Times*, 6 December 2014


The old dear rings in a terrible state.

I go, 'Alright, Cruella de Vodka? What's up?'

She's there, 'Ross, something terrible has happened!' and her voice is all, I don't know, *shrill*?

'Let me guess,' I straight away go. 'You made the cover of *VIP*, but your forked tail was sticking out of the end of your palazzo pants?'

'No.'

'You asked the off-licence to honour the points on your loyalty cord and they had to close four branches and make fifteen staff redundant?'

'Ross . . .'

'Okay, give me a second here. The latest batch of blubber they injected into your forehead came from an orangutan and now you've an irresistible urge to eat ants off the ground and touch yourself inappropriately in public?'

She goes, 'Ross, will you please stop being unpleasant to me for one minute!' and she actually roars the following line at me. 'The children are missing!'

I'll give you a bit of background if you're new to this particular story. For as long as I can remember, my old dear has had her hort set on a Rehab People of the Year Award. Unfortunately, they don't give out prizes for ugliness, and year after year, she keeps getting passed over in favour of people who actually *deserve* to be honoured? So she hired a PR guru, who told her it was time that the public saw – I'm giving you this in quotes – 'the luminescent goodness of Fionnuala O'Carroll-Kelly'.

Which is why, for the past three weeks, she's been parading around Dublin with her ethnically diverse godchildren in tow – one black, one Chinese and one a little bit, I don't know, Eastern Europeany? She's had them in The Gables. She's had them in the golf club. She's taken them to the National Gallery and to Teddy's.

I saw them a week ago walking Dún Laoghaire pier in a high wind and she looked like Michael Jackson in the *Earth Song* video – except obviously with more plastic surgery.

I couldn't get that song out of my head for days.

She has the legs walked off the poor kids as well. And now they're . . . did she say missing?

'Yes, missing!' she goes. 'That's *exactly* what I said.'

I'm there, 'Okay, what do you mean when you say missing, though?'

'What the hell do you think I mean when I say missing?'

'Whoa, watch your focking tone there, Angelina Stoli. *You* rang *me*, remember? I wouldn't have any qualms about hanging up on you right now.'

'I'm sorry, Ross. I'm going out of my mind here!'

'That's no excuse. Let's keep the porty polite. You bet-down harridan. Now tell me what happened.'

'It's awful, Ross. I took them into BTs to make an appointment to see Santa Claus – we got the eighteenth of December – and when we got outside I remembered I'd seen a lovely faux-fur stole that I'd meant to pick up, but, well, it slipped my mind. So I asked the children to wait outside while I went back in. And when I came out, they were gone!'

'Whoa, whoa, whoa – you asked them to wait outside?'

'I was only gone ten minutes. Fifteen at the most, because I had to pick up a voucher for Lauraleen Connell to say thank you for all her hord work as lady captain this year.'

'You left three kids – of what age? – seven, six and four, outside BTs while you went inside to shop?'

'Oh,' she tries to go, 'so that makes me a bad person, does it?'

'Hey, I've got a daughter who's possibly psychotic and a son who wants to be a professional soccer player. I'm in no position to judge. But, yes, I would say that makes you an absolutely horrendous person.'

'Please, Ross. I've been crying for the last hour. My face is a mess.'

She's such a spoofer.

'Your face is a mess,' I go. 'I'll give you that one. But you haven't had any tear ducts since that botched crow's feet operation you had done in international waters back in 2005.'

She's like, 'What am I going to do, Ross?'

'Is it not obvious?'

'Perhaps we could put something on the Internet about them.'

'The Internet? Are you kidding me? Call the focking Feds!'

'Oh, I don't wish to involve the Gords in this matter.'

'I don't blame you. They'll probably chorge you with neglect.'

'Neglect? I love my godchildren. There's a definite bond.'

'I'm sure the judge will take that into account. Ring the Feds.'

'I can't.'

'If you don't ring them, I will.'

'Ross, I mean I *literally* can't. I can't report them missing because . . . look, I can't remember any of their names.'

I actually laugh at that one.

'You can't remember their names?' I go. 'Your own godchildren? These kids who you have a definite bond with?'

'I had the names written down and now I can't find the piece of paper anywhere. I think one is called Fu or Lu or something.'

I'm there, 'They're called Justice, Wu and Gheorghe.'

That rocks her back on her heels.

She's like, 'How did you do that? You barely know them. Is it some form of memory technique?'

'Yeah, no, it's called actually giving a shit about other people,' I go. 'And also thinking that kids are pretty focking fantastic if you take the time to get to know them and give them a bit of feedback and a bit of love.'

How I turned out to be such a lovely, lovely goy is one of the genuine mysteries of our time.

She goes, 'So it's Lewie, Dewie . . .'

And I'm there, 'It's Justice, Wu and Gheorghe! For God's sake, write them down, woman! Then ring the Gords. And the other thing you need to do is to ring their parents.'

She's like, 'Oh, I think it's a little bit early for all of that.'

And I'm there, 'Do it, you incontinent old hag – or, again, *I* will?'

Then I hang up on her.

I'm actually staring straight *at* her, by the way. She's outside Weir's, pacing back and forth, and her dilemma is obvious. As soon as she makes that call, the word will be all over town and she can say goodbye to one of those little statuettes forever.

Do you know what she ends up doing? For once – the right thing. She phones the Feds.

There's nothing to worry about. I should have possibly mentioned that to you earlier. About fifteen minutes ago, I was passing BTs and I saw Justice, Wu and Gheorghe, staring at the window display, obviously on their own.

They told me about the faux-fur stole and I went, 'She's un-fockingbelievable. Come on, let's hit Mackers.'

And it's from the window of the McCafé – wrapping our faces around a Big Mac and fries each – that we watch my old dear explain to a pretty shocked Lady Gorda how she managed to misplace three children.

And after enough time has passed, I go, 'Come on, let's put the old trout out of her misery.'

# 2015

Minister for Health, Leo Varadkar, becomes the first openly gay government minister in Ireland * In a referendum, Ireland votes to legalize same-sex marriage * NASA announces that liquid water has been found on Mars * Businessman Denis O'Brien sues the Houses of the Oireachtas Commission, the government of Ireland and the Attorney General over remarks made about him and his banking affairs in the Dáil * New Zealand rugby legend Jonah Lomu dies * The ferry service between Dún Laoghaire and Holyhead comes to an end after more than 200 years * Ireland beat Scotland 40–10 in Edinburgh to snatch the Six Nations Championship on the final day * Conor McGregor, a former plumber from Crumlin, establishes himself as the biggest star in the world of mixed martial arts * A new political party, Renua Ireland, is launched * A new national postcode system called Eircode is introduced *

Meanwhile . . .

> 'She's obviously one smitten kitten,
> in fairness to the girl.'
> *The Irish Times, 14 February 2015*

We're having risotto for dinner. Risotto from the Italian word *risot*, which means to sell baby food to adults for two euros per spoonful. We'll know that the country is finally back on its feet again when we're all suddenly back eating it.

Sorcha goes, 'So who was the Valentine's cord from?'

The woman is like Sarah Lund. Misses fock-all.

'Valentine's cord?' I make the mistake of going.

And she's like, 'I'm not a fool, Ross. You practically ran down to the letterbox this morning and then I saw you hide something inside your shirt.'

'Oh, *that* Valentine's cord,' I go, trying not to smile.

She's like, 'So who sent it to you?'

'There was, like, no name on it – a secret admirer.'

'It's from *her*, isn't it?'

*Her*, just to fill you in, is Abnoba Kennedy, the Deputy Head of Commercial Lettings with Hook, Lyon and Sinker, who has a bit of a crush on the old Rossmeister General.

I'm like, 'Who's *her*, Babes?'

She goes, 'You know who I mean, Ross.'

'Yeah, no, I think I know who you're talking about now.'

'She's very good-looking.'

'I have to admit, I've never really thought about her in that way.'

I would let Mathieu Bastareaud punch me in the face for an hour and a half just to drink the run-off from the washing machine that cleaned her smalls.

Sorcha goes, 'I'm just wondering what kind of a girl sends a Valentine's cord to the home of a man she knows is married?'

I'm there, 'It's just a bit of hormless fun, Babes. She's obviously one smitten kitten, in fairness to the girl.'

'And I suppose you did nothing to encourage that?'

'You know me. I'm a people person, Sorcha.'

'A *people* person?'

'That's the expression I'm using . . . risotto for dinner, is it? And they said Ireland was focked for generations to come!'

That's when Honor suddenly steps into the kitchen.

'Was there any post?' she goes.

I laugh and I'm like, 'Don't mention the war, Honor! A cord for me! It looks like your old man's still got a few moves!'

I'm pulling up my sleeves to kiss my guns when Honor suddenly turns on her heel without saying a word – there's no 'Fair focks!', no 'Fully deserved!', no nothing – and back up the stairs she stomps.

Sorcha goes, 'Oh my God, Ross, are you *really* that insensitive?'

'Er,' I go, 'I'm tempted to say yes, Babes, because I've no idea what you're talking about.'

'She was asking did any Valentine's cords arrive for *her*!'

'They didn't, though. There was just one. And it was for me.'

'Do you not remember what it was like to be that age and to have a crush on someone?'

'Who's she got a crush on?'

'I don't know. But she was obviously waiting for a cord from *someone*. Oh my God, certain things are storting to suddenly add *up* now?'

'As in?'

'Well, we were in Dundrum last weekend and she queued up to pay for something with her own money.'

'She never pays for anything with her own money. A lorm bells must have been certainly ringing.'

'I asked her what she was buying and she pushed this little bag inside her jacket and said, "You don't have to make such a big deal of it!" and then she called me a knob and stormed off – oh my God – all *embarrassed*?'

Sorcha suddenly hands me my cor keys and goes, 'Ross, you know what you have to do.'

I'm like, 'Er . . .'

'Go out and buy your daughter a Valentine's cord.'

'What? She wouldn't want one from me.'

'It's not going to *be* from you. We'll write it ourselves and sign it from a secret admirer.'

'I don't know, Babes – isn't lying supposably wrong?'

'So is growing up with self-esteem issues.'

'Here, while I'm out, will I get something to go with the risotto – like fish and chips, for instance, or two snack boxes?'

'Just go, Ross – we'll have dinner when you come back.'

So off I head, into the night.

Shopping for a cord the night before Valentine's Day is a bit like dating in your early forties – most of what's left out there is wrecked-looking.

Seven petrol stations I end up having to try before I find a decent cord. It's got, like, a rose on the front and then a lot of romanticky shit inside it.

I sit in the forecourt and I write the thing. It's like, 'To Honor, with lots of love, from your secret admirer x.'

Luckily, my handwriting is actually *like* an eight-year-old's?

So the next trick, when I get home, is to convince the girl that someone just stuck the thing through the letterbox.

'Honor!' I shout up the stairs.

She appears on the landing.

She's like, 'What the fock do you want?' in an absolute fouler.

I'm there, 'Yeah, no, I just found this in the letterbox. It's for you. I've no idea what it is. It's a genuine mystery.'

She comes down the stairs, snatches it out of my hand, looks at it, then disappears back upstairs to her room.

And that ends up being that, until about an hour later, when I'm scraping my risotto into the Brabantia – and I suddenly notice the cord, ripped up, at the bottom of the bin. I reach in and I pull out the four pieces and that's when I notice that it hasn't even been opened yet?

Sorcha goes, 'Oh my God, I wonder does she know it was you?'

I'm like, 'Me? You were the one who told me to do it.'

'I don't want this to fracture her trust in us as adult role models. Ross, call her downstairs.'

Which is, again, what I end up *having* to do?

Ten seconds later, Honor reappears in the kitchen, going, 'Sorry, I'm trying to think up horrible things to say to Little Mix on Twitter – will this take long?'

Sorcha goes, 'You tore up your cord, Honor, without even *opening* it?'

Honor just shrugs. She's like, 'Er, it's a Valentine's cord? Valentine's Day is for knobs, losers and saps.'

'I know you don't think that,' Sorcha goes. 'I saw you buying a cord last weekend in Dundrum.'

And that's when Honor says it.

'That?' she goes. 'That was a joke. I sent it to Dad so that he'd think he had a secret admirer!'

They both look at me and they go . . . well, you know what they go.

They go, 'Hill! Air!'

## 'You look like . . . Denis O'Brien!'
### *The Irish Times, 12 June 2015*

There's something different about my old man. There's something *definitely* different about him – I just can't put my finger on what it might be.

'So,' he goes, 'what do you think of this Siteserv business?'

This is while I'm still standing on the front doorstep, by the way.

He goes, 'I was just talking to Hennessy. I said, "Ross, will have a take on this. Something suitably satiric, no doubt – you see if he doesn't!"'

I just, like, stare at him – literally *no* idea what he's talking about – then he suddenly bursts out laughing.

'You don't even need to open your mouth!' he goes. 'You've gone and said it with a look! I'm going to ring Hennessy this instant! Your best one yet! Oh, where would you and I be, Ross, if we didn't have politics in our lives?'

I go, 'I need money.'

He's like, 'Well, of course you do!' like there's no other reason I'd show up at his door at, like, ten to twelve on a weekday morning. And, of course, there isn't. 'Let's go and see what's in the safe, shall we?'

I follow him into the house, then down to the study. I'm there, 'You're in great form, by the way. It's kind of annoying. There's something different about you as well.'

He's there, 'You see, that's what made you such a great number ten, Ross – you're observant to an almost supernatural degree.'

'I'm obviously not,' I go, 'because I don't know what the fock it is.'

'Well, I'll say nothing,' he goes. 'See how long it takes for the world-famous penny to drop.'

He bends down to key the code into the safe. He goes, 'How much are you looking for?'

I'm like, 'Twenty grand.'

He goes, 'Twenty grand? Why do you need twenty grand?'

I'm there, 'What are you, an auditor? Mind your own focking business.'

'Quite right!' he goes. 'I know how expensive it is to run a big house. I think I was the only man who watched Pádraig Flynn's famous *Late Late Show* interview and came away thinking, "Three houses? On *his* salary? The chap's a bloody well miracle-worker."'

He takes the money out of the safe – four wads of presumably five Ks each.

'Oh my God,' I hear myself suddenly go, 'you've got hair!'

He laughs.

I'm actually just pointing at his head, going, 'What the fock?'

He goes, 'Do you like it?'

It's, like, a wig. It's an *actual* wig. I try to come up with something genuinely hurtful to say, except I actually can't.

'It's . . . it's incredible,' I go, grabbing him by the shoulders and turning him around. 'You look like . . . you look like . . . Denis O'Brien!'

He laughs. He goes, 'Uncanny, isn't it? At least five times a day I catch my reflection in the mirror and I have to do a bloody well double-take. I keep thinking I'm looking at the great man himself.'

I'm like, 'It doesn't even *look* like a wig. I mean, that's why it took so long for me to cop it. It looks like actual hair. I'm trying to think of something really negative to say, but I'm genuinely struggling, in fairness to you.'

He goes, 'Terribly kind of you to say, Ross.'

'I honestly can't come up with a single decent line to wound you. When did you decide to stort wearing a wig? I didn't think you minded that your head looked like a focking rugby ball.'

There it is. I've got my mojo back.

'I didn't,' he goes. 'Until the moment I put this thing on.'

I'm like, 'So where did you get it?'

'Would you believe me if I told you that I found it?'

'Found it?'

'In Helen's attic. I was rooting around for an old 45 by *The Crystals* that we both used to enjoy . . .'

'Whoa, whoa, whoa,' I go, at the same time laughing. 'You found a wig in an attic and you just, what, put it on your focking head?'

He goes, 'I tried it on for size, yes. And I discovered that – well, as you can see – it rather suited me.'

He walks over to the mirror and studies himself for a few seconds. He clearly likes what he sees.

'Oh, the chap has his critics,' he goes, 'alleging this, that and the other. But I always say to people, "Do you know the *real* reason why Denis is such a bloody titan when it comes to business? Look at his hair, for heaven's sakes! That great, proud mane of his!"'

'Yeah, no,' I go, 'he's got good hair alright.'

'He has MAGNIFICENT hair!' he practically roars at me. 'MAG! NIFICENT! His is *real*, of course. I should know. I'm one of the lucky few who's touched it.'

I'm there, 'So, what, this is going to be, like, a permanent thing?'

'Yes, indeed!' he goes. 'And people better get used to it! Without wishing to sound melodramatic, having this hair has given me, well . . . *powers*.'

I'm there, 'Powers? What are you shitting on about?'

'Well,' he goes, 'I pulled into a Topaz this morning and there was a chap standing there waiting to fill up the Kompressor for me before I'd even got the door open. I said, "Well, this is a turn-up! I can't remember the last time I had a pump attendant fill up the cor *for* me!"'

I'm there, 'Doesn't Denis O'Brien, like, *own* Topaz?'

'Yes, indeed! As he filled up my tank, another chap, who was getting out of a Toyota Avensis of all things, walked up to me, shook my hand and said, "Thank you! Thank you for bringing Johnny Sexton home!" Quote-unquote, Ross!'

I'm like, 'And did you tell him that it wasn't you?'

'Well, to be honest,' he goes, 'I was rather enjoying the praise.'

I'm there, 'Even though it wasn't intended for you?'

'The point I'm trying to make,' he goes, 'is that I suddenly feel like a man of substance, a man of power, a man not to be trifled with. I have a feeling that finding this wig is going to be the single greatest thing that has ever happened to me.'

'Er, with the exception of your son winning the Leinster Schools Senior Cup,' I go.

But he stares past me, at his reflection in the window behind me, and he goes, 'Perhaps greater than even that.'

### 'Mixed Mortial Orts? Okay, you're ripping the piss now.'
#### *The Irish Times*, 18 July 2015

So I'm showing three couples a house in Stoneybosher and I'm driving along the quays, practising my spiel for them:

'A great opportunity for a plumbing, plastering and roofing enthusiast at the hort of Dublin's very own Notting Hill!'

I've just crossed over whatever that bridge is called, not far from the Four Courts, when I suddenly spot a familiar figure, checking himself out in the window of a solicitor's practice on Blackhall Place.

I'm like, 'Ronan?'

He turns around and he cops me. Except I end up having to do an actual double-take when I notice what he's wearing – we're talking a powder-blue suit. From this distance, it looks like he's also had his hair cut – or at the very least *combed*?

I'm there, 'I didn't know you were in court this morning. You should have said something.'

It shows you how much faith I have in my first-born.

He laughs. He's there, 'Ine not in cowurt, you doorty-looken doort boord. Ine in thraining.'

He storts walking towards the cor.

I'm there, 'Training?' and I'm hit by this sudden sense of dread.

I suddenly notice that his hair is long on top, except shaved at the sides and the back – not unlike Ian Madigan's. And he's got a few wispy hairs on his chin that, if allowed to grow unchecked for another six or seven months, may eventually resemble Dorce's famous beard. Somehow, I already know that it's not rugby training he's talking about?

I'm there, 'Ro, what have you got yourself mixed up in?'

I'm talking to him through the window on the *driver's* side?

He goes, 'Ine doing Mixed Meertial Eerts, Rosser,' like it's the most natural thing in the world.

I'm like, 'Mixed Mortial Orts? Okay, you're ripping the piss now.'

He goes, 'Ine not, Rosser. Ine in the gym this morden – it's up above Beergintowun.'

I'm there, 'Up above Borgaintown? Jesus, I'd nearly prefer if you *were* up in court.'

For the first time in my life, I genuinely feel like I've failed as a father. The MMO crowd have got their claws into my son.

I'm there, 'Ro, it's not too late for me to put your name down for Clontorf. I could ask Cian Healy to bring you out there – show you the facilities. I'm a hero to him.'

He goes, 'Don't be giving me bleaten rubby, Rosser. This is a real man's gayum. Here, look at this,' and he suddenly makes a fist out of his right hand. Except his little finger is sticking out of it at an, I don't know, whatever-degree angle. I end up having to turn my head away for fear of spewing my breakfast muffin.

'Oh my God,' I go, 'that's disgusting!'

He laughs. He's there, 'I broke it, Rosser – pucking the lug off some bleaten sham in the gym the utter week.'

'Pucking the lug?' I go. 'God, you sound like – what's his name?'

His face lights up. He's like, 'Are you talking about Codor McGregor?' taking it as an actual compliment. 'Sure, that's who Ine modelling meself on, Rosser.'

I'm there, 'Fock off!'

He goes, 'Ine a good-looking fedda – almost too good-looking – but Ine also a killing machine. Ine breaking necks and Ine collecting cheques. And pucking the lug off shams.'

I'm there, 'Where did you get the suit?' even though I can probably guess.

'Offa Louis Copeland,' he goes.

I'm like, 'Yeah, no, I thought as much. Me and Louis will be having words next time I see him in Dundrum.'

Ronan suddenly launches into a spiel then.

He's there, 'I look damn good, but – there's no denying that, Rosser. Ine a freak of nature. You step into the Octagon with me, you better make sure you've had yisser dinner. Ine a looker. I've got the complexion and I've got the connections. Ine gonna shake up the wurdled. And if any sham gets in me way, I'll rip he's lower leg off and batter him into a toorty-year coma with he's own bleaten foot. That's authomathic – one thing foddows the utter.'

I'm just there, 'I blame myself. I just hoped you'd eventually realize that egg-chucking was the game for you all along.'

He's hunkered down now and he's checking out his reflection in my wing mirror. 'I know you're upset,' he goes, grabbing handfuls of his facial hair, willing it to grow.

I'm like, 'I'm not upset, Ro. What kind of father would I be if I got upset because my son is following his dream? I'm just very, very, very disappointed in you.'

He stands up again and he nods like he understands.

I'm there, 'Anyway, I've got to go. I'm showing a house up in The Bosher at eleven.'

'Here,' he goes, 'what are you doing two weeks on Toorsday, Rosser?'

I'm there, 'I don't know – why?'

He goes, 'Ine habbon me foorst fight – it's in the car peerk of the Broken Arms in Finglas. Some bleaten sham is about to get the lug pucked off him. I'd luven if you were there.'

I just shake my head.

'Ro,' I go, 'of course I'm going to be there. Just because I disapprove of what you're doing, it doesn't mean I won't be supporting you every step of the way while constantly reminding you how let down I feel.'

He's delighted. We get on like you wouldn't believe. He's there, 'Thanks, Rosser. When I win the wurdled title, Ine gonna dedicate it to you.'

And I'm like, 'Hopefully, it'll never come to that. I'm still hoping it's a phase and you'll drop this nonsense when you go back to school in September.'

He laughs.

He goes, 'I doatunt think Castlerock are godda take me back, Rosser,' and, as he's saying it, he storts unbuttoning his shirt. He suddenly pulls it open to reveal – oh my literally God – a massive Conor McGregor-style tattoo across his chest. 'Not since I got this little beauty done.'

'Your current hairstyle . . . is the exclusive property
of Mr Denis O'Brien.'
*The Irish Times, 1 August 2015*

Sorcha asks me if I'd be interested in going to Lecky Picky this year. She actually *calls* it that as well?

I'm like, 'Yeah, whatever,' barely even listening to the girl.

'It's just that Honor's got this Mandarin Immersion Programme coming up,' she goes. 'And I thought, well, before she goes off to China for six weeks, it'd be – oh my God – *so* amazing for the three of us to spend some quality time together, doing something that we'll always remember – as, like, a *family*?'

I'm just there, 'Yeah, no, cool.'

'A girl I sort of knew in UCD is, like, selling her tickets,' she goes.

I'm like, 'Yeah, no, that's great.'

And that's when she goes, 'Ross, what's wrong?'

Sorcha can read me like a book. I've been married to the girl for twelve years – at this stage, she knows me nearly as well as some of my old rugby teammates.

I'm there, 'I've got three weeks to save my job in Hook, Lyon and Sinker, Sorcha.'

She's like, 'Okay, what are you talking about?' because deep down we both know that the economy hasn't yet recovered to the point where people like me can afford to do fock-all, all day, every day. 'I thought JP's dad was talking about making you a portner?'

I'm there, 'Well, now he's talking about sacking me. Look, if you must know, I got on the wrong side of the New Land League. Selling all those repo-ed gaffs up in Killiney and – typical me – showboating while I was doing it. Now, they want to destroy me. We had this, like, distressed property auction and they basically disrupted it to the point where we had to actually *abandon* it? Then, last week, they stuck a picket on this development of gaffs we were trying to offload in literally Kinnegad. Estate agents should be given Taser guns. It should be the law.'

Sorcha – calm as you like – goes, 'So what are you going to do about it?'

I'm there, 'What can I do? Selling gaffs is the only thing I've ever been good at, aport from obviously playing rugby and getting women to fall in love with me.'

'What I mean is, are you going to spend the three weeks just feeling sorry for yourself. Because that's not the Ross O'Carroll-Kelly I know.'

'I like the way you're talking to me, Sorcha. I still haven't a clue what I'm going to do about the problem, but I like the way you're making me feel.'

'What were you always taught growing up? Whenever you have a problem in life . . .'

'Phone my old headmaster,' I go. 'But Father Fehily died ten years ago.'

She's like, 'And if your old headmaster isn't around?'

I'm there, 'Phone my old man!' and the answer suddenly hits me like Courtney Lawes. 'Of course! He'll sort these fockers out! He's got this new wig! People just look at him these days and they literally crumble!'

I kiss Sorcha on the cheek and I tell her she's a genius and thirty seconds later I'm pointing the cor in the direction of Ailesbury Road. I've got to stop thinking about my old man as just an ATM. He's actually more than that – although I probably will ask him for a couple of grand while I have him.

I let myself in and straight away I hear his voice coming from the study. He's actually shouting, going, 'I don't believe it! Of all the people to turn on me!'

I tip down to the study and I push the door. I'm surprised to find him alone, pacing back and forth, a piece of paper in his hand.

I'm like, 'What's going on? Actually, forget that, I don't care. I need two grand – no, three grand – and I also need you to get the New Land League off my back.'

He totally ignores the point I've just made.

'I've had a cease and desist letter!' he goes, waving it at me. 'From our friend.'

I'm like, 'What friend? Why do you have to make everything about you?'

'He's threatening me with a bloody well injunction!' he goes. 'And I thought we were friends! Here, have a listen to this,' and he storts, like, reading this, like, *letter* to me?

He goes, *'We have been instructed by our client, Mr Denis O'Brien, to inform you that your current hairstyle – hereinafter referred to as "Denis O'Brien Hair" – is the exclusive property of Mr Denis O'Brien and that your wearing of Denis O'Brien Hair is a clear infringement of his intellectual property rights.*

*'You are hereby put on notice and instructed to cease and desist from having, wearing and/or using for the purposes of business advancement, and/or any other reason or reasons, Denis O'Brien Hair, including any related hairstyle that seeks to replicate the colour, shape and manner in which Mr Denis O'Brien wears his hair, including, without limitation, any colour that could be construed, by a right-thinking person, as "autumn-ochre", or any similar shade; any style that involves a side parting; and any volume that might be interpreted as "generous-bodied", or any variation thereof.*

*'Unless we hear from you in writing within three days from the date hereof, your receipt of this letter shall be deemed to be your acknowledgement and agreement to immediately cease and desist from having Denis O'Brien Hair. A*

*failure to comply with the terms of this letter will result in, inter alia, an application for injunctive relief, pending a court action, at which our client, Mr Denis O'Brien, will seek damages, including punitive damages, and his costs associated therewith, including, without limitation, all legal and professional costs, fees, expenses, duties and outgoings.'*

He looks up at me. I actually laugh. I'm there, 'And I thought *I* had problems.'

He goes, 'You know what I'm going to have to do, Ross?'

And I'm there, 'Er, give in, obviously.'

Except the power has clearly gone to the dude's head – because he takes the letter, rips it in half, then goes, 'I'm going to fight him every step of the bloody well way!'

## 'The place has the atmosphere of a cockfight.'
### *The Irish Times, 8 August 2015*

I never thought I'd see my teenage son back in nappies. I say it to him as well and he looks at me like I've just questioned his manhood.

'It's not a nappy,' he goes, 'you bleaten flute, Rosser. It's a peerda Tudo showurts.'

Trust me, though, it's a nappy – a *big* nappy, with a cup at the front, stuffed with Kevlar, to protect his testicles and no doubt future, unborn generations of O'Carroll-Kelly cage fighters.

I'm there, 'Of all the sports you could have picked, Ro, why did it have to be this?'

He goes, 'You said the sayum thing to me when I was playing ball.'

Meaning soccer. And, yeah, no, he possibly has a point. Whatever you think about the idea of two men kicking the humanity out of each other in a cage, roared on by three or four hundred salivating locals, at least it's not *that*.

We're in the cor pork of The Broken Orms in Finglas and it's literally heaving. There must be – like I said – three- or four-hundred people here and the place has the atmosphere of a cockfight.

Actually, there *was* a cockfight on the undercord. Godzilla beat The Coop Killer in a pretty one-sided contest – in as much as I'm a judge of these things.

Ronan is definitely the hometown favourite, judging from the encouragement that's being shouted in his general postcode.

'Boorst him, the doort boord!' and 'Rip he's bleaten throat out!' and variations on that theme.

If I could send one message to the Jesuits right now, it would be, 'Send rugby. Quickly. Because these people need something in their lives.' This is pretty much what Kildare would look like today if there'd never been a Clongowes.

I'm there, 'I'd, em, better let you go and warm up, or whatever it is you do before one of these things.'

Ronan's expression suddenly changes. He's staring over my left shoulder in what would have to be described as a *hateful* way?

He goes, 'There he is, the boddicks!'

I'm like, 'Who?'

He's there, 'The sham Ine fighting. The sham who's about to get the bleaten lug pucked off him by the Man of the bleaten Moment hee-or.'

I turn around and I end up getting one of the biggest frights of my literally life. Ronan's opponent is a man – as in, like, a *grown* man? We're talking late twenties, six-foot-two, maybe six-foot-three, and built like Yoann Maestri.

I'm there, 'You're not fighting *him*?'

'Two hits,' Ronan goes. 'Me hitting him, then him hitting the flowur.'

'Ro, look at the size of him. What is he, Romanian or something?'

'Bulgeerdian. He does the dowur on the nightclub upsteers.'

'Ro,' I go, putting my orm around him, 'I can't let you do this. There's always someone weaker than you to pick on. That's the best advice I can give you as a father.'

He shakes my orm off him. 'Rosser, Ine fighting Radoslav and Ine warden you – doatunt embaddass me.'

I'm like, 'Radoslav? Ronan, he's going to kill you.'

He's there, 'Go and sit dowun, Rosser.'

Which is what I end up having to do, because Ronan storts making his way towards the cage, then the announcer is suddenly on the mic, going, 'Laaadieees and gentlemeeen . . .'

There *are* no ladies here – let me just say that for the record.

'And now for the main event of the evening . . .'

A humungous roar goes up. I find my way to my seat. Ronan's put me sitting next to his old dear in the front row. She doesn't even acknowledge me as I sit down.

'If I'd had full custody,' I go, 'we'd be at Castle Avenue right now. Or Templeville Road. Or even – dare I say it – *Stradbrook*? Instead, it's all this.'

She doesn't even answer me. She storts shouting, 'Battorum, Ronan! Battorum!' through the bors of the cage, then everyone else gets in on the act as the announcer introduces the two fighters. They're all going, 'Ro-hnin! Ro-hnin! Ro-hnin!'

There's no doubt the crowd is on his side. But my hort is beating like a Kango Hammer when I see the famous Radoslav stripped to the waist. He's got abs like speed bumps and biceps like basic *beach* balls?

I'm there, 'I've got a bad feeling about this.'

The bell rings and they make a rush for each other. Ronan throws a punch, which misses his opponent by a couple of postcodes. And in that moment, Radoslav – standing on one leg – spins however-many-degrees-are-in-a-full-circle and delivers the most unbelievable kick to the side of Ronan's head.

There's, like, a loud crack. Ronan's legs buckle and he collapses on the floor like an empty glove puppet. The noise from the crowd suddenly dies. The Broken Orms hasn't known silence like it since the day I asked the landlord if he knew how to make a lychee bellini.

Radoslav is suddenly bearing down on Ronan, getting ready to finish him off. I'm up off the seat like it's on fire and my orse is catching. I grab onto the bors of the cage and I stort literally shaking them, going, 'Leave him alone! He's had enough! He's my son and I love him!'

And that's when, from out of this little fallen bundle in the corner of the cage, a leg suddenly appears and kicks Radoslav full on the knee. I hear the most unbelievable snapping sound. Radoslav's orms drop and he falls to one side, his right leg sticking out at possibly the most horrific angle I've ever seen – and I've been in some messy rucks.

Ronan's up off the deck immediately, then he's suddenly on top of the dude – as he'd say himself, pucking the lug off him, until the referee decides that he's seen enough and he drags him off him, then lifts Ronan's hand to declare him the winner.

The crowd goes totally ballistic – it's pretty obvious they've found a new Mixed Mortial Orts hero – but all Ronan can do in his moment of glory is give me what would have to be described as a *withering* look?

Then he mouths a single word at me – and that word, I'm sad to say, is, 'Spanner!'

'The old man has become a monster
and he has to be stopped.'
*The Irish Times*, 15 August 2015

So I'm in bed on Tuesday afternoon, rewatching Ireland against Wales and obviously taking a few notes, when my phone all of a sudden rings and it ends up being Helen – as in, my old man's second *wife*?

'Ross,' she goes, 'it's about your father.'

I'm there, 'I hope you've finally wised up and left the knob,' because she's way out of his league. I actually said it the day they got married – in my best man speech. But that's when I hear the tears in her voice and I go, 'Helen, what's wrong?'

She's there, 'Ross, I don't think I could bear the stress of a court case.'

I actually *laugh*? I'm there, 'There won't *be* a court case, Helen. This is Denis literally O'Brien we're talking about. The old man will cave.'

'He won't,' she goes. 'The power has gone to his head. Ross, he's talking about countersuing.'

I'm there, 'Denis's lawyers will make shit of him on the witness stand. It'll be funny. A day out for us all.'

She goes, 'I need you to talk to him . . . Please, Ross.'

I'm like, 'I'm kind of working here, Helen. There's a World Cup coming up.'

Except all I can hear then is, like, *sobbing* on the other end of the phone? She's not a fan of the game. How could she possibly understand? So I end up having to get dressed, then I drive on over there.

The old man is in the study with Hennessy. 'I'm just having a legal consult with your godfather,' he goes when I arrive. Hennessy, I notice, is scribbling notes on a yellow legal pad. 'I've thought of another one,' the old man goes, at the same time running his fingers through his big mane. 'A few weeks ago, a chap was filling up my Kompressor in one of those Topazes of his – the one at Newlands Cross, if you don't mind! – and the pump was a little on the urgent side. I ended up with half a bloody well pint of Super Unleaded down the front of my trousers, then had to endure a day of incontinence jokes from the chaps at the Kildare Hotel and Golf Club – yourself included, Hennessy!'

Hennessy's there, 'We'll demand €500 for the trousers and €500 million for emotional distress.'

'Make it a good letter,' the old man goes. 'One of your specials. Lots of forthwiths and hereafters and what-nots. That should wipe the bloody well smile off Denis's face.'

He wanders over to the window and looks out.

'Oh, and another one,' he suddenly goes. 'That – inverted commas – water meter that his crowd installed out there. The new concrete they laid doesn't match the old concrete. It's a totally different shade, for heaven's sakes!'

Hennessy goes, 'We could argue that it's taken – what? – €3 million off the value of the house, then claim another €30 million for mental anguish.'

The old man's there, 'Write it up, old chap.'

'Stop!' I hear myself suddenly go. 'Just stop!'

They both look up at me.

I'm there, 'Why don't you just tell Denis O'Brien's solicitor that you'll stop having Denis O'Brien Hair?'

He looks at me in total disgust. He's like, 'Where the hell is this coming from?'

I'm there, 'You've been on some crazy power trip ever since you put that focking wig on your head. Your wife is upset. And her upset is affecting my World Cup preparations.'

He stares at me, his face turning quickly red, then he shouts, 'HELEN!' and he storms out of the study and down to the kitchen, with Hennessy following close behind. I go after them.

Helen is cooking dinner. The old man opens up on her. He's there, 'How DARE you go behind my back like that!'

She's like, 'Charles, we could lose our home! We could lose everything we own!'

The old man goes, 'Hennessy, I want you to send my wife a letter.'

Helen actually laughs in, like, a *bitter* way? She's there, 'Oh, you're going to sue *me* now, are you?'

The old man goes, 'Save your breath to cool your porridge – you're getting a letter! Instructing you to cease and also desist from going behind my back . . .'

Hennessy actually storts scribbling the words down on his yellow legal pad. He must be focking coining it with all the fees.

'Malicious slander,' the old man goes. 'Breach of wifely duties. Psychological torment . . .'

Helen bursts into tears and I suddenly can't listen to any more of this. The woman is right. The old man has become a monster and he has to be stopped.

My hand reaches out – sort of, like, *instinctively*? – and makes a grab for the wig. I give it a serious yank. He must be using some pretty heavy-duty adhesive because I end up pulling off half his scalp with it.

The dude screams.

They've got one of those, like, American-style gorbage disposal units next to the sink and I think, yeah, no, I'll stick it in there, then switch it on and it'll be a case of – *literally*? – good riddance to bad rubbish.

The old man's watching all of this in slow motion, going, 'Noooooo!!!'

I dance around the table – a throwback to the glory days when I used to do the same to Senior Cup defences – and I stretch out my hand, getting ready to dump that wig once and for all.

And that's when I feel the breath leave my body and I find myself suddenly falling to the floor. The old man – no slouch himself back in the, whatever, 1950s – has tackled me around the waist.

I hit the deck and I drop the wig – although if you were being technical, you'd probably call it a knock-on. It's lying on the floor a few feet away. We both scramble for it, but I'm still winded, and the old man reaches it before I *manage* to?

And I know in that moment that my only chance of saving the old man from himself is gone.

He puts the wig back on his head, then stands up, shaping it with his fingers, so that the old volume quickly returns.

'Ross,' he goes, 'you'll be hearing from my solicitor.'

### 'This is what going to Electric Picnic is all about!'
*The Irish Times, 5 September 2015*

Honor takes one look at our tent slash tipi and I know exactly what's going through her mind. Because it's the exact same thing that's going through mine.

'I'm not staying in a focking tent,' she goes.

But Sorcha just whips back the flap and in we go. It's all, like, cushions and rugs and beanbags and mood lighting. She stretches her two orms out, crucifixion-style, and does a full, three-hundred-and-whatever-degree twirl, with a big, stupid grin on her face.

'Look at this place!' she goes, hoping that we'll somehow see what *she* sees in it? 'This is what going to Electric Picnic is all about!'

On balance, I'd say my wife's least attractive quality is her enthusiasm for trying new things.

I'm like, 'Seriously, Sorcha, there are many things in life that I would consider myself above – and one of them is definitely, definitely camping.'

'It's not camping,' Sorcha tries to go. 'It's what they call *glamping*!'

Honor whips out her phone.

'I'm going to see if I can get a suite in Castle Durrow,' she goes. 'Yeah, that's what they call Five Star Hoteling.'

Sorcha's there, 'Ross, speak to your daughter. There's no point in even *being* at a festival unless you're going to, like, immerse yourself in the whole festival *experience*? Come on, let's go out and soak up the atmosphere.'

So she walks out of the tent and we end up having to just follow her. She looks a focking state, by the way, and I'm saying that as her husband. She's wearing, like, a short, white gypsy dress, black Hunters, white, hort-shaped shades and a straw boater.

And she's talking in this, like, continuous stream, going, 'If we only do one thing today, can we definitely go to the Theatre of Food? I want to try the famous goat's milk ice cream and also this, like, pressed apple juice made from twenty-eight varieties of apple, all of them grown in Mayo. And there's a band that Garret and Claire told me to go to see – no one has ever heard of them, but Garret says they're going to be bigger than *The Script* and they've only just done the Junior Cert! And, oh my God, in the Mindfield area, there's a woman who sings the poems of Thomas Kinsella to Andrew Lloyd Webber tunes – *so*, so random, but definitely worth catching, according to *The Ticket* – and there's also a theatre group from Tuam who tell the story of a home repossession through interpretive dance. Again, the *Irish Times* described it as brave and – I think – important?'

Honor turns around to me and goes, 'Okay, *how* old are all these people?'

I'm like, 'Thirties? Forties?'

And she goes, 'Why didn't they just enjoy themselves more when they were younger?' and I end up having to laugh, because she's pretty much nailed Electric Picnic right there.

There's suddenly a squeal out of Sorcha. 'Oh my God,' she goes, staring down at her phone, 'there's a Junior Shakespeare Workshop this year! Let's look for it. Come on, Honor, you love drama!'

She's very much her mother's daughter in that regard.

The tent is easy enough to find, because it has 'Junior Shakespeare Workshop!' on the side of it in, like, massive letters, with two masks – one smiley, one sad – on either side. In we go. The dude in chorge is called Aodhan and there's a group of maybe fifteen or sixteen kids listening to him blabber on.

Honor wanders over and joins them.

'When I tell people that I teach Shakespeare to children,' he goes, 'the response is always the same. They say, "How can children understand Shakespeare?" And in response to that, I always quote Berthold Brecht, who said, "For children, only the highest themes are high enough."'

I'm looking around me to see if there's a bor.

'Ross, try to remember that quote,' Sorcha goes. 'Berthold Brecht. Actually, put it into your phone if you still have battery power. I'm going to go out and get us something to eat. I'm storving!'

So Sorcha heads off and I sit down with the other parents. 'The play we're going to tackle today is *Julius Caesar*,' Aodhan goes, 'one of several written by Shakespeare that were based on real-life events.'

I suddenly get this tap on my shoulder. When I turn around it ends up being a dude called Linus Ormsby, who played full-back for Belvo back in the day. We're both like, 'How the hell are you?' and we instantly high-five each other – the differences in our backgrounds totally forgotten – and he introduces me to his wife, who's called Pyper.

She's not great, in case you're wondering.

They've got, like, a picnic basket with them.

'Here, you look like you could use a drink,' Linus goes, pretty much reading my mind, and he pours me a plastic beaker full of cava. I throw it into me.

Pyper's there, 'Electric Picnic is *such* an escape, isn't it? Have you tried the goat's milk ice cream?'

I'm like, 'Er, no, it's definitely on the list,' which it obviously isn't because it sounds focking revolting.

'And – oh my God – you *have* to see the woman who looks like Amy Winehouse and sings "Mirror in February" to the tune of "Another Suitcase in Another Hall" while her husband plays the saw.'

Linus smiles at me and rolls his eyes.

'I have to endure this every year,' he goes. 'I'm just here to see Florence and the Machine and the Riptide Movement and to get seriously messed up in between.'

I like his attitude, Belvo or not. He tops up my beaker. You'd have to say fair focks to the dude.

That's when Sorcha suddenly arrives back.

'I bought Crêpes Suzette from a man on stilts!' she goes, all delighted with herself, then she storts looking around her with a confused expression on her face. 'Ross, where's Honor?'

I'm like, 'Who?'

She goes, 'Er, our *daughter*?'

Yeah, no, the cava has gone straight to my head.

A woman sitting in front of us goes, 'Is she the little girl who said, "This is focking lame!" and then walked out – about ten minutes ago?'

I'm thinking, that's a pretty good description of our daughter alright.

'Oh my God,' Sorcha goes, dragging me to my feet, 'Honor is missing! Ross, we have to find her!'

## 'Do you have any idea how focking pathetic you people are?'
### *The Irish Times*, 12 September 2015

Our daughter is missing at Electric Picnic. I'll say that again – just in case you missed it.

Our daughter . . . is missing . . . at Electric Picnic.

Me and Sorcha are suddenly running through crowds of people in the pissings of rain, searching for her, the panic rising in our chests.

'Anything could have happened to her!' Sorcha keeps going – although, if I'm being totally honest, I'm one per cent worried about Honor and ninety-nine per cent concerned for the general public.

'Honor!' Sorcha is screaming. 'Honor!'

We end up running around for an hour, maybe more, covering every mucky inch of the place, but there's no actual sign of her.

We pass a tree completely covered in CDs – hundreds of them have been literally nailed to the trunk for no good reason – and a man with a t-shirt that says, 'I Prefer Their Early Stuff' with a child on his shoulders wearing pink ear muffs that look like headphones, and two sumo ballerinas rolling around in the mud, cheered on by maybe fifty or sixty men, women and children – and all the time, Sorcha is crying out, 'Has anyone seen our daughter? Someone must have seen our daughter!'

We pass grown men and women sliding down a muddy bank on their orses and their bellies, while their kids look on, then a fast food van called the Osama Kitchen, offering a Jihadi Special (kebab, chips and a can of Coke for nine-eleven), then a woman from a drama group based in Oranmore looking for child volunteers to form themselves into a forest of angry trees in protest at the political and financial establishment's betrayal of their generation, then four men in banana suits queuing for a chemical toilet, then a girl walking around ringing a cowbell, but without actually making any point, just ringing the focking thing.

We pass a maze made up of half a million VHS cassettes, then some old friends of Sorcha's from UCD who are off to absorb the energy current in the Zen gorden and try to drag us with them, then a dude in full Elizabethan costume down on his hands and knees being sick in a field, then a dude I know from Goatstown who asks us if we're coming to Leviathan to watch David McWilliams, Paul Sommerville and Nick Webb reconstruct the night of the bank guarantee using Punch and Judy puppets.

But Honor is nowhere to be seen and Sorcha suddenly stops, then stands rooted to the spot, her head going from side to side, just sobbing. She goes, 'Where is she, Ross?' tears running down her face. 'Where is our beautiful daughter?'

That's when I suddenly spot a huge mass of people crowding around outside one of the tents in, like, the Mindfield area.

I've spoken many times in the past about my ability to, like, *anticipate* shit? It's like a fifth sense that I've been given. And that's exactly what kicks in at that moment in time.

'Over there!' I go.

Sorcha looks over her shoulder. She's like, 'Where?'

And I go, 'Come on. I've just got one of my world-famous feelings.'

We run into the Mindfield area and over to where a humungous crowd is trying to squeeze itself into the tent.

'What's going on here?' Sorcha asks this random dude with a goatee standing outside.

'It's Speakers' Corner,' he goes. 'It's, like, a stage and, well, anyone can get up there and say whatever they want. There's a little girl in there . . .'

And without the dude even needing to say another word, I instantly know that we've found our daughter.

Me and Sorcha push our way through the throng and we manage to get inside.

And there, standing on the stage, one hand on her hip, the other holding a microphone – with that famous fock-you expression that will be familiar to all South Dublin parents – is Honor.

She's going, 'Do you have any idea how focking pathetic you people are?'

The first thing I notice when I look around the tent is that quite a few of the two hundred or so people there have their heads down, their eyes fixed on their feet. I recognize that look straight away. All you can do when Honor storts ripping into you is choose a point on the floor, the ceiling or the wall, then keep staring at it until it eventually passes.

And Honor *is* ripping into them, in fairness.

She's going, 'I mean, seriously – take a good look at yourselves. You're wearing t-shirts with the names of bands on them. You're drinking in front of your children at, like, eleven o'clock in the morning. You haven't showered for days. And you're – oh my God – convinced that you're having this amazing, like, spiritual experience together. Er, breaking news – you're *not*? You're just a bunch of unfulfilled, middle-aged people, drinking in a field and trying to remember a time when you were young and what you thought about anything mattered to anyone. And, by the way, you smell like a focking soup kitchen.'

I turn to Sorcha and I go, 'It's like that scene in the Bible – you know the one where Jesus goes missing as a kid and they find him in the temple, literally calling it.'

Honor's still up there going, 'My so-called mum and dad are just like you. All the way down here, they were talking about what a great escape Electric Picnic is. And I'm thinking, an escape from what? From your responsibilities? From the fact that you're supposed to be grown-ups? Maybe you didn't enjoy yourselves enough when you were younger. Hashtag – tough shit. You can't relive it. It's over. Dermot O'Leary has his orm around you and he's saying, "Let's look back at your best bits!"

'But look back at them knowing that it's never going to be that good again for you. So stop trying. Grow up, pack up your tents and go home.'

She puts the microphone back on the stand, then steps off the stage to this, like, deafening silence. I look around at all the faces – two hundred people cut to the core. Two hundred people's weekends totally ruined.

Sorcha's like, 'Ross, maybe we should do what she says.'

And I go, 'That's the most sensible thing I've heard all weekend.'

## 'Pang? What the fock is Pang?'
### The Irish Times, 12 September 2015

It's here. A day I thought would never come. Our daughter is going to China for three months as port of a thing called the Mandarin Immersion Programme. We're on our way to Mount Anville, where the bus is waiting to take Honor and forty other students to the airport to embork on the adventure of a pretty much lifetime.

'Slow down,' Sorcha goes. 'Ross, why are you driving so fast?'

I'm there, 'I don't want them to leave without her.'

Honor, sitting in the back of the cor, looks up from her phone and goes, 'He can't wait to get rid of me. He's been up since, like, four o'clock this morning.'

I'm there, 'I just think it's an amazing opportunity for you to sample a different culture and another way of life. And I'm saying that as someone who always regretted not signing for Connacht when it became obvious that Leinster didn't want me because of my work-hord, drink-hord reputation.'

I'm suddenly thinking about the weekend ahead. Ireland against Canada in their first match of the World Cup. I'll be able to watch it in my tight-fitting Ireland jersey without Honor drawing attention to my Minka Kelly hanging over the waist of my Cantos.

Sorcha goes, 'Ross, that was a *red* light you just drove through?'

In fairness, my wife is a lot more upset than I am. She spent so long helping Honor to pack her six suitcases that she forgot to give her any of the crucial life advice that she's going to need during her three months away from us. So now she's furiously scrolling through Pinterest to find some words of wisdom to give her.

'Courage is what it takes to stand up and speak,' she, for instance, goes. 'But it's also what it takes to sit down and listen.'

Honor looks at me and goes, 'You really should think about putting your wife on daily hormone injections.'

Three months without having to listen to lines like that. I'm on the record as saying that the birth of my children was the best (non-rugby-related) thing that has ever happened to me. But my daughter moving to the apparently other side of the world for twelve weeks is right up there with that.

'You never know,' I go. 'You might even like it over there and decide to stay until Christmas. I'm just throwing it out there.'

'Even if I love it over there,' she goes, 'I'll come back just to spite you – just to continue making your life a total focking misery.'

I already feel sorry for her host family – even though I've blocked their number in my phone.

We pull into the school. The cor pork is full of Volvo S6os and Volkswagen Touaregs and Mercedes S Classes and parents saying goodbye to their kids.

I pull up.

Honor goes, 'Don't you dare embarrass me in front of my friends.'

Sorcha goes, 'Always keep your hort open . . . Own who you are.'

'Focking spare me,' Honor goes, opening the door and climbing out of the cor.

I know they're worried about the problem of overpopulation in China, but wait till they get a load of our daughter. The whole country will turn celibate.

Me and Sorcha get out of the cor as well. I take the cases out of the boot two at a time, while Sorcha wraps herself around Honor like a boa constrictor, going, 'I'm going to miss you! I'm going to miss my little angel girl!'

When it comes to my turn, I kiss her on the forehead and I go, 'I'll see you in November,' and she must cop the joy in my face because she goes, 'I'm going to be ringing you, like, *all* the time,' and she means it as an actual threat.

I must make sure to block *her* number as well.

Off she goes, into the bus. We wave her off, then we get back into the cor. Sorcha is sobbing her hort out, while I go, 'Waaa-hooo!' and all of the other parents suddenly look, which is when I realize that I've left the sunroof open.

I stort the cor and we head off. We're actually back on the Stillorgan Dualler before either of us says shit.

I'm there, 'Oh my God, I'm getting an Ian Madigan haircut for the

World Cup. I'm just saying I'm totally free to do it now. I won't have Honor telling me that I'm having a midlife crisis.'

And that's when Sorcha's phone suddenly rings.

'Caller unknown,' she goes.

And I'm there, 'Don't answer it.'

'What are you talking about?'

'They might have changed their minds about taking her. But the deal is done. We don't do returns. I'm begging you, Sorcha. Please don't answer that phone.'

She's like, 'Ross, don't be ridiculous,' and she ends up answering it anyway.

Her phone is synced with the hands-free in my cor, so the voice comes over the speaker. It ends up being Xu Yanlu, Honor's Mandarin teacher.

'It must have been very emotional,' she goes, 'seeing the bus leave.'

I'm there, 'It's definitely gone, is it? You're not ringing to say the deal is off?'

She laughs.

She's there, 'No, I'm just ringing to tell you that you forgot Pang.'

I'm like, 'Pang? What the fock is Pang?'

'Pang is your exchange student. She's going to be living with you for the next three months. Anyway, she's here now if you want to come and get her.'

Sorcha looks at me, her hand over her mouth. In our rush to get rid of our daughter, we didn't even bother reading the small print.

I'm like, 'Yeah, no, fock that.'

'I beg your pardon?' Xu goes.

I'm like, 'Hang up, Sorcha! Hang up!'

Which is what Sorcha ends up doing.

I'm there, 'This is a bunch of focking bullshit – to quote Honor.'

Sorcha goes, 'I'm just reading back through the emails from the school. It does say it's an exchange programme.'

'Well, they should have made it clearer.'

'Ross, we're going to have to go back to the school.'

'Not a focking chance. We don't know the first thing about looking after a kid from China.'

'Ross, turn the cor around! Now!'

So – yeah, no – at the next traffic lights, I end up doing a U-ey and heading back to Mount Anville.

I'm there, 'Always read the small print. How many times do you hear people say that?'

Sorcha's like, 'Come on, Ross, whatever this Pang is like, it can't be any more challenging than looking after Honor.'

Ten minutes later, we're back at the school. I spot Xu in the playground, standing next to this – okay, it's racist – but Chinesey-looking girl?

'This is Pang!' Xu goes.

I shake my head. I still feel totally suckered, like when you get a supermorket trolley with a wonky wheel.

'Hello, Pang!' Sorcha goes in her plainest English. 'I'm Sorcha! And this is my husband, Ross! We're going to be your host family!'

But Pang just fixes me with a look and goes, 'Hey, Fatso – go get my bags.'

## 'Er, I wonder should you be smoking, Pang?'
### *The Irish Times, 10 October 2015*

'Okay,' Pang goes, 'where the fock are we?'

I should tell her that's not how an eight-year-old exchange student should be speaking to her host family, except I'm wondering the exact same thing.

Sorcha thought it'd be a good idea for her to see some of Ireland's – random word – *heritage* and somehow we've ended up here.

'This is Kilmainham Jail!' she goes.

It's a genuine tumbleweed moment for all concerned.

Pang goes, 'Yeah, I can read the sign. I'm asking what actually *is* it?'

I'm there, 'No one really knows for certain,' which was a holding answer I used to give whenever I was asked a difficult question at school. 'Different people say different things. It's kind of whatever you want it to be.'

Sorcha, who once captained Mount Anville to three consecutive victories in the Ides of March Classics Table Quiz, is only too happy to fill in the blanks in my knowledge of history slash trivia.

'This was the prison where the leaders of the 1916 Easter Rising were executed,' she goes. 'They were, like, *our* Founding Fathers.'

Pang rolls her eyes and shakes her head and checks her phone and sighs in a bored way, all at the same time – multitasking for the modern child.

'I need some air,' she goes. 'The excitement is killing me.'

Off she wanders. Sorcha looks about as sad as I've ever seen her.

'I just wanted her to see something of our history,' she goes, 'so she'd maybe understand where we're coming from – as, like, a *people*?'

I'm there, 'We should have taken her to Mountjoy Prison instead. At least my old man was actually *in* there. I could have shown her the spot on the canal where Ronan used to throw footballs over the wall to him, stuffed with cans of tuna belly and Courvoisier miniatures.'

That suddenly cheers her up. She laughs. I'm a catch – I don't think anyone's denying that.

I'm there, 'I better go and check on Pang,' and I head outside to look for her.

I find her standing in what appears to be the prison yard, leaning up against the wall, talking to three or four boys – Irish ones, about her own age. She sees me coming and she goes, 'That's him – the fat one in the green shirt!' and the boys look at me and laugh, like I'm somehow a *punchline*?

What I happen to be wearing is the Ireland jersey that Johnny Sexton wore against Scotland in the 2010 Six Nations: a gift from the man himself, even though – as the kid said – it's a slightly snugger fit on me than it was on him.

There's something different about Pang that I can't immediately put my *finger* on?

I'm like, 'So what's going on here?'

She goes, 'Nothing – we're just talking.'

'Talking, huh? So what port of Dublin are you guys from?' playing the protective father.

'Ongar,' one of them goes.

I just nod. I had no idea that Ongar was an actual place. Any time I see 'Ongar' on the front of a bus, I just presume it's Irish for 'Out of Service'.

'Ongar,' I go. 'That's very –'

Oh, Jesus, I suddenly realize what's different about Pang. I don't know how I missed it, because it's so obvious now. She's got a cigarette in her mouth.

Obviously, I'm there, 'Er, I wonder should you be smoking, Pang?'

She's like, 'Why shouldn't I be smoking?'

'I don't know – you're eight years old and it looks kind of weird.'

'I don't care how it looks.'

'Well, that's just my view.'

'Well, keep your views to yourself.'

The other kids all laugh.

I'm there, 'Yeah, no, I'm just thinking, Pang, that maybe you should, like, put it out,' and I go to grab it from her.

She ends up having a total conniption fit, there on the spot. She's like, 'Get your focking hands off me!' at the top of her voice.

I'm there, 'Pang, give me the cigarettes,' because I notice she has a whole pack in her hand.

'This is my culture,' she goes.

That suddenly throws me.

I'm like, 'What?'

She's there, 'All children in my country smoke.'

I'm like, 'That doesn't *sound* true – *is* it true?'

'Yes, it's true. And by trying to stop me smoking, you are a racist.'

Oh, no. I look around.

I'm there, 'I'm not a racist, Pang!' obviously whispering it.

She goes, 'You are! You are a racist! You are a racist man!'

This is at, like, the top of her voice with a prison yord full of people listening, a lot of them foreigners. So what can I do, except go, 'Okay, just hurry up and smoke the end of that one, then follow me back inside.'

I walk off. And that's when I get the tap on the shoulder.

It ends up being a woman who's about my age – average looks-wise, because I know that's what you're wondering.

'Is that your daughter?' she goes.

I'm like, 'Does she *look* like my daughter?'

I'm guessing she's a teacher.

She goes, 'I'm asking, are you in charge of her?'

'Supposably,' I go. 'Slash supposedly. I can never remember which of those is an actual word.'

'Do you think it's right that she's smoking?'

'I asked her the exact same thing and she said it was her culture. I don't want to be a racist.'

'How could it be racist to tell a child not to smoke?'

'I've no idea, but I'd rather not take the risk.'

'She's playing you for a fool. If you don't take those cigarettes from her this instant, I shall call the Guards.'

The woman is definitely a teacher. I try to stare her down, except she takes out her phone like she's about to ring the Feds.

I'm like, 'Okay, okay,' and then I shake my head and wander back over to where Pang is standing, showing the boys how to blow smoke rings.

I'm there, 'Pang, give me those cigarettes.'

She goes, 'Get away from me, you racist!'

I end up actually shouting at the girl. I'm like, 'Racist or not, I'm telling you to put that actual cigarette out – now!'

She knows I'm not messing around here. She looks me straight in the eye, then she takes the cigarette and she stubs it out on the badge of Johnny Sexton's jersey.

She's like, 'There! Satisfied?'

## 'The thrick is to break the ribs, Rosser.'
### *The Irish Times, 3 October 2015*

I find Ronan in a slaughterhouse on Saint Morgaret's Road, beating up the corcass of a cow, which is hanging from the ceiling by a chain. Apparently, it's how Rocky trained – Balboa rather than Elsom – although I have to admit I've never actually seen any of those movies. My old man didn't want me exposed to other sports in case it derailed my interest in rugby.

Ro goes, 'The thrick is to break the ribs, Rosser,' dancing around on the blood-soaked floor, throwing jabs, hooks and the odd kick, while calling the dead cow a poxbottle, a scumfook and a doorty-looken doort boord.

I'm like, 'Who even owns this place?'

The sign on the roof says 'Meat Your Maker'.

'Nudger's brutter-in-law,' he goes. 'He's a fan of moyen. He won a fowertune on me last fight.'

I'm there, 'Yeah, no, fair focks,' and then I try to change the subject. 'So did you see your famous Dubs, Ro?'

He's like, 'Ta Tups? What about them?'

'I'm just saying they beat Kerry, didn't they? They won the whole, I don't know, *thing*?'

'It's called the Oddle Arelunt, Rosser.'

'The All Ireland, yeah. Pretty inspiring stuff, I would have thought. I mean, it made *me* nearly proud to be from Dublin. And that's saying something.'

He suddenly stops beating up the dead animal. He goes, 'I know what your gayum is, Rosser.'

I'm like, 'Game? I have literally no idea what you're talking about.'

'You're throying to get me inthordested in the Gah again – you think if I steert going to see Burden It Brogan and the boys again, Ine godda lose inthordest in the spowurt of mixed meertial eerts.'

'Well, I'm still not a hundred per cent convinced it *is* a sport?'

'What do *you* call a spowurt? Throwing a ball backwards to each udder, then putting it behoyunt a line?'

'Exactly. There's a serious point to the exercise. But mixed mortial orts seems to be about, I don't know, just beating the lord out of each other for no actual reason. A general rule for me is that it's not a sport if you can do it on the upper deck of a number 40 bus.'

He goes back to punching, kicking and insulting the dead animal. 'I wontherstand you're woodied,' he goes. 'But Ine not godda get hoort, Rosser.'

I'm like, 'You don't know that.'

'Ine too good. There's not a man in the wurdled what can beat me. Ine breaking necks and Ine cashing cheques – and Ine pucking the lug off shams that get in me way. It's oately Sos Redmond standing between me and a crack at Josey Anto for the belt – and Ine gonna bleaten liquidate the doorty pox.'

I decide to just leave him to it. I find it hord to get through to my son when he's in character like this, so I tell him I'll see him on Hallowe'en Night for the – did he say Sos Redmond? – fight.

I head outside and I hop into the cor. I'm about to turn the key when I end up having one of my world-famous ideas. I actually laugh to myself at how actually *good* it is?

I whip out my phone and I ring Ronan's number. He answers on the tenth ring, out of breath.

He's like, 'Hello?'

And I go, 'Howiya, Ronan, it's Burden It Brogan,' who just so happens to be his all-time hero. 'Burden It Brogan offa the Dublin football team. What's the stordee?'

He ends up totally falling for it.

He's like, 'Ah, howiya, Burden It – how's things?'

I'm there, 'Notta bodder on me, Ronan,' really hamming up the accent. 'Ine just arthur being celebrating for the last nearly two weeks, so I am – arthur winning the, I don't know, Oddle Arelunt Celtic Sports Football focking Championships.'

'Ah, feer fooks to you, Burden It.'

'Feer fooks is right. What about you, Ronan? I hope you're still playing the gayum!'

Ronan goes, 'Ine not, Burden It. Ine arthur gibbon it up, so I am.'

I'm there, 'Ine veddy surprised to hear that. When you did me skills camp a couple of summers ago, you were veddy keen on it. I think I remember you saying the Gah was your one throo love, after smoking hash and militant republicanism.'

'Ine into the mixed meertial eerts now, but.'

'The what?'

'Mixed meertial eerts. UFC – all that.'

I'm like, 'Ine gonna have to be honest with you, Ronan, so I am – I wouldn't really class that as a spowurt.'

He laughs. He's there, 'Now you sound like me ould fedda.'

'Maybe you should listen to your ould fella,' I go. 'I oately met him the once, but he sthruck me as the kind of fedda who's never been afraid to consistently call it. Beerd in moyunt, he was also an incredible competitor in he's own spowurt and could've played rubby at the highest level if he'd oately met a coach like Joe Schmidt early odden in he's career.'

Ro goes, 'I suppose you've got a poyunt.'

I'm there, 'Thrust me, Ronan, give up that ould mixed meertial whatever the fook and go back to playing a real spowurt: eeder rubby, or, failing that, the Gah. You could end up winning an Oddle Arelunt Celtic Sports Football medal like what I've got.'

He's like, 'Do you know what, Burden It? You're after making me see the light!'

I'm there, 'Reedy?'

He goes, 'Reedy! Ine gibbon up this ould rubbish and Ine going back to the Gah.'

'Or the rubby – I wouldn't rule out the rubby, Ro.'

That's when I look up to see Ronan grinning at me through the front windscreen. I'm wondering has he copped it's me.

I try to bluff him. I put my hand over the mouthpiece of my phone and go, 'I'm just talking to Mads here, Ro. You know how much he values my advice.'

'Rosser,' he goes, 'when you ring me phowun, your nayum comes up on the screeyunt.'

Seriously, I'd have to be considered one of Ireland's thickest ever people.

He's there, 'When people on this soyud of the city thalk, Rosser, is that what you hee-or?'

I nod. I'm like, 'Kind of, yeah.'

He shakes his head.

He goes, 'You're some flute. I'll see you at the fight.'


## 'He's about to fight someone called Sos Redmond in a cage in a pub cor pork.'
### The Irish Times, 7 November 2015

So I'm making my way to my seat in the cor pork of The Broken Orms pub when I spot a familiar face in the crowd – it's, like, Gorda O'Floinn, as in the local Youth Diversion Officer? He recognizes me as well, which shouldn't come as any great surprise. I spent so much time talking to him when Ronan was growing up that I nearly asked him to be my best man.

'Rob O'Carroll-Kelly,' he goes.

I'm there, 'It's actually *Ross* O'Carroll-Kelly?'

Finglas isn't what you'd call a rugby town.

'Ross,' he goes. 'That's right. God, how long has it been?'

I'm there, 'I was just wondering the same thing – although it seems like only yesterday that Ronan was shouting, "Go back to Templemore, you fooken Fascist!" at you outside the courthouse on Porkgate Street.'

Gorda O'Floinn chuckles – I suppose the word would be *fondly*?

'He was a wild one alright,' he goes. 'Oh, there's no doubt about that.'

It has to be said that Gorda O'Floinn was always sound – think Officer Krupke except with George Webbs and a Leitrim accent.

'Well,' I go, 'you predicted that no good would come of my son – and you were bang on, in fairness to you.'

He looks at me like he thinks I'm mad. He's like, 'What are you talking about at all?'

'What am I talking about?' I go, having to laugh. 'He's about to fight someone called Sos Redmond in a cage in a pub cor pork.'

All around me, by the way, people are chanting, 'Ro! Hnin! Ro! Hnin! Ro! Hnin!'

He goes, 'Trust me, there's worse things he could be doing.'

I'm like, 'Well, I hope it'll just be the usual caution – provided he doesn't resist arrest. The old red mist still falls whenever he sees a man in uniform. Try to ignore whatever he calls you. Maybe stick the cuffs on him as well.'

'Cuffs? What are you talking about?'

'Er, I presume you're here to break up the fight?'

He laughs in my actual face.

'Not at all,' he goes, 'I'm here to *watch* the fight.'

I'm like, 'Watch it?'

'Watch it – like everyone else. You must be very proud of him altogether.'

'Er, not really, no.'

'Well, you should be. He's a hero in this community. We're very lucky to have him. Young people need positive role models – believe me, I see it every day in my work.'

'Dude, I can't believe that what's about to happen here is actually legal. It's basically a bor fight, al fresco.'

The next thing we hear is all this, like, *booing*? Sos Redmond is making his way to the cage.

'I hope he pucks the head off you,' someone behind me shouts. 'I hope he sends you back to Blanchardstown in an ambulance,' then he fires a plastic cup full of beer through the air and it explodes off the wire cage.

'Calm down, Father!' Gorda O'Floinn goes. 'It's only a fight!'

I turn my head and I literally can't believe my eyes. It's Father Gibbs, the local priest, who, only a few years ago, was preparing Ronan for his Confirmation.

'Father,' Gorda O'Floinn goes, 'have you met Ronan's dad?'

'Oh, yes,' the priest goes, instantly remembering my face. 'Ron O'Carroll-Kelly, isn't it?'

Rugby could do a lot for this town.

'Ross,' I go. 'And I can't believe *you're* in favour of what's happening here as well.'

He's like, 'Your son is one of the best things that has ever happened to this area! He is a wonderful young man who has given people pride in their community!'

A voice comes through the speakers. It's like, 'Laaadieees and gentlemeeen, will you please welcome to the Octagon, Ronaaan! Maaanslaaaughter! Maaasters!'

The place goes literally ballistic, as Ronan walks to the cage, all business. Into it he goes. He points at Sos Redmond and he tells him that he's going to boorst him and Sos Redmond says, no, *he's* the one who's going to end up getting boorsted here today, then Ronan says he won't be getting boorsted, because he'll be too busy pucking the lug off him.

And all I can think, while this fascinating exchange is taking place, is that my son's nickname is Manslaughter. I won't be mentioning that at the next Castlerock College Old Boys Reunion.

Suddenly, the fight has storted. Ronan chorges straight across the cage and decks Sos with a punch that *I* end up nearly feeling, standing thirty feet back from where it actually lands.

It's like, *Crrraaaccckkk!* and down he goes.

'Lights out!' Father Gibbs shouts. 'Good riddance, you prick!'

Gorda O'Floinn turns to him. He's like, 'Have you him backed, Father?'

The priest goes, 'I've five hundred on him at evens.'

'You were very lucky to get him at evens.'

Sos gets up, although Ronan floors him again, this time with a punch to the ribs, followed by a kick to the jaw. But this time Sos is up straight away and he panels Ro with a punch that catches him, like, *unawares*?

Ro staggers backwards against the far wall of the cage, trying to cover up, while Sos rains punches down on him. And then, from out of nowhere, Sos produces the most unbelievable roundhouse kick that puts Ro down.

The crowd are suddenly screaming at him to get up. They're all like, 'Gerrupta fook ourra that!' we're talking men and woman, we're taking young and old, getting totally sucked in by, I don't know, the brutality of the violence?

'Battor um, Ronan!' Tina, his own mother, is shouting. 'Battor the doorty pox!'

Sos bears down on him, trying to choose the punch that'll put my son into Connolly Hospital for a month. But then Ro suddenly manages to wrap his legs around Sos's neck and the crowd goes bananas. Sos's orms go limp and his eyes stort practically popping out of his *head*?

Gorda O'Floinn slaps me on the back.

'He has him!' he goes. 'He won't let go until the fella taps out!'

But all I can hear is a voice shouting, 'Kill! Kill! Kill! Kill!'

I turn around, presuming at first that it's Father Gibbs. He's got money riding on it, bear in mind. But then I realize, with a shock that almost stops my hort, that the voice is mine.

### 'Oh, look, you're right – a little Chinese girl!'
*The Irish Times, 5 December 2015*

So me and Pang are, like, decorating the house for Christmas. We've done the tree and now we've moved onto the Nativity figurines. I'm telling her that it's always a subject of debate in this house whether you put the Baby Jesus into the manger from the very stort or do you wait until Christmas morning?

I'm there, 'Sorcha prefers to wait, for reasons of, like, historical accuracy? She says He didn't arrive until Christmas morning. But then she puts the Three Wise Men in – and they didn't arrive until the sixth of January, the day everything goes back into the attic.'

'Put Him in now!' Pang goes – she's pretty adamant as well.

I'm like, 'Really?'

'Otherwise they're all just standing around staring at an empty crib – er, who *does* that?'

I have to admit, this kid has grown on me.

'I'll put Him in,' I go. 'Even though Sorcha will take Him out and hide Him somewhere until Christmas morning. And then, in retaliation, I'll hide the Three Wise Men until the whole thing's over. These are what we like to call Christmas traditions, Pang.'

And that's when the old dear suddenly shows up. She's there, 'Is Sorcha home?'

I'm like, 'What the hell are you wearing? You look ridiculous.'

'I don't have time for your unpleasantness. It's a Camilla pleated chiffon and lace gown by Vilshenko. Victoriana is very much "in" this year.'

'Victoriana?' I go. 'You look like something Dr Marie Cassidy should be going at with rubber gloves and a bone saw.'

Then – this is unbelievable – she goes, 'Well, *I* think it's a beautiful piece – what do you think, Honor? What do you think of what your grandmother is wearing?'

Pang looks over both shoulders, her face full of confusion.

I go, 'It's not Honor, you dope.'

She's there, 'What do you mean, it's not Honor?'

'It's our Chinese exchange student. She's called Pang.'

And Pang goes, 'Who is this ridiculous woman and how much has she had to drink?'

The old dear puts on her reading glasses and scrunches up her face. She's there, 'Are you absolutely sure it's not Honor, Ross, because she certainly *sounds* like her. Oh, look, you're right – a little Chinese girl!'

I'm there, 'Did you actually want something?'

She goes, 'Yes, I wanted to speak to Sorcha.'

'She's not home.'

'She reads good books, doesn't she?'

'I don't know. They're usually big, I know that.'

'It's just I've been asked by the *Irish Times* for my favourite books of 2015.'

'So, just tell them.'

'I couldn't do that, Ross. All the books I've read this year have been, well, just *books*. I don't want to come across as ordinary.'

'You're definitely not ordinary. Who else pours Hendrick's on their Alpen?'

'I'm ignoring that, Ross. No, for these types of features it's important to come up with something terribly oblique that no one else will have read. A coffee-table book called *Inuit Architecture in Western Greenland 1300 to 1450* or *In Him, We Live and Move and Have Our Being*, a first novel by a woman who's just called Aatukka, which was written in Finnish and translated into English via Russian and should have been on the Booker long list, except there were only thirty copies printed.'

I'm there, 'Why don't you say all of that, then?'

'Because those were the books I chose *last* year. I described the first one as "timely and important" and the second one as "humane and labyrinthine" – or maybe it was the other way around. What's Sorcha got on her bedside locker?'

'Echinacea tablets and a mouth-guard.'

'*I* know,' Pang suddenly goes. 'She's reading a book called *Gender Justice – 10 Essays on Modern Feminism* by Nahuel Rodrigo-Maidana.'

The old dear's face lights up. She's there, 'Oh, that sounds perfect. I've never heard of it. Plus, I'm a feminist, of course.'

I'm there, 'You're not a feminist. You're barely even female.'

'Ignore him, whatever your name is. Tell me the title and the author again.'

Pang repeats herself. As she does so, she slips me a magazine that I saw Sorcha reading at the breakfast table this morning. I give it the old left to right. The headline is: 'Argentine Academic Sacked for Controversial Views on Feminism'.

Then I read down through the story while the old dear tries to type the name of the book and the writer into her iPhone with her fingers like Hicks sausages.

I end up actually *laughing*?

It's like, 'One of Argentina's most well-known social commentators has been removed from his position at the University of Buenos Aires for expressing views of feminism that have seen him being likened to Adolf Hitler and Pol Pot. In his book *Gender Justice – 10 Essays on Modern Feminism* Nahuel Rodrigo-Maidana makes the case that life expectancy for men is 5.3 years shorter than it is for women. While the focus of equality campaigners has recently been on the areas of employment, education, pay and opportunities in the arts, the 97-year-old academic claims that if true balance is to be achieved between the genders, then it's necessary to close the mortality gap – by euthanizing between 40 and 50 million women per year.'

Oh! My God!

The old dear goes, 'What shall I say about this book?'

I'm there, totally straight-faced, 'Why don't you say that it's, like, really, really amazing and that you agree with every point the dude makes, even though a lot of people obviously aren't happy campers.'

'Well, I'll put that in my own words,' she goes, still tapping away at her iPhone. 'I'll say it's an inconvenient, even unsettling, book, but necessary, like all truths.'

She finishes typing. 'That's all I need,' she goes. 'Goodbye,' and then she flounces off.

I end up just, like, collapsing on the floor. I honestly haven't laughed as hord since the Christmas she got her pearl necklace caught in the Kitchen Aid. Pang is laughing so much, I think she might need CPR in a minute or two.

'You're worse than Honor,' I go, 'because you're cleverer.'

We high-five each other. And I realize for the first time that I don't want her to go back to China.

'Manslaughter Masters, as my son
calls himself these days.'
*The Irish Times*, 19 December 2015

'You're woodying about nuttin,' Ronan goes.

I'm there, 'I'd hordly call it nothing. I'm worrying about you – about, like, your safety.'

'Ine invincible, Rosser. I refuse to be beaten by addy man aloyuv. Ine breaking necks . . .'

'And cashing cheques. Yeah, I've heard your routine, Ro.'

'And pucking the lug off shams.'

'Pucking the lug – all of that. But this front you put on isn't going to protect you.'

We're in the gents' toilets in the Tipsy Wagon in Blanchardstown, where my son has changed into his fighting gear. He's staring into the mirror, talking himself up for his fight against Josey Anto for the vacant Irish Mixed Mortial Orts Bantamweight title.

He's like, 'The doorty pox is going down. Two hits. Me hitting him, him hitting the bleaten flowur.'

Through the wall, I can hear the noise building up in the cor pork outside. Ronan – or Manslaughter Masters, as my son calls himself these days – has brought quite a lot of support with him from Finglas.

I go, 'It's not too late to pull out, Ro. There's an emergency exit just beyond that door. We could slip out. I could hide you under my coat. My cor is pretty fast. Me and you could be in Kielys enjoying a couple of Dutch masters before anyone realized you'd totally bottled it.'

He's like, 'Pull out? Are you seerdious? This is me moment, Rosser.'

'Can I make a last-minute case for rugby? It's a great sport, Ronan. And one hundred per cent safe. Yes, there's the odd ear or finger lost in a scrum, but there's usually forty or fifty surgeons in an average rugby crowd.'

'This is me spowurt, Rosser. Mixed Meertial Eerts.'

'I just don't consider it a sport. It's like watching CCTV footage of a fight in a fast food restaurant.'

Ronan's cornerman, Buckets of Blood, sticks his head around the door of the jacks. 'Ronan,' he goes, 'it's toyum.'

Ro's there, 'See you back here in ten minutes, Rosser, when I'll be the Oddle Arelunt champion.'

I'm there, 'I'd be happier just to know you were still alive.'

I walk out and I take my seat at the side of the Octagon. Behind me, I hear someone go, 'That's he's aul lad there – the snobby-looking fedda in the yachting jacket,' meaning, I'm presuming, me.

I get a tap on the shoulder. I turn around and it ends up being some fat dude wearing a t-shirt with my son's face on it. He's there, 'You must be veddy prouth.'

And I go, 'I'm not actually. I'd nearly rather he was in prison. At least there's rules when people fight in there.'

He laughs like he thinks I'm joking. 'Go on ourra that!' he goes, then he hands me a warm, plastic pint glass full of Not Heineken. 'Get it inta ya, Cynthia!'

Josey Anto's name is called first. The announcer goes, 'Laaadddiiieeesss and gentlemen, will you please welcome, with a record of thirty-two wins from thirty-two fights, all by way of knockout – The Beast from Blanchardstown East, Joooseeey! The Widow-Maker! Annntooo!'

A huge roar goes up. Out he comes. The dude is ripped like an Abercrombie model and has a face like a sandblasted beetroot. He gets into the cage and he roars, 'Ine gonna rip his eerms off and beat him to death with them.'

You wouldn't hear the likes of that in rugby. Except maybe in Bruff.

Ronan comes out next.

The same dude goes, 'With a record of five fights and five wins, please show your appreciation for The Armageddon from Dublin 11, it's Roonaaan! Maaanslaughterrr! Maaastersss!'

It's hord to know who has the most support. The crowd goes literally mental as Ronan makes his way to the cage, his orms held above his head, showing no sign of fear whatsoever.

Into the cage he goes. He and the famous – yeah, no – Widow-Maker exchange insults and threats across the canvas – 'Ine gonna beat you into a coma, you doorty-looken doort boord!' and 'You're about to get your face rearranged, you bleaten clown.'

The word that Ronan's old man is in the audience has spread through the cor pork. People are coming up to me and shaking my hand and telling me it's an honour and that my son is a role model for children everywhere.

Then the two fighters are, I don't know, summoned to the centre of the ring. The bell goes and we're off. The noise is, like, deafening.

Ronan and Josey dance around each other for, like, twenty or thirty seconds, feigning punches, but mostly feeling each other out. Then Ro sees what he thinks is an opening and he makes a lunge for Josey, leaving his left hand dangerously low.

I shout, 'Watch his right, Ro!' except it's suddenly too late. The punch detonates on the side of Ronan's face with a sickening crack. His eyes stort spinning like pinwheels. I have no idea what keeps him upright, but Josey finishes him off with a kick to the leg that snaps Ronan's shin bone like a twig.

People actually turn away to avoid seeing it, while Ronan goes down like a dynamited building.

The referee waves it over before he even hits the deck. But there's just, like, silence from the crowd. No one seems to know how to be happy about this. I run to the cage, where my son is being loaded onto a stretcher, totally out of the game, spitting zeds.

One or two people tell me I should be ashamed of myself for allowing my son to take port in such a sport.

'It's barbaddick,' says one dude, who just so happens to be wearing a Manslaughter Masters headband. 'You're no kind of fadder letting him do that!'

Ronan is lifted out of the cage and I follow the stretcher as it's carried towards a waiting ambulance. I'm like, 'Ro, are you okay? Ronan, answer me! Please – answer me!'

He opens his eyes, his face totally twisted in pain and he goes, 'I want a rematch, Rosser.'


### 'Okay, Pang, it's time to go.'
*The Irish Times, 24 December 2015*

Pang goes, 'Okay, what's this?'

We're about to leave the gaff to drop her back to the school. She's going back home to China today and Honor is coming back home to us.

I notice the girl has got my famous Rugby Tactics Book open on her lap.

I'm like, 'Pang, please don't rip that up!'

She goes, 'I'm not going to rip it up! I'm interested! What is it?'

'It's what's known as a Rugby Tactics Book. It's basically a book in which I scribble down all my thoughts about rugby. That's why it's a disgrace that the IRFU has never found a role for me within the set-up – there's never a time when I'm *not* thinking about the game?'

'What are all these names?'

'I did those during the World Cup. They're, like, team line-ups. The XV that I would have picked to stort against Canada, Romania, Italy, France and Orgentina.'

'And what are all these diagrams?'

'These are just moves that I believe would have unlocked various teams in the competition. And this page here is just my thoughts on where certain teams had certain weaknesses.'

Pang reads from the page. She's like, *'Chris Robshaw is a focking prick with ears.'*

I'm there, 'Yeah, no, I don't know if that would go down as a *technical* weakness? Some of it was just, like, random thoughts that occurred to me on certain days.'

'So why do you keep this?'

'I don't know. Honor calls it my Sad Man Book.'

'You must know *why* you take all these notes.'

'Okay, I'll tell you. I have this dream that, you know, one day Joe Schmidt is going to see it.'

'Who's Joe Schmidt?'

You forget sometimes that China isn't a rugby country.

I'm there, 'Joe Schmidt is the Ireland rugby coach. I have this dream that one day he's going to see my Rugby Tactics Book, look through it, then go straight to the IRFU and demand to know why someone who's still got a massive, massive amount to contribute is sitting at home scribbling his thoughts in a notebook.'

Sorcha sticks her head around the door. She's like, 'Okay, Pang, it's time to go.'

Sorcha can't wait to see the back of the girl, but I've actually *warmed* to her? I carry her cases outside to the cor, then we all get in.

We're, like, nearing Mount Anville when Pang turns to me and goes, 'You should send it to him.'

I'm there, 'What are you talking about?'

'Your book. You should send it to this Joe man.'

'Do you mean send it unanimously?'

'The word is anonymously.'

Jesus Christ, she has better English than I do.

I'm like, 'Anonymously, then?'

She's there, 'No, put your name on it. Send it to him with a letter.'

'There wouldn't be much point, Pang. I'd be considered a bit of a joke in Irish rugby circles. I'm this goy who had this incredible, incredible – I'm going to add another one – *incredible* talent, but I loved the lifestyle that went with it too much. The booze. The women. They're not interested in my views.'

'People have to see what is in that book!'

'Can I tell you something, Pang? They don't. But it's actually an amazing thing for me that at least someone believes in me, even though you're someone who knows absolutely zero about the game of rugby.'

I can feel myself becoming emotional. I promised myself I wouldn't cry.

We pull into the cor pork of the school. There's thirty or forty other parents standing around, saying goodbye to their Chinese exchange students and waiting for their own children to be returned to them in time for Christmas.

We get out of the cor.

Sorcha says goodbye to Pang, but it's just, like, a handshake. There's no love, no sadness, at saying goodbye.

Sorcha goes, 'I'll let you two have your moment,' then she wanders off to talk to some of the other mothers, leaving us alone.

'It's going to be weird not having you around,' I go, 'even though I couldn't stand you at the stort. I actually thought you were God's revenge on us for sending our daughter away to another country.'

Pang goes, 'Can I tell you something?'

'Of course – you can tell me anything.'

'Do you remember I told you that I was allowed to smoke at home?'

'You said all kids in China smoked.'

'I was lying. My dad would be so angry if he knew.'

'Oh.'

'You're so much cooler than my dad.'

'That's a lovely thing for me to hear. People give out about kids smoking, but you never hear both sides of the argument. It *is* kind of *cool*, I suppose? And it helps keep the weight off. I hear Sorcha's friends say that all the time.'

'I'm going to miss you, Ross,' she goes.

I'm there, 'I'm going to miss you, Pang.'

She throws her orms around me and I realize that I'm crying.

I watch her get on the bus. She waves out the window to me and then, just like that, she's gone.

I tip over to Sorcha and the other parents. Sorcha goes, 'Are you okay?'

I'm there, 'Yeah, no, I can't believe she's gone.'

'You're looking forward to seeing Honor again, though, aren't you?'

'Not really, no.'

'Ross, that's a terrible thing to say!'

'Yeah, no, I'm *joking*, Sorcha?'

As one bus leaves the school grounds, another one arrives. The children stort piling off it.

I go, 'I actually think one of the positive things about having Pang here for the past three months is that it's taught me to possibly appreciate our *own* daughter a little bit more?'

Sorcha kisses me on the cheek and goes, 'That's terribly sweet, Ross.'

And seconds later, we both smile as we watch our beautiful little girl walking across the cor pork towards us.

'Oh my God,' Honor goes when she sees us, 'you two have got *so* fat!'

# 2016

Memorials commemorating the centenary of the Easter Rising take place throughout the year * Following a General Election, Fine Gael form a minority government with a number of independent TDs and the backing of Fianna Fáil * In football, Ireland beat Italy 1–0 at the European Championships to qualify for the second round, where they are beaten 2–1 by France * The United Kingdom votes in a referendum to leave the European Union * US President Barack Obama visits Cuba, the first US President to do so since 1928 * The augmented reality mobile game *Pokémon GO* is released, becoming an overnight sensation * Olympic Council of Ireland President Pat Hickey is arrested during the Olympics in Rio de Janeiro * US security intelligence agencies accuse the Russian government of using cyber hacking to interfere with the US election * The President of Cuba Fidel Castro dies * Ireland beat New Zealand 40–29 in Chicago, the country's first ever victory over the All Blacks in 111 years * The US and China join the Paris Global Climate Agreement * The government of North Korea conducts its fifth and biggest nuclear test * WikiLeaks releases thousands of private emails from inside the campaign of US presidential candidate Hillary Clinton * The year sees a high number of celebrity deaths, including those of David Bowie, Carrie Fisher, George Michael, Muhammad Ali, Glenn Frey, Harper Lee, George Martin, Johan Cruyff, Prince, Gene Wilder, Leonard Cohen and Debbie Reynolds * Donald Trump is elected President of the United States of America *

Meanwhile . . .

'Thanks to you, Hook, Lyon and Sinker
is now Ireland's number one seller of
repossessed homes in the €3 million
to €10 million category.'
*The Irish Times*, 16 January 2016

The Hook, Lyon and Sinker Excellence in Selling Awards have become
as familiar a part of the January routine as bringing my brat of a daughter to Dundrum to exchange her unwanted Christmas gifts for cash
and watching my wife walk up and down the Vico Road, swinging her
orms and muttering about the Women's Mini Marathon.

I'm saying the New Year wouldn't be the New Year without it.

When we arrive at JP's old man's gaff, the porty is already in full
swing. I hand JP's old dear the €5 bottle of *Shite Hole Neuf de Crap* that
we picked up in the petrol station on the way here and she looks at the
label with a fake smile that tells me it's going straight under the sink
with the cleaning products.

JP's old man is delighted to see me. And why wouldn't he be? I
must have stuck another five mills in his pension fund with the work
I did for him this year. He gives me what would have to be described
as a fatherly hug, then he says hello to Sorcha with an enthusiasm
that would be grounds for sexual harassment if he was paying her a
salary.

'What a year,' he goes. 'Not just for you, Ross, I'm hearing wonderful things about this little lady of yours. They're saying she might even
top the poll in Dublin Bay South.'

Sorcha smiles modestly and removes his hand from her bottom. She
goes, 'A lot can happen between now and the General Election, Mr
Conroy.'

Namely, she still hasn't told my old man yet that she's planning to
leave New Republic and run as, like, an *independent*?

JP's old man goes, 'Nonsense! Charles says you're going to romp home! Hey, it'll be great to have a politician on the payroll.'

It takes five or six seconds for this comment to land. Sorcha's like, 'Payroll?'

'Family,' he goes. 'It'll be great to have a politician in the Hook, Lyon and Sinker family.'

He gives me a little wink.

'Anyway,' he goes, 'I better get ready to make my speech. You nervous, Ross?'

I'm there, 'Nervous?'

'About the Seller of the Year Award. Hey, I'll put you out of your misery right now. It's you again!'

Now it's my turn to smile modestly. And remove his hand from my bottom. I'm there, 'Yeah, no, that's cool.'

'Well, who else was it going to be? Thanks to you, Hook, Lyon and Sinker is now Ireland's number one seller of repossessed homes in the €3 million to €10 million category.'

Sorcha goes, 'Oh my God, Ross, that's amazing!'

'It *is* amazing,' he goes. 'Let me tell you something about the kind of man you're married to. When the new planning guidelines were announced allowing for smaller apartments, he sat down with one of our developer clients and he showed him how to turn his plans for a development of twenty-seven apartments into a development of fifty-four apartments without laying a single additional brick. These apartments will be so small, there won't be room in them for two people to break wind at the same time. And they said those days were gone forever!'

I look at JP across the crowded living room. From his expression, it's pretty obvious that he knows that he's not getting the award. But then he played rugby with me. He knows what a beast I am when it comes to competition.

'You know,' his old man goes, 'I meant what I said a year ago. About my succession. I'm getting out of the game. Matter of fact, this is the last time I will ever host the Hook, Lyon and Sinker Excellence in Selling Awards. Because next year . . . you're doing it.'

I'm like, 'Me?'

Even Sorcha goes, 'Oh! My God!'

He's there, 'That's right. You're ready. I'm finishing up at the end of

March. I promised JP's mother I'd retire this side of my next heart attack. So from the first of April, you will be the new Managing Director of Hook, Lyon and Sinker. Congratulations, kid!'

I'm literally speechless. I'm there, 'I genuinely don't know what to say. But what about JP?'

It's just an expression. I don't mean it.

'JP is my son,' he goes. 'And, while I love him very, very dearly, he couldn't sell a dummy pass to a blind prop. He's not the man to lead the company through the next period of temporary economic buoyancy. No, that man is you!'

I'm there, 'Is this actually happening?'

'You better believe it's happening. In fact, I'm going to announce it right now!'

He taps his brandy glass with his wedding ring to bring hush to the room. 'Boys and girls,' he goes, 'it's great to have you here for the annual Hook, Lyon and Sinker Excellence in Selling Awards. There's no doubt that 2015 was an incredible year for the company. It's hard to believe that three or four years ago, so-called experts were saying that we would never again repeat the mistakes of the past. Well, we *are* repeating them – and I'm happy to say we're going to go on repeating them!'

Everyone cheers, then claps. It's pretty heady stuff alright.

'I'm predicting that 2016 is going to be an even bigger year for Hook, Lyon and Sinker. But it's also going to be a year of change. I have decided – in consultation with She Who Must Be Obeyed at All Times Without Question! – to relinquish the reins of Hook, Lyon and Sinker. But I am leaving the company in very capable hands . . .'

I look at JP. He has a look of just, like, *shock* on his face? Sorcha grabs my hand and squeezes it hord. I honestly haven't seen her this proud of me since Mary McAleese handed me the famous tinware back in the day.

I wait for JP's old man to say my name. Except he doesn't. There's just, like, silence. I turn around to him and I notice that he's clutching his left orm and he's, like, blue in the face. Then I look at JP again and he shouts, 'Someone phone an ambulance!'

And JP's old man suddenly falls face-first through the coffee table before I manage to even say the words, 'Oh, fock!'

I rub my two hands together. It's my first night away from Sorcha in I don't know how long – weeks, probably – and I am determined to enjoy it. She wasn't altogether crazy about the idea of me going out tonight, but the Friday before the stort of a Six Nations campaign has always been the night when we meet in Kielys of Donnybrook and I give everyone my analysis of how I see the championship panning out.

Mary has the pint glass in her hand the second she clocks me. I'm there, 'Yeah, no, pint of the old Tolerance Water, Mary. And Oisinn here will have the same.'

She reaches for the pump. She knows the stuff I mean. And that's when Oisinn says the most extraordinary thing. He goes, 'Not for me, Ross.'

I'm like, 'Excuse me?'

'Yeah, no, I'm off the drink until Paddy's Day.'

'Paddy's Day? That's in . . .'

'Morch.'

'I was going to say Morch. Why would you want to do that?'

'I suppose to prove that I can.'

'Oisinn, are you listening to yourself? This is crazy talk. That means you're not going to be drinking for, like, four of Ireland's five matches.'

'I don't mind,' he goes. 'I actually don't need it any more. Mary, what juices do you have?'

I'm there, 'She doesn't have any.'

She goes, 'We've got orange, apple, pineapple . . .'

I'm like, 'They're not for sale individually, though. They're just mixers. They're for putting in ladies' drinks. Tell him, Mary.'

'I'll actually have an apple juice,' Oisinn goes.

All I can do is just shake my head.

But then JP and Christian arrive and I think, Okay, here we go – the weekend storts here! I'm there, 'I'm presuming you two will have a pint?'

Christian – word for word – goes, 'Not me. I'm in training.'

I'm there, 'Training?'

JP's like, 'Yeah, we're both doing the Malin to Mizen Man of Steel

Challenge. It's one of these Ultra, Ultra, Ultra, Ultra, Ultra, Ultra Ironman events. You run from Donegal to Cork with a bicycle on your back, then you cut your own Achilles tendons and you cycle from Cork to Donegal, then you break both your tibia with a rock and you swim from Donegal to Cork again.'

'But do you have to go off the drink on the eve of a Six Nations to do this thing?'

Christian goes, 'That's how seriously we're taking it, Ross. I'll have an orange juice, Mary.'

JP's there, 'I'll have the same.'

But then suddenly I don't mind too much because Fionn has just walked in. He's always been the voice of reason in our group. He'll get hammered with me. I'm there, 'Pint of the old Giggle Juice for the dude in the specs.'

But Fionn goes, 'No, I'm not drinking these days, Ross. I've got my allergies. I'm actually off everything. Wheat, dairy, alcohol, salt, then obviously sugar.'

'This is getting ridiculous. It's like being on a spa weekend with Sorcha. I suppose you're having a juice as well, are you?'

'No, I actually had one before I left the house. Have you discovered the NutriBullet yet?'

'Dude. I'll stort taking my meals in liquid form when I'm a hundred and twelve and my teeth have fallen out. Until then, dinner is a meal. It's not a drink. Heineken is a drink.'

'Some of these juices are really tasty, Ross. I just had one with kale, jalapeños, pineapple and Himalayan Pink Salt.'

Himalayan Pink Salt. This is a man who played rugby.

I can't listen to any more of this. I have to hit the jacks. As I step into Trap One, my phone rings and it ends up being Sorcha.

She's like, 'Ross, where the hell are you?'

I'm there, 'I'm in Kielys. Don't worry, I'm coming home.'

'Kielys? I thought we discussed this. We were supposed to be meeting my parents for dinner.'

'There's no point in continuing this argument, Sorcha, because I've already said I'm coming home. I was supposed to give the goys my traditional Six Nations analysis, but they're all off the sauce. Seriously, I'd have been better off bringing your granny out. At least *she'd* have a Sandeman's.'

'You don't need drink to enjoy yourself, Ross.'

'I'm not going to comment on that, Sorcha. I'll leave you to think about what you just said.'

'Well, why *aren't* they drinking?'

'They're either worried about their unit intake, or they're worried they might put on an ounce of body fat, or they're worried that beer might contain sugar or salt or wheat or any of the other things that were fine to eat two years ago but are now supposedly poison. What's happening to the world? I genuinely think that's why so many people are turning their backs on religion – there's a million other things to feel guilty about instead. Sorry for being deep.'

'Are you crying?'

'I'm not crying . . . I'm a little bit crying. It's just, I don't know, my pre-Six Nations analysis was something they used to look forward to from pretty much Christmas onwards. And maybe I'm a bit, I don't know, down in the dumps, because I've realized that I'm another Six Nations older and the IRFU still hasn't found a place for me within the set-up. I've got all this knowledge and it's just there in my head. For instance, I think Scotland could turn over England tomorrow.'

'That sounds interesting, Ross.'

'That's nice of you to say, Sorcha, but you wouldn't know a rugby ball if one hit you on the head. Look, I'm just going to go and say goodnight to the Juice of the Month Club. I'll see you in a bit.'

I pull the door of the toilets open and I hear the laughter straight away. Everyone in the whole of Kielys is staring straight at me. I look at Fionn, Oisinn, Christian and JP and the first thing I notice is that they all have pints in their hands. They hold them up and everyone goes, 'Suckered!'

I laugh. I can't help it. I have the best friends in the world. Someone puts a drink – an *actual* drink – in my hand and everyone gathers around, their faces full of expectation, to hear what the Rossmeister has to say.


'I know we played rugby together. But that's
not an excuse for everything.'
*The Irish Times*, 12 March 2016


I arrive to work at my usual er-yeah-whatever o'clock and I cop it the moment I swing the old Five Serious into my porking space outside. It's gone. I'm talking about the sign above the shop. It's been, like, *removed*? And all that remains in its place is a slight discoloration on the wall where the letters used to be – the big, brass ones that once spelt out the words Hook, Lyon and Sinker.

I push the door and in I go. JP looks at me and goes, 'Ah, Ross,' then makes a big show of looking at his watch, to try to make the point that eleven a.m. is no time to be breezing in to work. 'Glad you could join us!'

I go, 'Are you taking my nine-year-old daughter's correspondence course in Passive-Aggression or something?'

He laughs, even though he's not amused, then he goes, 'We're about to have a staff meeting.'

I'm like, 'Dude, where's the sign gone? As in, why doesn't it say Hook, Lyon and Sinker above the door any more?'

His voice suddenly drops to, like, a *whisper*? 'Ross,' he goes, 'I would appreciate it if you didn't call me Dude any more – certainly not in front of the staff.'

I'm like, 'I've been calling you Dude since we were, like, six years old. Jesus, we played rugby together!'

'I know we played rugby together. But that's not an excuse for everything, Ross.'

'Well, it certainly used to be. So what am I supposed to call you – Mister Conroy?'

He doesn't answer – just lets it hang in the air between us.

I'm there, 'You're dreaming! You're *actually* dreaming!'

He goes, 'I think it would help everyone come to terms with the fact that I'm now running the show – including you.'

'You're only running the show until your old man gets better.'

His old man had, like, a hort attack a few weeks ago.

He goes, 'That won't be happening – as in, he won't be coming back to work. So everyone needs to understand that I'm in chorge of this estate agency now.'

I'm there, 'The thing is, Dude, I had this conversation with your old man – it was, like, five minutes before he keeled over – and he clearly said that he wanted *me* to take over the running of Hook, Lyon and Sinker if anything ever happened to him. I mean, has he mentioned anything to you about that?'

'He's not thinking about work, Ross. He's thinking about getting better.'

'Dude, if I could just talk to him – even for, like, five minutes.'

'That's not going to happen. And again – the whole Dude thing?'

'Look, JP, I honestly can't picture myself ever calling you Mister Conroy.'

'Well,' he has the cheek to go, 'there are lots of *other* estate agencies in this city where you could work. There's one three doors down. They call each other Dude – they also chest-bump each other when they make a sale.'

I'm like, 'Whoa! Are you saying you're banning the chest-bump?'

He doesn't respond, just claps his hands together twice, then at the top of his voice goes, 'Okay, everyone, staff meeting – take off your headsets. I want everyone's full attention.'

People finish whatever it is they're doing and they pull over their chairs. I'm just staring at this dude I no longer recognize as my friend and former teammate, thinking, If he's crazy enough to think he can take the chest-bump out of selling houses, he's crazy enough to do anything.

'Okay,' he goes, 'as you all know, my father is, em, indisposed at the moment due to illness. On his behalf, I'd just like to say thank you to all of you for your kind messages wishing him a speedy recovery. I also wanted to let you all know that I'm going to be taking over operations on a permanent basis and there are going to be some changes in the way we do things, effective from today. For twenty years now, Hook, Lyon and Sinker has been a byword for unscrupulous practices in the areas of selling and letting.'

We're all just, like, nodding. We worked hord to build up that reputation.

'Well, from today,' JP goes, 'that's all going to change. I want people to think of us as the ethical estate agency.'

Everyone's just, like, looking at each other, wondering has he been drinking.

He goes, 'I want us to be one hundred per cent straight and above board in our dealings with customers. For instance, we don't use flowery language to exaggerate the merits of our properties.'

I'm there, 'Can I just check? You *are* the same JP Conroy who first called Mullingar the Gateway to Dublin, are you? Because there are people in this country who have to get up at midnight to stort the commute to work because of you – and I'm saying that as a compliment.'

He's like, 'I know what happened in the past, Ross. I'm talking about what's happening now. We don't exaggerate the merits of our properties and we don't inflate prices to over and above what our properties are actually worth. We don't lie to prospective buyers about the level of interest in a property. We don't pretend they're in an auction situation when they're actually not.'

I go, 'Dude –'

He's like, 'It's Mister Conroy.'

'Yeah,' I go, 'I'm not calling you Mister Conroy, so get that out of your head. Look, I respect you as an estate agent. You were the one who came up with the idea that Ranelagh, Rathmines and Rathgor could be Dublin's TriBeCa – I mean, you invented the phrase RaRaRa. But this is crazy talk.'

'Crazy or not, this is how it's going to be. Ross, those new aportments you're selling from the plans? You're not selling them any more.'

'Can I ask why?'

'Because there isn't room to turn a blind eye in them. If people want to buy a kennel, they can go to a pet shop. We don't deal in repossessed Killiney mansions either. And, as to your earlier question, Ross, yes, I'm banning the chest-bump.'

Someone else goes, 'Why has the name gone from above the door?'

And JP's there, 'Because this estate agency is no longer called Hook, Lyon and Sinker. From this day forward, we'll be known as Bloodless, Human, Good.'

I'm giving it a month.


'He wants us to be known as the ethical estate agency.'
*The Irish Times, 26 March 2016*

My phone rings. The first thing I hear when I answer it is the sound of heavy breathing – like Tony Soprano carrying a wheelie bin up three flights of stairs. After thirty seconds, a voice goes, 'Ross . . . Ross, it's me.'

*Me* ends up being JP's old man.

I'm there, 'Mr Conroy, where are you? I've been worried.'

'I'm stuck in this bed,' he goes. 'JP and his mother have got me under house arrest – eating lettuce and drinking Complan.'

This is since his hort attack two months ago.

He goes, 'I need to see you.'

I'm there, 'How? JP won't let me anywhere near the gaff.'

'You're Ross O'Carroll-Kelly,' he goes. 'How many bedrooms have you climbed in and out of over the years?'

I feel instantly proud. It's nice that people still remember what a complete and utter dirtbag I used to be.

'Okay,' I go, 'I'm on the way.'

Twenty minutes later, I'm pulling up outside the gaff on Nutley Road. I spot the copy of the *Irish Times* property supplement in the window, where he said it'd be. I look to the left and there's, like, a wooden wall trellis with ivy growing out of it. I grip it with my hands, then I stort clambering up it, my teenage years coming back to me in a sudden flash of memory.

Did you ever wonder why ivy on the front of houses went out of fashion in the late nineties and early noughties? Now you know.

When I get to the top, I reach across for the window, which is already open a crack. I pull it fully open, then I slip inside.

JP's old man is sitting up in the bed. The dude looks horrendous. He's as white as Oscars night and you'd find more meat on an eggbeater.

I'm like, 'Mr Conroy?'

'Ross,' he goes, his head turning towards me, 'come closer so I can have a look at you.'

The sight of me seems to give him a bit of a lift. I did make millions for him.

'What's happening with the estate agency?' he goes. 'JP won't tell me anything.'

I'm there, 'I don't know if *I* even should? I don't want to give you another hort attack.'

He grabs my hand and he squeezes it hord. 'Whatever it is,' he goes, 'I need to know.'

I just nod. 'Okay,' I go, 'he's changed the name – from Hook, Lyon and Sinker to Bloodless, Human, Good.'

'You're shitting me.'

'I wish I was.'

'Bloodless, Human, Good? What kind of a name is that?'

'He wants us to be known as the ethical estate agency.'

He closes his eyes. I think a little bit of him dies in that moment.

I'm there, 'I probably shouldn't say any more than that.'

'No,' he goes, 'I want to hear it all. What does an ethical estate agency look like?'

I'm there, 'Well, he's given us each a code of conduct.'

'Jesus!'

'Things we *can* and *can't* do? For instance, we're not allowed to sell aportments that are smaller than 55 square metres.'

'But Alan Kelly said –'

'It doesn't matter what Alan Kelly said. JP says that if people want to live in greyhound traps, they can go to another estate agent. The other thing is, well, you might as well know everything . . .'

'Tell me.'

'He's banned words like compact, bijou and cosy.'

'What? There's no other way of describing –'

'Small. He wants us to use the word small.'

The dude just shakes his head. He goes, 'What happened to the boy? I mean, you two were close.'

I'm there, 'Yeah, no, we *used* to be? But we don't see that much of him any more. The goys call him Julian Assange, because he never goes out.'

'He's too damn nice. It was always his problem. I said it to his mother. Why can't he be more like Charles O'Carroll-Kelly's boy? Completely and utterly bereft of basic human empathy.'

'I'm going to take that as a compliment.'

'It was meant as a compliment. It's why I wanted you, not him, to take over the running of Hook, Lyon and Sinker. Because an estate agent with a conscience can do more damage to a country than a global economic recession. We need to do something about him. What about a woman?'

'A woman?'

'Is he doing it with anyone at the moment?'

I laugh. I'm there, 'The last time JP had his hand on a breast it came out of a bucket with Colonel Sanders's face on it. No disrespect.'

'Well,' he goes, 'you could introduce him to someone. A woman can have a leavening effect on a man. My father used to say, it's not who rules the roost that counts – it's who rules the rooster. Do you get me?'

'Not really. I'm famously slow, though.'

'You introduce him to a woman. She gets inside his head. And once she's in there, we tell her what levers to pull.'

'Okay, I'm beginning to understand you now.'

'But you've got to be quick.'

'Quick?'

'Something I didn't tell you – before I got sick. There's an estate near Carrickmines. Vulturestown Heights.'

'I know it. We're the rental agents, aren't we?'

'That's right. Well, just before Christmas, all of the developer's loans were acquired by an investment bank called Pillages, Plunders and Sacks.'

'They sound like good people.'

'They've given 370 tenants six months to clear out, then they're putting the houses on the market. And guess who they want to sell them?'

'Are you going to say Hook, Lyon and Sinker?'

'You better believe I'm going to say Hook, Lyon and Sinker! And not Bloodless, Human, Good.'

'JP might have a few, I don't know, moral issues with people being thrown out of their homes by an investment bank.'

'That's why you have to destroy him.'

I just nod.

'Don't worry,' I go. 'I think it was Matt Williams who once said of me: "What he lacks in intelligence, he more than makes up for in stupidity." I like to think what he meant by that was that Ross O'Carroll-Kelly doesn't know when to give in. Leave it to me, Mr Conroy. Give me three months and I'll have the words Hook, Lyon and Sinker over the door again.'

### 'We're doing a modern-day version of *West Side Story* and I'm writing it.'
### *The Irish Times, 2 April 2016*

I walk into the orangerie and I find my daughter sitting at the upright piano. I realize that's the most middle-class sentence I've ever written, but it's also a *fact*?

'Honor,' I go. 'There you are. Your mother says you've to come and watch the Easter Rising commemoration with us.'

She looks at me like I've offered her pâté and given her cat food. She's there, 'Er, *why*?'

'Yeah, no,' I go, 'she says she wants us to celebrate our Irishness together as a family. That's an actual quote.'

Honor goes, 'Granddad says we'd have been better off, both economically and morally, if we'd remained port of Britain.'

'Look, I know we've been brought up to believe that,' I go, 'but Sorcha says that today we have to be proud to be Irish. And from the way she said it, it doesn't sound like we've a lot of choice in the matter.'

'Well,' she goes, 'I can't indulge the woman and her fantasies of family life this morning. I'm busy.'

She storts playing a tune. Honor is naturally gifted on the piano. She'd want to be – we've spent about twelve grand on lessons for her.

'What are you up to?' I go, because they do say that you should always take an interest in what your kids are doing.

She sighs like she's already bored of me.

'If you must know,' she goes, 'I'm writing a musical.'

I laugh.

I'm there, 'A musical?'

'It's for school. We're doing a modern-day version of *West Side Story* and I'm writing it.'

I notice a school copybook on the piano stool beside her. I pick it up. I'm there, 'Do you mind if I have a look? I'm just showing an interest here – the whole caring parent routine.'

She goes, 'Whatever.'

So I open it up. On the first page, it's like, '*South Side Story* is a musical set in Dublin's prosperous southern suburbs and explores the bitter gang rivalry between the children from Educate As One, a multi-denominational school in Sandycove, and Gaelscoil Naomh Eithne, a Catholic National School in Glasthule. In particular, it focuses on the love story between Tony, a boy from a devout pluralist background, who has been brought up to respect all religions with the same ambivalence, and Maria, a girl who believes that only Catholics who speak fluent Irish can get into Heaven.'

I'm there, 'Honor, did you write this?'

She goes, 'Yeah – so?'

'So? I'm saying it's focking brilliant.'

'Do you think?'

Positive feedback is another thing that children need. God, I should teach this shit in a classroom.

I'm there, 'When are you putting this musical on?'

She's like, 'In May.'

'Well, *I'll* definitely be there to see it. Provided it doesn't clash with the rugby. Seriously, Honor, you've got a genuine talent.'

'Will you run lines with me? This particular scene I'm writing – I need to hear it out loud.'

'Of course,' I go, sitting down next to her. 'Anything to get out of watching that whole 1915 thing. Where do you want to stort?'

She takes the copybook from me, opens it out and puts it up on the music stand. 'Here,' she goes. 'Act One, Scene Five. I'll be Maria and you be Tony.'

'Okay,' I go. 'Tell me a little bit about my character.'

'What?'

'Because I was thinking he's probably a bit of a ladies' man – but then, at the same time, a lovable chormer? I think I can actually bring something to this role.'

'Look, just read it in your normal voice, Dad.'

Yeah, I was actually *going* to read it in my normal voice.

'It's night-time,' Honor goes – at the same time, tinkling the old ivories. 'A suggestion of buildings. A fire escape, climbing to the rear window of an unseen aportment. Tony looks up at Maria's window, wishing for her. She appears on the fire stairs.'

'Maria!' I go. 'Oh, Maria!'

'Ssshhh! My parents will hear you!'

'I don't care who hears me! Come down here!'

'No! You're a heathen and your father is on the board of governors of a school that hates Catholics!'

'We don't hate Catholics, Maria! We're just really smug people who happen to be committed to pluralism and diversity and disagree with the denominational nature of the existing Irish education system!'

'You sacrifice donkeys on Dalkey Island!'

'We don't sacrifice donkeys! That's Protestants! What we do is we learn about the rites, ceremonies, celebrations, beliefs, values and key figures of all the major world religions, including Islam, Christianity, Judaism, Buddhism, Hinduism and Sikhism, while also giving equal weight and attention to Atheism, Agnosticism and Humanism!'

'Exactly! You treat religion as a subject of academic interest rather than a matter of faith!'

'Oh, Maria, I wish you could see that our ways and your ways aren't so different! We follow an Ethical Education Curriculum, in which we're taught the importance of moral and spiritual values, as well as justice and equality!'

'But you don't believe in one supreme being as the source of all moral authority!'

'I don't believe in God, Maria – no! But I believe in you!'

'It's not enough! You have to believe in God! And, also, you have to believe that the Catholic Church has a vital role to play in the Irish education system, especially at primary school level! And you have to speak Irish!'

'If that's what I have to do, Maria – then that's what I shall do!'

Honor suddenly ramps up the music. She turns to me and goes, 'I'll sing these next lines from Tony, okay?'

I'm like, 'Yeah, no, cool.'

She goes, '*Maria! I've just met a girl named Maria! And suddenly agnosticism, has lost all its exoticism, for me! Maria! A God-fearing girl named Maria! And suddenly I wish, that I could speak Irish – mo chroí! Maria! Say it loud and there's music playing! To win her heart, I'll soon be praying! Maria! I'll never stop saying . . . Maria!*'

I'm literally in tears at the end. I haven't been this proud of my daughter since she tripped up three girls to win the egg-and-spoon race in Montessori.

'Honor,' I go, 'I think all of the parents are going to love it!'


'This isn't the type of musical I had in mind
when I asked you to write a South Dublin
version of *West Side Story*.'
*The Irish Times*, 23 April 2016


'Come on, Ross!' Sorcha goes. 'Where's the horm?'

I'm there, 'It just feels like, I don't know, *spying*?'

'Don't be ridiculous – this is our actual daughter we're talking about! And she's about to teach the Mount Anville Musical Society the songs she's written for the school musical!'

This is the famous *South Side Story*, Honor's modern-day, South Dublin take on the original, exploring the bitter gang rivalry between the children from Educate As One, a staunchly multi-denominational school in Sandycove, and Gaelscoil Naomh Eithne, a Catholic, Irish-speaking national school in Glasthule.

Sorcha goes, 'All we're going to do is listen from outside the door. If she sees us, we'll just say we came to give her a lift home and we must have got the time wrong.'

So into the school we go. We stand at the door of the concert hall, looking through the little window. Honor is onstage, sitting at the piano, while all of the other girls are filling the first five rows of seats, songsheets in their hands, hanging on her every word.

'Okay,' she goes, 'this next song is sung by the Educate As One kids. It comes just after Tony has serenaded Maria on the fire escape and promised to become a Catholic and learn Irish so they can be together. This is their statement of who they are and it's sung to the tune of "America".'

Sorcha is grinning at me like an idiot.

She goes, 'Oh my God, Ross, that's our little girl up there!'

Honor storts playing the piano and singing.

She's like:

> *Life is okay when you're secular!*
> *No need to pray when you're secular!*
> *No Allah, no God, we are secular!*
> *No Jews and no Prods, we are secular!*
>
> *A new kind of school, we are secular!*
> *We're smug and we're cool, we are secular!*
> *A flat playing pitch, we are secular!*
> *Our parents are rich, we are secular!*

All of a sudden, a voice shouts, 'Stop!'

Sorcha's face just drops. 'Oh my God,' she goes, 'that's Miss Pallister, Honor's music teacher.'

This old biddy steps out of the wings and onto the actual stage. She goes, 'You can't sing that song! I won't allow it!'

We both watch Honor's little shoulders horden. She goes, '*Excuse* me?'

I already feel sorry for Miss Pallister – for what she's about to invite upon herself.

'This isn't the type of musical I had in mind when I asked you to write a South Dublin version of *West Side Story*,' she goes. 'Do you not realize that these songs could offend people?'

'But I offend both sides,' Honor – not unreasonably – goes. 'Believers and non-believers. I haven't sung you the Catholic Gaelscoil song yet.'

She storts playing the piano then and singing:

> *I feel guilty,*
> *Oh so guilty,*
> *I feel guilty and sinful and bad,*
> *And I pity,*
> *Any girl without God for a dad.*

'Stop it!' Miss Pallister shouts. 'Stop it this instant! Girls, tear up those songsheets! Do it! Do it now!'

All of the girls rip up the lyrics that Honor spent literally hours at the piano writing.

'Oh my God,' Sorcha goes, 'this isn't going to be pleasant to watch.'

Honor's face turns beetroot red.

I'm there, 'Let's just go back to the cor.'

Except we don't get a chance to move, because Honor all of a sudden explodes. She rips into Miss Pallister with a fury I've honestly never seen before. She calls the poor woman every B name, F name, M name and – yes – C name under the sun.

It's not the kind of thing you expect to hear from your ten-year-old daughter. Fifteen, maybe – when she's arrived home from supposedly studying in a friend's house, dressed like a hooker and smelling of spirits. But not ten!

Miss Pallister just stands there with her mouth open. That's all you can do when our daughter storts ripping you – just hunker down and wait for the storm to pass.

Eventually, it does. Honor jumps down off the stage and storts stomping towards the exit – which happens to be the door we're, like, *standing* behind? There's no time for us to hide. She pushes it and we step backwards. She sees us standing there, except she's in such a rage that she just storms past us and out of the building.

Sorcha goes, 'Oh! My God! I am *so* embarrassed!'

I'm like, 'Leave this to me, Sorcha. This is a job for her dad.'

I follow her outside to the cor pork, where I find Honor dragging a key along the side of a cor – presumably Miss Pallister's. She stops when she sees me.

I go, 'Where did you learn language like that?'

She's there, 'Have you ever listened to yourself watching rugby? Swearing at that man?'

I laugh because I know she's talking about Dan Biggar.

I'm there, 'Doing the Macarena – just kick the focking ball, you stupid prick!'

She laughs – she tries not to, but she *does*?

I'm there, 'The first thing I want to say to you, Honor, is – believe it or not – fair focks to you for standing up for yourself. The second thing is that you need to go in there and apologize.'

She goes, 'Er, *why* would I apologize?'

'Because you're cleverer than this. You're going to go home and write some new songs – just to keep the woman happy. But you're also going to secretly rehearse the old songs with the cast. Then, on the night, when the concert hall is full and it's too late for her to do anything about it, you're going to put on the show that you want to put on.'

She stares at me for a long time, then suddenly, out of nowhere, she throws her orms around my waist and she hugs me very hord.

I used to think God put me on this planet to win Heineken Cups and Six Nations championships. I was wrong. It turns out that my job was to be an amazing, amazing father – and, much as I hate patting myself on the back, it's pretty clear that I'm nailing it.

'Come on,' I go, taking her by the hand, 'let's go and say sorry to the stupid bitch.'


'I think we said our priority was to raise a daughter
who doesn't take S, H, one, T, from anyone.'
*The Irish Times, 21 May 2016*

These are the moments you dream about as a parent. We're sitting in the concert hall in Mount Anville with three or four hundred other moms and dad, all of us grinning like idiots. The curtain has just gone up on *South Side Story*.

We're, like, five minutes into it and the girls and boys from the Educate As One gang launch into their first number, 'When You're Co-Ed'.

> *When you're Co-Ed,*
> *You're Co-Ed all the way,*
> *From your first Lego set,*
> *To your last dyin' day.*

> *When you're Co-Ed,*
> *You're not frightened of girls!*
> *You grow up gender blind!*
> *The best school in the world!*

Sorcha turns around to me with a look of, like, *shock* on her face? She's like, 'Oh my God, Ross, what are they doing?'

I'm there, 'What are you talking about?'

'Honor was told by Miss Pallister to rewrite this song because the lyrics could potentially offend . . . I don't know, *someone*? Why are they all singing the first version she wrote?'

'I don't know – maybe because Honor is the writer and director of this musical and we raised our daughter to stick to her principles.'

'Excuse me?'

'Like your great hero. Mandinka.'

'His name was Madiba, Ross. Oh my God, you didn't actually encourage her to do this, did you?'

'To do what?'

'To tell Miss Pallister that she was going to change the lyrics, then arrange with the other girls to perform the original songs on the night?'

'I think we said our priority was to raise a daughter who doesn't take S, H, one, T, from anyone.'

'I never said that. I wanted to raise a daughter who does what she's told and looks on me as, like, her best, best friend.'

We're both suddenly looking at Miss Pallister, the music teacher, who's playing the piano with a look of, like, horror on her face, as it suddenly dawns on her that our daughter has put one over on her here. She keeps on playing, though.

> *Some folk get us wrong!*
> *They say we're atheistic!*
> *But that's way too strong!*
> *Our curriculum is holistic!*
> *We're kind of humanistic!*
>
> *So now you're Co-ed,*
> *With a capital C!*
> *Just a small donation!*
> *No, we don't call them fees!*
> *When you're Co-ed,*
> *You stay Co-ed!*

The song ends. Everyone in the audience stares at the person sitting next to them, in just, like, open-mouthed silence. Then they all clap.

'Oh my God,' Sorcha goes, 'people are offended, Ross. They're clapping out of politeness, but there'll be letters to the *Times* about this.'

I'm there, 'Who focking cares if there's letters to the *Times*?'

'Honor's going to be expelled.'

'Look, she hopefully won't be. She's done way worse than this in her time. We'll explain that to them if it comes to it.'

I'm looking at Honor. I can see her standing in the wings of the stage, one hand on her hip, the other giving Miss Pallister the famous one-finger salute, just letting her know that she's the winner here.

It's the same gesture I used to give to the haters back in my Senior Cup days. My daughter is so like me, it sometimes makes me want to cry.

Of course, Miss Pallister doesn't want to let herself down in front of all these parents, so she keeps on playing the piano, with a face on her like she's trying to pass a laundry ball through her urinary tract.

She plays on through the scene where Maria, the girl from the Catholic Gaelscoil, falls in love with Tony, the heathen boy from the mixed school where the children are taught to respect all religions with Parity of Indifference. And the scene where Tony stands at the foot of the fire escape and vows to convert to Catholicism and learn Irish to win her hort.

I look at Sorcha. I swear to fock, she's on her phone, Googling other schools.

She goes, 'I wonder would Teresian's take her?'

Miss Pallister plays on through the scene where the two rival schools hold a war council in the sushi bar in Dundrum to discuss what weapons to use for the big fight. The Catholic kids choose guilt and threats of eternal damnation, the Educate As One kids choose absolute certainty and condescension.

In the aisle to my right, I can see teachers furiously whispering to each other, obviously debating whether or not they should drop the curtain now and apologize to everyone. But, of course, this being Mount Anville, they'd have to ring someone first to find out their legal position.

And then suddenly it's too late for them to stop it because we've come to the final scene, the one where Tony is shot and Maria, in her grief, chases away the priest who attempts to minister the Last Rites to him, with a Plenary Indulgence nailed on in an effort to save his non-believing soul. Then Maria cradles her dying boyfriend in her orms, renounces her religion and says she's going to join a co-educational, equality-based, child-centred, multi-denominational school. She sings:

*Hold my hand and we're halfway there,*
*It costs no more than what you can spare.*
*Respect . . .*
*Diversity . . .*
*Inclusion . . .*

The lights go out. In the dorkness, I can hear Sorcha go, 'If Teresian's don't want her, we could always try Loreto on the Green.'

The lights come on again and all the actors are standing at the front of the stage. And that's when the most incredible thing happens. The entire audience gets to its feet. They clap and they roar and they shout the word 'Author!' over and over again.

Honor eventually steps out of the wings. Between bows, she smiles at Miss Pallister in a way that says, 'You can't touch me – and you so know it!'

And I have to tell you, I've never been more proud of the girl.

## 'Oilgate was a scandal alright – but it was also one of JP's finest moments as an estate agent.' *The Irish Times, 7 May 2016*

I've always thought Oilgate was a pretty random name for a village. Oilgate sounds like a scandal – and of course, looking back, that's exactly what it *was?*

*Vicarage Manor is an exciting development of ultra-modern residences in a highly desirable area with enormous growth potential – a suite of homes that manages to combine the excitement of urban life with the sedateness of the countryside, in the process setting the template for a new type of living, a pleasant, scenic commute from Dublin City Centre.*

You could count the lies in that sentence, then read it back and still find two or three you missed the first time. Yes, Oilgate was a scandal alright – but it was also one of JP's finest moments as an estate agent.

It's, like, three o'clock on Thursday afternoon and Vicarage Manor is quiet. But then it's always quiet, on account of the fact that it's ten miles from anywhere else and no one wants to actually live here.

Only six of the thirty-seven highly desirable residences have actual humans in them. The rest were bought as, like, investment properties – and, well, you can probably guess how that went. The banks are in the process of repossessing most of them, although it's a fair bet that the elements will take them first.

'What are you selling?' a voice goes. 'Salvation, is it?'

I turn around. There's a dude standing in the driveway of number 6 – one of the supposed three-bedroom houses, which are actually two-bedroom houses. The third one is tiny – if you wanted to fart in bed, you'd have to do it in instalments.

'Salvation?' I go. 'What are you talking about?'

He's like, 'I'm just wondering what crowd you're with? You're not the Jehovah's Witnesses because they were here this morning. And you're not with the Mormons because we'd them at the weekend.'

I notice he's checking out my suit. I'm there, 'Dude, you've got the wrong end of the stick.'

Not for the first time, I *could* add?

He's there, 'Have I? We can't get tradesmen to come. The supermarket won't deliver. But once a week, without fail, one of your crowd is here, asking do we ever pray. I suppose there's great potential for you in human misery.'

I'm there, 'Dude, I'm not actually *any* religion?' which isn't strictly true, of course. I put 'Leinster' on the Census form. 'I'm actually an estate agent.'

His mouth falls open. He looks over his shoulder and goes, 'Ailish! Ailish, come quickly! Your prayers have been answered!'

Ten seconds later, a woman appears at the door behind him.

'This fella here is an estate agent!' he goes. 'He's here to ask are we interested in selling! You said this place would come back, Ailish! Although I had my doubts, especially after that sinkhole took numbers 33 and 34.'

I'm there, 'Dude, you're borking up the wrong tree. I'm not here to tell you that someone wants your house.'

Seriously, you'd pay half a million for a gaff in Westeros before you took a gift of one in Vicarage Manor.

Ailish goes, 'So why *are* you here?'

I'm there, 'I'm wondering do you remember the estate agent who sold you this place? His name was JP Conroy.'

Suddenly, a faraway look comes over their faces. It's the same expression you see on me when I'm trying to figure out which of the five remote controls on our coffee table switches on the TV.

'JP Conroy,' he goes. 'That's a name I'll not forget in a hurry.'

His wife goes, 'He told us lies.'

I'm there, 'You and a lot more like you.'

She goes, 'The prospectus he showed us had a lake with swans on it.'

Swans were everywhere during the Celtic Tiger. You'd wonder whatever happened to them. Like a lot of others, they're keeping their heads down.

'More than swans,' the dude goes. 'We were promised shops, an adventure playground, a civic theatre.'

'Look,' I go, 'I can't give you any of those things. But what I can offer you is a chance to settle old scores. Would it surprise you to hear that the same JP Conroy is still working as an estate agent?'

The dude's there, 'No, it wouldn't. Because estate agents don't die – they just come back with pointier shoes.'·

'Well, were either of you also aware that you can actually complain about estate agents now? As in, if you feel you were, like, missold a gaff, you can bring it up with a crowd called the Something Something Regulatory Authority. They can fine them up to a quarter of a million shecks and even revoke their licence to operate.'

The two of them just look at each other. They're like, 'Really?'

I hand them a piece of paper and I go, 'I've taken the liberty of print-ing out their address, phone number and email details for you. And I've written a sort of sample letter that you might consider using if you're going to complain.'

*She* goes, 'Why are you doing this?'

And I'm there, 'Because I care. And because I think crooks like JP Conroy should be run out of the business.'

*He* goes, 'Thank you. Thank you so much.'

I say my goodbyes, then I tip back to the cor. I'm turning the key when my phone all of a sudden rings. Speak of the devil, it ends up being JP.

He goes, 'Where are you?'

I'm there, 'I'm in, em, Malahide.'

'That's funny,' he goes, 'because I'm in Vicarage Manor in Wexford and I'm looking straight at you.'

I look up. His cor is porked, like, nose-to-nose with mine and he's grinning at me with the phone clamped to his ear.

'Er, yeah, no,' I try to go, 'I was just taking a trip down memory lane, remembering some of the stunts you pulled before you decided we should become an ethical estate agency.'

He's there, 'I've been following you since nine o'clock this morning, Ross. Shillelagh. Coolboy. Ballyhill. Oilgate. You've been visiting my old clients, trying to get them to complain about me.'

I'm there, 'I don't know where you got that idea.'

'You've been wasting your time. The legislation only came in in 2011. It doesn't cover that period. Oh, and one other thing, Ross.'

'What?'

'You're fired.'


## 'Get out of that bed and help me zip this dress up.'
### *The Irish Times*, 14 May 2016

I wake up in the middle of the day to find Sorcha standing at the foot of the bed, pulling on her wedding dress.

I go, 'Did I, em, forget to put something in the diary for today?'

She rolls her eyes and goes, 'I knew you'd forget. Even though I've been talking about this day for, like, *months* now?'

I'm there, 'Refresh my memory, Babes, because there's a chance I wasn't listening to you.'

The secret to a good marriage, I've always said, is a good spam filter.

She goes, 'Yeah, it's obvious you weren't listening to me, Ross. Today is our *wedding* anniversary?'

I'm there, 'Er, yeah, no, I knew that,' wondering could I slip out to the petrol station to get her a cord.

She goes, 'What did I say we were going to do on our wedding anniversary?'

I'm there, 'You better tell me. I think it may have ended up in the old junk folder.'

'I told you I was going to put on my dress and we were going to watch our wedding mass on DVD. And don't give me that look, Ross.'

'What look?'

'Like you think I've lost the plot. I know – oh my God – *loads* of girls who do this every year on their anniversary. Now, get out of that bed and help me zip this dress up. I want to make sure it still fits before the girl arrives to do my hair and make-up.'

Yes, she did just say that. But, like Queen Elsa from *Frozen*, I let it go.

I climb out of the bed. Sorcha turns her back to me and lifts up her hair and that's when I realize that we've got a problem here. Let me see if there's a delicate way to say this – there's a lot more Sorcha than there is dress.

I try the zip, but I can't get it up any higher than, like, mid-back? Sorcha's going, 'What are you doing back there? Oh my God, Ross, you're all fingers and thumbs!'

I'm gripping the two sides of the dress and I'm trying to pull them together then hold them in place to try to force the zip up another half an inch, but it's no good. She might have fitted into it on our wedding day, but now, well, it's like trying to stuff a double mattress into a shower cubicle.

'It doesn't fit,' I go.

And of course you can imagine how that goes down.

She's like, 'What do you mean, it doesn't fit? Of course it fits – it's a Vera Wang.'

I'm there, 'I'm just saying, you know, we got married a long time ago. A lot has happened.'

Eddie Rocket's storted delivering – that's just one example.

'Oh my God,' she goes, 'I know what it is.'

'Are you going to mention the Super Nachos?' I go. 'Because I think those things should come with a health warning.'

'The dress has shrunk, Ross! It must have been the cleaners I took it to in Blackrock. Grab your cor keys.'

'Why?'

'Because we're going back there to complain. I'm just going to throw on my Juicy tracksuit.'

There's no point in arguing with the girl. I realize that. Sometimes, you've just got to go through the whole process.

So, half an hour later, we're standing in the dry cleaners in Blackrock and the dude behind the counter is going, 'Good afternoon!'

Sorcha's like, 'I wish it was a good afternoon,' as she puts the dress box on the counter and whips out the dress. 'I handed this in to be dry-cleaned and you shrank it.'

He's like, 'Shrank it?'

'Yes, it's shrunk – as in, it doesn't *fit* me any more?'

He smiles sort of, like, *knowingly*? He goes, 'Well, shrinkage might not be the only reason it doesn't fit you any more!'

He's got the courage of Jon Snow, this dude. I refuse to make eye contact with him, though, in case Sorcha takes it as a sign that we're on the same side.

She's like, 'Sorry, what is that supposed to mean?'

He's there, 'I'm just saying there could be another explanation, that's all. I've been in this business thirty years and I've never known a wedding dress to shrink.'

'Well, it's happened now,' she goes, 'and I know my rights.'

She did an online correspondence course in Consumer Law.

He grabs his order book. 'Okay,' he goes, 'when did you leave it in?'

Sorcha goes, 'It was 2003.'

He actually laughs. 'Did you just say 2003? That's, like, thirteen years ago! Our records don't go back that far, I'm afraid.'

'Well, that doesn't affect my statutory rights. I'm actually *qualified* in this area?'

'Can I ask you a question? Is it your wedding anniversary?'

'Yes, it's today. But I don't see what that has to do with anything.'

'Like I said to you, I've never known a wedding dress to shrink. But at least once a month, I have someone in here telling me they put on their dress to watch their wedding video and it didn't fit them any more. Do you know what I'm saying to you?'

'I do – and I don't like your tone.'

He grabs a tape measure. 'Look,' he goes, 'I'm going to measure it for you – what waist size was the dress originally?'

But Sorcha quickly stuffs it back into its box. 'Oh my God,' she goes, 'you are *so*, so sued. I actually feel sorry for you, because you don't even realize yet how sued you actually *are*?'

She storms out of the shop. The dude looks at me – not unsympathetically – and goes, 'Seriously, one a month.'

I follow Sorcha outside. She's spitting nails. She storts quoting various pieces of consumer legislation at me. When I don't say anything back, she goes, 'Do *you* think I've put on weight?'

I don't give her a straight answer. I know better. Instead, I go, 'Whether you have or not, Sorcha, you're more beautiful to me today than you were the day I married you. And that's not me being sarcastic.'

She smiles at me.

I'm like, 'Come on, let's go home and watch this famous DVD.'

'You take the cor,' she goes. 'I'm going to speed-walk home.'

Which suits me. It'll give me a chance to buy her a cord.

The Westbury is rammers. Men in tuxes and women in ball gowns. The sign on the board says it's the Annual Ethics in Business Awards, sponsored by It's Accrual World Accounting Solutions.

I'm suddenly wondering why JP's old man wanted to meet me here.

'Drink?' he goes.

I'm there, 'Yeah, no – pint of the obvious.'

*He's* drinking just, like, water? At least I hope it's water. The dude's supposedly recovering from a hort attack, bear in mind.

I'm like, 'You're looking well.'

'You're a liar,' he goes. 'A bare-faced liar. It's what made you the best estate agent I ever had.'

I'm there, 'Look, I'm sorry. I had a plan to get rid of JP, except he found out about it and sacked me.'

'What, so you're just going to give up?'

'Dude, I don't even work for Hook, Lyon and Sinker any more.'

'Don't you mean Bloodless, Human, Good?'

'I refuse point-blank to call it that. It'll always be Hook, Lyon and Sinker to me.'

He smiles to himself. Then he goes, 'You know he hasn't sold a single house since the start of March?'

I'm like, 'Morch? Are you serious?'

'Serious as a – well, you know what I was going to say. It's a seller's market out there. There's a fortune to be made again for people like us. And my son has decided to become an honest estate agent. I mean, isn't that what they call an oxymoron?'

'Don't ask me. There's very little going on in my head. A monkey dressed as a butler. Holding a tray. Waiting for instructions. Blinking.'

'Well, now we know where telling the truth gets you. The place will be closed by the end of August. Still, at least he'll have his award to console him in his retirement.'

'What award?'

He laughs. 'You don't know?' he goes. 'Right now, my son is in the Grafton Suite, receiving an Ethics in Business Award.'

'Jesus.'

'An Ethics in Business Award. My own flesh and blood. I won't be able to show my face in Doheny & Nesbitt's again.'

'No one wants that for their children.'

He suddenly stands up. 'Come on,' he goes.

I'm like, 'Where?'

'Let's go see this for ourselves. If I have another heart attack, make sure and tell my son what a disappointment he was to me in the end.'

'It's the least I can do.'

We head down to the Grafton Suite. I push the door open a crack and we look in. JP is standing at the podium, a humungous crystal vase in his hands – happy as a dog with a boner. He's going, 'For years, estate agents have been the punchline to a joke that a great many of us found offensive. I hope if this award proves anything, it's that it is possible to operate in the property business without making exaggerated claims, without artificially inflating prices, without pulling any of the strokes for which estate agents have become notorious.'

I look at JP's old man. His eyes are full of tears.

'Dude,' I go, 'I don't think you need to hear this.'

He's there, 'Do you know how long it took me to build that business up?'

'It says "Since 1976" over the door, so I'm presuming it's, I don't know, however many years it is *since* then?'

'*Prime Time Investigates* did three programmes on us!'

'I know.'

'Three!'

'And no one can take that away from you. That will always stand.'

'*He's* taking it away from me. Everything I worked for – forty years.'

Forty. I was guessing fifty.

JP's still up at the podium, banging on. He's going, 'There is nothing wrong with telling customers the truth. It should be a first principle of business, whether it's selling tins of beans or selling houses. We believe there is nothing wrong with telling a client: "This is a poorly maintained house in an area with a high incidence of crime. That's reflected in the low price of the property." Or "This is an apartment that is so small as to be almost uninhabitable and is isolated by the poor public transport service in the area."'

That gets an actual round of applause.

He goes, 'At Bloodless, Human, Good, this is what we do. Our mission, if I may call it that, is to take back the property business from the fast-talking spivs in the tight suits and the pointy shoes. I want to dedicate this award to all estate agents who are committed to doing business with empathy and humanity. Thank you.'

The dude ends up getting a standing ovation. I let the door close. JP's old man falls back against the wall, his breathing all heavy. For about thirty seconds, I'm convinced it's his ticker again. I'm, like, loosening his tie and undoing the top button of his shirt.

'Breathe,' I go. 'Just try to, like, breathe.'

All of a sudden, the door of the Grafton Suite opens and out JP steps, clutching his phone to his ear and the crystal vase to his chest. He's obviously doing an interview with one of the papers, because we hear him go, 'Lies will earn you quick money, sure. But they hurt the property business in the long term – and, yes, you can quote me on that.'

He's standing at the top of the stairs, chatting to this journalist, and, at the same time, he storts admiring his vase, looking at it like you or I might look at, say, a Leinster Schools Senior Cup medal.

'Do something,' JP's old man goes.

I'm there, 'Like I said, it's hord. I don't even work for him any more.'

'Okay,' he goes, 'if you won't, then I will.'

I can't actually believe what happens next.

He walks towards him. JP has his back to him. He's going, 'I'm glad you asked me that question. Yes, it's challenging being an estate agent that tells the truth, but I think the benefits will come as our reputation grows.'

JP's old man puts his hand on his son's back and he shoves him, head-first, down the Westbury stairs.

### 'I want you to take over the running of Bloodless, Human, Good.'
*The Irish Times, 11 June 2016*

I shouldn't laugh, but JP *is* a comical sight? He's got plaster casts on both legs – we're talking, like, ankle to hip – and on both orms – we're talking from his shoulders to the tips of his fingers. 'I've got two broken tibia,' he goes, 'a broken fibula, a cracked patella, a broken radius and two broken ulnas.'

I give him my best fake sympathetic face. 'And if that wasn't bad enough,' I go, 'you've got two broken orms and two broken legs as well.'

He gives me a look – it's like I've just offered to give him a bed-bath. He goes, 'Yeah, I'm *talking* about my orms and legs. God, you're so thick.'

I don't know if it's that I'm thick. I'm from that generation that thinks there's no point in filling up your cupboard space with CDs when all the music you could ever want is out there and available to download illegally at the press of a button. And, in the same way, I've always felt there's no point in filling your head with knowledge and facts when you can find out anything you need to know online. By the way, I came up with this theory back in the 1990s, when no one had even heard of Wikipedia, so I *could* tell JP that, educationally, I'm actually years ahead of the pack.

But I don't. Instead, I go, 'It could be worse, Dude. At least you're in the Blackrock Clinic. I had a sneaky peak at the menu on the way in – er, rack of Wicklow lamb with horseradish potato dauphinoise and a natural jus?'

'Yeah,' he goes, 'I have to be spoon-fed each and every mouthful.'

'Swings and roundabouts,' I go. 'Swings *and* roundabouts. So, anyway, what happened – as in, like, actually?'

'I don't remember much. I was in the Westbury. I'd just collected my Ethics in Business Award and I was walking through the hotel lobby, talking to the *Irish Times* on the phone, explaining how I hoped the way that we do business at Bloodless, Human, Good could set a new template for the relationship between estate agent and customer. And that's when I felt –'

'What?'

'A hand on my back. Someone pushed me down the stairs, Ross.'

'That's crazy talk. I'm going to put this conversation down to whatever drugs you're on.'

'Think about it,' he goes. 'I mean, it stands to reason. The property morket is booming again. There's fortunes to be made. Then along *we* come and we're suddenly telling customers the truth about properties. We were a threat to the big goys.'

'Yeah, you haven't sold a single house or aportment since you brought that whole honesty is the best policy thing in. I'm not knocking you here – I'm just making a statement of fact.'

'Things were beginning to turn, Ross. We were getting a lot of publicity for being straight-talkers. That frightened a lot of people in the industry. I had to be taken out. Whoever pushed me did so on behalf of various vested interests – it's like that dude, what's his name, who shot Kennedy?'

Don't look at me. I don't even know who Kennedy is. I decide to move the conversation along. We can both Google it later. Well, one of us can. I've still got the use of my thumbs.

'So,' I go, 'the duty nurse rang me – she said you wanted to see me.'

He's like, 'Yeah, I did. Look, I realize you and I haven't exactly been getting on lately.'

'Are you talking about you sacking me from my job?'

'Dude, don't make this hord for me.'

'No, because I was just going to say, I wouldn't allow something as trivial as a sacking to come in the way of our friendship. Dude, we played rugby together. Thankfully, we still live in a world where that means something.'

'I'm glad to hear you say that. Because I've got a favour to ask you.'

'I wonder what this could be. Continue.'

'I want you to take over the running of Bloodless, Human, Good – just until my bones have healed and I'm fit to return to work.'

'Are you serious?'

'You were the most senior member of staff I had until – well, you know. And you're someone I can trust. I mean, you said the word, Ross – rugby.'

'There's no arguing with rugby.'

'But I need to ask you a second favour. I need you to keep the good work going. My philosophy. My commitment to telling customers the truth. It'll yield fruit in time. Tell me you won't let the agency return to the old ways.'

'You have my promise.'

'We've got a very young staff, Ross. They're hungry, but they're also very impressionable. They need a good role model.'

'Well, you're in luck, because being a good role model is one of the things I'm genuinely amazing at. That's me patting myself on the back.'

'Thanks, Ross.'

I say my goodbyes, then I point the cor in the direction of Balls-bridge. I throw the thing in the spot morked 'Managing Director' and then into the office I trot.

The staff all look miserable. You wouldn't blame them. Most of them haven't had a cent in commission all year. But they all brighten up when they see me walk through the door.

One of them, a girl who has a bit of a thing for me, goes, 'Oh my God, are you back – as in, like, *back* back?'

I don't say a word. I walk straight past her to the little room at the back of the office that's used as, like, a storage cupboard. I find the big brass letters that once hung over the window. I gather them up in my orms – the H, the K, the L, the S – and I carry them out onto the office floor, then I drop them on the corpet. They make a hell of racket.

I go, 'Are any of you familiar with the TV programme *Countdown*?'

Of course they are – most of them were in UCD like me. They're all like, 'Yeah.'

I'm there, 'Okay, let's see who can put these letters together to spell out the name of what was once – and will soon be again – the greatest estate agents in the world?'

'There's nothing criminal about this enterprise. If anything, it's just a little bit, well, immoral.'
*The Irish Times, 19 November 2016*

I swing into the old man's gaff to collect my ticket for the All Blacks match. He's in his study. He's sitting on one side of the desk, with Hennessy opposite him. And sitting on the desk between them is a lorge, grey breeze block.

I don't know what it says about my relationship with my old man that my first thought is that it's for weighing down a body.

'Kicker!' the old man goes when he sees me. 'I need to pick that world-famous brain of yours for a moment.'

That's just something he says, by the way – he knows I'm as thick as, well, that brick there.

'Hennessy and I are preparing a tender for a project,' he goes. 'How many of those blocks do you think we'd need to build a wall? Height, twelve feet. Depth, four feet. Length, oh, about the length of the border between the United States and Mexico.'

I'm like, 'Excuse me?'

'What's your best guesstimate, Kicker?'

'Are you serious? Are you *actually* serious?'

'Someone's going to have to build the thing. Let's not get caught up in the hows, the whys, the what-nots and the however-you-might-says.'

'That sounds suspiciously like the speech you made from the dock when they sent you down for corrupting the planning process.'

Hennessy throws in his two yoyos' worth then. 'There's nothing criminal about this enterprise,' he tries to go. 'If anything, it's just a little bit, well, immoral.'

I'm there, 'And that's what *you* said in the old man's defence before the judge put him away. You two are unbelievable. I was looking at that brick, thinking, Yeah, no, they're probably just trying to work out how many of those it'd take to drag a body to the bottom of the sea. Instead, it's *this*?'

The old man goes, 'Drag a body to the bottom of the sea? Is that what you think of me, Kicker?'

'I think you two are capable of anything when you put your heads together.'

'I'll take that as a compliment.'

'Don't. Seriously, don't. Do you know how upset Sorcha is about this whole, I don't know, election thing?'

'She was a fan of Ms Clinton – yes, we've debated on the subject.'

'She was more than a fan. It's all I've been hearing about for the last six months. Hillary this and Hillary that. She took down the poster in the utility room of all the dipshit things that George W. Bush said and replaced it with a poster of all the dipshit things that Donald Trump said.'

'She's always been political.'

'And now she's devastated. She's been in her pyjamas for a week.'

'I think it was John F. Kennedy who said that politics was the something-something of something-something else.'

'I don't think that's going to come as any consolation to her. She hasn't cooked in a week. The staff in Kingsland are sick of the sight of me.'

'The fact remains,' Hennessy goes, 'that someone is going to build this wall – and it might as well be us.'

'That's right,' the old man goes. 'And in four years' time, if the Democrats retake the White House, they'll probably be looking for someone to knock it down again.'

'And we'll tender for that job as well.'

'*Vitam regit fortuna, non sapientia!*'

'Virgil!'

'I think you'll find it was Cicero, old bean. Now, by my reckoning, Hennessy, we're going to need something in the region of a billion of these blocks . . .'

I can't listen to any more of this. I grab my ticket from on top of his drinks cabinet. As I'm going out the door, the old man shouts after me. He's like, 'Probably best if you don't tell Sorcha about this, Ross. Especially if, as you say, she's still grieving for Hillary.'

As I'm driving home, I'm thinking to myself, actually, no, I'm going to tell her. Why should I keep his secrets for him when I've difficulty enough keeping track of my own lies?

I walk through the front door and I end up meeting her in the hallway. She goes, 'Hi.'

I'm like, 'Hey,' and I smile because I notice that she's actually dressed for the first time in a week.

'How are you?' I go.

She's like, 'The grief keeps coming in waves. It's kind of like a *death*?'

'Right. Bummer.'

'The death of someone – oh my God – really, really close to me. But this afternoon, I actually realized something. I have no more tears left to cry. I've done my mourning. And now my grief is ready to transform into something more useful.'

I put my hand on her back and I go, 'Cooking always helps you take your mind off things,' and I stort trying to subtly steer her in the direction of the kitchen.

It's not me being sexist, it's me being storving.

'It's like Aaron Sorkin said,' she goes, 'four years will fly. And we'll be ready next time – as in *properly* ready? And, in the meantime, we'll be vigilant. We won't let them get away with anything. How's your dad, by the way?'

I'm there, 'Yeah, no, I was actually just getting to that.'

'What?'

'I walked into his study and there was, like, a *breeze* block on his desk?'

'A breeze block? What would your dad be doing with a breeze block?'

I look at her and I realize in that moment that I can't tell her the truth. It's portly because I'm ashamed of him and portly because I know it'll set her recovery back a week.

'It's nothing,' I go. 'I think him and Hennessy are thinking of killing someone.'

'Oh,' she goes. 'I was thinking of making my Jamie Oliver tomato, red wine and chorizo risotto for lunch.'

And I'm like, 'Sounds good to me.'

# 2017

Millions of people all over the world take part in the Women's March in response to the inauguration of Donald Trump as US President * Taoiseach Enda Kenny rejects the idea that Ireland should follow the United Kingdom in leaving the European Union * North Korea fires a ballistic missile across the Sea of Japan * British Prime Minister Theresa May calls a snap General Election, which results in the Conservative Party losing its parliamentary majority * The US government announces its decision to withdraw from the Paris Climate Agreement, a move that is condemned internationally * The government announces that it will formally recognize Irish Travellers as an indigenous ethnic minority * The United Kingdom triggers Article 50 of the Lisbon Treaty to begin the formal process of leaving the European Union * Robert Mueller begins his investigation into alleged Russian interference in the 2016 US presidential election * Former Deputy First Minister of Northern Ireland, Martin McGuinness, dies * Enda Kenny, Fine Gael's longest-serving Taoiseach, announces his retirement. He is succeeded by Leo Varadkar * Former Chairman and Chief Executive of Anglo Irish Bank, Seán FitzPatrick, is acquitted of twenty-seven charges relating to his conduct while at the bank * Gerry Adams announces he will stand down as leader of Sinn Féin * US President Donald Trump reiterates his election promise to build a wall between the United States and Mexico * Catalonia declares its independence from Spain * The Luas Cross City begins operating, connecting the Red and Green lines *

Meanwhile . . .

> 'Maybe we shouldn't keep telling them that an
> evil man has taken over the planet.'
> *The Irish Times, 28 January 2017*

Like a lot of parents, my old pair used to try to scare me straight by warning me about The Bogeyman. One of my earliest memories, in fact, is my old dear telling me, 'If you don't fix me a Martini – four ounces of gin, one ounce of dry vermouth, served in a chilled cocktail glass with a twist of lemon – The Bogeyman is going to get you!'

These days, of course, parents don't need to tell their kids about The Bogeyman, because they have the President of the United States of America.

Sorcha has spent the past six months telling our children all about the nasty orange man who was going to undo all the amazing, amazing things that Barack Obama did for the world. And now the triplets can't sleep. They're waking up at, like, three o'clock in the morning, screaming with nightmares.

'This is all down to *him*,' Sorcha went the night after the inauguration, as we got up for the third time to tell Leo, Brian and Johnny that everything was going to be okay in about four years' time.

I was like, 'Maybe it's kind of down to us as well, though.'

And Sorcha went, 'Excuse me?'

'I'm just saying, maybe we shouldn't keep telling them that an evil man has taken over the planet. They're only, like, two.'

She gave me *the* most unbelievable filthy then. 'You see to the children,' she went. 'I need to tell people about this on Facebook and Twitter.'

This has been the general vibe since the dude won the whole, I don't know, *thing*? I've been getting by on about two and a half hours of sleep per night while at the same time hoping that things will hopefully get back to normal soon. Which I genuinely thought they were beginning to – until the moment Honor arrived downstairs for breakfast wearing a sweatshirt bearing the words Make America Great Again.

Sorcha was just sitting there with her mouth wide open – like the shork that ate Robert Shaw in *Jaws*.

'Honor,' she went, trying *not* to lose it with her? 'Where did you get that?'

And Honor was like, 'I bought it – online.'

'It could be worse,' I went. 'At least it's not a Munster jersey!' just trying to introduce a little *humour* to the moment?

Sorcha was like, 'Are you wearing that to upset me?'

But Honor went, 'Oh my God, get *over* yourself! Everything doesn't have to be about you!'

'So why would you wear it – after everything I told you about that man?'

'I actually like him. I like the way he pisses people off. I can see a lot of myself in him.'

'Oh, so that's the kind of role model you want, is it? Someone who makes people – oh my God – so angry that they morch in, like, their *millions*? Honor, take it off.'

'No – you're always going on about how freedom of expression is a fundamental human right.'

'Yes – if used responsibly.'

'Oh, so everyone's entitled to free speech as long as they agree with you?'

'I know what you're doing. You're trying to twist my views and use them as a weapon against me.'

Honor stood up from the table. 'Yeah,' she went, 'I'm *bored* with this conversation? I'm going to go and wait in the cor!'

We were supposedly going shopping.

Sorcha looked at me. 'Ross,' she went, 'there is no way she is walking around Dundrum Town Centre wearing that sweatshirt.'

I was like, 'Sorcha, do you not think it's possibly time we all got over the whole Donald Trump thing?'

'This coming from the man who wet the bed for a month after Johnny Sexton left Leinster?'

'That's a low blow, Sorcha. I was drinking a lot and I genuinely thought it was a backward step for him in terms of his development as a ten.'

Sorcha stood up and picked up her cor keys. 'I know she's only doing it for a reaction,' she went. 'And the worst possible mistake you can make with trolls is to give them the attention they're looking for.'

So we all headed to Dundrum. Honor put 'My Way' on her iPhone and we ended up having to listen to it on repeat the entire way there. Sorcha said nothing, obviously deciding to just rise above it.

It has to be said, the sweatshirt drew quite a bit of comment over the course of the next two hours. 'Disgusting!' people typically said. 'What kind of a parent dresses their child up like that?'

And Sorcha – bizorrely – ended up becoming Honor's defender, going, 'If you must know, *she* chose it! And, by the way, we're fortunate enough to still live in a liberal democracy where people are entitled to express their views, however egregious they actually *are*?'

And in between these moments, she tried to use subtle arguments to try to get Honor to take the sweatshirt off. 'I think a round neck makes you look chunky,' she went, 'and that's not me being a bitch.'

Or it was like, 'Red is definitely *not* your colour! I just think it washes you out and makes you look ill!'

Honor just went, 'Look at the way these people are looking at me! I love it!'

To cut a long story short, me and Sorcha were sitting in front of the TV that night when Honor arrived downstairs in her pyjamas.

'I'm beginning to think I might go into politics,' she went.

Sorcha was like, 'You're just fishing, Honor – like all those trolls on social media who said I shouldn't be warning infant children about the threat that Donald Trump poses to the planet. But I hope I proved a point to you today – that debate is a far more effective tool than coercion.'

'Not really,' Honor went, 'because I'm going to wear it tomorrow as well – and the day after that and the day after that and the day after that.'

Sorcha sad-smiled her, stood up and went, 'Excuse me for a moment,' before leaving the room.

Thirty seconds later, we heard all this angry shouting coming from upstairs, followed by the sound of three babies suddenly crying.

'I'm only guessing,' I went, 'but I think your mother is ripping your sweatshirt to shreds.'

And Honor laughed and went, 'I don't care. I've got three more just like it.'

'As you know, Hennessy and I are tendering
to build a portion of this famous wall that
Donald Trump wants to build.'
*The Irish Times*, 4 February 2017

So the old man rang me earlier this week and he said, like, *the* weirdest thing? He went, 'I had a taco for the first time tonight, Ross, and I didn't enjoy it one little bit.'

I was like, 'What? Are you leathered or something?'

'No, I'm merely stating that Helen made tacos for dinner – and I found them frankly unsatisfying and a touch on the stodgy side. And – if you have the time – just too downright finicky by half. The ingredients are thrown onto the table and you end up having to prepare the bloody thing yourself!'

'Yeah, I'm kind of *busy* here?'

I was lying on the sofa, playing with my phone, changing my settings to get Siri to address me by different names, including Stud, Winner and Golden Balls. Her little robot voice just does it for me.

The old man didn't take the hint, though. He went, 'I find Mexican food grossly overrated – like much of what comes from that country.'

I was like, 'What are you talking about?'

'I'm simply observing that I don't really enjoy anything that comes from Mexico. Tequila is a dreadful, dreadful drink. Their music is offensive to my ears. And as for avocados – they taste of nothing and they make you fat!'

'You love a good Mexican wave. I'm remembering you at Neil Diamond in Croke Pork in '92. You were up and down so often, you had to go and sit in a St John's Ambulance for half an hour. They gave you a lollipop to suck.'

'I have no idea what you're talking about, Ross. I've never done the Mexican wave in my life. Anyway, I've really enjoyed this conversation.'

Then he hung up.

Two nights later, I was sitting at the kitchen table, scribbling a few notes in the back of my Rugby Tactics Book. I was actually writing a fantasy best man speech for Rob Kearney in the event of him one day asking me to do the honours. That's when my phone rang. It was the old man again.

'Isn't that Meryl Streep a hopeless actress?' he went.

I was like, 'What?'

'Meryl Streep. She's terribly overrated. Well, it's that type of acting that insists upon itself, isn't it? Everything's overcooked. Just dial it down a notch, Meryl! Just dial it the hell down!'

'You loved her in *Mamma Mia!*'

'I've never seen *Mamma Mia!* in my life!'

'You own it on DVD. You insist on putting it on every Christmas.'

'Like I said, Ross, overrated in the extreme! And I don't find her in the least bit attractive. I know some men do. Wouldn't be my kind of thing. I'd say she's bloody hard work as well. Forget her birthday and I expect she'd kick up bloody hell. And even doing that she wouldn't be convincing. Anyway, Kicker, I really enjoy these chats – must go!'

Then he hung up.

A day or two later, I happened to be in town when I ran into the famous Hennessy Coghlan-O'Hara, his solicitor and best friend. He was standing outside the Shelbourne, smoking a Cohiba the size of a rolling pin and loudly making the point that women shouldn't be allowed to drive motor cors. This was while watching a woman trying to parallel pork.

I morched up to him and I was like, 'What's going on with my old man?'

He was there, 'Charlie? What are you talking about?'

'He rings me up the other night and he storts banging on about Meryl Streep's movies to me – critiquing her acting. Before that, he was on about how he'd just had a taco and he found it – I want to say – *unsatisfying*? Have they upped his meds or something?'

Hennessy just laughed. 'There's nothing to worry about,' he went. 'There's a very simple reason for it.'

I was like, 'Okay, I'm listening.'

'Well, as you know, he and I are tendering to build a portion of this famous wall that Donald Trump wants to build. We're hoping to build the bit from Ciudad Juárez to Heroica Nogales.'

'So why is he pretending he's never seen *Mamma Mia!*? Jesus, he used to walk around the house singing the songs. Helen thought he was about to come out of the closet. She told me that herself.'

'All companies tendering for the job are subjected to a vetting process.'

'Okay.'

'And your father is convinced that the National Security Agency is monitoring his phone calls.'

'Who?'

'American intelligence.'

'Random. And *are* they?'

'Who knows? But we're going over there next week. And I told him, to be on the safe side, if he's using the phone, not to say anything impolitic.'

'Is that a definite word?'

'Yes, it's a definite word. It sounds to me like your father is probably overcompensating.'

'Well, it's focking annoying. I've a busy lifestyle. That's what he fails to see.'

Then I walked off.

That night, I was sitting at home, writing a list in my head of all the girls I've slept with who were named after months of the year. January. April. May. June. Could I count Julie for July?

That's when my phone suddenly rang and it was him again.

He went, 'What do you think of stairs, Ross?'

I was like, 'What?'

'Stairs. You know – steps. Why do we bloody need them? The older I get, the more I think, what is our obsession with these infernal things? If it was up to me, I'd get rid of them.'

So I went, 'I hear you and Hennessy are off to the States next week?'

He was like, 'Yes, we're heading to Washington on Friday for, let's just say, *business* reasons!'

'Can I give you a few things to bring over?'

'Things? What type of things?'

'It's just a few bags of Tayto for a few mates of mine who are stuck over there – overstayed their visas.'

'Er, Ross, I rather think . . .'

'Are you going to be seeing Fazil and Aabidullah while you're over there?'

'Who?'

'Your mates, Fazil and Aabidullah? Actually, is Aabidullah even out of prison?'

'Who is this? I'm sorry, Ross, I rather think we have a crossed line here.'

'By the way, that was great joke you told about Donald Trump over dinner last night.'

And the line went thankfully dead.

# 'I'm here to watch Denis O'Brien
## wipe the floor with you.'
### *The Irish Times*, 11 March 2017

The old man gives me a big smile. He's like, 'Thank you for coming, Kicker! It's wonderful to know that I can count on your support!'

I'm there, 'I'm not here to support you. I'm here to watch Denis O'Brien wipe the floor with you.'

The old man turns around to Hennessy and goes, 'You can see what he's doing, can't you, old scout? He's playing the role of devil's advocate, just to make sure his old dad's wits remain shorp for the legal swordplay to come.'

I'm like, 'No, I'm genuinely on Denis O'Brien's side. He gave us Johnny Sexton back. What have you ever given the country?'

The answer to that question, of course, is the square root of fockall. Suddenly, a hush descends on the court and in he walks – Denis himself – flanked by his legal team.

He takes one brief look at my old man, then he sits down. The old man carries on staring him, at the same time primping up his hair slash wig with his hand, pretty much *goading* the dude?

'*Allez Les Bleus!*' I shout across the courtroom. Denis just blanks me. Bigger things on his mind, I suppose.

The whole thing eventually kicks off. One of the dudes representing Denis storts outlining the case against my old man.

'My client,' he goes, 'had a hairstyle that – in respect of colour, length and arrangement – was unique to him. It was his signature style. You could see him cast in silhouette and still recognize him.

'In March 2001, he applied to the Irish Patents Office to register this design – including specific features, such as the lines, contours, colour, shape, texture, volume and bounciness – as *his* industrial property. He was successful in this application.

'In the autumn of 2015, Mr Charles O'Carroll-Kelly – a disgraced property developer and the proprietor of what might loosely be called a document disposal service –'

The old man is suddenly on his feet.

'I'm a bloody well entrepreneur!' he shouts, staring straight at Denis. 'And let the court record reflect it!'

The judge tells him – in polite legal terms – to sit the fock down and the dude representing Denis carries on hammering him.

'Mr Charles O'Carroll-Kelly,' he goes, 'for the purposes of career advancement, took to wearing a wig that is, in every respect, identical to the style over which my client has design protection, including such characteristics as the shade of autumn-ochre; the volume, defined by the patents office as 'generous-bodied'; the overall shape, defined as rotunda-like; the position of the side-parting and its geometrical relation to the main body of the hair; and the orientation and general aspect of the side-comb feature.

'It is our contention that this wig represents a breach of my client's intellectual property rights and has caused him considerable embarrassment in both his personal and professional life, for which he is seeking substantial punitive damages.'

'Fair focks!' I shout. 'You definitely have me convinced!'

The judge stares at me and says something about, I don't know, possibly jailing me for contempt of court in the event of, like, *further* outbursts?

Various expert witnesses are called by both sides then. Appearing for my old man, Mr Naseem Khan, a Professor of Geometry and Applied Mathematics with the Massachusetts Institute of Technology, says that he studied fifty photographs of Charles O'Carroll-Kelly and Denis O'Brien, focusing specifically on the structural similarities between their hairstyles.

He says that, firstly, he compared the steepness and curvature of the main hemispherical surface area of both men's hair using traditional formulae for measuring quadric surfaces. In the case of Denis O'Brien's hair, he says, it satisfied all the mathematical criteria of a spherical cap dome – in contrast to Charles O'Carroll-Kelly's hair, which was more paraboloid in character.

There's suddenly a lot of muttering in court. I presume everyone else, like me, is struggling to follow what's being said. A lot of legal types go to rugby schools as well.

With regord to the angle at which the two men's respective hairs are combed, Professor Khan says he calculated a mean differential of fourteen degrees in the angle of the side-porting in relation to the main body of the hair.

'What this means,' he goes, 'is that the hairstyles of these two men are *not* the same.'

Under cross-examination, he ends up being asked whether, in his expert opinion, the two hairstyles might satisfy the provision under patent law as being aesthetically similar. Professor Khan says he is not an expert in patent law. He is asked whether a layman might consider the two men's hair to be aesthetically similar. He says he has not been called to testify as a layman – he has been asked to testify as an expert in geometry and that answering as a layman would require him to give a wilfully ignorant answer.

The judge tells him – again, using legal niceties – to stop acting the dick. So the dude agrees that, yes, to the untutored eye, the two men *could* be said to have similar hairstyles.

Appearing as a witness for Denis O'Brien, Pamela Fry, a Master Colourist with Peter Mork on Grafton Street, says that my old man's hair and Denis's hair are identical in colour. But, under cross-examination, she bursts into tears and admits that, in a certain light, the old man's hair is possibly more cinnamon-honeywheat than autumn-ochre and the judge suggests a short recess to allow Pamela to gather herself, while the old man shouts, 'Strike out with costs to the plaintiff! Strike out with costs to the plaintiff!'

During the break in proceedings, I turn around to the old man and I go, 'Why don't you just give this up? Just admit that you haven't had one good day since you put that thing on your head.'

'What,' he goes, 'and deny myself the sweet taste of victory against my old nemesis? Never!'

And suddenly there's another hush in the court, as Pamela is dismissed, and Denis O'Brien himself is called to the witness box. I clap my two hands together and I'm like, 'Here we go! Hammer time!'

## 'That hurts, Denis! Like salt in the proverbial wound!'
### *The Irish Times, 18 March 2017*

Denis O'Brien is giving evidence. His barrister goes, 'How long have you known Charles O'Carroll-Kelly?'

And Denis is there, 'I don't know Charles O'Carroll-Kelly. I don't know him at all.'

The old man shouts, 'That hurts, Denis! Like salt in the proverbial wound!'

The barrister goes, 'This is *despite* his claim that you were once friends. *Good* friends, according to his account.'

'I may have met him once or twice over the years,' Denis goes. 'I remember he walked up to me at Leopardstown one Christmas and asked if he could touch my hair.'

'He asked . . . if he could touch . . . your hair?'

'He said he'd admired it for years and he wanted to pat it with his hand just to test its tensile strength.'

'A rather strange thing to ask, wouldn't you think?'

'That's why I made an excuse and left.'

'And did you ever encounter him again?'

'Yes, about a year later, in the Shelbourne Hotel. Again, he was fixated on my hair. He said that in all the acres of coverage given over to the Moriarty Tribunal, not one journalist had mentioned my magnificent hemispherical mane – his words – as the true source of my success as an entrepreneur. Then he asked again if he could touch it.'

'So you know that your hair was something that Charles O'Carroll-Kelly coveted?'

'He seemed obsessed with it.'

'How did you feel when you first saw him *with* Denis O'Brien hair?'

'I was a bit annoyed. But it was later on, when people started to mistake *me* for Charles O'Carroll-Kelly, that I knew I had to do something.'

'It caused you a great deal of embarrassment – would I be correct in saying that?'

'Yes, you would. A man walked up to me when I was leaving the Aviva Stadium, for instance, and told me I'd spoiled his enjoyment of an Ireland rugby match by repeatedly shouting the word "Endure!" throughout the second half.'

I laugh. I'm there, 'The old man definitely does that. It's incredibly annoying. He also shouts, "Stealth!" He's been threatened with I don't know *how* many deckings?'

The judge tells me – again, in legalese – to basically butt out.

Denis goes, 'Another man approached me as I was walking into Brown Thomas and said he'd bought one of the O'Carroll-Kelly houses in West Dublin that were built in the 1970s on a floodplain. He said that he thought about me every time it rained and he and his wife had to use buckets to bail out the living room.'

'A gross calumny on my character!' the old man shouts. 'Exclamation mork! Exclamation mork! Exclamation mork!'

'Would it be true to say,' the barrister goes, 'that since Charles

O'Carroll-Kelly started wearing that wig, you have been caused considerable public embarrassment?'

Denis is like, 'Yes.'

'And held up to ridicule?'

'Yes.'

'Which is why you're demanding that he remove it from his head and give assurances that it will remain removed from his head in perpetuity?'

'Yes.'

'No further questions.'

There's a break for lunch. We all head for the Chancery Inn. I order a pint of Amsterdamage while the old man goes into a huddle with Hennessy and his barrister to discuss their strategy for cross-examining Denis.

The old man is going, 'Those houses were not built on a floodplain. They were built on a thing called hydric soil. I want you to make that very clear in the afternoon.'

The old man's barrister goes, 'With respect, Charles, the houses aren't really the issue in this case.'

'*I'll* decide what is and isn't an issue! I want the court record amended to remove any reference to flooding. They are subject to seasonal saturation. Remind me again how much I'm paying you?'

Two grand per minute would be my guess.

Hennessy storts looking at his phone, checking his emails.

I stare at the old man over the top of my pint and I go, 'The dude is wiping the floor with you in there. It's hilarious seeing you get your final comeuppance.'

He's like, 'Don't you worry your head, Ross. There's a twist or two left in this case.'

'Hey, I'm not worried. I told you, I'm on *his* side. I just think back to the time Johnny Sexton went to Racing Metro. Sorcha will tell you. I wasn't eating. I was drinking like a rock star. I was wetting the . . . well, let's just say my mattress was subject to seasonal saturation.'

'We were all upset, Ross. Hennessy and I arranged a candlelit vigil outside the French embassy.'

'Yeah, a candlelit vigil – and what did that achieve?'

'It let the French know, in no uncertain terms, that they should keep their grasping hands off our bloody well players – especially Messrs Heaslip, Kearney and O'Brien.'

'Well, while you were doing that, Denis O'Brien was putting his money where his literally mouth was and coming up with a plan to bring the great man home. And we should be thanking him for that – as a people. I genuinely feel like grabbing that wig right now and focking it in the Liffey. And it wouldn't actually bother me if you were still attached to it at the time.'

'I know it's difficult for you to understand, Ross, but this case, well, it's about a very important principle.'

Hennessy looks up from his phone. 'Trouble,' he goes.

The old man's like, 'Trouble? What is it, old scout?'

'An email from the Department of Homeland Security.'

Yeah, no, Hennessy and the old man have submitted a tender to build a portion of Donald Trump's famous wall between Mexico and, like, the States?

'What,' the old man goes, 'don't they like our tender?'

Hennessy's there, 'The tender is fine. It seems that President Trump . . . doesn't like your hair.'

'Doesn't like my hair?'

'Says it reminds him of someone.'

Hennessy stares at him, waiting for the penny to drop. In the end, he has to help him get there.

He goes, 'A friend of Bill and Hillary?'

The old man finally cops it. He's like, 'No!'

Hennessy's there, 'Yes!'

And with that, the old man grabs the wig with his two hands, and, closing his eyes against the pain, rips it from his head and drops it onto the bor.

He's there, 'Go ahead, Kicker – throw it in the river,' and then he turns to his barrister and goes, 'Tell Denis we're happy to discuss a settlement.'

I'm like, 'What about that very important principle?'

And he goes, 'Like you said, Ross, he did give us Johnny Sexton back.'

'In ten years' time, Crumlin will be
what Terenure is today.'
*The Irish Times,* 29 April 2017

I hate people talking down the property bubble – especially this one, which I genuinely believe could last for six or seven years, as long as we all stop constantly asking questions.

Like this pair. The Dolans. They're interested in a three-bedroom gaff that's just come on the morket – 'a mature property in a vibrant area that presents an exciting opportunity to the DIY enthusiast' – but the wife is wondering whether €490,000 is a bit pricey for a semi-d in Crumlin.

I actually *laugh*?

'In ten years' time,' I go, 'Crumlin will be what Terenure is today,' even though I make a point of not saying what *that* actually is? Like I said, some things are best left unquestioned.

'It's not that we don't like the area,' the husband goes, 'and it's not that we don't like the house, even though it does need a lot of work.'

'You say work,' I go. 'I say exciting weekend projects.'

He's there, 'I wouldn't consider replumbing an entire house an exciting weekend project. But the real issue is the price. It just seems a bit on the high side compared to other properties in this area.'

You still get people like this. The couples – typically in their early forties – who remember the last crash and are convinced that there's some kind of lesson we should have all learned from it. Despite all the reports saying we're going back to where we were twelve or thirteen years ago, they're still nervous. They read the Residential Property Price Register and they quote it to you like it actually *means* something?

The dude goes, 'The last place we bought is in serious negative equity and we don't want to get stung again.'

And I go, 'Dude, can I tell you a story?'

The wife's like, 'As long as it doesn't involve cranes!'

I'm there, 'What?'

'Oh,' the husband goes, 'it's just a joke that we have. The estate agent we bought our last place from – back in '03 – told us that if we had any doubts about the health of the Irish economy, all we had to do was look at the skyline and count the cranes.'

Oh God, I thought I recognized them.

'He was a bit of an idiot,' he goes. 'He said his father had a boat in Dún Laoghaire harbour. Sometimes they went out on it to – he had this phrase – take the nation's economic pulse or something. The week he sold us our apartment he said he'd counted a hundred cranes.'

*She's* looking at me now with her eyes narrowed and her head tilted to the side. She's like, 'Was it you?'

I'm there, 'It doesn't sound like me.'

'It was Hook, Lyon and Sinker as well. I'm nearly sure it was you.'

This happens occasionally. You meet couples on their second lap of the track and they remember the bullshit you told them last time. It's called blowback and it's port and porcel of the game.

'No,' I go, 'I'm, er, new to the property business.'

She turns to the husband and she goes, 'It's him, Mark! Same grin on his face, same ridiculous voice . . .'

Ridiculous voice?

'Okay,' I go, 'I'll knock five Ks off, seeing as we're old friends. Let's just say €485,000.'

But it's no good. I've lost the Dolans. They're out through the front door like the house has just caught fire. Which it could do at any moment – the wiring is in a jocker as well as the plumbing.

I'm going to admit something to you now. I end up having an actual crisis of confidence when I go back to the cor. Which isn't like me at all. I sit there for, like, twenty minutes, wondering am I actually cut out for this game? I'm supposed to be going out on my own. I've been stealing client files from the Hook, Lyon and Sinker office for the past few weeks with a view to hopefully setting up my own estate agency. But the Dolans have me suddenly questioning whether the Celtic Phoenix is even an actual thing.

I'm supposed to be showing another couple – the Raymonds – the same gaff in an hour's time. But I stort thinking about not bothering my hole. I don't have the magic any more. It's left me.

But then, as always happens when I'm at my lowest ebb, I stort to think about Father Fehily, my old schools coach, whose wisdom helped make me the man I am today. I genuinely believe that he's looking down from Heaven on me because I always seem to remember the right quote at the right moment.

'So Plan A failed,' he used to say. 'There are still –' and I can't remember whether it was twenty-five or twenty-six more letters in the alphabet. But you wouldn't believe the strength I suddenly get from that.

Ten minutes later, I'm in the Tesco Express on St Agnes Road, buying salt, cheap table lamps, wholemeal flour, margarine, low wattage light bulbs, lemons, limes and yeast. I'm thinking, this is how we did it during the Celtic Tiger. I'm going old school.

I go back to the house and I scatter the lamps around the place with the poor visibility bulbs in them, then I switch off all the overhead lights.

To sell a house, you have to create the right mood.

I take a clear glass vase out of the boot of the cor, which Sorcha bought in House of Fraser and I was supposed to return two weeks ago. I fill it with lemons and limes and I put it in the middle of the kitchen table.

Then I take the salt, the wholemeal flour, the margarine and the yeast and I stort making bread. All estate agents know how to make bread. It's one of the first things they teach you. Twenty minutes later, the place smells like an actual bakery and the Raymonds are at the door.

I let them in. They're young. They haven't been hurt before. They don't know the tricks of the trade. I see *her* eyes focus on the lemons and limes and I can nearly hear her thinking, 'What a great idea!' and I can see both their noses twitching, wondering what's in the oven.

He goes, 'It's actually nicer than it looked in the photograph.'

And I know straight away that this pair are putty – or dough – in my hands.

## 'They're sitting on the track, linking orms and singing "Nearer, My God, to Thee".'
### *The Irish Times*, 10 December 2017

The old dear is dressed in black. The colour of mourning. And even the two kilos of seal blubber and orangutan sperm she has injected into her cheeks and forehead every fortnight by one of the country's leading plastic surgeons can't hide the sadness in her face.

She looks at me with her head tilted to one side and her eyelashes flapping like mad. The full Diana.

She goes, 'Thank you for coming, Ross.'

I'm there, 'Don't flatter yourself. I heard you talking to Sean O'Rourke the other day and I came to rip the piss.'

Today is the first day of the Luas Cross City Service, linking the Red and Green lines. And it's a sort last stand for Luas Women, the old dear's pressure group who've fought for five years to stop it from happening.

There's about two hundred and fifty of the most expensively dressed protesters you've ever seen in your life gathered at the bottom of Dawson Street, where the first Cross City Luas is due to pass in, what, two *minutes* from now?

They're sitting on the track, linking orms and singing 'Nearer, My God, to Thee', except they've changed the lyrics and instead they're going:

> *Never the twain shall meet,*
> *Nearer to Marlborough Street,*
> *Nearer to Jervis Street,*
> *Nearer to Thee.*

I recognize most of them. There's all of her mates from the golf club and The Gables – the Stoli Dollies, as I call them. And there's quite a few veterans from her previous campaigns, especially 'Move Funderland to the Northside' and 'Build an Enormous Fan to Blow the Flue Gas from the Poolbeg Incinerator Towards the Likes of Kilbarrack and Raheny'.

'What they're proposing to do,' she goes, 'is dangerous in the extreme. Linking Ranelagh to Tallaght? Milltown to Smithfield? Leopardstown to Fettercairn? It's messing around with the unknown, Ross.'

I'm there, 'What do you care? You drive everywhere. Or you get taxis when you're too drunk to find your cor keys.'

'In this world, Dorling, there are People Like Us and there are People Like Them. As your father says, this city has been planned in such a way as to ensure that we lead parallel and mutually exclusive lives. What they're about to do will have the effect of bringing us closer together. And no one can predict what that will mean – other than that our homes are sure to be burgled.'

She really is a despicable human being.

I'm there, 'Look, you and your mates fought tooth and claw – or, more specifically, veneer and manicured nail – to stop it from happening. You have to accept that you failed.'

She goes, 'We haven't failed, Ross. Not until the very first Luas passes down this street. And we are still determined that it will not happen.'

> *Nearer to Phibsborough,*
> *Nearer to Drim-anagh,*
> *Nearer to Cab-ara,*
> *Nearer to Thee.*

There's some lovely voices in the crowd. There's obviously a fair few Protestants here and one thing you'd have to say about Protestants is that they know how to hold a note. It actually brings me back to my rugby days. Whenever you played the likes of Columba's, or Andrew's, or even Wesley, in the early rounds of Leinster Schools Senior Cup, you'd nearly be tempted to stop scoring try after try against them and instead just enjoy the close hormony singing of their supporters.

'Hang on,' I suddenly go, 'are you saying that when the first Luas comes around that corner, then down this street, all these people are going to stay sitting here?'

The old dear's there, 'Of course they are! It's like I told Sean O'Rourke, it's not a rail extension they should be building, it's a security wall! Twelve feet high and topped with broken glass!'

'But you'll all be killed.'

'We won't be killed, Ross. The tram will be forced to stop.'

'Do you know how long it takes for those things to brake? Have you never heard the warnings on the radio?'

'This is a test of our strength of will and purpose! *Those who resolve to conquer or die are rarely conquered!* Who said that? It was someone.'

I'm looking around at all these people putting their lives quite *literally* on the line? And that's when I see the Luas hurtling down Dawson Street towards them.

The old dear walks among them, shouting, 'Strength, everyone! Courage! Unity!'

*Nearer to Fortunestown . . .*

The thing is, like, thirty feet in front of them. The driver storts furiously ringing the bell, but everyone stays sitting.

*Nearer to Cheeverston . . .*

'Fortitude!' the old dear shouts. 'Fellowship! Valour!'

DING! DING! DING! DING! DING!

The driver is basically screaming at them to get out of the way.

I'm thinking, Jesus, if this lot are killed, Donnybrook Fair may as well just drop the shutters.

It's suddenly, like, twenty feet in front of them and it's obvious that it's not going to stop.

It's, like, ten feet in front of them now.

'That's it!' the old dear shouts. 'Let's show them what People Like Us are made of!'

DING! DING! DING! DING! DING! DING!

And then, at the very last second, they all roll clear.

*Nearer to Thee.*

Then, still lying on the ground, they turn and watch the Luas disappear onto Nassau Street, towards Westmoreland Street and into the great unknown.

# 2018

Ireland votes by an unexpectedly wide margin of 67 per cent to 33 per cent to repeal the Eighth Amendment of the Constitution, paving the way to the legalization of abortion in Ireland * Ireland beat England 24–15 to win the Grand Slam and the Six Nations Championship * Michael D. Higgins is re-elected as President of Ireland, winning more than twice as many votes as his nearest challenger, populist candidate Peter Casey * The wedding of Britain's Prince Harry to actress Meghan Markle is watched by a worldwide TV audience of almost two billion * United States President Donald Trump meets North Korean leader Kim Jong-un in Singapore, the first ever summit between leaders of the two countries * The state passes legislation to permit the sale of alcohol on Good Friday for the first time in more than ninety years * On a visit to Dublin, Brexit supporter Nigel Farage says there is a gap in the market for a political party that would push for Ireland to leave the European Union * People across Ireland are warned not to leave their homes as the so-called Beast from the East brings high winds and heavy snowfall from Siberia * Leinster beat French side Racing 92 by 15–12 to win their fourth European Cup * Ryanair Chief Executive Michael O'Leary becomes Ireland's latest billionaire * Pope Francis makes the first papal visit to Ireland for almost forty years. However, the crowds that turn out to see him are just a fraction of those that saw Pope John Paul II's visit in 1979 * Up to 10,000 people take part in a protest in Dublin in relation to the ongoing Housing Crisis * Former Chief Executive of Anglo Irish Bank, David Drumm, is jailed for six years after being found guilty of conspiracy to defraud and false accounting * A two-month hosepipe ban is introduced as Ireland experiences a summer heatwave * Leinster stand-in flyhalf Joey Carbery signs for Munster * Donnybrook Fair is bought by SuperValu owners, the Musgrave Group * The Ireland women's hockey team enjoy a fairytale run to the final of the World Cup, where they eventually lose to the Netherlands * More than 700,000 people march through London demanding a second Brexit referendum * Ireland beat New

Zealand 16–9 to record their first ever win against the All Blacks on home soil * Kielys of Donnybrook, Ross O'Carroll-Kelly's favourite watering hole and home-from-home, closes its doors in what Ross describes as 'South Dublin's Diana moment'.

Meanwhile . . .

'I swear to fock, she goes, "What's Dricmas?"'
*The Irish Times, 20 January 2018*

Lauren – the new Managing Director of Hook, Lyon and Sinker – wants a word with me. And, while I have no issue taking orders from a woman boss – absolutely none whatsoever – I make sure to wait a good five minutes before sticking my head around the door of her office and asking her what she wants.

She's there, 'Why are you sending around memos telling people that the office will be closed on Monday?'

'Yeah, no,' I go, stepping into the room, 'it was just a reminder that it's Dricmas on Sunday. And when Dricmas falls on a weekend, people are entitled to the Monday off.'

I swear to fock, she goes, 'What's Dricmas?'

I look around me, suddenly suspecting that this is one of those hidden camera shows.

I'm like, 'Dricmas is Brian O'Driscoll's birthday, Lauren.'

She goes, 'And why should people be entitled to a day off for Brian O'Driscoll's birthday?'

'Is that a serious question?'

'Do I sound serious to you?'

'You actually do. That's why I'm wondering is this some kind of set-up? Is *Naked Camera* back on the TV or something?'

'I've been told you threatened one member of staff with the sack last year when you found out she did some work from home.'

'It's one day of the year, Lauren.'

'She has no interest in rugby.'

'Who interviewed her for the job, then? That's what I want to know.'

'This has been going on for years, has it? No work on the twenty-first of January.'

'Brian O'Driscoll did things for this country. I don't think it's too much to ask people to set aside one day of the year to reflect on that.'

'What do you mean by reflect on it?'

'Hey, people mork the day in different ways. I sit down and watch my Grand Slam and Heineken Cup final DVDs. I know Oisinn and JP usually drive from supermorket to supermorket, moving all the tomatoes from the vegetable section to the fruit section. I've gone with them once or twice. It's a lot of fun.'

She looks down at her desk and goes, 'What's Rogmas?'

I'm like, 'Rogmas? Have you got my work diary there or something?'

'All work diaries are the property of Hook, Lyon and Sinker. I asked you a question, Ross. What's Rogmas?'

'Rogmas is obviously Ronan O'Gara's birthday. The seventh of Morch – the day he entered this world.'

'So he's another rugby player?'

'I can't believe you're asking me that. Your husband won a Leinster Schools Senior Cup medal because of me. I'm thinking of phoning him, by the way. I don't think you're well.'

She storts turning pages in my diary then. She's like, 'The twentieth of October?'

I'm there, 'What about it?'

'It's Pocmas, according to this.'

'Yeah, no, that's Paul O'Connell's birthday. One of my all-time heroes.'

'Another day the office is closed?'

'I might as well warn you, Lauren, there's Sexmas as well. The eleventh of July. And if you tell me you've never heard of Johnny Sexton, I'm calling an ambulance for you.'

'You have all of those marked down as Bank Holidays.'

'Yes.'

'Then you have all these other dates marked down as Holy Days of Obligation.'

'Correct.'

'The eighteenth of July.'

'Shane Horgan's birthday.'

'The twentieth of April.'

'Conor Murray's birthday.'

'The ninth of January.'

'The Big Man. Leo Cullen. I was thinking of upgrading that one to an actual Bank Holiday.'

'The twenty-sixth of March.'

'Rob Kearney.'

'The seventh of October.'

'The legend that is Cian Healy.'

'The fifteenth of December.'

'Jamie Heaslip.'

'The twenty-sixth of January.'

'Garry Ringrose. I call that Little Dricmas.'

'And these are compulsory days off as well, are they?'

'No, they're what I call Days of Religious Observance. People can have one or two pints at lunchtime if they want and I always turn a blind eye if they don't come back to work in the afternoon. I'm usually too shit-faced to notice anyway.'

She slams my diary shut.

'Well, not any more,' she goes.

I'm like, 'Excuse me?'

'Things are changing around here. I'm in charge now, Ross, and I'm telling you that this is all coming to an end.'

'You don't mean that.'

'I do mean it. This is a business I'm running. In case you haven't noticed, we're in the middle of another property boom. I'm not paying people to take off Bank Holidays that you invented.'

'I didn't invent them, Lauren. They're days on which very important people happened to be born.'

'Well, in future, if people want them off, they can take them at their own expense.'

I actually laugh.

'Lauren,' I go, 'if you tell those people out there that they have to work on Brian O'Driscoll's birthday, or on Johnny Sexton's birthday, or Ronan O'Gara's birthday, you are going to have a full-scale mutiny on your hands.'

She's there, 'I doubt that, Ross.'

'Okay, let's put it to the test, will we?'

'What are you doing?'

'Come on, let's make the announcement to the staff – see how it goes down when they find out that you're the Grinch Who Stole Dricmas.'

I walk out and I stand in the middle of the open-plan office. Lauren is standing behind me.

'Little announcement,' I go.

She's like, 'Ross, you're being childish.'

'Lauren here, as the new Managing Director of Hook, Lyon and

Sinker, has decided to cancel *all* your Rugby Bank Holidays – I think it's a word – *forthwith*? Not only Dricmas, but Rogmas, Pocmas and Sexmas as well.'

Graham – one of the best estate agents we have – goes, 'Thank God for that!' and this sets off a round of nodding and smiles of relief amongst all the other staff.

I'm there, 'Say that again.'

He goes, 'Most of us are on commission, Ross. If we don't work, we don't get paid. I'm not even that interested in rugby.'

'That's not what it said on your CV.'

'Well, it's a fact. All those days off. Then all those afternoons – I mean, it's someone's birthday at least once a fortnight – when you come back from The Bridge, stinking of drink and asking us what we're all still doing in the office?'

I can't believe what I'm hearing.

I'm like, 'Okay, it's three o'clock on a Friday afternoon. It's the day before Dricmas Eve. Who's coming to the pub with me?'

And literally no one moves.

### 'Young people these days – they have necks like Barry Geraghty's undercrackers.'
#### *The Irish Times*, 27 January 2018

So it's, like, Saturday morning and I'm strolling down Grafton Street with Honor when I notice – right in our path – a woman taking a photograph of her kids in front of the Disney Store. Of course, the polite thing to do in this case is to stop walking and wait until they've got the shot, then roll your eyes and continue about your day. *Or* just walk around them – yeah, no, that's the other option.

Except Honor does neither.

She walks *between* them – at the exact moment when the mother is pressing the button. The woman's like, 'Oh, for heaven's sakes!' and Honor – I swear to God – turns around to her and goes, 'What's *your* problem? Aport from the fact that you dress about twenty years too young for your age?'

I laugh – no choice in the matter.

The woman goes, 'You saw that I was taking a photograph and you deliberately walked into the shot.'

Honor's there, 'Sorry, what am I, a focking extra in the movie of your life or something?' then she carries on walking.

I just give the woman a shrug, as if to say, 'Hey – welcome to big school!'

Five minutes later, we're standing at an ATM at the bottom of Grafton Street and I'm like, 'I hope you don't mind me saying this, Honor, but I really admire the way you handled that situation.'

She goes, 'Excuse me?'

'People with their phones, making you feel like a nuisance just for walking down the street. I'm sick of it . . . Hey, Honor, look!'

The reason I tell her to look is that I spot a girl walking past carrying a snooker cue case, which almost certainly doesn't contain a snooker cue, but which in fact she's using as a handbag. It's a new fashion – I suppose – *trend* that Honor storted on her fashion vlog, as an experiment to see how many gullible people there are out there. Quite a few seems to be the answer. That's the fifteenth snooker cue case I've seen in Dublin since Christmas and there's a rumour that Saoirse Ronan is considering taking one to the Oscars.

I put my cord in the ATM and – I swear to God – I hear the dude in the queue behind us tut to himself. I have to say, I absolutely *hate* people who do that in queues – even though I always do it myself.

I'm keying in my PIN when Honor all of a sudden turns around to the dude and goes, 'What are you focking tutting for?'

The dude's there, 'Excuse me?' obviously not used to being called out – especially by a twelve-year-old girl.

'You keep tutting,' Honor goes. 'And it's focking annoying.'

The dude's like, 'It's just I'm waiting to use the ATM here – and you two are having a grand old chat.'

'So go and find another ATM.'

'No, I want to use this one.'

Honor suddenly takes my wallet out of my hand and goes, 'My dad has fourteen bank cords in here. Do you know what I'm going to do if you stay standing there? I'm going to use them, one by one, to withdraw ten euros each time. Then I'll do it again and again and again.'

The dude takes the hint and walks off, shaking his head.

Honor looks at me and goes, 'Tutting. *So* irritating.'

I just give her a little round of applause. I'm there, 'That's what I would call Vintage Honor! I just love the way you refuse to take S, H, one, T from people.'

Anyway, an hour later, we're back home. Honor troops upstairs to her room to record herself – *her* words – 'unboxing her purchases', while Sorcha tells me she wants a quick word with me in the kitchen.

She goes, 'Have you noticed anything different about Honor in the last few days?'

I'm there, 'It's funny you should mention that, Sorcha, but no. As a matter of fact, I was just patting myself on the back for the way I raised her to be just like me in terms of not taking bullshit from people.'

'You don't think she's been moody and irritable lately?'

'Honor came out of the womb moody and irritable, Sorcha.'

'But I think she's been getting worse. At first, I thought it was, well, you know – the obvious.'

'Okay, help me out here?'

'Hormones, Ross. She's going to be a teenager soon.'

'Well, I'm actually loving her at this age. She's horrible to everyone and not just us.'

'I've been a bit concerned about it, Ross. So I checked her Facebook page and her Twitter feed.'

'And?'

'Well, you know she's been talking about going to England next month for London Fashion Week?'

'No – but continue.'

'She's been writing to hotels over there, saying, you know, she was considering staying with them and what could they do in terms of offering her a complimentary room in return for a mention on her vlog, which has however many million followers.'

I just laugh.

I'm there, 'Young people these days – they have necks like Barry Geraghty's undercrackers. I'm saying that as a compliment to them.'

'Anyway, Ross, the manager of this hotel in Covent Gorden responded by saying no, she couldn't have a complimentary room, then he called her a freeloader who didn't want to work for anything.'

'We're from South Dublin, Sorcha – none of us wants to work for anything. I mean, that's the dream, isn't it?'

'He said she was everything that was wrong with young people today. And then, Ross – this is, like, the *worst* bit? – he posted *her* letter and *his* response on social media. They've gone, like, *viral*?'

All of a sudden, the kitchen door opens and in she walks. She doesn't say anything, just goes to the fridge and takes out a Diet Coke.

Sorcha goes, 'Honor, I just want you to know that we're aware of what's happened and that, as your parents, we –'

Honor's there, 'Are you talking about the manager of that hotel in Covent Gorden?'

Sorcha's like, 'What he said was *so* mean, Honor. But we don't want you to think that the entire world is full of dream-stealers like him.'

'Oh, don't worry,' Honor goes, in a tone of voice that gives me literally chills. 'I'll fix him.'


## 'It looks like one of those cones that dogs have to wear to stop them licking their bits, post-op.'
### *The Irish Times, 3 February 2018*

It's the day before Sixmas and I'm sitting up in bed with my famous Rugby Tactics Book open in front of me, mulling over one or two last-minute selection dilemmas for my fantasy Ireland team to face France tomorrow. I'm also flicking back through the pages of the book, thinking, 'I can't believe that Joe Schmidt isn't beating down my door to get his hands on this thing. I genuinely can't.'

That's when Sorcha steps into the room. I don't immediately look up. That's how focused I am on the job in hand.

'I've just realized that all fifteen of the players I've picked are from Leinster. I know people are going to accuse me of an anti-Munster bias, but I'm going with my gut here.'

I hear Sorcha go, 'What do you think, Ross?' and that's when I look up – and immediately laugh. On her head, she's wearing – I'm not making this up – one of those bonnets that Elisabeth Moss wears in *The Handmaid's Tale*. 'Does it suit me?'

I'm there, 'It looks like one of those cones that dogs have to wear to stop them licking their bits, post-op.'

'Honor's done an – oh my God – amazing vlog on how to get the June Osbourne slash Offred look without breaking the actual bank!'

Sorcha – in common with hundreds of thousands of others – hasn't figured out yet that Honor is using her YouTube channel to test the bounds of women's gullibility.

'Hang on,' I go, 'is that the light shade from the utility room?'

She's like, 'Yes, Ross, it's the light shade from the utility room. I told you, we're getting downlights in there eventually.'

'Are you *actually* going to go out like that?'

'Ross, *everyone* is wearing these! You've no idea what a powerful influencer your daughter has become.'

As she's saying it, there's a ring on the door.

'If that's Joe Schmidt, looking for this book,' I go, 'tell him to fock off,' but even as the words are coming out of my mouth, I'm thinking, Who am I kidding? If he asked me for it, it'd be his – there wouldn't even be a conversation.

Sorcha wanders over to the window and looks out. 'Oh my God,' she goes, 'it's the Gords.'

Now, having grown up as the son of one of Ireland's leading crooks, I'm not exactly *unaccustomed* to hearing those words? As a matter of fact, I'm suddenly listening to myself go, 'Turn on the shredder! I'll hand you pages and you feed them in!'

Sorcha's like, 'Ross, we don't have a shredder.'

And I'm there, 'Sorry, Babes, I still get flashbacks. Okay, I'll go and answer it.'

I tip downstairs and I open the door. The dude says his name is Detective Something or Other. He's basically CSI Ballycumber. I invite him in.

'If it's about my old man,' I go, 'I'm happy to implicate him in anything. Put a piece of paper in front of me and I'll sign it.'

He's like, 'I'm not here about your father. It's about your daughter.'

'Honor?' Sorcha goes, tipping down the stairs, sounding suddenly concerned. 'Is she okay?'

He's there, 'Do you ever inquire as to what she gets up to online?'

I'm there, 'Never. Mainly because I've always half expected a knock on the door from you goys one day. I'm proud to say – and I could swear this on a stack of Bibles – that I have no idea what my daughter does on the Internet.'

He goes, 'Then I think you'd better look at the video she posted three days ago.'

Which is what we end *up* doing? Sorcha gets the thing up on her laptop while I flick on the Nespresso machine and make myself a Clooneycino.

'That's the video there,' he goes.

And Sorcha's like, 'This is the one she put up in response to that awful, awful man who wouldn't give her a free room in that hotel in Covent Gorden. I've already watched it. I thought she was *so* brave.'

'Watch it again,' he goes.

The kitchen is suddenly filled with the sound of my daughter's voice – laying it on thick. 'As a girl,' she goes, 'I felt actually *triggered* when this person said these awful things about me online? But then I just thought, Oh my God, why would I want to stay in his stupid hotel? So he embarrassed me. Burn! It doesn't matter. Down deep in my heart, I know I'm a good person.'

Well, that's a definite exaggeration, I think.

'Did you hear that?' the dude goes.

Sorcha's like, 'What, the sound of my daughter deciding to take the high road and just live her best life?'

'The first word of each of the last three sentences she said. Listen to it again.'

He puts on the last ten seconds.

We hear Honor go, '*Burn! It* doesn't matter. *Down* deep in my heart, I know I'm a good person.'

Sorcha laughs like it's the most ridiculous thing she's ever heard. She's like, 'Come on, that's a serious stretch.'

'Burn! It! Down,' he goes.

'That's, like, a total coincidence.'

'There's no doubt she puts an inflection on those three words.'

I ask the question that *you're* probably wondering. I'm like, 'What's an inflection?'

Sorcha goes, 'Essentially, Ross, this man is suggesting that our daughter is sending out subliminal messages to her followers, urging them to avenge her honour by doing who *knows* what?'

She says it in a way that tries to make it sound ridiculous.

The dude's there, 'We had a call from our friends across the water. There's a woman in London – she found her daughter siphoning petrol out of the lawnmower. When she asked what she was doing, she said a girl on the Internet told her to do it.'

Sorcha, being your typical South Dublin mom, decides to defend her daughter against all the weight of evidence. She goes, 'How *dare* you come to my house making allegations like this? My dad is a solicitor.'

Which is true. Family Law and Small Claims.

The dude goes, 'You really should monitor your daughter's Internet use more closely.'

I'm thinking, there's not a chance – especially after finding this out.

When he's gone, Sorcha is still furious. She goes, 'How could any-one believe that a twelve-year-old girl could be that powerful?'

And I'm there, 'Your lampshade is crooked there, Sorcha.'

## 'I've joined this WhatsApp group that some of the moms set up.'
### The Irish Times, 29 September 2018

So – yeah, no – I'm walking down Anglesea Road on the way to watch Leinster against Edinburgh at the old D4tress when my *phone* all of a sudden beeps?

I whip it out of my pocket and it ends up being a message from Mallorie Kennedy, the mother of Honor's classmate, Courage Kennedy, asking if anyone knows a good – I've never even *seen* this word before – but immunodermatologist?

'Who's that?' JP goes.

I'm there, 'It's actually one of the Mount Anville moms,' and JP laughs in a real, I don't know, *knowing* way.

I'm like, 'Dude, it's nothing like that,' which it genuinely isn't for once. Since Sorcha went to work for LinkedIn, I've taken over a lot of her old jobs, including the school run and everything that involves. 'I've joined this WhatsApp group that some of the moms set up.'

'You did *what*?' Oisinn goes, sounding instantly worried about me.

I'm there, 'It's just to talk about school stuff mostly. Hockey. The musical society. They're doing *Goys and Dolls* this year.'

That's when my phone beeps again. It's Rebecca Leahy, Diva Leahy's old dear. She says no, she doesn't know a good immunodermatologist.

I'm like, 'Why does she have to do that? If she doesn't know a good – whatever that word is – why doesn't she just, like, not answer?'

Oisinn laughs. He goes, 'Dude, I know a lot of parents who've got suckered into joining those groups and they took over their lives.'

I'm there, 'I wouldn't say it's taken over my –'

But my phone beeps again. It's Grainne Power, Conwenna Power's old dear. She says she doesn't know a good immunodermatologist either. And, as I'm reading that one, Rachel Lynch, Eponine Lynch's old dear, says she thinks she left her sunnies in the Merrion Tree Bistro when we were having coffee the other day and did any of us notice them?

Into the stadium we go. We find our seats while my phone is still beeping like mad in my hand. Alva Crowe, Ginny Crowe's old dear, says she didn't see Rachel's sunnies. Then Grainne Lessing, Hester Lessing's old dear, says she's didn't see the sunnies either. Then Amanda Mangan, Tess Mangan's old dear, says she knew an ah! mazing! immunoderma-tologist but he retired three years ago and he might even be dead.

Helen Hall, Thia Hall's old dear, says she didn't see the sunnies. Cho Hye-ji, Jang Hye-ji's old dear, says she didn't see the sunnies but she really hopes she finds them. Then Orlaith Stapleton, Liesel Stapleton's old dear, says Liesel forgot to bring her biology book home from school and would someone in the group mind photographing the pages from the chapter on Photosynthesis and Plant Response?

It all goes very quiet then. I stick my phone in my pocket, then I look up and I realize that I've missed the first ten minutes of the match. I ask the goys what score it is and they say it's still nil–nil and I'm about to ask–how Jordan Larmour is playing when it all of a sudden storts again. My phone is hopping around in my pocket like a focking ferret on E.

I whip it out – my phone obviously. Cho Hye-ji has sent the twenty-three pages from the chapter on Photosynthesis and Plant Response. Alva Crowe has sent the twenty-three pages from the chapter on Photosynthesis and Plant Response. Helen Hall says she's in a gor-geous restaurant in Ranelagh that's owned by the sister of a woman she knows who's thinking of setting up a SoulCycle in Blackrock – and she'll send the twenty-three pages from the chapter on Photosynthesis and Plant Response when she gets home tonight.

I hear a humungous roar and I look up. I've managed to miss Fergus McFadden's try. I turn to JP and I'm there, 'What was it like?' and he goes, 'Incredible. Big Dev did all the work.'

I watch Johnny add the cheese and crackers, then my phone beeps again.

Sally-Ann Markey, Rioghnach Markey's old dear, wants to know what kind of sunnies they were. Orlaith Stapleton says thank you to Cho Hye-ji for sending the twenty-three pages from the chapter on Photosynthesis and Plant Response. Rachel Lynch says her sunnies were Céline Wayfarers. Rioghnach says, 'OMG! Want!'

Helen Hall says what's an immunodermatologist? Vanessa Mitch-ell, Treasa Mitchell's old dear, says she didn't see the sunnies. Mallorie Kennedy says an immunodermatologitst is a dermatologist who treats skin disorders caused by defective responses of the body's immune system. Helen Hall says, in that case, she doesn't know a good immunodermatologist.

Orlaith Stapleton says thank you to Alva Crowe for sending the twenty-three pages from the chapter on Photosynthesis and Plant Response. Vanessa Mitchell says she read somewhere that the new head of Céline has decided to drop the accent from the name and now it's just going to be Celine. Ferne Brannigan, Molly Brannigan's old dear, says she doesn't know a good immunodermatologist.

Alva Crowe says she's really sad to hear that about Céline and she hopes that Donnybrook Fair won't change now that it's been taken over by – I hope this doesn't sound racist – but people from Cork. Ferne Brannigan, Sally-Ann Markey and Mallorie Kennedy say some things about Cork and its people that would be unpublishable in a newspaper like this. Vanessa Mitchell says her mother is from Cork. Sally-Ann Markey says she didn't mean any offence. Mallorie Kennedy says she didn't mean any offence. Vanessa Mitchell says it's fine – her mother always kept it quiet anyway.

Orlaith Stapleton says she never saw the sunnies. Ferne Brannigan says she's delighted to hear that about SoulCycle because it's the kind of thing that Blackrock is crying out for. Amanda Mangan says Tess left her music book in her locker at school and does anyone have the sheet music for 'A Bushel and a Peck'? Helen Hall sends the sheet music for 'A Bushel and a Peck'. Sally-Ann Markey sends the sheet music for 'A Bushel and a Peck'. Amanda Mangan says sorry, she actually meant to say 'Take Back Your Mink'. Rebecca Leahy sends the sheet music to 'A Bushel and a Peck'. Rachel Lynch says she found her sunnies – they were on her head all the time.

JP nudges me. He goes, 'Are you okay?'

I'm like, 'I had no idea how difficult being a Mount Anville mom was going to be.'

'Let's get a pint,' he goes, 'it's half-time.'


## 'What, so you can never walk down Grafton Street again?'
### *The Irish Times, 6 October 2018*

Sorcha has decided she needs an entire new work wardrobe, so into town we go. I throw the cor into the Stephen's Green Shopping Centre cor pork, then down the escalators we come: me at the front, holding the triplets on their lead, while they bork and snorl like feral dogs; Sorcha two steps behind me, apologizing to the other shoppers for our children's language; then Honor, seven or eight steps further back, texting on her phone.

When we reach the ground floor, I stort heading in the direction of the main entrance, but Sorcha wants to go out the back door. I'm like, 'Er, that makes *no* sense? We're going to BTs. It's through the front door and straight down Grafton Street.'

She goes, 'I don't want to walk past Benetton, Ross.'

'Why not?'

'There's a girl who works in there who I was in UCD with and whenever I meet her it's just, like, weird.'

'Weird in what way?'

'Yeah, no, we're really good friends on Instagram – as in, she always gives me Likes for photos I put up, and vice-versa – but whenever we *actually* meet, we never know what to say to each other. It's, like, *so* awkward.'

'What,' I go, 'so you're going to spend the rest of your life never walking past Benetton in case she sees you?'

'Don't be ridiculous, Ross. I check her LinkedIn page every two or three days to see has she moved jobs yet.'

'How long has this been going on?'

'Three and a half years. Ross, can we just go out the back door without you making a major deal out of it?'

I tell her fine – whatever. Then out the back door we go onto South King Street.

'I don't know why you're pulling that face,' Sorcha goes, as the boys drag me – swearing like dockworkers – towards the top of Grafton Street. 'The walk is exactly the same length whether we go through the shopping centre or *not*?'

And that's when I suddenly stop walking.

'I've just remembered,' I go, 'we can't walk past the Disney Store.'

Sorcha's like, 'Why not?'

'Er, because the last time we were in there, the triplets smashed an eight-foot-high Chewbacca into about a million pieces and I left without paying for the damage.'

'You did what?'

'Hey, my old man says that rich people not paying for the things they broke is the rock on which the Celtic Phoenix was built.'

'What, so you can never walk down Grafton Street again?'

'Of course I can. I just have to avoid that little section of it.'

I whip out my phone and I call up Google maps. We stand in the doorway of Zara and we stort plotting a route to BTs that bypasses the top of Grafton Street.

'I've got it,' I go. 'We can head straight down South William Street as far as Wicklow Street and come at BTs from the other direction.'

But, straight away, Sorcha sees a problem. She goes, 'I can't walk that far down South William Street. I don't want to pass Brown Sugar.'

I'm like, 'The reason being?'

'Because I went somewhere else to get my hair done this month. I didn't have time to come into town. And if my regular hairdresser sees me, she'll notice that I have no root growth and she'll *know* I went somewhere else?'

'Okay,' I go, looking at the map again – and it suddenly brings me back to my rugby days when I used to have to think strategically to find a way through opposition defences.

I'm tempted to say, once a ten, always a ten!

'Okay,' I go, 'we can take Clarendon Street, then cut down Chatham –'

Honor decides to pipe up then. 'I can't walk down Chatham Street,' she goes. 'They've been holding a necklace for me in Loulerie since June and they keep ringing me every week to check that I definitely still want it.'

'Okay,' I go, 'why don't we take Chatham Row onto Clarendon Street, then cut through the Westbury –'

'I want to avoid the whole Westbury Mall area,' Sorcha goes. 'I tried to return a pair of burgundy gloves to Paula Rowan about six months ago because they turned out to be a different shade of burgundy to my burgundy coat. But they refused to take them because they could tell I'd worn them a few times. Ross, I'd be too embarrassed to see them again.'

I'm thinking, Okay, what would Johnny Sexton do? He'd find a way through in, like, five seconds.

I'm there, 'Why don't we take Drury Street, as far as Castlemorket Street, then hit Coppinger –'

Sorcha goes, 'We can't go near Coppinger Row because Honor was mean to that girl who did her Vinylux nails in Fifth Avenue. She made her cry, Ross.'

'Then we'll take Drury Street all the way to Wicklow –'

'We can't take Wicklow Street. Have you forgotten the incident with the boys in Murphy's Ice Cream?'

'We could avoid Murphy's by turning onto Andrew Street, then taking Suffolk –'

'I can't go near Suffolk Street. I ordered a picnic hamper from Avoca during the summer and I never paid for it or collected it. Okay, can *I* suggest a route?'

'Hey,' I go, 'I was the one who played out-half, but go on.'

She's there, 'It's kind of a long way around, but we could take Stephen Street as far as George's Street, then walk to the bottom of George's Street, turn right onto Dame Street, then go through College Green and right onto Grafton Street. Oh, hang on, I can't pass Weir's.'

'Er, why?'

'I was asked to leave because the boys were spitting on the display glass. It was so embarrassing, I honestly couldn't face them. Okay, instead of coming at Grafton Street from that end, we'll keep going along Nassau Street, then turn right onto Dawson Street, then turn right again onto Duke –'

'I can't go near Duke Street,' I go. 'There's a girl who works in The Bailey. And, before you say anything, Sorcha, me and you were on a break at the time.'

Honor looks up from her phone then. 'I've got the perfect solution,' she goes.

I'm like, 'Let's hear it, Honor.'

She's there, 'Let's all just go home.'

Me and Sorcha exchange a look. And in that moment, we both know that it's the best plan anyone is going to come up with today.

'The thing to always bear in mind about men is that there's a hell of a lot less to us than meets the eye.'
*The Irish Times*, 13 October 2018

I get the coffees in. We're talking a one-shot macchiato with regular milk, a two-shot macchiato with coconut milk, four skinny cappuccinos, one soy latte, one ristretto with almond milk and one flat white. Yeah, no, I'm in Cinnamon in Ranelagh with, I can't believe I'm even saying this, but The Girls – and, it has to be said, we're getting along like doughnuts and Blanchardstown.

'I was thinking of getting Invisalign braces,' Grainne Lessing – as in, Hester Lessing's old dear – goes, 'because, oh my God, I *hate* my teeth!'

I'm just like, 'Yeah, you're the last person in the world who needs those things.'

'What do you mean?'

'Er, you look like Rachel McAdams when you smile. And that's not me coming onto you. I thought it the first time I saw you.'

She's delighted. She flashes her upper and lower sets at me. I've got a genuine way with people.

I'm there, 'You should maybe get them bleached – but that's about it. Did you not see those two builders checking you out as we were coming in? Here, there's your coffee – better latte than never!'

All the other Mount Anville moms laugh like it's the funniest line they've ever heard. Sorcha always rolls her eyes when I say it, but they're all going, 'Did you hear what he said? Better latte than never!' quoting me back to each other, then going, '*So*, so clever.'

I get a text from Oisinn. I forgot I'm supposed to be playing golf with him in Milltown today and he's waiting for me in the clubhouse. I decide to just ignore it.

Rachel Lynch – as in, Eponine Lynch's old dear – goes, 'Okay, Ross, I want to get a male perspective on something. So we're, like, having a porty to celebrate my mom and dad's fortieth wedding anniversary and I'm having a hord time choosing the right tablecloths for it. I can't decide between baby powder white and cornsilk. When I asked Trev, my husband, for an opinion, he said he didn't mind either way.'

I'm there, 'And what port of that are you not understanding?'

'Well, which do you think he's leaning more towards? At first, I thought it was cornsilk. But then, from the *way* he said he didn't mind, I was thinking maybe his hort is set on Orctic snow and he doesn't want to hurt my feelings by saying it.'

'Look, Rachel, when Trev says he doesn't mind, what he means is that he *genuinely* doesn't give a shit. Was he watching something on TV when this conversation took place?'

'*The Walking Dead.*'

'See, the thing to always bear in mind about men is that there's a hell of a lot less to us than meets the eye.'

Orlaith Stapleton – as in Liesel Stapleton's old dear – goes, 'That's amazing!'

And I'm like, 'No, I'll tell you what's amazing – those pumpkin cinnamon cookies you made for me the last day!'

'You liked them?'

'Liked them?' I go, drumming my hands off my belly. 'I horsed the lot in the cor on the way home!'

She's like, 'Oh my God, I can't believe you liked my cookies! I'll make more!'

'Yeah, no, definitely do.'

My phone all of a sudden rings. I just presume it's Oisinn and I end up answering it without even looking at the screen. I'm like, 'Dude, go ahead without me. I'm out with The Girls.'

But it ends up not being Oisinn at all. It ends up being Sorcha.

'The Girls?' she goes.

I decide to step away from them to have the conversation.

I'm like, 'Er, hey, Sorcha. Yeah, no, I'm talking about some of the moms in the Mount Anville WhatsApp group.'

She goes, 'You're having coffee with them?'

'Yeah, no, they do it every Tuesday and Thursday and they sometimes drag me along. I'm trying to work out if you sound jealous.'

'Oh, I'm not jealous, Ross. Have you used your "better latte than never" joke on them?'

'No.'

'Because it's not as funny as you think it is. I'm just letting you know.'

'Well, *they* all laughed.'

'They're probably just patronizing you. You're still a novelty to them.'

'Is there a reason for this call, Sorcha? Because they're really helping to build my confidence up and you're knocking it down again.'

'I'm ringing to ask, have you checked your daughter's laptop lately?'

'You know my attitude, Sorcha. What Honor does on the Internet is her own business. You heard what Hennessy said, the less we know, the fewer lies we'll have to tell when the Gords inevitably call to the door again.'

'She's set up a website –'

'Sorcha, if you try to explain it to me, I'm just going to put my hands over my ears and shout, Bah, bah, bah, bah, bah . . . over the sound of your voice.'

All of a sudden, Grainne Lessing shouts over to me, 'Ross, I think I'm going to do a muffin – do you want one?'

I'm there, 'Yeah, no, banana and chocolate chip, thanks, Grainne.'

Sorcha goes, 'Is that Grainne Lessing – with the crooked teeth?'

I'm like, 'Personally, I just think they need to be whitened.'

'Oh, *she* would definitely be interested in this new website that your daughter has set up.'

'Seriously, I don't want to know.'

'It's a review site, Ross – called Rate My Playdate.'

'Excuse me?'

'It invites young people to post anonymous reviews about other young people they've been on playdates with. Have a listen to this: *Hester Lessing pretends to be a nice person but she's actually a two-faced cow. And she's totally self-obsessed – like her mother.*'

I look across at Grainne. She's going, 'Ross, they don't have banana and chocolate chip! Do you want Nutella and orange instead?'

I just nod sadly, then, under my breath, I go, 'Poor Grainne.'

Sorcha's there, 'There's already dozens relating to Mount Anville. Listen to this one: *Eponine Lynch came to my house for a playdate and afterwards my Pandora bracelet was missing. The next time I saw her, she was wearing the exact same one. My mum said it was no surprise given that Eponine's dad borrowed €18m from the bank and never paid back a single penny and they're still living in the same house and going on three holidays a year.*'

I look across at Rachel. She's licking cappuccino froth off the back of her spoon, knowing none of this.

And Sorcha goes, 'I wonder will *The Girls* still love you when they find out who's behind this website, Ross?'

### 'It wasn't Fear of Missing Out as much as Fear of Being Talked about Behind My Back.'
*The Irish Times*, 10 November 2018

It's, like, five o'clock in the morning when it storts. I'm still in bed when Grainne Lessing posts a message on the Mount Anville moms WhatsApp group to say there's a Gorda speed van on Newtownpork Avenue and be careful if we're passing.

Amanda Mangan says, 'Omg you're up early!!!' and Grainne says,

'Sorry everyone that message was actually meant for the Willow Pork swimming group not the Mount Anville moms group.' Orlaith Stapleton says, 'Go Shorks!' Vanessa Mitchell says, 'Go Shorks!!!' Amanda Mangan says, 'GO SHORKS!!!'

On the Mount Anville Mid-Term Trip to Dordogne WhatsApp group, Orlaith Stapleton says, 'By the way, in case you missed it, that was Grainne's not-so-subtle way of letting us all know that Morcus is on the Willow Pork swimming team this year.' Vanessa Mitchell says, 'Hilarious!' Rebecca Leahy says, 'LOL!'

I'm now a member of nineteen Mount Anville-related WhatsApp groups. It wasn't Fear of Missing Out as much as Fear of Being Talked About Behind My Back. So this is my life now. I don't know how I ever found time to work.

Orlaith Stapleton says, 'Omg just had the total fear that Grainne was in the Mid-Term Trip to Dordogne WhatsApp group!' and Sally-Ann Markey says, 'No, Grainne said there's no point in sending Hester on the trip because they own a place in Dordogne – with a vineyord!' Helen Hall says, 'Er, subtle much?' Vanessa Mitchell says, 'Lol.' Alva Crowe says, 'Go Sharks!' and then a few seconds later, 'Sorry, that was meant for the Willow Park swimming group. Garvan is a substitute on the team this year.'

Mallorie Kennedy messages everyone in the musical society group to say she's hearing rumours about a speed van on Newtownpork Avenue. Ferne Brannigan says, 'Thanks!' Cho Hye-Ji says, 'Thanks!' Emer Durnin says, 'Yeah just heard the same thing.'

Rachel Lynch tells everyone in the moms group that she was actually pulled over by a Gorda recently who accused her of texting while she was driving. Cho Hye-Ji says, 'That's terrible.' Helen Hall says, 'So unfair.' Mallorie Kennedy says, 'Have they nothing better to do, these Gords?' Rachel Lynch says she actually said that to him: 'I asked him would his time not be better spent carrying out imaginary breathalyser tests? Well, I didn't actually say that but I certainly thought it! The focking bogger!'

Helen Hall messages everyone in the orchestra WhatsApp group to say, 'Rachel Lynch is telling the story about being pulled over for texting! Lol!' Mallorie Kennedy says, 'The hilarious thing is that she WAS actually texting! AND she got two penalty points.' Grainne Power says, 'Not being a bitch but if anyone has anything to fear from an early morning breathalyser test, it's Rachel!' Helen Hall says, 'No way!'

Mallorie Kennedy says, 'Way!' Alva Crowe says, 'Well, you couldn't blame her, being married to that w\*\*ker.'

Orlaith Stapleton messages everyone in the hockey WhatsApp group, going, 'By the way, in case you didn't get Grainne Lessing's 5am message, HER SON IS NOW ON THE WILLOW PORK SWIM TEAM!' Rachel Lynch says, 'Lol.' Rebecca Leahy says, 'LOL!' Ferne Brannigan says, 'Morcus pushed Jemma into the pool in the National Aquatic Centre two years ago and she nearly drowned. When I brought it up with Grainne, she didn't even apologize. She just said, Oh, yes, Morcus was mortified by that whole business!'

Susan Brennan messages the moms group to say, 'Thanks for the info re the speed van. I'm on my way to Newpork now. I don't know if I mentioned that Dorra is on the swim team this year.' No one responds.

But Rebecca Leahy messages everyone in the drama group to say, 'Susan Brennan lol!' Alva Crowe says, 'Tone deaf!' Cho Hye-Ji says, 'Did you see the STATE of those runners she was wearing two coffee mornings ago in Gleego's?' Rebecca Leahy says, 'They were actually Balenciaga!' and Alva Crowe says, 'Yeah, they're actually MADE to look wrecked!' Vanessa Mitchell says, 'I didn't hear anything about coffee mornings in Gleego's.'

Rebecca Leahy messages everyone in the *Gaeilgeori* group to say, 'Vanessa knows about Gleego's! Cho just opened her big mouth!' Oonagh Ni Charthaigh says, 'Speaking of coffee mornings, has anyone else noticed that Alva Crowe always orders a huge muffin when we're in the Merrion Tree Bistro and then NEVER eats it? She puts it in her bag and 'supposedly' eats it at home!' Maire Ni Bhraonain says, 'And what's she like, ordering hot water?!!!' Alannah de Nais says, 'Lol!!!' Cait Needham says, 'That's why she has no arse!'

Breena Marron messages the moms group to say, 'By the way, where is the National Aquatic Centre? Obviously I lived abroad for ten years.' Grainne Lessing goes, 'Junction 6.' Rebecca Leahy goes, 'Junction 6.' Caroline Landers goes, 'Junction 6,' and then a few seconds later she messages the hockey group to say, 'Breena Marron asking where things are again! Because OBVIOUSLY she lived in the UAE for ten years! I don't know if she's ever mentioned that before!' Serena Bennett says, 'Lol!' Lucy Anders says, 'Lol!'

Then Lucy Anders messages the orchestra group, saying, 'Btw did we ever get to the bottom of who set up that Rate My Playdate site?' Helen Hall says, 'Honor O'Carroll-Kelly!' Mallorie Kennedy says,

'Honor O'Carroll-Kelly!' Maoliosa Byrne says, 'Honor O'Carroll-Kelly!' Alva Crowe says, 'Girls, not to embarrass anyone, but Honor's dad is actually IN the orchestra group.'

Mallorie Kennedy says, 'I was only joking, Ross!' Helen Hall says, 'Me too!' Maoliosa Byrne says, 'I actually knew you were in this group!' and then a few seconds later she messages the drama group, saying, 'Just got caught slagging off that little b*tch Honor O'Carroll-Kelly! Her dad is in the orchestra group so be careful!'

Liz Bryant says, 'I kind of fancy him a bit,' but then Beibhinn Murray says, 'My sister was with him back in the day – as in WITH with,' and then, beside it, she puts up a picture of what looks like a small sausage.

Liz Bryant says, 'Hang on, isn't he in the drama group as well?' and Maoliosa Byrne says, 'I knew that as well! I was only joking, Ross!'

I check the time. It's 5.20 a.m. It's going to be another long day.

## 'He's been talking to Peter Casey. Sounding him out about replacing me as the leader of New Republic.'
### *The Irish Times*, 17 November 2018

The third Wednesday of November is what my old man calls Golfmas. It's a day of the year when me, him and Ronan – three generations of the O'Carroll-Kelly family – have our annual day out in Portmornock. We play eighteen holes of golf while my old man sucks on his hip flask, shouts random things in Latin and makes increasingly sexist jokes about women golfers, women drivers, women bank tellers, and just women generally, with the occasional, 'Of course, you can't even *joke* about things like that these days,' before going on to joke about them loads more.

This year, though, he's not his usual chirpy self. I can tell from the moment his driver lifts his clubs out of the boot of the Kompressor for him. Something is definitely wrong. I'd ask what it is, except – honestly? – I don't actually care. Whatever it is, he'll hopefully get over it. But then, as we're about to tee off on the difficult third, Ronan makes the mistake of asking him.

'You doatunt seem yisser self, Cheerlie,' he goes. 'Is there something the mathor?'

Which is an invitation for my old man to share, of course.

'I've got a lot on my mind,' he tries to go. 'Weighty matters of state, exclamation mork.'

I'm like, 'Oh, well. We won't stick our noses in. Here, tell Ronan your famous story about the woman in the bank who accidentally gave you a draft for €33,000 that should have been for someone else!'

Ronan looks at me and shakes his head.

'Rosser, caddent you see that Cheerlie's got something on he's moyunt?'

'Yes, I can, Ro – but I'm caught somewhere between indifference and actively not giving a fock. You should let him tell you that story, though. He got the poor woman sacked.'

My son, who's actually kind – something I'd hoped he'd grow out of – goes, 'What is it, Cheerlie? What's bottering you?'

The old man's like, 'There are plans afoot, young Ronan. Dastardly dealings happening in the shadows. One of my own friends is planning to betray me. *Omnis homo mendax.* Virgil said that. Although, equally, it might have been Cicero.'

I throw my eyes skyward.

Ronan goes, 'Come on, Cheerlie, let's sit dowun for a midute. Let these wooben play troo.'

He helps the old man over to a bench a few yords away.

'Letting women play through,' the old man goes. 'God, I mustn't be myself, eh, Ross?'

Ronan's like, 'That's it. Sit dowun oaber hee-or. So what is it, Cheerlie? What's going on?'

The old man sits down and takes a deep drink.

'It's Eduard, Ronan. A man I've been friends with for nigh on fifty years. A man I invited into the party and made the New Republic candidate for Dublin Mid-West. *Nervi et artus sapientiae sunt, non temere credere.*'

'You'd want to lay off the brandy,' I go.

Ronan's there, 'What's he arthur doing on you, Cheerlie?'

The old man stares at the women teeing off. He's so upset, he can't even bring himself to comment on their swings.

'He's been talking to Peter Casey,' he goes. 'Sounding him out about replacing me as the leader of New Republic.'

'That's teddible,' Ro goes. 'The doorty-looking doort boord.'

'A snake in the grass, Ronan. A scheming traitor. Have you ever heard of anything so underhanded?'

'How did you foyunt out, Cheerlie?'

'Oh, I've been tapping the chap's phone for months now.'

That shocks even Ronan. And he's been around a few corners in his short life.

'Are you seerdious?' he goes. 'Is that not illegal, Cheerlie?'

The old man just shrugs. He's there, 'No more illegal than reading someone else's letters, I'd imagine. Yes, Hennessy arranged the whole thing. Trust, but see in whom you are trusting. *Fide sed cui vide* – eh, Kicker?'

I'm like, 'Any more Latin out of you and I'm taking that hip flask off you.'

'I'm sorry. It's just, I'm still in shock, that's all. I should have seen it coming – of course, I should! Peter Casey's been casting around for a political party to join for weeks now. He tried Fianna Fáil. There's been talk of Renua. I knew how much some of our chaps admired him. I should have sensed the mood in the room at our recent policy think-in.'

I'm there, 'Ah, well, you didn't. Bummer. Now, are we playing golf or what?'

'Picking on the Travellers,' he goes. 'It was absolutely inspired. It's the kind of thing I would have come up with myself except I stopped relying on my instincts. You see, a while ago, Hennessy and I retained the services of a company called Merrion Analytics. Oh, the work they do is very impressive. They can feed polling data into a computer and come up with profiles of marginalized people that it's perfectly okay to dislike. We were going to use the information to play on the prejudices of the electorate in certain, closely contested constituencies in the next election. They suggested *our* Bogey Group should be lactose-intolerant cyclists from the southern border counties.'

I laugh. He's a knob. Always was. Always will be.

He goes, 'Well, think about it, Kicker. They're tight with money and they're careful with what they say; they have no respect for traffic lights or the Rules of the Road; and they talk about the fact that they can't drink milk like it's some kind of achievement. Oh, we were planning to hit them hord. Issue the Garda Traffic Division with Tasers, power to seize their assets and so forth. Then Peter Casey steps forward, utters the word "Travellers" and suddenly he's got twenty per cent of the electorate on his side.'

Ronan goes, 'What does it mean, but?'

'What it means, Ronan, is that my political instincts are not what they once were! What it means is that I'm clearly not the man to lead the party into the next General Election! What it means is that I'm going to invite Peter Casey to assume the presidency of New Republic!'

## 'Whatever else I might be, Eduard, I'm still a believer in democracy.'
### *The Irish Times*, 24 November 2018

It's unbelievable. Ireland are leading the All Blacks by ten points with fifteen minutes to go. But the tension down on the pitch is nothing compared to the atmos in the old man's corporate box.

The old man has uncovered a plot to replace him as the leader of New Republic with Peter Casey. And yet Eduard, the chief plotter, is helping himself to the old man's scotch and his turkey and Brie mini ciabattas as if nothing was wrong.

Hennessy is fit to kill him – quite *literally* as it happens?

'Forty years ago,' he goes, 'I'd have cut his throat, thrown him over the rail and watched him bleed out in the West Stand Lower. I hate the way politics has gone.'

The old man's there, 'Calm yourself, Old Scout. I told you how I wanted to handle this thing.'

'It still makes me angry, Charlie.'

The All Blacks win a penalty. Me, JP, Oisinn, Fionn and Christian look at each other. We're all thinking the same thing. Not again. Beauden Barrett splits the chopsticks and suddenly it's a one-score game with ten minutes to go.

Eduard looks around him and goes, 'It's all beginning to look a bit inevitable, isn't it?'

And Hennessy can't stay quiet any longer. He's like, 'That's always been your fundamental problem, Eduard – your lack of faith.'

Eduard has no idea what the dude is even *talking* about? He goes, 'What's that supposed to mean?'

The old man shakes his head. 'Hennessy,' he goes, 'this isn't how I wanted to do this thing.'

Eduard's there, 'No, Charles, I'd like to know what Hennessy meant by that comment?'

'We *know*,' Hennessy goes. 'All about your contacts with Peter Casey.'

Oh, that shocks the dude. He turns pretty much *white*? He's there, 'I swear on the lives of my children that I have had no contact with Peter Casey.'

'I've been tapping your phone for weeks,' Hennessy goes. 'And reading your emails. Who's Aurora, by the way? Does your wife know about her?'

Outside, beyond that glass, the roar goes up as the hits go in. This is – honestly? – the greatest performance I've ever seen from an Ireland team and yet it's hord to know whether to watch what's going on out there or what's going on in here.

'Oh, so that's what this is?' Eduard goes. 'You're going to try to blackmail me, are you?'

Hennessy's like, 'Hey, if it was up to me, you'd be watching the end of this match from pitch-side, cheering Ireland on through a hole in your throat.'

'Was that a threat? Because there *are* witnesses in this corporate box,' and he immediately looks at Martell Bagnel, a dude the old man knows from Portmornock Golf Club.

Hennessy laughs. 'Of course,' he goes, 'the New Republic candidate for Cork South-Central is in on it too. Your grammar is atrocious, by the way.'

'I'll sue you for breach of privacy,' Martell goes.

'Stop!' the old man suddenly shouts. 'This isn't how I wanted this thing to play out.'

'My wife knows all about Aurora,' Eduard tries to go. 'We've had an open marriage since 2003.'

I wish I could record this and watch it straight after the match.

'No one's trying to blackmail anyone,' the old man goes. 'As a matter of fact, I'm more than happy for this matter to take its democratic course.'

Eduard's like, 'What does that mean?'

'Well, I presume you're planning to table some kind of motion of no confidence in me at the Ord Fheis in two weeks' time?'

The dude can't even look the old man in the eye.

'Yes,' he goes. 'I'm sorry to say it, Charles – I know we go back a long time – but I don't believe you are the man to lead the porty into the next General Election.'

Joey Corbery comes on for Johnny Sexton. 'For me,' I go, 'that was Johnny's greatest ever performance in an Irish jersey.'

Oisinn's there, 'You say that every time he plays.'

'And I mean it every time he plays.'

The old man just smiles at Eduard. 'I understand where you're coming from,' he goes. 'Peter Casey has arrived on the scene. He's younger than me. He's got more energy. I can understand how people might see him as the future of the porty and me as the past.'

'It's not personal,' Eduard goes.

'I realize that. Which is why I'm prepared to step aside as the leader of New Republic.'

'What? Really?'

'If you can show me over the coming days that there is an appetite for change among the membership, then I'll stand down before you even have to submit your motion.'

'That's very magnanimous of you, Charles.'

'Whatever else I might be, Eduard, I'm still a believer in democracy. Now, can I ask you to leave, please?'

'Leave?'

'This box.'

'But there's still two or three minutes left. I'd like to see how it ends.'

'Why don't you ring Peter Casey? See if *he* has a corporate box in the stadium?'

'He doesn't. I think he's more GAA.'

'Oh, well – it takes all sort, etcetera, etcetera. I'm sure he'll bring other qualities to the job. Now, please be gone – and take your co-conspirator with you.'

The two dudes leave, muttering to themselves.

'Shame,' the old man goes. 'I was considering Martell as my future Minister for Foreign Affairs.'

I watch with my hort in my mouth as the All Blacks stort pinging the ball around. I reach for a turkey and Brie mini ciabatta and the old man goes, 'Probably best you don't eat those, Kicker,' and then – I swear to God – Hennessy opens up a Tupperware container and tips what's left of them into it.

Hennessy goes, 'Get these out of here,' then he hands the container to some dude in a black suit, who puts the Tupperware box into a briefcase and walks out.

The old man stands beside me and stares down at the pitch. 'They're going to hold on,' he goes.

A second or two later, New Zealand drop the ball and it's all over.

And suddenly Martell comes running back into the box, going, 'Quick! Something's wrong with Eduard! He's fallen down the stairs!'

Nobody moves. And the old man goes, 'That's the wonderful thing about this team. They simply refuse to be beaten.'

## 'Dude, we're here to end your ordeal. We're here to bring you home.'
### Specially Commissioned Piece Written for the Munster Rugby Christmas Party, 2018

Joey Corbery's face fills the big TV screen in Kielys of Donnybrook Town.

He's talking about the first try he scored for Munster tonight. He's saying all the things that you're supposed to say – that other players created the space for him and the most important thing is that the team won tonight.

I'm there, 'If I scored a try like that, I wouldn't be sharing the credit with anyone else. I'd have my jersey off in, like, two seconds, then I'd stort playing my abs like they were accordion buttons, shouting, "Whooda man?" at the visiting crowd. It's the only port of his game that Joey really needs to work on.'

'And the only port of *your* game that you ever got right,' JP goes.

Everyone laughs. I pretend to as well because I like to think of myself as someone who can take a joke, even though I'll probably ring him tomorrow and remind him that he wouldn't have won a Leinster Schools Senior Cup medal if it wasn't for me and I possibly deserve a bit more respect.

For now, though, I just tell him to shut the fock up, because Joey's still talking.

'Yeah,' he goes, 'I'm really happy with the move. I'm playing with great players in front of these amazing supporters. And I'm really loving the life down here. Munster is very much home to me now.'

Now – usually? – I would just snigger at a line like that and presume that it's just Joey ripping the piss. But there's something about the way he says it that has me instantly concerned for the dude.

I'm there, 'Goys, does Joey seem frightened to you?'

Oisinn's like, 'Frightened?'

'Yeah, frightened. All that stuff about Munster having amazing supporters and how he loves the life down there. It's like he was being forced to read a statement from a cue cord.'

'Ross, you're being ridiculous.'

'Plus – I know you're going to say this is the drink talking – but he's blinking really fast up there.'

'He *is* blinking fast,' JP agrees.

'It's like he's signalling to us. Do any of you goys know Morse code?'

It turns out that they don't. We were all on the Castlerock College Senior Cup team, bear in mind. The only thing *we* learned at school was the square root of fock-all.

I'm there, 'Goys, I know I'm eight pints down the road here, but, to me, he's trying to put out a message. Jesus, he seems to be saying: Send help!'

Christian goes, 'A cousin of mine who lives in Cork said he saw Joey a couple of weeks ago in the English Morket. He was buying crubeens and chatting to the locals like he was one of them. He's totally assimilated.'

I'm like, 'Dude, are you pulling my wire?'

He's there, 'I'm not pulling your wire. As a matter of fact, this same cousin saw him another night drinking a pint of Murphy's.'

I'm like, 'What the fock is Murphy's?'

'It's Guinness for culchies.'

And that, for me, is the final straw. That ends up being the line that snaps my basic crayons. I put down my pint of Heinemite – and I stort heading for the door.

I'm like, 'Come on, let's go.'

The goys are all like, 'Er, where are you going, Dude?'

And I'm there, '*We're* going to Munster! We're going to snatch Joey Corbery back.'

A short time later, we're sitting in Christian's – quite literally – Volkswagen focking Passat. We're on the M7 and we're heading for Limerick.

JP goes, 'I can't believe we're about to kidnap a man.'

I'm like, 'We're not kidnapping him! We're *extracting* him! Like in one of those movies with Matt Damon in it.'

But I'm just as tense as the other goys. I've always been nervous of Limerick – ever since the time I asked for a Mojito in Flannery's and the borman punched me straight in the face.

We spend a good port of the journey down talking about our

favourite Joey Corbery moments. I mention his seventy-metre try for Leinster against Treviso.

'It was actually the best try he's ever scored,' I go. 'Even though the Munster fans will be banging on about tonight's one forever.'

Christian laughs. He goes, 'Yeah – it's a bit like them beating the All Blacks!'

I'm like, 'What the fock are you talking about?'

'Munster beat the All Blacks.'

'No, they didn't.'

'Yes, they did.'

'When was this?'

'I don't know. It was in, like, the 1970s or something.'

'Dude,' I go, 'that was a focking play! Jesus Christ, I went to see it in the Gaiety with Rob Kearney and Jamie Heaslip and we walked out halfway through. The most far-fetched thing any of us had ever seen.'

'Ross, I'm telling you, it actually happened.'

'And I'm telling you it didn't. Seriously, Dude, it's like my old man claiming he got a hole-in-one when he was playing in a celebrity programme with JP McManus and Morty focking Morrissey. Whenever it's mentioned, I just go, "Yeah, I'm sure that happened alright!"'

We drive on in silence until we see the signs that tell us we have entered County Limerick. I'm looking out at the passing countryside and I'm wondering are these the famous Fields of Athenry?

'No,' Oisinn goes, 'they're in Connacht.'

I'm like, 'What?'

'The Fields of Athenry. They're in Connacht.'

'Why are the Munster fans always banging on about them, then?'

'I've no idea. I think a lot of Cork and Limerick people have holiday homes in Connemara.'

'My old man has a holiday home in Quinta do Lago. You don't hear me constantly singing about it, do you?'

'You do mention it a lot, though, Ross.'

'I'm tempted to say that this is typical Munster. They stole their theme tune from Connacht and their out-half from Leinster. I'll tell you something, goys, I'm more convinced than ever that snatching Joey Corbery back is the best idea I've ever come up with – pissed or not.'

Christian goes, 'So how are we going to do it?'

I'm like, 'What do you mean?'

'As in, how are going to take him?'

'We'll knock on his door. I'll distract him by telling him one or two stories about my Leinster Schools Senior Cup days, then you throw a bag over his head, Oisinn will tie him up and we'll throw him in the boot of the Passat.'

'Is that not a bit extreme?' JP goes. 'We don't want to traumatize him.'

'Dude, you saw the look in his eyes on TV tonight. He's *already* traumatized. There's nothing we can do to add to it. We snatch him, we drive him back to Ballsbridge and we'll all be eating brunch together by eleven o'clock tomorrow morning.'

I'd say it's a long time since Joey had brunch. Breakfast in Limerick is a scratch of your balls and a drink of water straight from the tap.

'Okay,' Oisinn goes, 'it's a plan.'

Pretty soon, we arrive in Limerick actual City.

It doesn't look as bad as I thought it would be. They've definitely tidied the place up since *Angela's Ashes*.

We find Joey's gaff and we pull up outside. It's pitch dork out and all the lights in the house are switched off. We pile out of the Passat.

'Don't forget the hood for his head,' I remind Christian. He takes a Donnybrook Fair 'Bag for Life' out of the boot.

We approach the door. I tell the goys to stand to the side and await my signal.

I press the bell. A few seconds later, I hear someone coming down the stairs. I can see through the glass that it's the man himself. Answering his own front door. Jesus Christ, they really don't know how to treat players in Munster.

I can tell you for a fact that Cian Healy has a butler.

Joey whips open the door. He's in his pyjamas. They're not even Leinster pyjamas. God, it's worse than I thought.

He looks at me and he goes, 'Hey, how's it going, er . . . Rob?'

That's a thing that Blackrock College players always do. They pretend they don't know my name. Brian O'Driscoll still calls me Rodney even though I'm godfather to him and Amy's eldest.

Joey goes, 'What are *you* doing here?'

And I'm like, 'Yeah, *me* in Limerick, right? Yeah, no, I was just, em, passing. I thought I'd knock in and tell you that I thought you'd a great game today. That was some try you scored, even though it wasn't as good as the one you scored for us against Treviso.'

He looks at me like he thinks I'm drunk. I *am* drunk. I'm shit-faced.

He goes, 'Rob, it's midnight.'

I'm there, 'The name is Ross, Joey – stop pretending that you don't know it. Focking Blackrock.'

'I was about to go to sleep.'

'Dude,' I go, 'I saw the interview after the match tonight. Let's just say I got the message.'

He's like, 'What message?'

'The one you were sending out with your eyes. You were signalling to someone to come and rescue you.'

He has this look of confusion on his face. A pettier man than me might say that's *also* a Blackrock thing?

He goes, 'Is there someone there with you, Rob?'

I'm there, 'No.'

But he steps out of the house onto the doorstep and looks around the side. And that's when he sees the rest of the goys.

He's like, 'Seriously, what's going on?'

I'm there, 'Dude, we're here to end your ordeal. We're here to bring you home.'

'What's with the Donnybrook Fair "Bag for Life"?'

'We were going to put that over your head before we stuck you in the boot of the Passat.'

'You were going to drive me back to Dublin in the boot of a Passat?'

You can see why he's upset. He's supposed to be a brand ambassador for BMW Ireland.

I'm like, 'Dude, I'd have gladly brought you back in the boot of my X5 except Christian was the only one of us who wasn't drinking.'

'No,' he goes, 'what I mean is, why were you planning to kidnap me?'

I laugh. I'm there, 'Because you're miserable.'

He goes, 'I'm not miserable. I love it here. I love Munster.'

'Dude, is there someone behind that door with a gun pointed at you?'

'No.'

'Have they kidnapped your family? Is that it? I'm just trying to figure out why you're talking like a crazy person.'

'Rob, I love this town. I love the people. I'm playing the best rugby of my career.'

'Well, I disagree with that – but continue.'

'This is where I belong. This is where I want to be.'

Christian scrunches up the Donnybrook Fair 'Bag for Life' and hands it to me – the first sign that we're abandoning our mission here.

He goes, 'I think what Ross is trying to say, Joey, is that we miss you.'

That ends up being it. I just burst into tears. We *all* do? It's one of those moments when tears are called for.

There's so much change in our lives recently. Kielys is about to close down. Lillie's is soon to follow. Jesus, even Donnybrook Fair has been bought out by Musgraves and I don't know what to tell my children any more.

Joey goes, 'Things change. People change,' and I feel like he's breaking up with me – which, in a way, he sort of *is*? 'Guys, this is my life now. I'm very, very happy here.'

And we all silently think, The poor, brainwashed focker.

I do something pretty amazing then. I hand him the Donnybrook Fair 'Bag for Life' and I go, 'Here, you can use this to bring your boots to training,' because I can't imagine the Munster Branch give them actual kit bags. 'It'll be a reminder of home. It'll be a reminder of us.'

Although now that Musgraves own the place, I'm sure it won't be long before the name appears on the Munster jersey. They've stolen everything else from us – why not that as well?

We say our goodbyes – there on the doorstep. Then we pile back into the Passat – a focking Passat! – and Christian points the thing in the direction of Dublin.

Ten minutes later, I'm fast asleep and drunkenly snoring my head off. Suddenly, I hear Ryle Nugent's voice going, 'Tooommmyyy Booowwweee!!!'

I wake up. I'm like, 'Is that my phone?'

'Tooommmyyy Booowwweee!!!'

It *is* my phone.

I reach into my Henri Lloyd sailing jacket, but it's not in there. It's fallen out of my pocket into the back of the cor and JP has picked it up.

'Tooommmyyy Booowwweee!!!'

I'm there, 'Answer that, Dude, will you? And if it's Simon Zebo pretending to be Joe Schmidt and asking me to join the Ireland coaching set-up again, tell him I'm not in the mood.'

I'd consider Zeebs a close, personal friend of mine, but he is one sick bastard when it comes to practical jokes.

Christian answers the phone, then he hands it to me. He goes, 'Ross, it's your daughter.'

I take the phone from him. I'm like, 'Honor, what's up?'

She goes, 'Where are you?'

'I'm in Limerick – obviously, don't tell your mother.'

'That's hill-arious.'

'I know. I was on a rescue mission that was sort of rugby-related. Why aren't you in bed? It's after midnight.'

'I'm working on a project for school. I need to talk to you about something.'

'Could you maybe talk to your mother about it? My hangover is storting to kick in here.'

'Do you remember I told you about that project we were doing in school, where we all had to spit into a test tube and they sent it away to be, like, analysed?'

'Of course I remember.'

I *don't* remember. It sounds focking disgusting, though.

She's like, 'It's, like, a DNA Ancestry test. They can tell you everything about your ethnic make-up from studying your saliva – as in, who your ancestors were and where they came from.'

'Why are you telling me this, Honor? It's actually a bit boring.'

'Because I found out something that I thought you should know. I found out where *our* actual ancestors came from.'

My body turns instantly cold. Because I already know what she's going to say.

She goes, 'We're from Limerick, Dad.'

I'm like, 'No! Nooooooooo!!!' like Luke Skywalker did when he found out that Dorth Vader was his old man. 'That's not true! That's impossible!'

She's there, 'It's not impossible. This is actual science. We're from Munster. We're literally Munster people.'

I hang up and I stare out the window. For no reason whatsoever, the 'Fields of Athenry' pops into my head and suddenly I can't get focking rid of it. I'm hoping that this is just another one of my famous drunken dreams. But somehow, deep down, I know that it's real. And, after tonight, the Rossmeister General will never, ever be the same again.

# 2019

Ireland suffer an opening day Six Nations defeat to England in Dublin at the start of a year of disappointment for Joe Schmidt's team * Extinction Rebellion activists block the gates of Leinster House * Newly released figures reveal that the number of people who are homeless in Ireland has exceeded 10,000 for the first time * In the United States, Donald Trump becomes only the third US President to be impeached. He is accused of abusing power and obstructing Congress * Broadcaster Gay Byrne dies * The World Anti-Doping Agency votes to ban Russia from all international sport competition for four years due to doping violations * US President Donald Trump and First Lady Melania visit Ireland * A major fire destroys Notre-Dame Cathedral in Paris * *Avengers: Endgame* is released and breaks box office records across the world * British Prime Minister Theresa May announces her resignation after failing to get Parliament to accept her Brexit deal. She is succeeded by Boris Johnson * The UK Parliament is prorogued in the face of protests from many MPs. The UK Supreme Court later rules the move unlawful and void * British Prime Minister Boris Johnson calls a General Election – the UK's third in four and a half years – as he seeks a mandate for his Brexit strategy. He wins an eighty-seat majority * Fine Gael TD for Dún Laoghaire Maria Bailey is deselected as an election candidate after an aborted personal injuries claim involving a swing * Ireland suffers a shock defeat to Japan at the Rugby World Cup, condemning them to a quarter-final against the eventual winners, New Zealand * Joe Schmidt retires as Ireland coach *

Meanwhile . . .

'The boys shouted, "Fock England!" throughout
"God Save the Queen".'
*The Irish Times*, 9 February 2019

There are landmork moments in the lives of your children that you will remember forever. The day they sit the Leaving Cert. The day they get married. The day they have children of their own.

But all of those things, while no doubt special, are things that they can do over and over again. There are only a handful of truly great moments that you get to experience with them just once – and one of those is their first Ireland rugby match.

So – yeah, no – I decided last weekend that, being four years old, Brian, Johnny and Leo were ready to go to the Aviva for the first time. And what an occasion it promised to be. We're talking Ireland versus England in the opening match of this year's Six Nations Championship.

It was – I was pretty confident – the first step in what would be an incredible rugby journey. First match. Junior Cup. Senior Cup. Professional contract. Leinster debut. Ireland debut. Grand Slam. Lions.

Yeah, no, it was all ahead of us.

But in the days leading up to the match, I storted to feel that I wasn't seeing enough – believe it or not – *excitement* from the boys? I blame Sorcha's old pair for buying them those Match Attax trading cords when they were three years old and setting them on a bad road. It's been a long, hord struggle trying to wean them off soccer and onto rugby ever since.

I was at a genuine loss as to what to do about the lack of passion that I sensed in them. But, on the morning of the match, I invited Ronan over to the gaff to tell them about all the terrible things – non-rugby-related – that the English did to Ireland over the years.

Now, it'll probably surprise no one to hear that History wasn't the Rossmeister's *thing* at school. Between Cú Chulainn, Brian Boru and Michael Collins, I could never figure out who was real and who was made up. But it's a subject that my eldest son is into in a major, major

way – for instance he has the names of all the main goys from 1916 tat-
tooed on his upper orm.

As it turned out, a two-hour crash course from their older brother
on England's crimes against Ireland – I honestly didn't know the half
of it! – was all it took to turn Brian, Johnny and Leo into three snorling
monsters, who spent the entire cor journey to the match having a competition to see who could shout, 'Fock England!' the loudest.

We porked the cor in Ballsbridge, then we walked to the stadium –
me, Sorcha and our three little boys, them in their little green hats and
scorves, me with my famous Rugby Tactics Book tucked under my
orm and the usual butterflies in my stomach.

'Fock England!' the boys shouted as we passed a group of – yeah,
no – *actual* England supporters. They found it hilarious, in fairness, and
insisted on recording a video of them screaming it at the top of their
voices, which they were sure would go viral.

On we walked. We passed what was once the Berkeley Court and I
had a sudden flashback of being in there with *my* old man on match
days – him in his ridiculous coat and hat, sucking on his hip flask as he
queued for the bor and shouted random things like, 'What would life
be, ladies and gentlemen, without the Five Nations Championship to
shorten the winter?'

Into the stadium we went. A dude in a high-viz checked our Lemony Snickets.

'Fock England!' Leo shouted at him and Sorcha explained that we'd
decided, as parents, not to correct our children when they used bad
language for fear of creating taboos around certain words, which in
turn made them more attractive to them. The dude gave her a dubious
look and Sorcha ended up roaring at him: 'You can spare us the judgy
looks! This is the route we've decided to go!'

We eventually found our seats. The boys shouted, 'Fock England!'
throughout 'God Save the Queen' and – while everyone around us was
of the opinion that this was very, very funny – I storted to worry that
Ronan had maybe filled them with a bit *too* much passion?

As the game storted, I was like, 'The time for mindless, verbal abuse
is over now, goys. Once the match storts, it's time for analysis,' and, as
if to emphasize the point, I opened my Rugby Tactics Book across my
lap and sat there with my brand-new pen at the ready.

The match kicked off.

Various people behind, beside and in front of us storted shouting,

'Have you storted taking notes there, Rosser?' because it's something I'd be famous for in the West Stand Lower. People laugh, but at the same time they respect me for how seriously I take the game.

But no sooner had I written down the names of the two XVs than Ireland had conceded a try.

'It was Jonny focking May,' I went – even before the stadium announcer said it.

There was, like, silence in our section of the crowd, until the boys storted shouting, 'Fock you, Jonny May!' which went down an absolute storm.

Everyone was cracking their holes laughing at it.

'Okay,' I went, 'here comes Owen Farrell,' as the dude stuck the ball in the cup and got ready to kick the extras.

There was, like, a deathly stillness in the stadium as the dude lined up the kick, doing that weird thing he does with his eyes. And then, out of the silence, came the voices of my three little boys, going, 'Fock you, Owen Farrell!'

There were gasps all around me. Which I could totally understand. I mean, even *I* was speechless?

Sorcha turned to the boys and explained to them that it was customary – no matter how much you hate the opposition – to maintain a respectful silence for the kicker. She knows this from experience. She once booed Morgan Parra and we spent six months sleeping in separate beds.

We ended up having to see a marriage counsellor.

'The reason being that kickers are ortists,' I went, 'and it's a privilege to watch what *they* – slash, *we* – do. While you've heard me shout some not-very-nice things about Owen Farrell when he's on the TV, the respect I have for him is absolutely massive, the focking wanker.'

'Fock you, Owen Farrell!' they continued to shout as the dude finished lining up his shot.

I was like, 'Goys, seriously, knock it off.'

'Fock you, Owen Farrell!' they carried on shouting as he ran at the ball.

'I blame the parents,' some dude behind me went.

I was there, 'Goys, you've no idea how seriously, seriously out of *order* you're being here?'

'Fock you, Owen Farrell!' they shouted as the ball sailed between the posts.

'Sorcha,' I went, 'will you bring them home?'

And, as she ushered them out of their seats, I'm going to be honest, I couldn't even bring myself to look at my own children.

Too soon, I thought.

Yeah, no, we'll try again in about five years' time.

### 'He got no-platformed before a public meeting a few weeks ago and he wasn't *happy* about it?' *The Irish Times*, 2 March 2019

So it's, like, the middle of the afternoon when the old man rings. He asks me if I'm at home, then he tells me to come outside because he has a little surprise waiting for me. The surprise ends up being – quite literally – a white Transit Van. The old man is sitting in the front passenger seat, with the famous K . . . K . . . K . . . K . . . Kennet at the wheel and Hennessy wedged in between them, sucking on a cigar as long as – it sickens me to say it – the Blackrock College senior cup roll of honour.

I'm like, 'What the fock is this?' the same question that everyone on the Vico Road will be asking right now.

'This,' the old man goes, 'is the Charles O'Carroll-Kelly Truth Bus!'

I actually laugh. I'm like, 'The what?'

He goes, 'Oh, you heard me right, Ross! There are none so deaf as those who won't listen!' and then he holds something like a walkie-talkie up to his mouth and goes, 'BUT I'D LOVE TO SEE THEM IGNORE ME NOW!'

I end up jumping backwards with fright. The old man's voice is coming out of four speakers mounted to the roof of the – again – Transit Van.

I'm like, 'Wait a minute – is this about UCD refusing to accept your offer of an O'Carroll-Kelly building?'

He's there, 'No, Ross, this is about the student body's refusal to hear my reasons for wanting to make them such a gift.'

Yeah, no, he got no-platformed before a public meeting a few weeks ago and he wasn't *happy* about it?

'So what's the plan?' I go. 'You're not going to drive around the Belfield campus just bellowing insanely at passers-by, are you?'

He's like, 'That's exactly what I intend to do, Kicker! Charles O'Carroll-Kelly isn't about to be silenced by a bunch of bloody well teenagers who've been brought up to believe that they don't have to listen to the opinions of others! This is real life – and, unfortunately for them, real life doesn't have a Block or Mute button!'

I slide open the side door and I climb into the back of the van. I'm there, 'I'm not missing this for the world.'

Twenty minutes later, we take the left turn off the Stillorgan Dualler into actual UCD. Kennet goes, 'Wh . . . Wh . . . Wh . . . Wh . . . Wheer am I th . . . th . . . th . . . th . . . thriving to, Cheerdles?'

The old man goes, 'Straight ahead, Kennet. There's a cor pork next to O'Reilly Hall. We'll drive a few circuits of that while I get my voice warmed up. *Veritas liberabit vos* – eh, Hennessy?'

Hennessy has a little chuckle to himself. He's like, 'Even the great Livy, in all his wisdom, couldn't have put it better.'

The old man holds the walkie-talkie thing up to his mouth and suddenly his voice storts coming out of the speakers. He's like, 'LADIES AND GENTLEMEN, BOYS AND GIRLS, THIS IS CHORLES O'CARROLL-KELLY SPEAKING! SEVERAL WEEKS AGO, I MADE PUBLIC MY INTENTION TO GIFT TO YOU – AND TO FUTURE GENERATIONS OF UCD STUDENTS – A BRAND-NEW BUILDING THAT WOULD BE AS IMPRESSIVE AS IT WOULD BE LORGE!

'THE REASON BEHIND THIS EXTRAORDINARY ACT OF PHILANTHROPY IS ONE OF GRATITUDE! IT'S MY WAY OF SAYING THANK YOU TO THIS WONDERFUL SEAT OF LEARNING – THANK YOU FOR HELPING TO MAKE CHORLES O'CARROLL-KELLY THE MAN HE IS TODAY!'

I'm going to be sick. It's, like, dizziness from doing circuits of the cor pork, although the old man's so-called speech isn't exactly helping my stomach either.

I'm like, 'Pull over, will you? I'm about to vom.'

Kennet stops the van. And that's when I spot the cavalry coming. A crowd of sixty, maybe seventy students tipping down the steps towards the van.

'Sh . . . Sh . . . S . . . Sh . . . Shut the bleaten door,' Kennet goes – and I don't need to be told twice.

They obviously have some kind of loudhailer themselves because I hear a girl's voice go, 'LEAVE THIS CAMPUS IMMEDIATELY! YOU HAVE NOT BEEN INVITED TO SPEAK HERE TODAY!'

Instead of winding down the window, the old man decides to talk to her through the speakers on top of the van.

He's like, 'I DON'T NEED YOUR PERMISSION OR THE PERMISSION OF ANY OF YOUR BLOODY WELL SNOWFLAKE FRIENDS TO SPEAK! YOUR FEELINGS ARE NOT THE MOST IMPORTANT THING IN THE WORLD – EVEN IF YOU THINK THEY ARE!'

The girl goes, 'WE WILL NOT ALLOW FASCISTS TO DISSEMINATE THEIR POISONOUS VIEWS ON THIS CAMPUS!'

'*YOU'RE* CALLING *ME* A FASCIST? OH, THAT'S RICH! THE DENIAL OF FREE SPEECH IS A CENTRAL TENET OF FASCISM, I WOULD HAVE SAID – EH, ROSS?'

I decide to just stay out of it, though.

The girl goes, 'YOU ARE THE LEADER OF A POLITICAL PARTY ESPOUSING RIGHT-WING VIEWS THAT ARE MISOGYNISTIC AS WELL AS RACIST!'

He goes, 'IT'S NOT RACIST TO SAY THAT CAVAN PEOPLE ARE CAUTIOUS WITH THEIR MONEY AND THAT LEITRIM PEOPLE DON'T LIKE OUTSIDERS!'

'LEAVE THIS CAMPUS IMMEDIATELY! WE DON'T WANT FASCISTS HERE!'

'I THINK YOU'LL FIND THAT YOU'RE THE FASCIST!'

'NO, ACTUALLY, *YOU'RE* THE FASCIST!'

'NO, IT'S ACTUALLY YOU! *ACTA NON VERBA*, EH, HENNESSY?'

'YOU'RE A *LITERALLY* FASCIST, THOUGH?'

'THERE ARE A GREAT MANY FASCISTS HERE – AND I CAN TELL YOU NOW THAT NONE OF THEM IS IN THIS TRUTH BUS!'

I'm sitting in the back of the van wondering why they can't just have this conversation on Twitter like normal annoying people.

And that's when I feel the van move. It's, like, only slight at first, but then the thing storts actually rocking and it's obvious that the crowd outside have storted shaking the thing. It's when I feel the wheels on the left-hand side lift off the ground that I stort to get *seriously* worried?

The old man should probably shut his mouth at this point, but he decides to ramp it up. He goes, 'THIS COUNTRY SAT AND WATCHED THE REST OF THE WORLD FIGHT A WAR TO GUARANTEE YOUR RIGHT TO FREE SPEECH! AND THIS IS WHAT YOU CHOOSE TO DO WITH THAT RIGHT!'

The rocking becomes more violent and suddenly I'm being thrown back and forth across the floor of the van.

'FASCISM IN ACTION!' the old man shouts. 'FASCISM IN ACTION!' until eventually – inevitably – Charles O'Carroll-Kelly's Truth Bus is tipped over onto its side.

## 'I knew it was a bad idea letting her watch that Amal Clooney documentary on Netflix.'
### *The Irish Times*, 13 April 2019

'Unbelievable!' Sorcha goes, picking up her cor keys. 'Un-focking-believable!'

I'm like, 'What's wrong?'

She's there, 'I just had a phone call from the Montessori, telling me to come and collect Brian, Johnny and Leo.'

I sigh. It's the only thing you *can* do when you've got kids like ours. I'm there, 'What have they done now?'

And Sorcha goes, 'Why do you automatically assume it was something *they* did?'

'Er, have you met them, Sorcha?'

'Excuse me?'

'I'm just saying that they're three little yobs.'

'I can't believe you would describe your own children as yobs.'

'Yeah, they were banned from the Disney Store last week for kicking the shit out of Dumbo.'

'It was a giant stuffed toy, Ross. And I still say the only reason Brian attacked him was out of fear. Anyway, are you going to just stand there slandering them or are you going to come with me and be an actual advocate for our children?'

An *actual advocate* for our children? I knew it was a bad idea letting her watch that Amal Clooney documentary on Netflix.

I decide to accompany her to Little Apples – if anything, to try to talk her down during the course of the drive.

'I don't like asking questions of us as parents,' I go when we've been in the cor for, like, five minutes, 'but I wonder are we in any way responsible – even accidentally – for the way they've turned out?'

She's like, 'What's that supposed to mean?'

'I'm talking about us not correcting them when they use bad

language. Or when they pull the ears off an innocent elephant. Or when they spit over the side of the escalators in Dundrum.'

'That was the approach we decided to take, Ross. We both agreed that we didn't want to create taboos around certain words or behaviours in case they made those words or behaviours more attractive to them.'

'I just think that, two years on, we need to maybe ask ourselves is that approach definitely working?'

She goes on the big-time defensive then. She's like, 'And where did our sons *learn* all of the disgusting words they know, Ross?'

I'm there, 'Er, from their sister?'

'And where did Honor learn them?'

'You can't say this is my fault just because I drop the occasional F-Bomb. If anyone's to blame, it's your old pair for buying them those Manchester Something Something soccer jerseys.'

'Okay, I'm struggling to see the connection.'

'Yeah, no, that's pretty obvious. Look it up. There's an actual link between soccer and anti-social behaviour – not to mention crime of the non-white-collar variety. I'm going to use the words slippery slope, Sorcha. I'm *going* to use them – end of.'

'Okay, Ross, I don't think you and I should fall out over this. I think we need to walk in there this morning and show a united front. I mean, our boys are *far* from the most badly behaved children in Little Apples Montessori.'

Then we sit there in silence for a good five minutes trying to think of a kid who's worse.

Sorcha goes, 'What about Hugo White?'

I'm there, 'Is that Hugo whose old man is a portner in –?'

'No, that's Hugo Murray.'

'Oh, is Hugo White the kid with the sticky-out –'

'No, that's Hugo Leary.'

'Is it Hugo with the –'

'No, that's Hugo Bailey.'

'Right. Why is every second kid these days called Hugo, by the way?'

'It's the new go-to name for parents who want their children to be mistaken for Protestants.'

'Makes sense, I suppose. And you're saying this Hugo – whoever he is and whatever he's done – is definitely at least as bad as our three?'

'He's awful, Ross.'

'That's good. Well, at least we've got that to fall back on.'

We drive on in silence.

Then Sorcha goes, 'I think the so-called teachers in this place have some questions to answer as well, don't you?'

I'm like, 'Questions, as in?'

'The reason we sent our boys to Little Apples was because they *claimed* they could help discover their special gifts.'

'I'm wondering do they even have any, Sorcha. They seem pretty useless to me.'

'Of course they have gifts, Ross!'

Sorcha is one of *those* South Dublin mothers – if her kid pissed on the floor of the Vatican, she'd be looking for signs of genius in the splash patterns.

She goes, 'We need to ask the school why, after however many months it's been since they were enrolled, none of them is playing a musical instrument or producing a piece of ort that suggests genuine talent?'

She throws the Nissan Leaf into the cor pork, then I follow her – Sorcha O'Carroll-Clooney – into the school. She morches straight for the Principal's office, with me running beside her to try to keep up with the length of her stride.

She knocks on the door – three no-nonsense knocks – and Mrs Perezynski goes, 'Come in!'

Which we then do.

Brian, Johnny and Leo are sitting next to each other at the far wall of the office, looking seriously shamefaced. They turn their eyes away when I look at them. I don't know what they've been accused of doing, but it's *obviously* bad?

Mrs Perezynski stands up. She's like, 'Thank you both for coming in to see me this morning. I wanted to talk to you about –'

But Sorcha cuts her off.

She's like, 'How about *I* talk and *you* listen for once? Because I am – oh my God – sick to death of receiving phone calls and letters from this school, offering me tittle-tattle about the things my boys have supposedly done. And, while it's too early for me to stort talking about solicitors, I would like to know how my children had the time to do this thing that you're alleging they've done. Perhaps if you were spending actual time with them, helping them to discover who they are and what makes them unique as individuals, they wouldn't have time for mischief. It's teaching you're supposed to be doing, not crowd control.'

Mrs Perezynski smiles at her patiently and goes, 'Mrs O'Carroll-Kelly, I asked you here today because –'

'Oh, this should be good!' Sorcha goes. 'I can't *wait* to hear what you have to say next!'

And Mrs Perezynski goes, 'Your children have nits.'

## 'Wait a minute . . . How come you know so much about head lice?' *The Irish Times*, 20 April 2019

Sorcha is crying in the cor. 'How could something like this have happened?' she keeps going – over and over again.

It reminds me of the time, at the height of the recession, when she miscalculated her Brown Thomas reward cord points and ended up losing her platinum status for a year.

'What does this say about *me*, Ross?'

She said that back in 2011 as well.

I'm there, 'It doesn't say anything about *you*, Sorcha. Lots of kids get head lice.'

She's like, 'Not kids who go to Little Apples Montessori, Ross!'

'Yes, *even* kids who go to Little Apples Montessori.'

'What, even though it's six hundred euros per week, per child?'

'The head lice don't know that, though. Anyway, they're not a sign of, like, uncleanliness. They actually only *like* clean hair?'

'Don't be ridiculous. That's just something people say to make you feel better when your children have head lice. Oh my God, can you *imagine* what the other parents are saying about us right now?'

Brian, Johnny and Leo are sitting in the back, delighted to have been sent home from school early. Leo leans forward between the two front seats and goes, 'Me want ice cream!'

And I'm there, 'Let's ask your mother can we go to Dundrum, will we?'

'No,' Sorcha goes, 'we are *not* going to Dundrum. Because we are not running the risk of infecting another family. As a matter of fact, Leo, sit back in your seat. I don't want to catch them from you.'

'Fock you!' Leo goes.

And Sorcha's like, 'No, Leo, *fock* you!' which is very out of character for her. She never swears at the children. That's usually my job.

I'm like, 'Sorcha, calm down.'

'How can I calm down?' she goes. 'We're going to miss the Easter Bonnet Parade in Dalkey on Sunday!'

'We won't have to miss it. They'll have hats on, Sorcha. Their heads will be covered.'

'Wait a minute,' she goes, suddenly looking at me suspiciously. 'How come you know so much about head lice?'

I'm like, 'Sorry?'

'All that stuff you were saying a minute ago about them only liking clean hair?'

'It's just a fact I happen to know.'

'Oh my God, you *had* them, didn't you? You had head lice!'

There's no point in lying to the woman. But I give it a go anyway. I'm like, 'No.'

'Yes, you did!' she goes. 'I can tell from your face!'

'Yeah, no, I had them when I was a kid. I barely even remember it.'

'Oh my God, so that's where the boys got them!'

'Yeah, they don't run in families, Sorcha.'

And that's when I feel it. My head is suddenly itchy. I don't know whether it's, like, a genuine itch, or if it's just paranoia from all this talk of head lice, but my scalp feels like it's suddenly hopping with the things. I try not to scratch it, but then my eyes stort watering and suddenly I can't resist the urge. I stick my nails into my head and stort going at it like a crazy person.

Sorcha *literally* screams? 'Oh! My God!' she goes. 'That's it!' and she turns the wheel right and swings the cor across two lanes of traffic, then onto Westminster Road.

I'm like, 'Where are you going?'

She's there, 'You're going to your mother's and you're taking the boys with you. You can ring me when you're all nit-free.'

'I don't have head lice, Sorcha. I'm just itchy from all this talk about them.'

But she refuses to listen. Sixty seconds later, she's dumped us outside the old dear's gaff and driven off in the Nissan Leaf.

'This is some bullshit,' Brian goes – and who am I to contradict him?

Into the gaff the four of us go. I find the old dear in the kitchen. I'm there, 'Are you sober?'

She goes, 'What kind of way is that to greet your mother? Oh, look at, em, the lovely boys!'

She still can't remember their names.

I'm there, 'Do you remember when I was a kid and I had, like, head lice?'

She goes, 'Oh, that saga! I'll never forget it! The shame! People say they only like clean hair but no on really believes that – especially around here!'

'How did you get rid of them?'

'What happened was, I washed your hair using a rug shampoo that someone recommended. It was Turkish or something. Funnily enough, I found the bottle in the utility room the other day –'

'Okay,' I go, cutting her off, 'pleasantries over. I've got work to do. Come on, boys. Let's leave your grandmother to mix her lunch.'

Brian, Johnny and Leo follow me down to the utility room. It doesn't take me long to find the bottle with the foreign writing on it. I get the three boys to stand on chairs and lean over the sink, while I wash their heads using the – I don't know if it's even racist to actually say the word – but *Turkish* shampoo.

It builds up quite a lather, it has to be said, but I use the little sink hose to wash all the suds off, while Brian and Leo go, 'Pack! Of! Focking! Shite!'

Still, ten minutes later, I have all their hairs washed and I'm pretty delighted with myself. But it's only when I'm toweling them dry that I discover the problem . . .

Their hair is falling out. Their hair is falling out in great, big chunks.

I look up and I see the old dear standing in the doorway of the utility room, a mortini in her hand.

I'm like, 'What the fock?'

And she goes, 'Yes, that's what happened when I used it on you!'

'You could have told me.'

'I thought you'd remember. You were shedding hair like a German Shepherd.'

Celine Dion. It's all coming back to me now.

I'm there, 'So what did you do in the end?'

She goes, 'I had no choice. I had to shave your head. I still have the electric razor upstairs somewhere. Will I go and get it for you?'

I'm like, 'Yeah, no, please do.'

I look at the boys. Their faces are all lit up at the thought of having their heads shaved.

'Your old dear is going to go spare,' I go. 'I think you're going to be wearing those Easter bonnets until the summer.'

'She's the rudest, most obnoxious little
madam I've ever met.'
*The Irish Times*, 11 May 2019

Sorcha tells me to look at the time. Which I do. It's, like, six o'clock in the evening and I'm not really sure where this conversation is going.

'Honor's been at a birthday porty for the last three hours,' she reminds me. 'And we still haven't had a call from the parents demanding that we come and take her home.'

'Why do you always do that?' I go. 'Why do you always believe the worst of our daughter?'

'Okay, *how* many playdates has she been on that resulted in us receiving solicitors' letters?'

'One or two.'

'Yeah, try nine or ten, Ross.'

'*Someone's* obviously keeping count.'

'Someone *has* to. I mean, you're, like, *wilfully* blind to her faults? She's got you wrapped around her finger.'

'Yeah, that's called parenting, Sorcha.'

'Is it, Ross? What, allowing your children to manipulate you into giving them everything they want while allowing them to do whatever they want to do?'

'Exactly. And I happen to be very good at it.'

Which kills her. I know deep down she actually hates that I'm the cool parent.

She's like, 'Go and collect her, Ross.'

I'm there, 'Me? I was about to grab a stick of Heinemite and scribble down my thoughts on the Sarries match. It's the final this weekend, Sorcha. The goys are going to be looking for my analysis.'

She goes, 'Your *analysis* is going to have to wait,' and she says 'analysis' like she doesn't believe it's an actual thing. 'The porty finishes at six.'

I'm like, 'Where? As in, where am I getting her from?'

'It's a house in Watson Pork.'

So I grab my cor keys and I head for Watson's. The whole way there, I think about my daughter and how she's very like Owen Farrell in a lot of ways – as in, she has her critics and there's something about her face that tends to rub people up the wrong way, but I wouldn't swap her for anyone in the world, except obviously Johnny Sexton and maybe Beauden Barrett when he's on form.

Halfway up Watson Pork, I spot the house. There's, like, balloons on the gateposts out front. I pork the cor outside. The door is wide open, so I let myself in. The gaff is full of kids. I walk through the noisy throng down to the kitchen, where I can hear, like, grown-ups talking.

I'm about to walk in there and introduce myself – being very much a people person – but then I hear something that stops me dead in my tracks. It's, like, a woman's voice, going, 'She's the rudest, most obnoxious little madam I've ever met. And the parents have no control over her – she's allowed to just run riot.'

'That's no surprise,' I hear another woman's voice go, 'given who her father is. He's some rugby player. Or *failed* rugby player. Yeah, no, my husband remembers him when he was a teenager. Every bit as awful as the daughter, *he* said.'

'Apparently,' some dude goes, 'her brothers are even worse. They're allowed to do whatever the hell they want.'

I stand in the doorway of the kitchen and I clear my throat to get their attention. They all just look at me.

They're like, 'Oh, hello!'

I end up just glowering at them until one of the women – I'm presuming it's *her* actual gaff – goes, 'Is everything okay?'

I'm like, 'That's my focking daughter you're slagging off!'

The atmos in the kitchen suddenly changes. They're all like, 'Er . . .' nearly choking on their prosecco.

I'm like, 'You should be ashamed of yourselves. She's only a kid. And let me tell you something else – she's a focking great kid. Did you know, for instance, that she has her own fashion vlog with, like, 94,000 subscribers?'

They didn't. That much is obvious from their reaction.

I'm there, 'And those brothers of hers who you *also* slagged off? Would it surprise you to hear that she's actually an amazing sister to them?'

The woman whose gaff it is – she's, like, morto – just goes, 'I'll go and get her for you.'

And there ends up being a seriously awkward silence in the room then.

I'm there, 'I'm glad you're all embarrassed,' helping myself to a slice of birthday cake and a glass of prosecco. 'Slagging off a little girl who you haven't even bothered to get to know. I actually feel sorry for you that you're never going to get to see my daughter's amazing, amazing qualities. As a matter of fact, I pity you – every single one of you.'

And that's when my phone storts vibrating in my pocket. I whip it out. It ends up being Honor. I answer it.

She goes, 'Where the fock are you?'

I'm like, 'I'm downstairs in the kitchen.'

'No, you're not,' she goes. '*I'm* downstairs in the kitchen.'

I look around. There's no sign of her. And a horrible feeling suddenly comes over me.

I'm like, 'Your old dear said the porty was in Watson Pork.'

Honor goes, 'Yeah, she's actually losing it. I told her, like, twenty times it was Watson Drive, the stupid focking bitch.'

At that moment, the woman of the house returns to the kitchen with a girl of about ten, who – I hate to be judgemental – looks like a complete and utter wagon.

'Now, Begnet,' the woman goes, 'your dad's here!'

The kid looks me up and down and goes, 'He's not my dad!'

My body turns instantly cold.

The woman's there, 'Now don't like be like that, Begnet. I've got a little porty bag for you to take home.'

Begnet goes, 'I don't know who this focking asshole is – but he's not my dad.'

'Do you know what?' I suddenly go. 'You were actually right. She *is* awful. You can hang onto her.'

Then I knock back my prosecco and I walk out of the house.

I've still got Honor on the phone, by the way.

She goes, 'What the fock is going on? Who were you talking to?'

And I'm like, 'No one, Honor. God, there's some really focking obnoxious kids around here, isn't there?'

'Well, just to warn you in advance,' she goes, 'I upset someone at the porty and you're probably going to be getting a solicitor's letter.'

And I'm like, 'Not a problem, Honor. I'll get Hennessy to send them one right back. See you in a minute.'

'This is the only video footage that exists of the
Munster versus All Blacks match from 1978.'
*The Irish Times, 21 September 2019*

So I invite the goys around to watch the opening match of the World
Cup and – typical me – I end up pushing the boat out in a major way.
We're talking the full nine *yords* here?

I decide to give the morning an actual Japanese theme, so I buy
eighty bottles of Sapporo, then I obviously tip the contents down the
sink and fill them up with Heineken. I've also got fifteen or sixteen
boxes of sushi from Morks & Spencer. And then – a nice touch, this – I
answer the door to the goys wearing Sorcha's pink kimono with the
pandas and pagodas on it and I put my hands together as if in prayer
while bowing to greet them. Which, according to Fionn, makes me
guilty of a thing called 'cultural appropriation'.

He also has a problem with me pronouncing all my R's as L's and all
my L's as R's, which he says is 'er, *kind* of offensive?' so I drop it after a
quick round of 'Herro's'.

We get comfortable in front of the TV and stort watching the opening ceremony. JP goes, 'Er, Ross, you know your kimono is open?'

I'm there, 'Yeah, no, it's actually Sorcha's? She bought it in the spa in
Monort – it's, like, so silky that the belt refuses to stay tied.'

'Would you not –?'

'What?'

'– put some underpants on?'

'Hey, it's cool. I kind of *like* the airy feeling?'

He goes, 'Dude, seriously, either you put on a pair of boxer shorts or
I'm going somewhere else to watch the match.'

Unbelievable. All the effort I've put in to make it seem like we're in
*actual* Japan and this is the thanks I end up getting. I stand up – everyone
averts their eyes – and I head upstairs to throw on some kacks.

As it happens, I don't make it that far, because there ends up being a
ring on the doorbell. I answer it and it's, like, the old man.

'Ross,' he goes, 'the very chap I need to see!'

I'm like, 'What the fock are you doing here? I'm about to watch the
match.'

He goes, 'Is it an important one?'

And I'm like, 'Er, it's *rugby*? They're *all* important?'

I feel like I'm talking to my wife here.

He's there, 'Yes, of course! Sorry, Kicker, I've been rather preoccupied with this,' and he holds up his laptop.

I'm like, 'What is it?' but he doesn't answer me. He just steps past me into the gaff. I follow him down the hallway and into the living room.

He goes, 'Oh, look, all your chaps are here! Well, that's a stroke of luck because I want to get your opinion on something!'

And that's when – I swear to God – he literally switches off the TV and opens up his laptop.

I'm like, 'What the fock?'

He goes, 'This is very important, Ross.'

And I'm there, 'So is Japan versus, I don't know, whoever they're playing today.'

He's like, 'I want you all to look at something. This is the only video footage that exists of the Munster versus All Blacks match from 1978.'

'Not this again!' I go. 'Yeah, no, he's become a Munster Truther, goys. He's trying to prove that the supposedly miracle match never actually *happened*?'

Oisinn goes, 'Oh, it definitely happened. I know someone who claims to have been at it.'

The old man's there, 'I'm not saying it didn't happen, Oisinn. I'm saying it didn't happen the way the Mainstream Media have told you it happened. And at last I have the evidence to prove it!'

'Okay,' JP goes, a big smirk on his face, 'let's see this evidence,' and the goys all gather around his laptop. They're worse for encouraging him.

The old man storts playing the footage. It's, like, after the match. There's, like, hundreds of supporters on the pitch, surrounding the Munster players, who all have their orms in the air – in, like, *triumph*?

'So this is the aftermath of the match,' the old man goes. 'The Munster players celebrating. Now, I want you to look at the great Tony Ward. There he is there. You'll recognize him, Ross – you being a fan and everything. Now, look at his face – he has a five o'clock shadow, you see? And here, in this window, is a photograph of the chap converting Christy Cantillon's try – where he's clean-shaven.'

Fionn's there, 'I have to be honest, Charles, I don't see what you're seeing.'

'Also,' the old man goes, 'look at the great Ginger McLoughlin celebrating at the final whistle! You see? Look how dry he is! And yet we can all see from the footage that it was raining for most of the match! Look, here's a photograph of him in the second half! See? The chap was bloody well covered in mud!'

I'm there, 'So what does all of this prove?'

He goes, 'The celebrations were staged, Ross.'

'Staged?'

'Quote-unquote. Possibly the following day. But certainly some time afterwards. They got the players and a crowd of fans together and they faked a scene of celebration to convince the world that they actually won the match.'

JP goes, 'This is great work, Charles,' and for some reason it annoys me to see the dude ripping the pistachio out of my old man like this.

Fionn's there, 'But Munster *did* win the match, Charles. I've actually watched it.'

'No,' the old man goes, 'what you watched was a carefully edited and cleverly cut version of the match. Watch this. If I pull the footage back a bit. Okay, it's the seventy-eighth minute. There's the legendary Pa Whelan with the ball, yes? Now, watch what happens next! There!'

I'm like, 'It was turned over.'

He goes, 'It wasn't turned over, Kicker. The footage jumped. And it jumped because the film has been cut. There are two missing minutes from the game, during which we – and, by we, I mean the Society of Munster Truthers – believe that the All Blacks scored and converted two tries to level the match.'

I stand up and I'm there, 'Okay, put the actual rugby back on. You've lost it. You've lost it in a serious, serious way.'

But he goes, 'I haven't lost it at all, Ross! My eyes are suddenly open! And so is your kimono, by the way!'

<br>

'I just – oh my God – love the literary theme!'
*The Irish Times, 28 September 2019*

Me and Sorcha are out celebrating, I don't know, *something* or other? It's, like, an anniversary of some sort – definitely not our wedding anniversary because I forgot that back in June. Yeah, no, it's the anniversary of the first time I ever smiled at her, or the first time I ever bought her a drink, or the first time we ever kissed. Sorcha has them all in her head. I generally just take her word for it and go along with whatever she has planned.

So we're in a restaurant on, like, Fumbally Lane that's so cool it doesn't even have a name. There's literally fock-all written over the door and everyone just refers to it as, 'Oh my God – the *new* place?'

The tables are basically old school desks, repurposed – and by 'repurposed' I mean removed from a skip and wiped down with a biodegradable, citric wet wipe – and all of the chairs are mismatched.

Yeah, no, you get the general idea.

I'm having The Infidel – which is basically pulled pork on a toasted Acme roll with a gorlicky, lemony mayo and a side of sausage-doughnuts, served on a 1986 edition of the oi telephone directory. Sorcha is having the Panko-fried chicken skewers, locally sourced, with a maple mayo dip and a side of kale fries, served on a VHS copy of *Honey, I Shrunk the Kids*.

'Oh my God,' Sorcha goes, 'I have to say, the word of mouth was *so* not wrong about this place!'

But I'm like, 'Meh!' because I'm way more sober than I need to be to enjoy it.

She goes, 'I can't believe you're still sulking just because they don't serve Heineken.'

They don't serve alcohol at all. I'm drinking juice made from thirty-seven varieties of pear – all of them grown sustainably in Wicklow – and served in a Batchelors Baked Beans tin.

She goes, 'I just – oh my God – love the literary theme!'

I'm like, 'What literary theme?' and I genuinely *mean* it?

'I'm talking about all the shelves of books over there, Ross. They're all, like, previously loved. You can bring one and take one.'

I'm there, 'People and their books. Ridiculous. Okay, I need a slash,' because the pear juice is running straight through me.

So I tip down the stairs to the jacks. And that's kind of when the *trouble* storts? There's, like, two doors in front of me. On one, it says, 'George Eliot', and on the other, it's like, 'Charles Dickens'.

And – yeah, no – there's literally no further information.

So I end up standing there for a good five minutes, wondering – probably like the rest of you – which of these is supposed to be the men's jacks and which of them is supposedly the women's?

Of course, in the end, I have no choice other than to just take a punt – like I said, my tonsils are floating – so I push the door morked 'George Eliot' and in I walk.

My error becomes apparent pretty much straight away when I cop the general cleanliness of the place. One of the thousands of things I love about women is that they don't feel the need to urinate on the floor just because they're in a toilet that someone else is going to be cleaning. You could eat your dinner off those floor tiles – and, let's be honest, I wouldn't be surprised if that's how the dessert is served.

I'm chuckling at this line, thinking what a pity it is that no one else is here to enjoy it, when all of a sudden the door of Trap Two opens. A woman walks out, cops the Rossmeister General standing there and let's out what would have to be described as a piercing scream.

Now, back in the day, much was written – especially in these pages – about my turn of speed from a standing stort. And the poor woman ends up being a witness to the fact that I've still got it – certainly in terms of pace. I turn on my heel and I'm out of there and up the stairs like I'm running from gainful employment.

I rush over to the table and I go, 'Come on, Sorcha, let's hit the road!'

But she's like, 'We haven't had dessert yet! Oh my God, I'm dying to try their scrambled egg crème brulee with a bacon-flavoured, caramelized sugar top!'

Suddenly, I hear a voice behind me go, 'That's him! In the blue rugby jersey and the chinos! He was in the women's toilets!'

Every conversation in the place suddenly stops. People are suddenly looking up from their Sika deer sliders and their kimchi tacos and their foraged raspberry fools to find out, basically, what the *fock*?

And – yeah, no – Sorcha is kind of curious herself.

She goes, 'Ross, what's she talking about?'

And I'm like, 'I didn't know it was the women's toilet. It actually said George Eliot on the door.'

'Yeah, George Eliot was a *woman*, Ross?'

'I didn't know that. I'd never heard of him – slash her.'

'Oh my God,' a girl at another table goes, 'are you saying you've never read *Middlemorch*?'

I'm there, 'I've never read anything! Is that, like, a book he wrote?'

'*She* wrote. And, yeah, it's only the greatest novel ever written in the English language.'

'Well, I'm going to have to take your word for that. Sorry, can I make a point here? There are signs for women's and men's toilets that are known all over the focking world. Why do we have to always complicate things?'

The manager decides to get involved then. 'There's nothing

complicated about it,' he goes, suddenly on the big-time defensive. 'How could you not know that Charles Dickens was a man?'

I'm there, 'Because I've never heard of him either.'

The woman goes, 'Okay, that's it. Call the Guards. How could anyone *not* have heard of Charles Dickens?'

Sorcha's like, 'Look, I know it's not an excuse, but my husband *was* on the senior rugby team in school.'

You'd want to see the looks of sympathy I'm suddenly getting.

She goes, 'We had a similar incident in a restaurant in Ranelagh last year when he walked into "Billie Holiday" instead of "Dizzy Gillespie".'

I'm there, 'And *I'm* supposedly the weirdo? Seriously, I don't know what the fock is happening to the world. Come on, Sorcha, let's get out of here.'

## 'Dude, save your breath. You had me at "free drink".' *The Irish Times*, 19 October 2019

The old man asks me what I'm doing on Thursday night. He goes, 'I'm having a bit of a soirée, Kicker! I've booked the famous Stephen's Green Hibernian Club for a private dinner to celebrate Ireland's relationship with the – inverted commas – Land of the Long White Cloud!'

I'm obviously there, 'The Land of the what?'

He goes, 'I'm talking about New Zealand, Ross! On Saturday, we are World Cup opponents, but let us not forget that we are also friends with much in common – our population size, our landscape and the friendliness of our peoples!'

'And this affects me how exactly?'

'I've got those ten cases of Framingham's F-Series Riesling Trockenbeerenauslese that I picked up in Rotorua during the 2011 World Cup! As I said to your mother, they're not going to drink themselves! Plus, Hennessy has the full carcass of a Booroola Merino lamb in his coffin-style freezer! He strangled the thing with his own hands – just after he hit it with the Bentley while driving over the Wicklow Gap! An act of mercy – poor little chap! Still, if eating his poor, broken body, medium-rare, helps to solidify the relationship between the country of his birth and the country of his forebears, then I'm sure he'd agree that his sacrifice will not have been . . . etcetera, etcetera!'

'Yeah, no, I'm in.'

'I thought I'd invite a couple of hundred of my closest friends and acquaintances along! Michael McDowell obviously! Dick Spring! Hooky and Popey! Good old Gerald Kean! Thought I'd ask the New Zealand ambassador to Ireland – maybe even the entire staff of the embassy! They're on Merrion Row, don't you know!'

'Dude, save your breath. You had me at "free drink".'

'That's wonderful, Ross! And bring your chaps as well, won't you?'

So Thursday night, I rock up with Oisinn, Fionn and Christian in tow. The place is, like, rammers. We sit at our table and various friends of my old man swing by to ask me for my thoughts on the match. I tell them all the exact same thing. Ireland will beat the All Blacks. End of analysis. It seems to send everyone away hopeful.

Anyway, the dinner is going well. We've, like, finished our mains and we're waiting for our desserts when, all of a sudden, my old man steps up to the mic to make what everyone presumes is going to be one of his usual boring speeches.

He goes, 'Mr Ambassador, friends and colleagues, ladies and gentlemen . . .'

He obviously doesn't mean that literally – there are no women here.

He goes, 'Thank you all for coming tonight! I want to say a special thank-you to my legal adviser and long-suffering golf portner for supplying the meat for this evening! Those of you who spotted Bridgestone tyres morks, especially on the shoulder cuts, may have come to certain conclusions as to its provenance – and you'd be absolutely right!'

Everyone laughs. I forget sometimes that a lot of people actually *like* my old man? Fock knows why.

Oisinn goes, 'He's very funny – in all fairness.'

But that's when my old man's facial expression suddenly changes. 'What I haven't told you yet,' he goes, 'is that I had – let's just say – an ulterior motive in inviting you here tonight.'

The room suddenly dorkens as all the lights are dimmed. A projector screen comes down on the wall beside him. On it, there's a rugby match that looks like it happened in the olden days – and it's, like, paused.

He's there, 'This Saturday's match against the world-famous All Blacks is, I think, an opportune moment to correct, once and forever, a grave, historical, sporting injustice! Some of you will be aware that I have recently become a founding member of the Society of Munster Truthers – an organization that believes that province's so-called victory over the All Blacks in 1978 was, in fact, a hoax!'

That doesn't go down well. People are either groaning or actually shouting, 'Give it up, Chorles!' and 'I think we all know what this is really about!'

Yeah, no, he's had a bee in his bonnet ever since Munster Rugby turned down his offer to buy the naming rights to Thomond Pork. My old man is nothing if not a petty and vindictive man.

He goes, 'Please, my friends, hear me out! I think all of you will join me in questioning the official narrative when you see what I am about to show you!'

Christian goes, 'What is it, Ross?'

I'm like, 'Dude, I'm as much in the dork as the rest of you.'

The old man's there, 'It has long been rumoured that, in the final stages of the match, the All Blacks scored and converted two tries to draw the game, although these have been edited out of the official footage! Those of you who've watched it as closely and as many times as I have will be familiar with the subtle jumps in the footage!'

There's, like, boos throughout the room. People stand up from their tables with the intention of walking out.

The old man goes, 'So I offered one million euros – a bounty, if you will – to anyone who could provide me with the missing footage! And now – at last – I have it!'

Oh, that gets their attention. Everyone's like, 'What did he say?'

There's suddenly, like, total silence in the room. Hennessy presses Play and we watch the footage, which – I'm going to be honest – *seems* to show the All Blacks scoring then converting a try, then gaining possession from the restort, then scoring and converting another try.

You could hear a pin drop when it finishes.

Then someone shouts, 'Someone's doctored the footage! That's from another match altogether!'

It's a Cork accent – no surprise there.

Fionn turns around to me and goes, 'What the fock? Did your old man pay someone to make a fake video?'

If he did, they did a very good job. I mean, most people in the room seem to agree that the footage looks real – as in, like, *actual*?

Others aren't happy bunnies, though – especially the ones who come from down that way. They're going, 'It's fake news, boy! It's fake news!'

The old man just goes, 'Some people can't handle the truth! But this video proves it conclusively! Ireland may well beat the All Blacks on Saturday. But Munster certainly didn't in 1978!'

# 2020

Four 153-year-old statues are removed from the front of the Shelbourne Hotel in Dublin in the belief that they represent slaves. They are later reinstated * The government cancels an event to commemorate the RIC and the Dublin Metropolitan Police in the face of an angry public backlash * A General Election results in huge seat gains for Sinn Féin, whose candidates top the poll in many constituencies * Following months with a caretaker government, Micheál Martin succeeds Leo Varadkar as Taoiseach in a three-party coalition involving Fianna Fáil, Fine Gael and the Green Party * The year is defined by the COVID-19 pandemic, which leads to social and economic disruption on a global scale * Mass public gatherings are cancelled in Ireland as the government orders two Level 5 lockdowns of the country * The IRFU, GAA and FAI announce the suspension of all events due to the COVID-19 pandemic * The live register of unemployed people rises to 513,350, the highest in the history of the state * Amazon CEO Jeff Bezos becomes the first individual in history to enjoy a net worth of $200 billion * The impeachment trial of US President Donald Trump results in his acquittal * The Leaving Cert and Junior Cert examinations are cancelled, with students awarded predicted grades * Protests in response to the killing of George Floyd break out in America and all over the world and the Black Lives Matter movement gains huge international support * The wearing of face coverings becomes mandatory on public transport, in retail outlets and in many public spaces * Irish people are urged not to travel abroad and to instead 'staycation' in Ireland * The United Kingdom formally withdraws from the European Union, though talks on the terms of the country's withdrawal continue * A number of high-profile attendees of an Oireachtas Golf Society event, including Health Minister Dara Calleary and European Commissioner Phil Hogan, are forced to resign after it is revealed that the event breached public health guidelines * Nobel Peace Prize Laureate John Hume dies * The worldwide death toll from COVID-19 surpasses 1.3 million * Donald Trump announces the United States will suspend funding to the World Health Organization in protest at its handling of the COVID-19 crisis * Joe Biden is elected as the 46th President of the United States, beating incumbent President Donald Trump, who refuses to accept the result * Pfizer and BioNTech announce that their COVID-19 vaccine has been found to be 90 per cent successful in trials *

Meanwhile . . .

### 'You are *not* bringing Covid-19 into this house.'
### *The Irish Times, 21 March 2020*

In times of, I don't know, crisis, whenever I stort to feel anxious about the future of the world, I always find it helps to remember the words of the late, great Father Denis Fehily: '*Iucunda memoria est praeteritorum malorum,*' which roughly translates as, 'Whatever shit goes down, there will always be rugby.'

But we can't be certain of even that any more.

I'm watching Brian, Johnny and Leo. They're gobbing on the kitchen window, then cheering their spits on as they dribble down the glass in a race to the windowsill. With the Six Nations suspended, the O'Carroll-Kelly Saliva Stakes is the closest thing we have to live sport now.

Sorcha has all the pots and pans on the go, cooking enough dinners to see us through months of self-isolation. I grab the wooden spoon and I go to have a mouthful of her famous Donal Skehan's Beef and Guinness stew, except she snatches the spoon from me and goes, 'That isn't Today food, Ross!' Then she spoons the entire thing into a Pyrex dish and, with a black Shorpie, she writes on the lid, 'February 2021'.

Jesus Christ.

For five days now, I've been stuck in the house with my wife, my children and my old man – who's chosen the lockdown as the perfect time to separate from my old dear – and I can't help thinking, God, my family are annoying.

I'm there, 'I'm going out.'

Sorcha's like, 'You're not going out.'

'I'm going off my rocker, Sorcha. It's supposed to be Paddy's Day.'

'I don't care, Ross. You are *not* bringing Covid-19 into this house.'

Who said anything about me coming back?

'What was that?' she goes.

I'm like, 'Sorry?'

'You said something under your breath – about not coming back.'

'Yeah, no, you must have misheard me. I'm going to see what Honor's up to.'

So I tip up the hallway to the living room, where I find her and the old man playing – believe it or not – Monopoly on the coffee table. I have this sudden flashback to my own childhood. The old man insisted we played every Sunday afternoon because he said it would teach me about – and I quote – 'capitalism in all its wonderful glory'.

And, right enough, I notice that the old man has piles and piles of cash in front of him, while Honor is basically broke and looking utterly miserable.

I'm like, 'Monopoly, huh?'

And Honor goes, 'Oh my God, I *hate* this focking game!'

The old man's there, 'I'm teaching your daughter about capitalism, Kicker – in all its wonderful glory!'

I notice that some of the names on the board have been crossed out in biro and new names have been written in underneath. I see that 'Kimmage' has become 'Harold's Cross' and 'Crumlin' is now 'Terenure'.

I'm like, 'Why have you written in new names?'

The old man's there, 'I've, em, gentrified some of the areas I bought.'

'And when I land on them,' Honor goes, 'I have to pay him *twice* the amount that it says on the cord.'

I'm like, 'Why did you agree to that?'

'Honor got herself into a little bit of financial bother about twenty minutes ago,' the old man goes. 'Overextended herself. I agreed to re-finance her – and, in return, she allowed me to upgrade the value of some of the properties in my own portfolio.'

I'm suddenly remembering how he likes to make the rules up as he goes along.

Honor rolls the two dices, slash, I don't know, *die*? She gets, like, a one and a two. She moves the little top hat along the board, going, 'One, two, three . . .'

'Capel Street!' the old man goes. 'I'm sure that's one of mine!'

Honor's like, 'Er, it's not – it's, like, *mine*? And I want to build a house on it.'

'On Capel Street?' the old man goes, chuckling at the very idea. 'Well, you know what you have to do first.'

She takes a hundred from her little pile of money and she puts it into – hilariously – a little brown envelope.

I'm like, 'What are you doing?'

The old man points at a square on the board. The words 'The Electric Company' have been crossed out and in their place he's written 'The Political Establishment'.

'The very first thing I bought!' he goes.

She hands him the envelope and he slips it into his pocket – or 'offshore', as he calls it.

Then she hands him the dosh for the gaff and he adds it to his pile.

I'm like, 'Whoa, is that money not supposed to go to the bank?'

'I bought the bank,' the old man goes, biting the end off a humungous Cohiba. 'Yes, it was experiencing a little liquidity problem just before you walked in, so I agreed to take on all of its assets and liabilities.'

I'm there, 'Honor, this is how he plays – he makes up the rules to suit himself.'

The old man rolls the – okay, I'm just going to say – dices, then he moves the cor along the board and lands on 'Go to Jail'.

I laugh.

'Hilarious!' I go. 'Now you're banged up – like you were in real life! Justice at last!'

The old man's there, 'Fortunately not, Ross. I also own our friends in the Four Courts!' and he points at the square that used to say 'Water Works' and now says 'The Judiciary'.

I'm there, 'Honor, I can't believe you're letting him cheat like this.'

She rolls the dices. She's like, 'Nine, ten, eleven . . .'

'Shrewsbury Road!' the old man goes. 'That *is* one of mine. And you owe me precisely . . . one thousand euros!'

Honor's there, 'I don't have one thousand euros.'

'Then I shall have to acquire one of your properties.'

I notice Honor try to slip a cord up her sleeve.

'What about Dundrum Town Centre,' the old man goes, lighting his cigor, 'formerly Busárus?'

Honor's like, 'You're not having Dundrum Town Centre! It's not for sale!'

'I don't really see that you have any option. Unless you want to discuss restructuring your loans with the bank. But then I own that too.'

Honor ends up suddenly losing it. She grabs both sides of the board and she tips it all over the old man's lap.

'Stupid focking game,' she goes, then she storms out of the room.

I'm there, 'How are we all going to survive this thing?'

And the old man takes a long pull on his cigor and goes, '*Iucunda memoria est praeteritorum malorum*, Ross!'

## 'Some HSE person phoned and told her that she'd been in contact with somebody who has this *thing*.'
*The Irish Times, 4 April 2020*

I ring the old dear. No idea why. They're saying this Covid-19 thing is bringing out the best in people and it's a side of myself that I don't actually recognize.

I'm there, 'I'm just ringing to find out if you're okay.'

As it turns out, she doesn't recognize it either.

She's like, 'Who *is* this?'

I'm there, 'It's Ross.'

'Ross who?'

'Er, your *son*?'

'Why are you speaking that way?'

'What do you mean?'

'Usually, when you phone, you say something awful about my drinking, or my writing, or the work I've had done on my face, even though I've never had *any* work done on my face.'

'I don't know. They're saying we all have to look out for each other now.'

'Who said that?'

'That Varadkar dude. He was on TV. So I'm just ringing to find out – yeah, no – how you're *coping* and blah, blah, blah? And to wish you a belated Happy Mother's Day for, I don't know, whenever that whole thing was.'

I swear to God, she goes, 'How do I know it's you?'

I end up suddenly losing it with her. I'm there, 'Look, can we stort this conversation again?'

And she's like, 'Yes, I think it would be best all round if we did.'

So we both hang up, then I ring her back. She lets the phone ring seven or eight times, then she answers it by going, 'Hello?'

I'm like, 'Took your focking time answering, didn't you? What are you doing, you gin-crazed, blubber-filled phoney – writing more of your dirty books for sexually frustrated, old bints like yourself?'

She goes, 'Hello, Dorling!'

'Was that better?'

'Much better! I didn't like whoever you were trying to be just then. You sounded smarmy and insincere.'

'Well, normal service has been resumed – you rubber-faced, permanently pissed, pedaller of porn.'

'I'm glad to hear it.'

'So how *actually* are you?'

'Oh, we're all fine up here, Ross. As I said to Delma on the phone, I just can't imagine this thing coming to Foxrock.'

'Yeah, it's not public transport, Mom. Or a drive-thru Krispy Kreme. It's a global pandemic – and you're not going to stop it by writing to the council and saying we don't consider such things appropriate for an area like this.'

'You just called me Mom.'

'What?'

She sort of, like, chuckles to herself.

She goes, 'I don't think I've heard you call me Mom since you were a little boy.'

I'm there, 'Do you want me to hang up and stort again?'

'No, I think I liked it. It's not often I think of myself as a mom. Poor Delma's in an awful state, by the way.'

'What's wrong with Delma?'

'Oh, some HSE person phoned and told her that she'd been in contact with somebody who has this *thing* and that she wasn't to leave the house under any circumstances.'

'What's wrong with that? That's good advice.'

'What's wrong with it is that this HSE person simply refused to tell her who this *somebody* was.'

'Why does it matter who it was?'

'I said to Delma, I bet it was Ginny McIlwaine. Lives next door to her. You know, she once accused me of filling in an incorrect scorecord – the year I won the Lady Captain's Prize in Foxrock!'

'Yeah, it's not a witch-hunt, you know?'

'The reason my ball ended up in that divot was because *she* focking stood on it. I said to Delma, "Let's be honest, none of us would be the least bit surprised if it turned out to be her."'

Did you ever regret phoning someone?

I'm there, 'Delma should be staying in anyway. And so should you, by the way.'

She goes, 'Me? But I don't *have* this thing. If I saw Ginny coming, I'd cross the road, pandemic or no pandemic.'

'I'm saying you should be staying in because of your age.'

'My age? What's wrong with my age?'

'There's nothing wrong with it. They're just saying that all people over the age of seventy should stay home.'

There's, like, five seconds of silence on the other end of the phone.

'Ross,' she goes, 'I'll have you know, I'm a *long* way away from seventy.'

I'm there, 'I know you are – you're three years past it. I was at your porty, remember?'

'That was my sixtieth.'

'Yeah, you keep telling yourself that, Benjamin Button. But don't go out again, Mom.'

'Mom! There it is again!'

'I mean it, okay?'

'When is this ghastly business going to be over, Ross?'

'Nobody knows.'

'You know I haven't had the house cleaned in two weeks? Stefania says she's *social distancing*. That's a quote.'

'Jesus, would it kill you to hoover your own gaff for once?'

'I don't know how it all *works*, Ross.'

'You don't know how to use a hoover?'

'Well, I know you push it about the place. It's just that I've tried pressing the On button and nothing seems to be happening.'

'Have you got it plugged in?'

'Does it *have* to be plugged in?'

'Of course it has to be plugged in! What do you think it runs off? The evil in your soul?'

She laughs at that line, in fairness to her. I think I've given her a genuine lift by ringing her. I'm not going to make a habit of it, but I definitely won't leave it two weeks next time.

'Anyway,' I go, 'I've got shit to do. Honor's home-schooling me. I'm thinking of having another crack at the Leaving Cert, by the way.'

She goes, 'How interesting!' but I know if I asked her to repeat what I just said, she wouldn't be able to. She has one of those minds that automatically sifts out anything that doesn't directly affect her.

I'm there, 'Do you want me to tell Dad you were asking for him?'

She's just like, 'No, it's fine.'

'Okay,' I go, 'I'll hopefully talk to you again soon. Look after your-self, okay? I worry about you.'

She's like, 'Please, Ross – let's not leave things like that.'

'Okay,' I go. 'Look after yourself. I worry about you – you talentless, vodka-soaked, whale sperm-infused excuse for a mother.'

And she's like, 'Thank you, Dorling!'


### 'I've made her some banana bread . . . it's Nigella Lawson's.'
*The Irish Times*, 11 April 2020

We're one of those families. You might be one of those families your-selves. When we're filling the supermorket trolley every week, we're not shopping for us – we're shopping for the family we'd like to be. Which usually means buying thirty or forty kilos of fruit and vege-tables that we know we'll never eat.

'Yes,' I think, dropping a watermelon into the trolley every Thurs-day night, 'I *am* the kind of man who'll chop and eat this at some point over the next seven days.'

Then, before the week is over, I'm putting it in the bin, having decided the whole thing was too much focking trouble.

The need to pretend you're a healthy family is even greater when you shop online. As Sorcha says, the last thing you want is some ran-domer filling your trolley and thinking ill of your choices.

Which is how we reached a point this week where we found ourselves with seventy-seven bananas that no one showed the slightest interest in eating, especially since most of them were turning black. And that's when Sorcha announced – with the serious tone of, I don't know, a prime minister declaring war – that she was going to make banana bread.

'Oh my God,' she went, '*everyone* on Instagram is doing it!' which – in my wife's world – means we have no choice but to comply too. 'I'm going to do Donal Skehan's one!'

So she got to work. Within an hour, she had made fourteen freshly baked loaves of banana bread. And that was when I reminded her that no one in this house even likes the stuff.

'*We're* not going to eat it,' she went. 'We're going to give it to the neighbours. Put your mask and gloves on, Ross – drop one in to Gwen and one in to Joy.'

So I get suited and booted, grab the two banana breads – still warm – and set off. A few minutes later, I'm ringing the Loschers' bell.

Through the door, Gwen goes, 'Who is it?'

I'm there, 'It's Ross O'Carroll-Kelly.'

She's like, 'Who?'

They're not rugby people.

I'm like, 'Er, Ross from next *door*?'

'Oh,' she goes, 'Sorcha Lalor's husband?'

And I'm there, 'Yeah, no, that's one way of looking at it. Sorcha's made you some banana bread.'

She's like, 'Oh, dear.'

I'm there, 'What?'

'Well, I've made her some banana bread as well. It's Nigella Lawson's.'

'Ours is Donal Skehan's.'

'Are you wearing gloves?'

'Yes, I'm wearing gloves.'

'Well, leave it on the doorstep,' she goes, 'then take ten steps backwards. I'll open the door and take yours in, then I'll leave mine on the doorstep and you can take it once I'm safely back inside.'

So that's what we do. It's like a hostage exchange. For focking banana bread.

Sixty seconds later, I'm back on the Vico Road and – probably like you – I'm thinking what has happened to the world we once knew? I think this lockdown is storting to seriously affect me. I got a pop-up on my laptop yesterday that said, 'There are hot women in your area who want to meet you!' and my first thought was that a high temperature is a symptom of Covid-19 and that women in their condition shouldn't be meeting anyone.

That's when I spot a woman, wearing gordening gloves and a Hermès scorf covering the lower half of her face, putting something in our post box at the gate.

I'm like, 'Halt! Who goes there?' because I can be very funny.

It turns out it's Joy Felton, the neighbour from the other side.

She goes, 'I made you some banana bread. It's the Happy Pear one.'

I'm there, 'I was just coming to see you. We've got Donal Skehan's.'

'Oh,' she goes, sounding disappointed by this turn of events. 'How shall we do the exchange?'

I'm there, 'You put that one in the post box and I'll leave this one on the path on the other side of the road.'

She's like, 'Okay. Have you just come from Gwen's?'

'Yeah, no, she's got Nigella Lawson's.'

'Well, maybe I'll just leave mine in her post box too. I don't want to disturb her.'

A minute or two later, I'm back in the gaff.

I'm like, 'That's our good deed done for the year, Sorcha.'

She steps out of the kitchen. She goes, 'Ross, I know you're mocking me, but little neighbourly gestures are important at a time like this. What have you got there?'

I'm like, 'Banana bread. Gwen Loscher and Joy Felton made you some.'

'Oh, for fock's sake!' she goes, suddenly losing it. 'We're trying to get *rid* of banana bread?'

'Okay, what happened to little neighbourly gestures are important at a time like this?'

Suddenly, there's a knock on the door. I shout through it. I'm like, 'Who is it?'

A voice goes, 'It's Anthea Shotton,' who lives five houses down. 'I've made you some banana bread. It's the Jamie Oliver one.'

I'm there, 'Er, just give me a second to think, Anthea.'

Sorcha goes, 'What the fock, Ross? I sent you out with two banana breads and you've come back with three!'

'I've got an idea,' I go. 'I'll give her the one Joy Felton gave me. It's the Happy Pear one.'

Sorcha's like, 'What?'

'Seriously, she won't know that you didn't make it. It all tastes the same anyway.'

So I'm standing there with my back against the door.

I'm like, 'We've got some banana bread for you as well, Anthea.'

'Oh,' she goes, sounding disappointed.

I'm there, 'Leave yours on the doorstep, then take ten steps backwards. I'll open the door and put this one out for you. Do you need me to repeat that?'

'No,' she goes, 'I understand.'

So I leave Joy's banana bread out and I take Anthea's banana bread in. And Sorcha looks definitely relieved.

'Okay,' she goes, 'at least we're back to square one.'

But that's when, suddenly, we hear Anthea's voice outside, going, 'Ross? This is actually *my* banana bread you've given me.'

I'm there, 'It probably just *looks* the same, Anthea. Banana bread is banana bread.'

'But it's got Joy Felton's name on it,' she goes, 'in *my* handwriting.'

Sorcha grabs me by the wrist and drags me down the hallway to the kitchen.

'Ignore her,' she goes. 'Hopefully this thing will drag on for months and it's September before we see her again.'

## 'What kind of a rugby father am I?'
### *The Irish Times, 18 April 2020*

Sorcha has decided that, for as long as this lockdown lasts, we should all get dressed every morning as if it's just a regular day. She's not saying it explicitly, but I suspect this has something to do with the Zoom call with her family on Easter Monday, when I stood up – totally forgetting that I was wearing boxer shorts – and apparently 'popped out'.

I know Sorcha's old dear was upset about it, because I could hear Sorcha on the phone to her afterwards, going, 'Breathe, Mom! Breathe!'

Simon Harris can talk about the 'new normal' until he's blue in the face, but there's no way to prepare any woman in her seventies for the experience of being flashed by her son-in-law – even *if* her daughter tries to persuade her subsequently that she was hallucinating on her blood pressure meds.

Anyway, Sorcha called a family conference that afternoon and pointed out that – much like the fly of my favourite Jockey briefs – we'd all become a bit too slack in recent weeks. The upshot was that she wanted us all to wear clothes – trousers were specifically mentioned – for as long as this Corona crisis lasts.

So, twenty minutes later, I'm dressing little Leo and I'm struggling to fasten the top button on his chinos.

I'm like, 'Sorcha, have these shrunk?'

She's there, 'What?'

'Er, Leo's trousers – they won't, like, *close*?'

'That's because he's put on weight, Ross. Did you see how much chocolate the boys ate over the weekend?'

I did. The Easter egg hunt was pure focking terrifying. The three of them went through the gorden like shorks scenting chump. I watched Leo and Johnny lift Sorcha's Nissan Leaf off the ground so that Brian could check under it for chocolate.

Sorcha's there, 'We're all in the same boat, Ross. We've been stuck in for nearly five weeks now. We've been eating, like, twice what we normally would, plus not *exercising*?'

She's actually right. I notice Brian's belly hanging over the waistband of his trousers like an untrimmed pie.

'Jesus,' I go, having a moment of, like, serious parental guilt, 'what kind of a rugby father *am* I?'

Sorcha's there, 'What are you talking about?'

'Letting them get out of shape like that. I might give Fla a ring.'

'Who's Fla?'

I laugh. I'll tell him she said that.

I'm there, 'Fla is the great Jerry Flannery. A hero of mine and, I'm proud to say, one of my best friends in the world on the rare occasions that he's actually talking to me. There's nothing he doesn't know about strength and condition . . . Okay, I've just remembered, he's *not* actually talking to me.'

Yeah, no, he focked me out of the bor last summer for heckling the singer while he was performing 'Limerick, You're a Lady' – a statement to which I apparently took drunken exception.

'We don't need Jerry Flannery,' Sorcha goes. 'We'll just use Joe Wicks.'

I'm there, 'Who's Joe Wicks? As in, who did he play for?'

'He didn't play for anyone – as far as I know. He's the Body Coach. He's on, like, TV and – oh my God – *all* over social media. He's doing online workouts for kids during the lockdown. Nine o'clock every morning.'

'Jesus Christ, nine o'clock is very early, Sorcha.'

'Well, I know from Instagram that Lauren is doing it every morning with Ross Junior and Oliver. And JP is doing it with little Isa. And William Whelehan is doing it with Currer Bell.'

She knows exactly what she's doing, because this suddenly awakens the competitor in me. So the following morning at, like, ten to nine, I'm shaking the boys awake and telling them that it's PE time.

'Get the fock out,' Leo goes, 'you fat bastard.'

'Yeah, *you're* the fat bastard,' I remind him. 'That's *why* we have to get up at stupid o'clock to exercise.'

He's not wrong, in fairness. My Leinster training top is definitely a bit snugger on me than usual. I may have gone too hord on the chocolate myself. Still, as I tell the boys while I'm setting up the laptop in the kitchen, I could burn off a stone in two weeks back in my rugby-playing days after a summer on the serious piss.

So anyway, a few minutes later, we're doing our warm-up with the famous – yeah, no – Joe Wicks. At the beginning, it's mostly just lunges and I'm being a bit more Sorgeant Major than Joe with my instructions.

I'm like, 'If it's not hurting, you're not doing it right, Johnny! Come on – hip flexor, hamstring, hip flexor, hamstring! That's it! Feel the burn!'

It's the same while we're doing the table-top stretch, the orm swings and the whole running on the *spot* thing? I'm going, 'Move your orse, Leo! You're supposed to be backs! I don't want you goys coming out of this lockdown looking like a hooker and two props! Move it!'

It's while we're bending down to supposedly touch our toes that I stort to feel weirdly faint. I stretch my right hand down as far as my – being honest – left shin and I can suddenly hear what sounds like rushing water in my ears. I'm also out of breath and I'm wondering is it because I've been shouting at the *boys* so much?

'Okay,' Joe Wicks goes, 'that's our warm-up completed. Now, let's do our first exercise.'

Our first exercise? I'm already focked. Seriously, my hort is beating like a jack-hammer and I'm sweating pints.

'Right,' Joe Wicks goes, 'a nice gentle exercise to start us off. Knees together. We're going to do two lateral jumps to the left, then two vertical jumps. Can we do that?'

Jesus, my breathing is seriously ragged now and I think I'm going to genuinely vom.

I'm like, 'That's it . . . goys . . . Jump – no, Johnny . . . left is . . . that way . . . One, two,' and suddenly I notice this, like, black border around the edges of my vision. 'Now, goys . . . jump up . . . into the air . . . Pretend . . . you're big . . . Devin T–'

And that's when everything goes suddenly dork.

The next thing I remember is feeling the hordwood floor against my back and a cold face-cloth on my forehead. And hearing Sorcha go, 'No, we're not going to bury your daddy in the gorden, Leo. He's not dead – he's just not as fit as he used to be.'

'You can't throw him out . . . There's a
pandemic going on out there.'
*The Irish Times, 9 May 2020*

So – yeah, no – I walk into the dining room to be confronted by a sight
I never thought I'd see. My five-year-old triplets are playing cords with
my old man, each with a lorge brandy in front of him and a cigor long
enough to inseminate a whale wedged between their tiny fingers.

I'm like, 'What the fock is going on here?'

The old man goes, 'I'm teaching the chaps how to play poker, Ross.'

'I'm not talking about the cords. I'm talking about them drinking.'

'Oh, it's just water with a bit of food colouring in it! It's a bit of fun,
that's all!'

'And the cigors?'

'They're not lit, Kicker.'

'Er, *Brian's* is?'

The old man suddenly notices that the kid is smoking like a focking
gorse fire.

'Brian, I told you to leave my lighter alone,' he goes, taking the cigor
from him. He puts it out in the ashtray, then hands it back to him.

I don't like the influence that my old man has been having on my
children since he storted self-isolating with us. Which is why I end up
having to say something.

'I don't want you turning my kids into miniature versions of you,' I
go. 'The last thing the world needs right now is three more Chorles
O'Carroll-Kellys.'

'Oh, Ross,' he tries to go, 'what horm is it? I'll see your two hundred,
Johnny – and I'm going to raise you three hundred!'

I look at the table. There must be, like, five grand on it.

I'm there, 'Is that *actual* money you're playing with?'

He goes, 'Don't worry about it, Kicker. I've explained to them that
we're not playing for keepsies. Although Leo there is a wily one. He
keeps slipping fifties into his pocket when he thinks his granddad isn't
looking!'

Leo – I swear to fock – goes, '*Parvus pendetur fur, magnus abire
videtur.*'

'That's right!' the old man goes. 'The small ones are hanged, the big
ones are not touched!'

'Quote-unquote!' Johnny goes.

I'm like, 'What the fock is going on under my own roof?'

I head for the kitchen. Sorcha is sitting at the table with the Singer sewing machine that her granny left her.

I'm there, '*He* has to go.'

She's like, 'Who?'

'The old man, Sorcha. He has to go.'

'You can't throw him out, Ross. There's a pandemic going on out there.'

'Out where?'

'Er, out in the *world*?'

'Well, I'm worried about the effect he's having on our children. You know they're playing poker with fake brandies and cigors? And real money?'

'I know. Oh my God, it's *so* cute the way they idolize him.'

'And you're perfectly okay with him teaching them Latin, are you?'

'Ross, I think it's amazing that they're getting to spend all this time with their grandfather. If this crisis has taught us anything, it's the importance of these, like, intergenerational *moments*? As a matter of fact, I'm going to ask Honor if she wants to help me with *my* project.'

She stands at the kitchen door and shouts up the stairs: 'HONOR? HONOR?'

I'm there, 'What's this project anyway?'

She goes, 'I'm making designer facemasks!' and she says it like it's the most natural thing in the world. 'It looks like these things are going to be port of our lives for a long time to come – so we might as well turn them into, like, *fashion* accessories? Loads of celebrities in the States are making them and selling them for, like, a thousand dollars each.'

'Is that your good Chloé dress you're cutting up?'

'It's for a good cause, Ross. I'm going to give the money to this amazing, amazing charity that's working to restore the urban tree canopy and improve levels of *climate* literacy?'

Honor walks into the kitchen then.

She goes, 'Why do you have to shout? I told you before, if you want me for something, just text me the details and I'll decide if it's important enough for me to come downstairs.'

Sorcha's there, 'Honor, I just wondered did you want to help me make designer facemasks?'

'No,' Honor goes, 'I'm busy with my *own* business?'

'Business? What business?'

'I'm selling supermorket delivery slots online.'

That ends up going down about as well as you'd expect.

Sorcha's there, 'You're doing *what*?'

'I've been booking hundreds of supermorket delivery slots weeks in advance,' Honor goes, 'then, as the time gets closer, I'm selling them for twenty euros each.'

Sorcha's like, 'But those slots are for people who can't get out and who have to do their shopping online!'

'Welcome to the horsh realities of the free morket,' Honor goes.

I recognize the line – just as surely as Sorcha does. She suddenly stands up from her sewing machine and morches up to the dining room, with me following closely behind.

'Chorles,' she goes, bursting into the room, 'did you encourage Honor to pre-book hundreds of supermorket delivery slots online?'

*He's* there, 'There's no need to thank me, Sorcha!'

'I wasn't *going* to thank you, Chorles. I was going to say how dare you teach my daughter to profiteer during an emergency.'

'As the great Hennessy Coghlan-O'Hara is wont to say, any old fool can make money when times are good. To make money during a time of crisis takes real entrepreneurship.'

I notice that Brian has relit his cigor and is puffing away on it like Columbo. No one seems to care.

'It's no different from you and those facemasks,' the old man goes. 'How much did you tell me you were selling them for? Five hundred euros apiece, wasn't it?'

'Chorles, I'm doing it to support an amazing, amazing charity. Plus, they're genuine Chloé.'

'Come on, Sorcha, we all know there's no such thing as a truly selfless act.'

'She's doing it because she wants people to think she's a good person,' Honor goes. 'She's doing it for Likes and Reposts on Instagram.'

The old man's there, 'It was the great Winston Churchill who said, "Some people regord private enterprise as a predatory tiger to be shot. Others look on it as a cow they can milk. Not enough people see it as a healthy horse . . . pulling a sturdy wagon!"'

'Quote-unquote!' Brian goes, fat Cohiba burning between his fingers.

Sorcha turns on her heel and storms out of the dining room, stopping only to say, 'He has to go, Ross!'

337

## 'I'm not performing some lame dance.'
### *The Irish Times*, 20 June 2020

So, yeah, no, I'm enjoying some quality time with my kids – as you do. Me and Honor are watching a YouTube video of wedding day fails, while Brian, Johnny and Leo are rolling around on the floor, basically killing each other.

A groom – very clearly hungover – spews his breakfast right down the front of the bride's dress while they're exchanging their vows and me and Honor nearly herniate ourselves laughing.

Suddenly, Sorcha walks into the room. She's like, 'Okay, everyone,' pulling the boys aport, 'we're going to do something together this morning – as a family.'

Me and Honor are both like, 'Excuse me?' straight on the defensive.

She's there, 'We're going to do a TikTok dance!'

I'm like, 'A TikTok dance? Is that not a bit, I don't know, six weeks ago?'

'Exactly,' Sorcha goes. 'We're pretty much the only family I know who *hasn't* done one yet? Julie from yoga did one with her daughters, Bayley and Madison, and it's – oh my God – so cute! And I was thinking, wouldn't it be an amazing souvenir to have of, like, the *lockdown*?'

'Oh my God,' Honor goes, 'watch this one, Dad – the mother of the bride falls face-forward into the cake!'

I laugh. Six tiers – totally obliterated. It takes four people to pick the woman up. I'm like, 'Let me see that one again, Honor.'

But Sorcha closes over the laptop and goes, 'You can watch that later, Honor. Come on, everyone, we're going to do Blinding Lights.'

I'm there, 'Sorcha, I'm not sure we're that kind of family.'

'What,' Sorcha goes, 'a family who likes fun? Of course we are. Now, I'll show you the steps. Boys, watch me,' and she storts jumping around like an aerobics teacher on coke. 'You bounce on your right foot while tapping your left foot in and out. You keep the motion going and then dab with your hands while continuing to tap your left foot out. Next, you're going to lift your hands together and –'

This *happens* from time to time? Sorcha gets a sudden burst of enthusiasm for something and we end up having to dampen it down.

'Yeah, take the focking hint,' Honor goes. 'We're not interested in your bullshit.'

But even that fails to put the fire out completely.

Sorcha's there, 'I just think it'd be a nice thing to have in years to come – a positive to come out of the pandemic.'

'I'm not performing some lame dance,' Honor goes, 'just so you can pretend to your friends on social media that we're this, like, cutesy family living this dream life. How old are you – ten?'

Leo laughs. He's like, 'Yeah, how old are you – ten?'

I watch Sorcha's eyes fill up with tears. She turns on her heel and she storms out of the room. A few seconds later, I hear the front door slam.

I'm there, 'Honor, that was possibly a *bit* horsh?'

She goes, 'Got the message, though, didn't she?'

'No, I mean it, Honor. You really upset her.'

'She wants all her mates on social media to think she has this, like, perfect family – she's so focking needy.'

'So what, Honor? Is it too much to ask to let her have her little thing? Jesus, the amount of stuff she does for us. She's the one who's kept the show on the road since this whole Corona thing happened. Cooking meals, overseeing the home-schooling, doing the online shop, while also trying to work from home. It's only a few dance steps, Honor.'

'You've never spoken to me like this before.'

'Well, maybe it's time I storted. She's your mother, Honor. And, in case you've missed it, she's a pretty focking amazing person. Even though she *can* be annoying a lot of the time.'

With that, I just, like, storm out of the room as well. I tip downstairs and then outside. Sorcha is sitting on the bench halfway down the gorden, staring out at the sea. I sit down beside her. I don't say anything. I just put my orm around her.

This is the Rossmeister that my critics never get to see.

She doesn't look at me. She just goes, 'Are we bad parents, Ross?'

I'm there, 'We give our children literally everything they ever ask for. I fail to see what else we can do.'

'God forgive me for saying this, Ross, but they're not nice kids.'

'I know that – but they're not finished yet. They're, like, a work in progress. Who knows *how* they'll turn out.'

'Have a look at Julie from yoga's Instagram. Bayley and Madison have brought her breakfast in bed every single day during the lockdown.'

'They sound like dorks, in fairness.'

'They're not dorks. They're beautiful little girls who have an amazing, amazing relationship with their mother.'

'You think it's like that all the time? Trust me, there must be days when Julie sees them coming with the breakfast tray and thinks, "Jesus, not these two focking dickheads again."'

'Do you really mean that?'

'Sorcha, it's Instagram. It's people showing you the very best version of their lives. Sorry for being deep, but it's not reality – as in, it's not *actual*?'

She doesn't say anything for ages. Eventually, she goes, 'I don't know if it's, like, cabin fever – or if it's just everything that's going on in the news right now – but I've storted to wonder did we do the wrong thing bringing children into this world?'

'Hey, that's port of what it is to be a parent, Sorcha. To always be asking yourself that question. Again – deep.'

All of a sudden, her phone beeps. She stares at it for a few seconds, then she goes, 'It's from Honor. It's a video.'

I'm like, 'Open it,' which is what she ends up doing.

We sit and we watch it together. The girl is standing in a line with her three brothers and they're singing, 'So long, farewell, Auf Wiedersehen, goodnight,' with all the waves and the bows and the twirls in the right places.

Sorcha puts her hand over her mouth. 'Oh my God,' she goes, because *The Sound of Music* is literally her favourite movie.

'I hate to go,' they sing, in perfect harmony, 'and leave this pretty sight . . .'

I feel a tear slip from my eye, just as I watch one slip from hers, because the question of whether we did the right thing has been well and truly answered. For today.

### 'I habn't addything for Foxrock until the Twenty-Sixth Sunday in Ordinary Time.' *The Irish Times*, 11 July 2020

I'm watching Ronan working four mobile phones at the same time, plus the – believe it or not – *house* phone?

'Ine soddy,' he's going, 'I habn't addything for the Choorch of the Apostoddles for this Sunday. You're arthur leaving it veddy late in the day, so you are. I can get you into St Alphonsus and Columba Choorch, if that's addy use to you. Yeah, it's the one in Baddybrack Viddage.'

The old man, I notice, is just, like, staring at him – we're talking, like, *totally* mesmerized? We've got, like, the pair of them, plus Sorcha's old dear, living with us at the moment. They're saying this lockdown is going to be a big challenge for unhappily married couples and don't we focking know it? Honalee is like a focking shelter for separated spouses at the moment.

I'm there, 'What's going on?'

'Well,' he goes, 'it seems that young Ronan here is doing a line in black morket tickets for Masses and other church services.'

I'm like, '*Excuse* me?'

'You see, the fifty-person limit on indoor gatherings has apparently made tickets for Sunday Masses the most sought-after commodity in Ireland today – even more than hand sanitizer and facemasks. I'll tell you something for nothing, Ross – this country won't stay down for long, not with entrepreneurs like your son around.'

Ronan puts a caller on hold to answer another one of his phones. 'Mass tickets,' he goes. 'Buying or sedding?'

He listens for a few seconds, then he's like, 'Foxrock? You're habbon a laugh, ardent you? I habn't addything for Foxrock until the Twenty-Sixth Sunday in Ordinary Time. I'll tell what I've got for this Sunday, but. I've two for ten o'clock mass in the Choorch of the Guardian Angels on Newtownpeerk Abenue. They're for the South Transept. Hodestly, I've nothing for the Nave this side of the Assumption. Although I can put you in the Nave in the Choorch of St Thérèse in Mount Meddion at midday if you've addy inthordest in that?'

I end up just shaking my head.

'Okay,' I go, 'speaking of things that are wrong on every possible level, I need to talk to you about what happened the other day.'

'The other day?' the old man *actually* tries to go. 'What happened the other day?'

I'm there, 'Are you genuinely going to make me say it? You and Sorcha's old dear were bumping uglies in the back of my rented RV.'

'Oh,' he goes. 'That.'

And I'm like, 'Yes, Dad – *that*!'

He's there, 'I thought I explained at the time, Ross, that nothing untoward happened. Sorcha's mother and I were merely looking around the vehicle, admiring the leather upholstery and so forth. Then the thing started moving. We tried to alert you to the fact that we were inside, but you couldn't hear our shouts. I expect you were listening to the famous Snoopy and the Doggy Dogs with the volume up high.'

I'm there, 'The bed had been slept in and you had lipstick all over your ear. Don't even *try* to bullshit me of all people.'

Ronan's going, 'I've two Premium Seats for the Choorch of the Hody Tridity in Doddamede this Sunday. Eleben o'clock Mass. They're fifty eurdos each, but – not a woord of a lie – they're so close to the altar, you'll practically be saying Mass yisser selves.'

I'm there, 'I seem to be the only one in this family with a working moral compass. I mean, how did *that* happen?'

'Okay,' the old man goes, 'I admit it. We were both of us seized by a moment of passion.'

'Jesus.'

'Obviously, though, we'd both appreciate it very much if Sorcha never found out about what happened.'

'Your sordid little tryst in the back of a camper van?'

'There was nothing sordid about it.'

'Er, it's *incense*, Dad.'

'Yes, you've reached for a word there, Ross, and taken the wrong one down from the shelf. For the record, there was nothing incestuous about it either. Sorcha's mother and I are not related except through the marriage of our children.'

'Well, you can rest easy, Dude. I'm hordly likely to shout about it from the rooftops. Although Honor is the one you need to worry about. She'll almost certainly blackmail you.'

'She did blackmail me. I gave her a thousand euros this morning.'

'A thousand yoyos?'

'Your children really are a credit to you, Ross.'

Ronan's on the landline, going, 'Foxrock? For when? You're pudding me woyer! Are thee Nave? How far back? Much do you waddant for them? What do you think I am – greeyun?'

'Enterprise!' the old man shouts.

I'm there, 'Dude, I just need to know that what happened was a one-off.'

'What do you mean?'

'Er, I need to know that it's not going to happen again. As in, you and her. Okay, it might not be incense, but it's certainly weird.'

'Look, Ross, the last few months have been hord on us. Your mother and I are going through one of our famous separations, while Sorcha's mother is absolutely adamant that her marriage to Sorcha's father is finished. We both have needs, Ross.'

'Don't.'

'Physical needs that demand satisfaction. Sorcha's mother is a very attractive woman – I don't know if you've ever noticed.'

'I don't think about my mother-in-law in that way. Because I'm not a deviant.'

'Well, it's a fact, Ross. You know, in a certain light, she's always reminded me of Diane Keaton, except with obviously thicker legs.'

Her legs aren't her best feature, in fairness to her.

I'm there, 'My point is, whatever *needs* you two supposedly have, you're going to have to find some other way to meet them. Because that is definitely not going to be happening under my roof.'

He goes, 'Like I said, Ross, it was a moment of pure lust. Two lonely people making a desperate grab for each other in a time of existential crisis.'

I'm there, 'I'm glad to hear it.'

'I've only got standing tickets for St Odiver's in Navan this Sunday,' Ronan goes, 'but you'd be way down back, practically in the Narthex. Now, I *can* let you have two Premium Nave seats for nine o'clock Mass in St Mary's. Only thing is, but, they're part of a Combi Package. You'll have to block book them until the Thirtieth Sunday in Ordinary Time.'

The old man goes, 'There's just one small problem, Kicker.'

I'm like, 'What's that?'

'In the midst of our more than satisfactory lovemaking, romantic fool that I am, I may have mentioned that I loved her.'

> 'I'm not holidaying in Ireland. I'd
> rather nail my eyelids shut.'
> *The Irish Times*, 18 July 2020

'I say let's drive the entire thing,' Sorcha goes, 'from Malin Head to Mizen Head. Ross, are you even listening to me?'

I'm *not*, by the way? Me and the boys are throwing the old Gilbert around the gorden.

Honor is sitting in her egg chair. She's the one who actually cops it. She looks up from her phone and goes, 'Are those the names of places in Ireland that you're saying?' and there's the sound of genuine concern in her voice.

Sorcha's like, 'Yes, Honor! I'm talking about us driving the Wild Atlantic Way!'

I'm there, 'What?' because I'm definitely listening now. 'Why? As in, why the fock?'

'The last few months have been unbelievably stressful,' she goes. 'On top of the whole lockdown thing, we've got my mom, your dad and Ronan all living under our roof. We actually *need* a holiday at this stage?'

I'm like, 'So what's wrong with Quinta do Lago?'

She goes, 'Quinta do Lago is in Portugal, Ross.'

This may or may not be true. I've never thought about it *being* in any specific country? All I know is that my old man has a massive penthouse aportment there and we've stayed there every summer for the past, like, ten years.

'Even presuming what you're saying is true,' I go, 'what's wrong with Portugal?'

Sorcha's like, 'We've been through this already. We agreed that because of the whole, like, pandemic thing, we'd holiday in Ireland this year. Ross, I told you to cancel the flights.'

I'm there, 'And Honor told me not to.'

She's like, 'What? Why?'

Honor goes, 'I'm not holidaying in Ireland. I'd rather nail my eyelids shut.'

'Honor,' Sorcha tries to go, 'Ireland is one of the most beautiful countries in the world!' and then we all wait around for a good sixty seconds for Sorcha to follow up with something. She doesn't.

I'm there, 'Er, is it possible to go into, like, specifics, Sorcha?'

And she goes, 'I'm not going to go into specifics, Ross. I'm just saying that Keeva Rowell from my Glee Dance Class did the whole, like, Wild Atlantic Way thing in June and it looked – oh my God – ah! mazing! Certainly on Instagram!'

Honor sort of, like, sniggers to herself.

'What's so funny?' Sorcha goes. 'If Keeva and her family can staycation in the national interest, then we owe it to the country to staycation as well.'

Honor's there, 'If everyone on Instagram's who's *claiming* to be doing the Wild Atlantic Way was *actually* doing the Wild Atlantic Way, you wouldn't be able to move on it for cors.'

I'm there, 'Hang on, are you saying she's lying, Honor?'

'I'm saying *everyone* is lying!'

'What,' Sorcha goes, 'all these people who are on social media talking about – okay, I'm trying to think of something specific – the Blasket Islands, or – yeah, no – the Aillwee Cave –'

'Yes, they're all in Quinta do Lago.'

'Honor, there's no way Keeva would lie about something like that.'

'We met her coming out of Morton's in Ranelagh yesterday – she had an actual suntan.'

'So?'

'Er, it's been raining in Ireland since the end of May.'

'Yeah, no, she said they had one or two sunny days in Donegal.'

Honor laughs. 'Yeah,' she goes, 'you keep telling yourself that.'

'But why would she lie, Honor?'

'Because she wants to go on holiday and she doesn't want people like you being all judgy-judgy about it.'

'You're so cynical, Honor.'

'And you're not cynical enough. Okay, let's just imagine for a second that Dad is having another one of his affairs.'

I'm like, 'Whoa, steady on, Honor. I'm on *your* side, bear in mind?'

'I'm just saying, what does Mom do when she suspects that you're cheating on her? She goes looking for the evidence.'

That's actually true. She's like Jessica Fletcher when she has the sniff of dishonesty in her nostrils. I watch Sorcha's face turn suddenly serious.

'Well, that's the port of her brain that she needs to engage right now,' Honor goes. 'Because we'll be eating soup with blankets around us in focking Drizzle Mór, County Galway, next week, while everyone else from South Dublin will be sipping piña coladas, looking at our pictures and saying, "Thank fock that's happening to them and not us!"'

Sorcha whips out her phone and suddenly her thumbs are just a blur of activity.

She's like, 'I still don't think Keeva would go to the trouble of – ,' and then she suddenly stops. 'Oh my God, I've just checked the weather app. The sun – *literally*? – hasn't shone in Donegal for, like, six weeks.'

'Told you,' Honor goes in a singsong voice.

'Okay, I'm going into her Instagram account and I'm going to check if . . . There, see, she couldn't be lying, Honor, because there she is in Dingle, having dinner in Out of the Blue – with Breffni, look! And there they are on the boat, with the kids, going out to see the famous Fungie!'

'Er, those pictures could have been taken *any* time?' Honor goes.

I'm like, 'Well said, Honor,' because I'm a massive believer in positive enforcement. 'She's not so sure any more – look at her face.'

Because suddenly Sorcha is staring at her phone with her jaw unhinged. 'Oh my God,' she goes, 'look at her hair! It's long! Oh! My! God! These pictures were taken *last* summer!'

Honor's there, 'Quinta. Do. Lago.'

'So if *she's* lying about staycationing in Ireland,' Sorcha goes, 'does that mean Dochara Stephens who I work with is *also* lying?'

I'm there, 'It's not lying if you're trying to stop people finding out things you don't want them to know about you,' as my old man told the judge at his perjury trial.

Sorcha's thumbs go to work again. Thirty seconds later, she goes, 'Oh my God, Dochara isn't even *in* any of these photographs. One or two of them have the Fáilte Ireland logo on them! She's taken these from the Internet! Hang on, there's one here of two glasses of champagne. First day of the holiday, it says. Oh my God, I recognize that countertop. Ross, that's Flutes in Dublin Airport! They're all lying. Everyone is lying.'

I'm there, 'Does that mean we're going to – if you're to be believed – Portugal?'

And Sorcha's like, 'Too focking right it does.'

## 'I thought you were one of those fakecationing families.'
### *The Irish Times*, 25 July 2020

'Oh my God,' Sorcha goes – this is while we're sitting in the airport departures lounge, 'what if someone, like, recognizes me?'

I'm there, 'Sorcha, you're wearing Ray-Bans, a facemask and a baseball cap. How is anyone going to recognize you?'

'Sorcha! Lalor!' a voice goes. It ends up being Stephanie Spangler, a girl she was in, like, *school* with? 'I haven't seen you in – oh my God – years!'

Sorcha's like, 'Oh my God, Stephanie! You look ah! mazing! – as in, like, teeny-tiny! You're obviously still going to spinning classes.'

'I'm actually an *instructor* now. So where are you goys flying to today?'

I'm there, 'Quinta do –'

'Farranfore,' Sorcha quickly goes.

Stephanie laughs. She's like, 'Quinta do Farranfore? I've never heard of it.'

'Yeah, no,' Sorcha goes, 'it's just our little staycationing joke. Because we usually go to, obviously, Quinta do Lago. But this year we're doing the whole, like, Wild Atlantic *Way* thing?'

'Is that not a bit random for you?'

'Well, we just felt that – given the whole Coronavirus thing – holidaying abroad was definitely the wrong thing to do.'

'You always had a really strong sense of social responsibility,' Stephanie goes, 'and that's not me being a bitch. I remember when you chaired the Mount Anville Peace and Justice Committee.'

'Yeah, no, I was the one who actually set it up.'

'That's like, oh my God.'

'Thanks.'

'So the Wild Atlantic Way? I've heard good things – again, not being a bitch.'

'Yeah, no, we're going to rent a camper van and really take our time doing it, aren't we, Ross?'

I'm like, 'Er, yeah,' but at the same time I'm actually shocked at how easily the lies are tripping off her lips behind that mask. She'll have to be watched more closely in future.

Honor and the boys arrive back from the shop then – perfect timing.

Honor goes, 'I got the factor fifty, Dad.'

'Factor fifty?' Stephanie goes. 'I hope you get the weather you're expecting!'

Sorcha's like, 'It can get really hot in Kerry, Stephanie.'

Honor's there, 'But they didn't have any mosquito repellent.'

'Mosquito repellent?' Stephanie goes. 'Er, do they even *have* mosquitos in Kerry?'

Sorcha's like, 'Oh my God, massive ones! A girl I know from Erasmus got bitten in Sneem.'

'That's like, Oh! My! God!'

'That's exactly what I said at the time, wasn't it, Ross?'

I'm like, 'Words to that effect, yeah.'

Leo is just, like, staring at Stephanie, his big Coca-Cola bottle glasses fogging up above his mask. He has a definite eye for the ladies – takes after you know who.

'Who's this focker?' he goes.

Stephanie puts her hand on her chest and acts all shocked. You'd swear she'd never heard a five-year-old drop a fock-bomb before – and her from, originally, Glasthule.

Sorcha's there, 'Please don't react to it, Stephanie. We're trying not to create taboos around certain words in case it makes them more attractive to them.'

'Yeah, who the fock *is* she?' Johnny goes.

I'm like, 'This is a friend of Mommy's from school – who I *also* knew back in the day?'

Stephanie once gave me a love bite up at the Witch's Hat and I had to tell Sorcha that I got it playing paintball, although I decide to not add that detail.

Brian goes, 'We're going to Quinta do focking Lago.'

Stephanie's like, 'Excuse me?'

'Again,' Sorcha goes, 'please don't respond to it, Stephanie. We don't want to derail all the years we've put into ignoring the problem.'

'It's not the swearing,' Stephanie goes. 'He said you were going to Quinta do Lago.'

Sorcha's there, 'Errr,' because we've been busted here in a major way.

'Yeah, *in* make-believe,' Honor goes, suddenly rescuing the situation. 'Just because we're not *going* to Quinta do Lago doesn't mean we can't pretend we're all there in our minds.'

'Exactly,' Sorcha goes. 'The best caldo verde I ever had was in Milltown Malbay.'

'Because for a minute there,' Stephanie goes, 'I thought you were one of those fakecationing families.'

Sorcha's like, 'Fakecationing? As in?'

'Oh my God, you must have heard about the fakecationers. All these people who are pretending that they're holidaying in Ireland because they're ashamed to let people know that they're actually in, like, France, or Spain, or Portugal.'

'That's so random,' Sorcha goes. '*So*, so random.'

Stephanie's there, 'And – oh my God – the lengths that some of them go to just to maintain the lie. My sister knows a girl who was posting other people's photographs on her Instagram to convince everyone that she was in West Cork when she was *actually* in Ibiza – obviously the nice bit.'

Yeah, no, in her orchive, Sorcha has Amie with an ie's photographs from her caravanning holiday in Connemara, as well as Claire from Bray's photographs from her sponsored cycle around the Ring of Kerry, ready to post.

'That's, like, oh my God,' Sorcha goes.

Stephanie's there, 'You took the words out of my mouth, Sorcha. But then there's, like, no way you'd do something like that – er, former Chairperson of the Mount Anville Peace and Justice Committee?'

'And founder.'

'You're just one of those people who always, always, always does the right thing.'

'Thanks.'

'And that's not intended as a criticism.'

'No, it's a genuinely lovely thing to hear. Oh my God, I'm so rude, I haven't even asked you where *you're* jetting off to – somewhere amazing I'm guessing.'

And, without missing a beat, Stephanie goes, 'Quinta do Lago.'

Sorcha's there, 'Excuse me?'

'I know, I know, I know,' Stephanie goes, 'none of us should be travelling to countries that aren't on the green list. But Graham and I had a really good think about it and, in the end, we just thought, Fock what anyone else thinks. Anyway, I'd better go. We're on the six o'clock flight.'

I'm there, 'The six o'clock flight?'

'To Faro,' she goes.

In other words, *our* flight.

She goes, 'Enjoy Farranfore. And watch out for those mosquitoes!' and then off the girl focks.

Sorcha sits there saying nothing for a good sixty seconds as we watch Stephanie join her husband in the queue for the gate.

I'm like, 'What happens now?' because there's no way Sorcha is going to get on that plane now.

'We're going back to the cor,' she goes.

I'm there, 'There might be a later flight. We can just switch.'

'What, and bump into Stephanie walking through Quinta do Lago?'

'So are you saying we're not going on holidays?' Honor goes.

And Sorcha's like, 'We are. But we're going to Kerry.'

> 'Er, the thing is, we're not actually *from* America?
> We're from, like, South Dublin – the accents
> would be definitely similar.'
> *The Irish Times*, 1 August 2020

'Can I have a glass of wine?' Honor goes.

And I'm there, 'I don't see why not.'

'Er, she's, like, thirteen years *old*?' Sorcha reminds me. '*That's* why not, Ross.'

But Honor goes, 'I know – oh my God – *loads* of girls who are allowed to have a glass of wine with their dinner when they're on, like, holidays.'

Sorcha's there, 'Well, *we're* not the kind of parents who allow our children to call us by our first names and buy them condoms with the weekly grocery shop. You're in Mount Anville, Honor – not a certain *other* school I could mention?'

Newpork.

I'm there, 'My friend Christian's old pair used to let him have wine with dinner from the time he was, like, ten years old. Although he ended up an alcoholic, so he's probably not a great example of what Honor's talking about.'

'Ross, our daughter is not having wine,' Sorcha goes. 'Now, can we please, like, *drop* the subject?'

This is us, by the way, sitting in A Fishy Business, a restaurant in Dingle recommended to us by Claire from Bray of all places.

Honor's there, 'I hate it here.'

'It's got, like, *two* Michelin stors,' Sorcha goes.

'I'm talking about Kerry. It's always, like, raining and it gets dork at, like, midday.'

'Er, *slight* exaggeration? It was still bright at, like, five o'clock today?'

'The only way I'm staying here is if I can, like, drink through it. If I can't have wine, can I have a gin and tonic, then?'

I'm there, 'Where do we stand on gin and tonics, Sorcha?'

That ends up storting the boys off.

Leo goes, 'I want a gin and tonic!' at the top of his voice. 'I want a focking gin and tonic!'

And that's when the owner of the place decides to stop by our table for a quiet word.

'Hello there,' she goes – she's smiling, but you can tell she doesn't mean a word of it.

Sorcha's like, 'Oh my God, hi!' like Meghan Morkle meeting the Queen for the first time. 'I've been dying to try this place for – oh my God – *so* long? I've heard only good things about your barramundi thermidor.'

'Do you mind me asking you,' the woman goes, 'when did you arrive here?'

Sorcha looks at me.

'Er, last night?' she goes. 'We went to see, like, Fungie the dolphin today – didn't we, goys? – and we're going to take a drive out to, like, Slea Head tomorrow.'

'You know you're supposed to be quarantining?' the woman goes.

And that's when I pick up on the fact that every conversation in the place has stopped and everyone is just, like, *staring* at us?

Sorcha's there, 'Er, *excuse* me?' in her best L&H Society voice.

'The rules are that if you come here from America,' the woman goes, 'you're supposed to stay in for two weeks.'

Sorcha laughs. She's like, 'Er, the thing is, we're not actually *from* America?'

'You sound like you're from America.'

'Oh my God, I get that *all* the time! We're from, like, South Dublin – the accents would be definitely similar.'

The woman looks like she *might* be about to buy this when Honor all of a sudden pipes up.

'Why are you telling everyone that we're, like, Irish?' she goes, in an accent that's, like, pure *Beverly Hills 90210*. 'I'm, like, *proud* to be an American?'

That ends up drawing a few howls of anger from our fellow diners.

The owner goes, 'You do know, don't you, that you are endangering the lives of everybody in this restaurant?'

Honor looks at her phone and goes, 'Oh my God, you will not *believe* who Casey is taking to Junior Prom!'

Sorcha's there, 'You're not, like, *helping* here, Honor?'

'I'm sorry,' the owner goes, 'I'm going to have to ask you to leave.'

'But we're not *actually* American,' Sorcha tries to go.

'Please leave or I'll call the Guards.'

There's suddenly a shout of, 'Go home, Yank!' from a table on the far side of the restaurant and a sense that this could get ugly.

I'm there, 'Sorcha, we should maybe, like, *split*?'

'No,' Sorcha goes, 'I'm not going anywhere. I'll have the barramundi thermidor, please.'

'And I'll have a focking gin and tonic,' Leo goes.

The owner turns on her heel and focks off – presumably *not* to get my wife the main course she ordered, or my son his G&T.

There ends up being – I can't help but notice – a bit of an atmosphere in the restaurant after that. Sorcha folds her orms, like she's on one of her Mount Anville Peace and Justice Committee lunchtime sit-ins, while Honor looks at her phone and shouts out updates about the lives of Jaydon and Brandon and all her other imaginary High School friends.

'Probably Trump voters as well,' a man at the next table goes.

I'm going to be honest with you here – I'm actually *relieved* when the Feds show up? It ends up being two Gords – a Man Gorda and a *Bean* Gorda.

'Hello,' it's the *Bean* who goes. 'Is there some kind of problem here?'

'There's no problem,' Sorcha goes. 'Except I placed my order, like, twenty minutes ago and it still hasn't arrived.'

'Where are you from, do you mind me asking?'

'We're *from* the Vico Road!'

'And what state is that in?'

Sorcha ends up suddenly losing it. She goes, 'Are you saying you've never heard of, like, the Vico Road?'

They don't even bother answering her. Instead, the Man Gorda goes, 'Was it not explained to you on your arrival in Ireland that you were expected to self-isolate for two weeks before you went out into the community?'

'We're not American!' Sorcha roars. 'This is just how we, like, talk!'

Honor's there, 'Oh my God, Harper has mono! She's going to miss cheerleading camp!'

The Man Gorda looks at me then and goes, 'Where are yee staying?'

I'm like, 'The Corca Something or Other Guesthouse.'

'I know it well. I'm going to escort you back there now. And I'm going to be checking on you every day to make sure you're still quarantining.'

Sorcha goes, 'Oh my God, I can't *actually* believe this is happening!'

As we make our way to the door, everyone in the restaurant storts clapping. Honor turns around to the owner and she's like, 'Can I get a bottle of Cab Sav – to, like, *go*?'

> 'We could be in DeVille's tonight, enjoying
> a Sheelin Rib Eye among people who *get*
> where we're coming from.'
> *The Irish Times*, 8 August 2020

*Verbum Domini Manet in Aeternum* is a phrase that won't mean much to most people. But anyone who has ever passed through the French-polished, lavender-smelling hallways of Mount Anville Secondary School will recognize it as the motto of the Mount Anville Peace and Justice Committee, which – roughly translated – means, 'You want to see stubborn? I'll show you focking stubborn!'

My wife – the Committee's founder and Honorary Life President – quotes it to me on a regular basis. Like last summer, when she stayed up for four days and nights to make 1,600 cupcakes for a bake sale in aid of the Foxrock Children Without Skis Foundation, fuelled by caffeine suppositories and licking the top of a nine-volt battery to shock herself awake every time she felt her eyes close.

And like now, sitting in the Corca Something or Other Guesthouse in Dingle, where we've been told we have to quarantine for a fortnight because the natives – including the local Feds – heard our accents and mistook us for Americans.

The sensible thing to do at this point would be to follow the advice of the King's Hospital motto, which is to accept defeat early and try to get back on the road before the traffic gets bad. Except Sorcha is having none of it.

'Ross,' she goes, not even looking up from her iPad, 'I am *going* back to A Fishy Business and I am *having* their world-famous barramundi thermidor – even if I have to sit in this room for two weeks.'

I'm there, 'Sorcha, we *will* have to sit in this room for two weeks. There's a squad cor at the gate out there. I think you may have unnecessarily escalated the situation by threatening to report them to GSOC.'

'I will be reporting them to GSOC,' she goes, looking up from whatever it is she's reading. 'The Gords are supposed to be, like, a highly sophisticated crime *detection* agency? Those two out there can't tell the difference between, like, an American accent and, like, a South Dublin accent – that's like, er, *hello*?'

I'm there, 'I know it's like, er, *hello*? But are we not, like, cutting off our noses to, like, spite our faces here?'

'As in?'

'As in, why don't we just go home? We could be in DeVille's tonight, enjoying a Sheelin Rib Eye among people who *get* where we're coming from. Literally the Vico Road.'

'Ross, we said we were staycationing in Ireland and *that* is what we're doing.'

I look out the window. Through the grey mist and horizontal rain, I can see that a second squad cor has arrived.

'They're doing a shift change,' I go.

Sorcha's like, 'They're about to find out the meaning of the words, *Verbum Domini Manet in Aeternum.*'

I'm there, 'Sorcha, you won't last. You'll go absolutely bonkers stuck in this room for two weeks.'

'Oh, I've got plenty to keep me occupied,' she goes, her nose back in her iPad. 'There's a rumour on the Dalkey Open Forum that The Queen's is going to be turned into a massive Dealz and – oh my God – you can *imagine* how that's going down?'

I'm there, 'You can't spend two weeks of your life on the Dalkey Open Forum,' but, even as I'm saying it, I know how crazy I sound.

She totally could.

There's suddenly a loud knock on the door. It ends up being Maidhc, the *fear an tí*, with our breakfast.

'I ordered it to the room,' Sorcha goes. 'I thought it might be nice to have it in bed.'

'I'm about to come in,' Maidhc goes. 'Can yee put on yeer masks and stand against the far wall?'

Sorcha's like, 'Come on, Ross – it's just social distancing. It's the same everywhere.'

So we end up doing what we're told.

I hear Maidhc shout over his shoulder at his wife, 'I'm giving the Yanks their breakfast – I've only the one pair of hands!' and then into the room he walks.

I can't actually *believe* what I'm suddenly seeing? Maidhc is wearing, quite literally, painting overalls on top of his clothes and – I shit you not – a motorcycle helmet, a sort of makeshift hazmat suit to protect himself from the alien invaders.

'Turn around and face the wall!' he shouts. 'You're not in California now!'

So we turn and we face the wall.

'Answering only yes or no,' he goes, 'do yee want me to pour the tea for yee?'

'Er, no,' Sorcha goes, 'I'll do that.'

He's like, 'When yee're finished the breakfast, knock twice on the door, then put yeer masks on and stand facing the wall until I come to collect the tray. See, that's how we do things in *this* country,' and then off he focks.

Sorcha goes, 'Oh my God, the kippers smell amazing – although they're probably going to stink up the room.'

I'm just there, 'I'm going next door to see how the kids are getting on.'

I'm expecting them to be absolutely murdering each other, but I end up being surprised. They're all just, like, sitting up in their beds, staring at their devices, to the point where they don't even notice me come into the room.

I'm there, 'God, can you believe your old dear wants us to stay here for two weeks?'

'I don't mind,' Honor goes. 'I'm actually enjoying myself.'

I'm like, 'Okay, *how* could you be enjoying yourself?'

She looks up from her iPhone. 'I storted a rumour on the Dalkey Open Forum,' she goes, 'that The Queen's is going to be turned into a massive Dealz. I've been up all night debating the issue with your wife.'

That ends up being the last straw. Out to the kitchen I morch. Maidhc – I swear to fock – dives for cover behind the table when he sees me.

He's like, 'Jesus, Mary and the understanding husband, you'll kill us all, Yank!'

I'm just there, 'Where's your modem?'

He goes, 'It's on the counter there,' and he points at it.

I walk over to the box and I flick the switch to Off.

Maidhc goes, 'What in the name of God are you doing?'

I'm just like, 'Wait,' and we both stand there for, like, sixty seconds, just listening.

All of a sudden, I hear it. Honor goes, 'The focking WiFi is gone!'

And then twenty seconds after that, Sorcha's like, 'Ross, bring the cor around. We're going home.'

'He's totally poisoned our minds so that we think of – oh my God – *everything* in terms of conflict.'
*The Irish Times, 17 November 2020*

Amie with an ie says she can't believe he's gone. Sorcha blows her porty horn and everyone cheers.

'I was thinking tonight,' Chloe goes, 'that it's like that time in *The West Wing* when Jed Borlet had to step down after Zoey was kidnapped and John Goodman became the President and he was – oh my God – *such* a dick.'

'I said that!' Sorcha goes. 'I said that four years ago after Hillary was robbed.'

Chloe's there, 'Did you?'

'Er, *yeah*? I said I hated Donald Trump even more than I hated Glen Allen Walken. I said it in this very room.'

'Well, the point *I'm* trying to make is that the relief I feel now is the same as the relief I felt when Zoey was rescued and President Bortlet returned to the Oval Office.'

'Yeah, that's pretty much the same point *I* made? Again, four years ago. You've just, like, *reframed* it?'

Sophie is like, 'Oh my God, you two, does it *matter* who said it first? Surely all that matters now is that *he's* gone!' and then *she* blows *her* porty horn.

Chloe's there, 'You're actually right – er, *why* are we fighting?'

Sorcha goes, 'That's the thing about . . . actually I'm going to stop saying his name. He's totally poisoned our minds so that we think of – oh my God – *everything* in terms of conflict.'

And then she mutes her Zoom call and goes, 'Ross, you heard me say that, didn't you? About John Goodman?'

I'm there, 'Er . . .'

'It was four *focking* years ago, Ross! We were all in this room. Honor was walking around with the blond wig and the Make America Great Again sweatshirt, trying to upset me.'

I'm like, 'Er, yeah, no, it's all coming back to me now,' because she's three quarters of the way through a bottle of Moët & Chandon and she was getting by on two hours' sleep a night while they were still counting in Pennsylvania. 'What a total wagon.'

That's when Honor sticks her head around the door of the living room and goes, 'Er, the *kitchen's* on fire?'

And Sorcha's like, 'Yeah, nice try, Honor. Oh my God, you are so *not* ruining this night for me?' and she goes back to her Zoom porty.

Honor looks at me and goes, 'Dad, the kitchen really *is* on fire.'

And I'm there, 'Like she said, maybe don't push her buttons tonight. You know what a cranky drunk she can be.'

Honor just goes, 'Fine,' and off she focks.

Lauren's there, 'Do you know what I did tonight? I made Jill Biden's Pormesan chicken for dinner – the recipe was on the Forbes website. And – afterwards? – we had Ben & Jerry's Peanut Butter Cup ice cream!'

A long moment of silence follows and you can tell that Sorcha and the others are wishing they'd thought of it themselves.

'Oh my God,' Chloe, in fact, goes, 'we should have *all* done that!'

Sorcha's like, 'Is that his *actual* favourite dinner, though? Because I read a piece years ago in the *New Yorker* – you've probably all forgotten that I was a major fan when he was, like, *Vice*-President? – and it said his favourite food was pasta fra diavolo and that's not me being a bitch, Lauren.'

'I've just Googled it,' Amie with an ie goes, 'and it just says his favourite food is pasta with red sauce.'

'Er, that's what focking pasta fra diavolo *is*?' Sorcha goes and I move the champagne bottle beyond her reach.

'I'm just saying, it doesn't say that specifically,' Amie with an ie goes. 'And his favourite ice cream is actually salted peanut butter with chocolate flakes.'

'Yeah,' Lauren goes, 'but that was the nearest thing to it in Donnybrook Fair, Amie with a focking ie.'

Again, it's Chloe who goes, 'Oh my God, will you *listen* to us! You'd swear we *lost* or something?'

And Sorcha's like, 'I know. That's how bad he was for the world – it's, like, we've forgotten what happiness actually *feels* like?'

Honor sticks her head around the door again. She goes, 'Okay, I've managed to get the boys outside and I've phoned the fire brigade.'

Sophie's like, 'Oh my God, what's that about?'

'Oh, don't worry,' Sorcha goes, 'it's just Honor looking for attention as per usual.'

Lauren's there, 'Do you remember when we had the Wake for

Hillary and she was walking around with a Donald Trump mask and a MAGA sweatshirt?'

'It was actually a Donald Trump *wig*,' Sorcha goes, 'and your kids are hordly focking perfect, Lauren.'

Honor's there, 'Okay, I'm going outside now.'

'Honor,' I go, 'have you ever heard the story about the boy who cried wolf? If there *was* an actual fire, the smoke alorm would have gone off.'

'Except you took the batteries out of it last Christmas to put them in the Rock 'n' Roll Santa Claus who played the drums. And, secondly, do you know what happened at the *end* of the story of the boy who cried wolf?'

I don't, as a matter of fact. There's not a lot in my head – focking bingo balls.

Off she focks again.

Sophie's there, 'My grandmother was originally from Mayo, even though we kept it quiet for obvious reasons.'

'That's nothing,' Chloe goes, 'my dad knows a woman whose maiden name was Blewitt, even though they're the Enniscorthy Blewitts rather than the Ballina Blewitts and I think they might even spell their name B, L, U, E, T.'

'I'm sorry, *what* is the point of that story?' Sophie goes.

'I just thought it was interesting, that's all.'

'Well, *I* was making the point that I have *actual* Mayo blood in my veins – again, that's just between ourselves – and you interrupt me to tell some bullshit story that has, like, zero relevance to me possibly having the same, like, genealogy as the President Elect.'

Sorcha's phone all of a sudden beeps. It's, like, a text message. She reads it and she goes, 'Oh! My God!'

I'm there, 'What's the Jack? What's wrong?'

'It's Joy Felton next door,' she goes. 'She says our kitchen is on fire.'

# 2021

Ireland locks down for the third time in nine months as the number of COVID-19 infections increases substantially following a Christmas relaxation of government restrictions * Joe Biden is inaugurated as the 46th President of the United States, the oldest individual to hold the office * Ireland is removed as a tournament host for the UEFA European Championships due to a lack of guarantees on spectator numbers * The Jerusalema Challenge becomes the newest social media viral sensation * A coup in Myanmar removes Aung San Suu Kyi from power and restores military rule * The traditional St Patrick's Day meeting between the Taoiseach, Micheál Martin, and US President Joe Biden takes place virtually due to the pandemic * President Michael D. Higgins celebrates his 80th birthday * The government announces plans for Mandatory Hotel Quarantine for certain passengers arriving in Ireland from a list of high-risk countries * A record-breaking heatwave in Canada intensifies fears that the process of climate change is now irreversible * Leinster are beaten by Ronan O'Gara's La Rochelle in the semi-final of the European Champions Cup * The rollout of Covid vaccinations begins in Ireland * Political tensions between Ireland and Britain are heightened over the position of Northern Ireland post-Brexit * Labour's Ivana Bacik wins the Dublin Bay South by-election, following the resignation from the Dáil of former Fine Gael Housing Minister Eoghan Murphy * Ireland experiences a mid-summer heatwave as temperatures soar to above 25 degrees Celsius for five consecutive days * Irish jockey Rachael Blackmore becomes the first woman to win the Aintree Grand National * The Department of Health and Health Service Executive confirm that they have both been the victim of a ransomware cyber attack *

Meanwhile . . .

> 'Chorles has been reading up on it . . .
> It seems it's all port of some big conspiracy.'
> *The Irish Times, 23 January 2021*

It'd be fair to say that the old pair have never really gotten the hang of the whole, like, *Zoom* thing? Yeah, no, *she* still talks like she's shouting into a cave, while *he* keeps shaking his head and laughing to himself every sixty seconds, then saying shit like, 'Foxrock to Killiney! And look at that picture! H. G. Wells couldn't have predicted it!'

'So how have you both been?' Sorcha goes, just trying to come up with things to say.

The old man's like, 'Oh, you know – enduring, the same as everyone else! Can they still hear us, Fionnuala, do you think?'

'Yes, we can still hear you,' I go. 'Jesus, it's not two tin cans with a piece of string connecting them.'

'Oh, well,' Sorcha goes, trying to jolly things along, 'at least you'll be getting the vaccine soon.'

The old dear's there, 'OH, I WON'T BE GETTING IT FOR A LONG TIME, SORCHA.'

I'm like, 'Seriously, why are you shouting?'

'I SAW THE SCHEDULE,' the woman goes. 'THEY'RE DOING ALL THE OLD AND SICK PEOPLE FIRST.'

I'm there, 'And what do you think you are?'

'I *BEG* YOUR PORDON?'

'Let's not bother arguing over sick – we'll leave that to the Amazon reviewers who've read your books. But you're definitely old.'

'SIXTY ISN'T OLD ANY MORE, ROSS.'

'Yeah, no, seventy-five is, though.'

'SEVENTY-FIVE? WHAT ON EARTH MAKES YOU THINK I'M SEVENTY-FIVE?'

'Oh, little things. Like the fact that I was at your seventieth birthday porty – and it was five years ago. You do the focking maths. As my daughter says when she's home-schooling me.'

'I THINK YOUR MEMORY IS PLAYING TRICKS ON YOU, ROSS. THAT WAS MY *FIFTIETH* BIRTHDAY PORTY.'

'Yeah, you keep telling yourself that, Benjamin Buckled.'

Sorcha's there, 'Fionnuala, please don't tell me that you're deliberately placing yourself at the back of the queue for reasons of vanity.'

She like, 'IT'S NOT VANITY, SORCHA. IT'S JUST A FACT. I'M A LONG WAY OFF SEVENTY.'

'Yeah, a long way *past* it,' I go. I'm not trying to insult her. I'm just trying to make her see reason. 'You're older than dirt – and twice as ugly.'

Sorcha's there, 'Chorles, please talk some sense into your wife.'

'I would,' the old man goes, 'except I shan't be getting the vaccine at all!'

'Excuse me?'

'CHORLES HAS BEEN READING UP ON IT,' the old dear goes. 'IT SEEMS IT'S ALL PORT OF SOME BIG CONSPIRACY.'

Me and Sorcha are both, like, suddenly silent.

*He* goes, 'I think we've lost the connection, Fionnuala! Hello? Hello? No, I knew it was too good to be true!'

'We can hear you perfectly well,' Sorcha goes. 'We're just in, like, *shock* here?'

'Well,' the old man goes, 'shock doesn't even begin to describe my reaction to what I've discovered over the past few weeks! It seems this *thing* – let's not even dignify it by giving it a name, eh, Kicker? – was created in a laboratory as port of the Great Reset!'

I'm like, 'The great what?'

'The Great Reset! Oh, come on, you two, you must know about the plan by the world's political and financial elite to temporarily cripple the planet, socially and economically, so as to create the conditions that will allow a restructuring of how the world is governed?'

'Okay, how come I've never heard about this? Mind you, I wouldn't even walk into a room if I thought the news was on in there.'

'Oh, you won't hear about this on the news, Ross! You see, *they* don't want you to know the truth! They don't want you to know that this so-called Covid-19 was created on a petri dish as port of a plan to place the entire planet in a two-year cryogenic freeze, during which time the people of the world would come to accept military-style, stop-and-search policing as being in their own best interests – chaps with red hair, Ross, not out of Templemore a wet weekend, asking you where you're going and whether you consider a simple Cohiba Robusto to be an essential item!'

'And while we're all forcibly confined in this state of suspended animation, a shadow planetary government is hord at work, creating a new world order that will abolish personal ownership and property rights, rule by mortial law and subject us all to regular – inverted commas – *vaccinations* that will turn us all into Godless, sustainable-energy-loving liberals!'

Sorcha puts our microphone on mute.

'Oh my God,' she goes, 'your dad has learned how to work the Internet!'

I'm there, 'Well, maybe we should listen to what he has to say, Sorcha. He certainly has *me* convinced.'

'Er, no, we shouldn't, Ross. Your dad has disappeared down a misinformation slash disinformation rabbit hole.'

'So why don't we just tell him he's talking S, H, one, T, then?'

'Because I read an orticle in *The Gordian* about this – people who slip into this, like, alternative *reality*? And confronting them head-on never works. It simply hordens their views and increases their sense of being uniquely aware of what *they* see as the truth.'

He's still banging *on*, by the way?

He's going, 'The vaccine will be used to plant a microchip in your cerebrum so that this secret cabal will know everything about you, from whether you've changed your brand of cigor, to whether you're thinking of hiding money offshore, to what you had for lunch – right down to the nearest alcohol unit!'

'THEY'RE ALSO USING IT,' the old dear goes, 'TO TRY TO FORCE PEOPLE TO SAY THEY'RE OVER SEVENTY WHEN THEY'D CLEARLY PASS FOR FIFTY.'

I'm there, 'So what are we going to do?'

Sorcha goes, 'We're not going to make an issue out of it. I just think challenging your dad a didactic way is not the most effective way to combat this.'

'So pretty much the same approach to our children using bad language, then?'

Upstairs, I hear Johnny go, 'Fock you, you focking fock!'

The old man goes, 'I can see your lips moving, Ross and Sorcha, but I can't hear any sound coming from your mouths!'

'IT MUST BE A CROSSED LINE,' the old dear goes.

Sorcha's like, 'Just hang up, Ross. We need to come up with a plan.'

> 'Twenty or thirty pages into *Wuthering Heights*,
> I storted to think, oh my God,
> this is basically the story of my life.'
> *The Irish Times*, 20 February 2021

Johnny is having difficulty throwing the ball off his left hand. He's not putting enough spin on it to give it, like, distance *and* accuracy? I knock on the window and tell him as well.

I'm there, 'You're not putting enough spin on it to give it, like, distance *and* accuracy?' but Honor tells me to sit the fock down, like she's my teacher – which, I suppose, she actually *is*?

'If you want me to home-school you,' she goes, 'you're going to have to learn to concentrate, okay?'

I'm there, 'But how come *they're* allowed to go outside to play?'

'Because they're five years old,' she goes, 'and they're not proposing to sit the Leaving Cert for – what is it? – the *third* time?'

'Okay, that was uncalled for.'

'Dad, just sit down and try to, like, focus. Okay, we're doing English now. Did you stort that book I told you to read the last day?'

'Er, not only did I stort it, Honor, I actually *finished* it?'

Oh, that rocks her back on her kitten heels. The last time she saw me with a book in my hands, it was the Littlewoods Ireland catalogue – and that's only because an ex of mine was modelling a velour hoodie and a pair of form-hugging joggers on the cover.

'You read *Wuthering Heights*?' she goes.

And I'm like, 'Yes, Honor – surprising as that may seem, I did.'

She picks my copy up off the kitchen table and flicks through it. 'What, *all* of it?' she goes.

And I'm there, 'Every single page, Honor. Nice move, by the way, telling me that the dude ends up playing rugby at the end. That was the main reason I persisted through the first, like, hundred or so pages. But then I ended up getting really into the story, to the point where I didn't actually *care* that there was no rugby in it?'

'Oh my God,' she goes, 'what are all these things you've underlined?'

I'm there, 'Mainly big words that I didn't understand. I was planning to Google them later to find out were they *actual*?'

She just, like, shakes her head. I'm a genuine wonder sometimes. 'I can't believe you read an entire book in, like, a weekend,' she goes. 'So what did you think of it?'

I'm there, 'Yeah, no, I loved it. I thought it was going to be like a Christopher Nolan movie – that I was going to have to ask Sorcha to explain it to me over and over and over again, until I got bored and just pretended that I knew what the fock was going on.'

'What did you like about it in particular?'

'The main dude. Heathcliff – was that his name?'

'You're saying you were sympathetic towards him?'

'In a major way. I mean, Heathcliff was kind of the Ross O'Carroll-Kelly of his day, wasn't he? And I hope that doesn't come across as big-headed. Here, Honor, what's that thing you always call me?'

'What, a knob?'

'No, not that one.'

'A sad sack, clinging to the delusion that he could have been a rugby player?'

'Keep going.'

'A norcissist?'

'Bingo! See, I've looked that one up once or twice after you've said it. They think everything is about them, don't they? Well, twenty or thirty pages into *Wuthering Heights*, I storted to think, oh my God, this is basically the story of my life.'

'Er, *how* exactly?'

'Like I said, Heathcliff was a good-looking dude who could be a bit of a dick, especially when it came to women. But then the reason he was like that was because of his, I don't know, *background*?'

'Keep going.'

'Well, that Mr Earnshaw took him in, even though Mrs Earnshaw wasn't keen. She wanted to fock him out onto the moors to fend for himself. And that was basically *my* old pair. As in, my old man really wanted me, but my old dear used to accidentally, on purpose, leave me in the National Gallery, or on the back seat of taxis.'

'This is good, Dad.'

'The only time in my childhood that I ever remember the woman smiling at me was when I was five years old and I mixed a strawberry Daiquiri for her in a way that pleased her. Anyway, so Heathcliff is, like, totally storved of love. And, like me, no one bothers their orse educating him. Plus, he's never allowed to forget the shame of his background.

In his case, it's that he was an orphan. In mine, it's that we lived on the affordable side of the Glenageary Road.'

Honor laughs. She's like, 'Keep going.'

'Heathcliff was in love with Catherine,' I go. 'And they were, like, totally attuned to each other – we're talking mentally, we're talking spiritually, we're talking, I don't know, whatever *else* there is?'

Honor's there, 'So, like, who's Catherine in your story?'

'Well, Catherine is obviously rugby,' I go. 'As in, the one true love of my life, who I wanted to, like, *be* with? Except – yeah, no – it was stolen away from me by Edgar Linton, who I pictured as either Declan Kidney, or Warren Gatland, or a combination of both – if you can imagine such a terrible thing.'

'Keep going.'

'So, instead, Heathcliff ended up marrying the naive and impressionable Isabella, who's basically your old dear. Don't tell her that, by the way. Like Sorcha, she was totally infatuated with her man, mistaking him for some kind of romantic figure, even though everyone told her he was a dick and she was making the biggest mistake of her life, including her old man, out of the corner of his mouth, even as he was walking her up the aisle of Foxrock Church.

'But even though Heathcliff married the girl, he was driven slowly mad with bitterness for the life that was stolen away from him and yearning for his one true love, crying out in his sleep at night – even as Sorcha lay in the bed beside him – "Rugby! Oh, rugby!" and "Fock you, Warren Gatland!"'

Honor just, like, smiles at me and goes, 'You can go outside and play, Dad.'

I'm like, 'Really?' jumping up from my chair.

And she goes, 'Yeah, you've earned it.'

'Honor, I hope we didn't raise you to believe that just because we live in a big house in Killiney, we should be allowed to use our money to skip the queue.'
*The Irish Times, 20 March 2021*

'Why don't they just give us all the vaccine?' Honor goes, with the innocence of a child. 'As in, why can't we just, like, pay to get it before everyone else?'

'The vaccine is being distributed on the basis of the greatest need,' Sorcha goes. 'We're not considered a priority.'

'What, even though we're rich?' Honor goes, and when she puts it like that – yeah, no – it *does* seem unfair?

Sorcha's there, 'Honor, I hope we didn't raise you to believe that just because we live in a big house in Killiney, we should be allowed to use our money to skip the queue.'

Honor goes, 'We use our money to skip every other queue. Why should this one be any different?'

Yeah, no, it's possibly our fault for spoiling the girl. We Fast Passed our way around Disneyland Paris when she was, like, five years old and we may have created an expectation that her entire life was going to be like that.

Sorcha just, like, sighs. Hey, she was the one who was worried that Netflix was – direct quote – turning our brains into *foie gras* and insisted on having two evenings a week when we sit around as a family and – again, her word – *talk*?

'Okay,' she goes, 'changing the subject, what about all the things we're most looking forward to doing when this whole thing is, like, *over*? Okay, I'm going to go first. I'm looking forward to having a lorge gin and tonic while I have my hair done. I'm looking forward to being able to hug my mom and dad and go to the National Concert Hall with them. And I'm looking forward to having a porty, here in the house, for – oh my God – all our friends!'

I'm there, 'Except for Gareth and Claire from Bray of all places.'

She's like, 'What's wrong with Gareth and Claire from Bray of all places?'

'I think you'll find the answer's in the question,' I go. 'But on top of that, I saw *him* on a petrol station forecourt two days after Christmas, filling up the Avensis while wearing shorts.'

'That's because he's thinking about doing a triathlon.'

'He's been thinking about doing a triathlon for ten years. These were, like, board shorts, though. And Havanas. In the middle of focking winter. I hate dudes who do that. It's just so, "Look at me!" and I was, like, *this* close to just decking him on a point of principle.'

'Well, if we're cancelling Garret and Claire on that basis, then we're also cancelling Christian.'

'Er, why?'

'Because he put up a photograph on Instagram of him having a picnic with the kids in Stephen's Green two weeks ago. And before you say anything to defend him, Ross, he lives exactly 5.3 kilometres from Stephen's Green, because I checked.'

Honor goes, 'I really cherish these evenings we spend together as a family.'

'Oh my God,' Sorcha goes, 'that's what we'll do! I was reading in – it might have even been the *Irish Times* magazine – about how a lot of people are using lockdown as an opportunity to purge their friend lists and let the relationships that no longer work for them just, like, *slide*?'

Straight away, I'm like, 'Amie with an ie.'

'What's wrong with Amie with an ie?'

'Two weeks ago, I was in SuperValu in Dalkey, standing at the checkout with a full trolley. Her and her old dear came up behind me and asked me if they could play through because they only had, like, five items.'

'What's wrong with that?'

'I don't think that's something you ask to do. Yeah, no, you take it if it's offered. So I told them to fock off and Amie with an ie's old dear storted muttering under her breath about how I was rude and it was no wonder our children turned out the way they did. No offence, Honor.'

'Well, if we're culling Amie with an ie from our friend list, then we're also culling JP.'

'JP? We played rugby together!'

'I saw him last week, Ross, and he was wearing his mask *under* his nose. He might as well have not been wearing it at all. Plus – and this has annoyed me for years – he says "Pacific" when he means "specific". And before you say it, rugby is not an excuse.'

'Okay, what about Simon and Rachael with two a's?'

'What about them?'

'We have dinner with them, like, three times a year, even though the only thing we have in common is that we met them on holidays in, like, 2009. And *he* insists on calling Dubai "Dubes", even though Dubes are things you wear on your feet. And if I have to sit through that anecdote again about how a waiter offered him five camels in exchange for Rachael, I'll end up glassing the focker.'

'Did you know that Oisinn had, like, a dinner porty in his house two weeks ago – for eight people with, like, zero social distancing? Plus, when he doesn't hear something you say, he doesn't go, "What?" or even "Pordon?" He goes, "The which?" and that – oh my God *so* irritates me.'

'Well, if Oisinn's cancelled, then so is your mate Sophie.'

'What did Sophie ever do?'

'She's always banging on about her *rescue* dog – like *she's* its focking saviour or something. She went to the pound, pointed at the cutest one and said, "I'll take it." I'm sorry, that is *not* a rescue situation, Sorcha. End of.'

The conversation continues in this vein for, like, an hour, the two of us ripping the backs off pretty much everyone we know. Chloe uses the word 'rosemantic'. Sorcha's sister and her boyfriend took us to a restaurant once where there's no actual menu and they serve you – I shit you not – 'whatever's in season', take it or leave it. Everyone we know ends up getting roasted.

And that's when I realize that Honor has been suspiciously quiet for the entire thing. I mention it to her as well. I'm there, 'What are you thinking about, Honor?'

'I was thinking,' she goes, a big, evil grin on her face, 'what a shame it would be if someone recorded this entire conversation and sent it to everyone in your contacts list.'

## 'So I urge you all – standing here, in the People's Pork – to REMOVE YOUR MASKS!'
### *The Irish Times*, 13 March 2021

The People's Pork in Dun Laoghaire is rammers and there's, like, a definite *tension* in the air? You can see that even the Gords are nervous.

I can hear drunken shouts of, 'Why don't you fock off back down the country?' like my old dear in the restaurant in Brown Thomas every eighth of December. 'You sprout-eating clods!'

And, meanwhile, my old man is doing what my old man does best – listening to the sound of his own voice in three-figure decibels.

He's holding a megaphone to his mouth and he's going, 'Ladies and gentlemen, we have been duped! We have been taken in by a plot to divest us of the fundamental human rights that were fought for – however misguidedly – by the patriots of Ireland's proud past! We have been rendered prisoners in our own homes!'

And suddenly, behind the masks, you can hear the low buzz of people tutting, going, 'The whole thing's ridiculous at this stage!' and the general hubbub of people being – as they say in this port of the world – up in orms.

'We are moving into our second year of living under mortial law!' He goes, 'We, the people, are being subjected to a level of control and repression that has never been experienced before in all of human history and we have not only submitted to it willingly, we have done so on the understanding that it is in *our* best interests! To be told where we can go, how we can worship, who we can see, how we can love!

'And, like dutiful sheep, we have gone along with it all! We have cut our social contacts down to only our closest family – our interactions with the outside world restricted to cloud-based, peer-to-peer, video-conferencing platforms, which *they* can switch off – and *will* switch off – when they deem the time is right!'

Sorcha turns around to me and goes, 'The atmosphere is getting ugly.'

I'm there, 'Yeah, no, he's certainly whipping the crowd up alright.'

'Maybe I'll shout something,' she goes, 'to invite people to consider, like, the *counter* orgument?'

'Which is?'

'That lockdowns do actually work if properly observed.'

'I don't think you should shout that.'

'Why not?'

'Because this isn't Mount Anville running rings around Muckross College in the All Ireland Debating Championships. This is, like, real life, Sorcha – as in, like, *actual*?'

'Look at us!' the old man goes. 'Look at the person to your left! To your right! Behind you! In front of you! Do you recognize him? Do you recognize her?'

He has an actual point. I haven't seen this many South Dublin people in masks since the night we accidentally ended up at an *Eyes Wide Shut* porty on Ulverton Road. Yeah, no, Sorcha somehow managed to miss the creepy vibes given off by a dude who was on her Renewable Energy and Environmental Finance course in the Smurfit Business School, until we'd been at the party for twenty minutes and a woman dressed as the Pope tried to set fire to my chest hair with a Zippo.

'They have ordered us to cover our faces,' the old man goes, 'with masks of non-woven material, to rob us of our individuality! To steal from us that which makes us unique as human beings! So I urge you all – standing here, in the *People's* Pork – to REMOVE YOUR MASKS!'

'NOOO!!!' Sorcha roars. 'LABORATORY STUDIES HAVE SHOWN THAT MASKS ARE UP TO NINETY-FIVE PER CENT

EFFECTIVE IN BLOCKING THE TRANSMISSION OF PATH-
OGENS SHED IN RESPIRATORY DROPLETS! PLUS, YOU
CAN STILL ASSERT YOUR INDIVIDUALITY BY CREATING
ONE OF, LIKE, YOUR *OWN* DESIGN?'

But it's no good. The old man has whipped this crowd up into an actual frenzy. They stort literally peeling off their masks while *he* goes, 'THAT'S IT! BREATHE! BREATHE IN THAT CLEAN AIR THAT THEY WOULD HAVE YOU BELIEVE IS FILLED WITH POISONS! NOW, LADIES AND GENTLEMEN, LET US SEND A MESSAGE TO THE CABAL OF LIZARD PEOPLE WHO HAVE TAKEN OVER DÁIL ÉIRE-ANN AND THEIR VOLE KING, JEFF BEZOS, THAT WE ARE NOT PREPARED TO PUT UP WITH IT ANY MORE! LADIES AND GENTLEMEN, LET US MORCH . . . ON LEINSTER HOUSE!'

It'll tell you something about the mood of the crowd that no one objects to the idea of actually walking into town – and I know people from Killiney and Dalkey who quite literally drive to their own front gates to collect their mail.

'Quick!' Sorcha goes. 'Let's lock them in!' and before I can try to talk sense into her, she's hared off in the direction of the Upper George's Street gate with the intention of, like, slamming it shut and holding three or four hundred people prisoner.

Unfortunately for her, the old man leads his supporters out through the Marine Terrace gate, which forces Sorcha to come up with a new plan.

'Let's get in the cor,' she goes, 'and we can head them off outside Meadows and Byrne.'

I'm there, 'Sorcha, this is, like, madness,' except I know there's no point in trying to talk her out of it.

Ten minutes later, we're standing at the bottom of Marine Road as the crowd comes towards us, the old man at the front with a giant, hippo turd of a cigor wedged between his teeth.

Sorcha runs out onto the road and goes, 'Chorles, you have to stop this!'

And he's like, 'Who's that?'

'It's Sorcha,' she goes, 'as in, like, your *daughter*-in-law?'

'Oh, I'll not be stopping anything!' he goes. 'Not until *they* stop sundering our economy and curtailing our personal freedoms to try to force us to take a vaccine that will allow them access to our innermost thoughts.'

'You've lost your mind, Chorles! You've lost your actual mind!'

But, as we pass Scrumdiddly's, Sorcha suddenly stops walking. She's like, 'Wait!' at the same time throwing her orm across my chest.

I'm there, 'What's wrong?'

'My phone just beeped,' she goes, 'to tell me that we've reached the edge of our five K limit,' and all we can do is stand by helplessly as the old man leads his supporters in the direction of town.

He looks back over his shoulder at us and goes, 'I think you'll find *you're* the one who's lost her mind, Sorcha!'


## 'Ross, you're not listening to me! I've been kidnapped!'
### *The Irish Times*, 17 April 2021

So I'm sitting in front of the TV when the old dear rings and storts literally *screaming* down the phone at me?

She's going, 'Ross, help me! I don't know where I am! I don't know where I am!'

At first I think nothing of it. Monday night is her Morgarita Night and she's been warned a dozen times about mixing tequila with her androgenic alopecia meds.

'Yeah,' I go, 'I'm sort of, like *busy* here?' because I'm rewatching Leinster versus the Exeter Chiefs and taking a few notes, just for my own records. 'Just stick your head under the cold tap for fifteen minutes and stay away from the stairs.'

But then she says *the* most random thing. 'Ross,' she goes, 'you're not listening to me! I've been kidnapped!'

I'm like, 'What?'

'Oh, you heard me right, Ross! Kidnapped!'

'Yeah, how much have you had tonight – rounding down to the nearest litre?'

'I haven't been drinking! Although I won't deny I need one right now!'

'You're saying *kidnapped*?'

'Yes, Ross, kidnapped!'

'And why are you ringing me and not the old man?'

'Because I'm going to need you to handle the negotiations at your end. Your father will fall to absolute pieces when he finds out.'

'Yeah, no problem. And don't worry, I won't go above ten grand for you.'

She goes, 'Ross, will please stop making jokes?' and then she suddenly bursts into tears. And that's when I remember that she's not actually *at* home at the moment. She's in, like, Kosovo, seeing the plastic surgeon slash organ trafficker who I recently heard her describe on *Ireland AM* as 'my rock'.

'Hang on,' I go, 'you're actually serious, aren't you?'

She's like, 'Yes, I'm actually serious.'

'Okay, well, just stay calm.'

'How can I stay calm?' she pretty much roars at me. 'I'm being held against my will in this ghastly . . . *ghastly* place!'

'Okay,' I go, remembering all the Liam Neeson movies I've seen in my time, 'is there a window in the room?'

'Yes, there's a window.'

'Right, make your way over to it.'

'It's no good, Ross, it's blacked out.'

'Blacked out?'

'Oh, my mistake – it's just dork out! God, I can't tell if it's day or night in this horrible prison!'

'Are you looking out?'

'Yes, I'm looking out.'

'What do you see?'

'There's a motorway.'

'Right.'

'With cors on it.'

'Okay, what else do you see?'

'Trees.'

'Describe the trees to me.'

'They're Sitka spruce.'

'Right, I don't know why I even asked that question. Can you, like, *open* the window?'

She goes, 'Yes, I think so. Hold on. No, it doesn't open!' and she suddenly storts losing her shit again. 'It doesn't open, Ross! I'm trapped! I'm trapped here like a bloody well rat!'

'Okay, try and keep it together, okay? I need you calm.'

'Wait a minute,' she goes, 'there's someone out there,' and then I can hear her hammering away on the window, going, 'Help! Help! Can you hear me? Please help me! I've been abducted!' and then there's, like, more tears. 'Why can't they hear me, Ross? Why can't they hear me?'

I'm like, 'Listen to me! Mom, listen to me!'

She suddenly stops shrieking.

'You never call me Mom,' she goes.

And I'm there, 'Well, I'm calling you Mom now. And I'm asking you to keep your shit together, okay?'

'Okay.'

'We're going to solve this like it's a puzzle. I've seen all the *Taken* movies, bear in mind, and I'm watching the TV series on illegal download.'

'Please just get me out of here!'

'Okay, can you describe the room for me?'

'I did – I said it was ghastly.'

'I'm possibly going to need *more* than that?'

'The walls are – oh, I can't even find the words. And I'm a writer.'

'Yeah, you're definitely pushing it now, but I'm going to let that one go, given the circs. Are they, like, dungeon walls?'

'Worse.'

'Worse?'

'They're . . .'

'Go on.'

'They're magnolia.'

'Jesus.'

'It's the colour they slap on the walls in an asylum. It's making me think of my mother.'

'What else can you see?'

'There's an L. S. Lowry painting on the wall. It's not an original either – it's a focking . . . *print*.'

'Keep talking – you're doing great.'

'There's a bed.'

'Describe it to me.'

'I don't even want to *think* about who might have slept in it. The top sheet is a sort of garish orange colour. Oh, I can already feel one of my migraines coming on!'

'Keep going. There's bound to be a clue that tells us something.'

'There's a kettle.'

'A kettle? What kind of kettle are we talking here?'

'A little plastic one. There's some little sachets of – good God! – freeze-dried coffee and – Jesus! – individually wrapped tea bags. And this looks like . . . oh, where is the humanity?'

'What is it?'

'I don't want to touch it!'

'Mom, what is it?'

'It's UHT, Ross.'

As slow as I am off the mork, I think that's the moment when the penny storts to *finally* drop?

'There's some tiny cups here as well,' she goes, 'that look like they wouldn't hold more than a mouthful. And a pack of three biscuits. Bourbon creams, it says on the wrapping, but they don't taste of bourbon at all.'

I'm there, 'When did you arrive back in Ireland?'

'About two hours ago,' she goes. 'They're saying I have to stay here for two weeks, Ross! Two bloody well weeks!'

'Yeah, you knew about the whole quarantine thing before you went away.'

'I just presumed that when it came to it, it wouldn't affect people like us. That's why I'm asking you to handle the negotiations. There must be *someone* we can give some money to.'

'Who?'

'Oh, come on, Ross, there's *always* someone we can give some money to.'

'Not this time. They seem to be taking it seriously.'

'Well, can't you ask that son of yours to phone in a bomb warning?'

'You want Ronan to ring up and make a fake bomb warning?'

'Yes, like he phoned one to Foxrock Golf Club the night Penelope Mangan challenged my Lady Captaincy over an honest mistake I made on a scorecord.'

I'm there, 'I'm hanging up on you now.'

'Ross, please,' she goes, 'I can't stay here for two weeks. These people who have me are sadists! There's a fridge in this room with no alcohol in it!'

But I'm just like, 'Goodbye.'

'As a politician, Ross, I'm fully entitled
to a public view and a private view!'
*The Irish Times*, 24 April 2021

They're porked the whole length of Brighton Road – we're talking BMW X5s of every colour. You'd never know there was, like, a global *pandemic* on?

The old man is surprised to see me at the door – although shocked is possibly more the word?

'Kicker!' he goes, quickly closing it over, so that he's suddenly talking to me through a gap about an inch wide. 'What a lovely surprise?'

I'm there, 'What are you doing?'

'Well, we're all supposed to be social distancing, aren't we? None of wants to catch this – quote, unquote – *thing*!'

'Er, I thought you didn't believe it even *was* a thing?'

'That's a slight misrepresentation, Ross. I said it was created in a laboratory with a view to inducing moral panic on a global scale and preparing the planet for a totalitarian world government! It's hordly the same thing!'

'Well, either way, I need to talk to you about the old dear.'

'What about her?'

'Er, she's being held hostage in a so-called stylish budget hotel on, like, a *motorway*?'

'Oh, yes! Awful, awful business!'

'It's got two focking stors,' I pretty much roar at him. 'She's living on chicken Kiev and chips and little screw-top bottles of Sauvignon blanc!'

He's there, 'This is the new world order, Ross! People treated like dangerous subversives for the simple act of travelling abroad! Policemen looking in your shopping bags and asking if your lamb cutlets were necessary! It's no wonder fear stalks this once great land!'

'Why aren't you doing something about it? The woman's ringing me, like, twenty times a day.'

'Hennessy and I will be in the High Court on Tuesday!'

'Tuesday? Her quarantine will be nearly over by then.'

'The wheels of justice move slowly, Kicker – if they move at all!'

'Are you not going to ask me in?'

'It's, em, not a good time, I'm afraid.'

I go, 'What are you up to?' and I give the door a firm nudge with my shoulder, sending him staggering backwards into the hallway.

I can hear voices in the gaff – we're talking a *lot* of voices?

I'm like, 'Does this have something to do with all those cors being porked out there?'

I head for the living room with him running after me, going, 'Ross, it really isn't a convenient time!'

I give that door a serious shove as well. The room ends up being full of all his dickhead mates. We're talking Aurelius Burke. We're talking Gordon Greenhalgh. We're talking Ambrose Rahilly.

If you set off a bomb in this room, you wouldn't see a sheepskin coat at Leopardstown this Christmas.

'The fock *is* this?' I go, asking the obvious question.

'If you must know,' the old man goes, 'it's a vaccine porty!'

'A vaccine porty?'

'Yes, a chap Hennessy knows was able to get his hands on some – left over at the end of the day, etcetera, etcetera!'

'What, so you're having brandy and cigors, followed by –'

'That's right! Aurelius is going to do the necessary, what with him being a qualified medical practitioner!'

'Isn't he, like, a horse vet?'

'Oh, it's just an injection, Ross! Although between you and me, he's not exactly happy about all of this! But, as the only eyewitness to his 1987 hole-in-one, commemorated on the board in Portmornock Golf Club, I threatened to tell the truth – that we'd made the entire thing up with drink taken!'

I'm there, 'Can you not see that this whole thing is – and it's a not phrase that I'd usually use – but morally *wrong*?'

'Oh, don't bring morals into it, Ross! Look around you! In this room are some of the most important people in Ireland! You don't honestly believe they should stand at the back of some bloody well line while those idiots in Leinster House try to figure out their left foot from their right, do you?'

'Hang on, you don't even believe in the vaccine. Isn't New Republic's position that the government is using it to read people's thoughts?'

'As a politician, Ross, I'm fully entitled to a public view and a private view!'

There's, like, a ring on the doorbell then, followed by a shout from Hennessy of 'The focking Guards are outside!'

How many times have I heard him say those words over the years?

Of course, it causes, like, *panic* in the room? Like the dude said, these are important people with a lot to lose.

'Stay calm,' the old man goes, 'and remain quiet! I shall deal with our friends!'

I follow him out to the front door. He opens it a crack and goes, 'What do you want?'

I hear some dude in a – not being racist – but country accent go, 'There's a lot of BMWs parked on the road out there.'

'Well, you're not in Leitrim any more,' the old man goes, 'or whatever rain-sodden grief hole you originally hail from.'

He can be alright sometimes, my old man.

'We're looking for Fionnuala O'Carroll-Kelly,' I hear the dude go. 'She absconded from her Mandatory Hotel Quarantine this morning.'

'I wouldn't blame her! Chicken Kievs? This government has a bloody well nerve! She's not here if that's what you're implying!'

All of a sudden I hear what would have to be described as a kerfuffle coming from the downstairs jacks. I hear shouting and banging and flushing.

The dudes at the door obviously hear this too because one of them goes, 'May we come in?'

The old man's like, 'No, you bloody well can't! They may not have taught you the finer points of Constitutional Law in Templemore, but if you wish to search my home, you will obtain a warrant,' before literally slamming the door in their faces.

I follow him down the hallway to the jacks then. Hennessy and six or seven others are standing outside, pounding on the door, shouting, 'Open this door now!'

The old man's there, 'Was it the cheese you ate, chaps?'

But Hennessy goes, 'Aurelius took fright. He didn't want to be caught in the same house as the vaccines. He's flushed the bloody lot.'

The old man just sighs, then goes, 'Pop upstairs, Ross! I'm sure your mother would love to see you!'

'If they're playing with shit players week in,
week out, they'll drag them down to their level.'
*The Irish Times, 8 May 2021*

So it's, like, Sunday evening and I'm sitting at the kitchen table, staring at my Maths homework, but unable to think about anything except Leinster versus La Rochelle.

Honor looks over my shoulder.

She goes, 'Oh my God, Dad, you've been sitting there for two hours and you haven't done a tap.'

I'm there, 'I'm just thinking about the match, Honor – replaying the second half in my head over and over again.'

'Dad, you've got a month to go until the Leaving Cert. You need to forget about rugby.'

I laugh – the very idea of it. And that's when my phone suddenly pings and I end up reading a WhatsApp message that tears me from my unhappy trance. It's from, like, Rob Railton, my sons' rugby coach, and it's like, 'Great news! Outdoor sporting activities can resume again! You'll see in the attached list that all of the kids have been divided into pods of ten for the return to rugby. Each pod has been assigned a bib colour. Please let me know if you would like your child switched to a different group.'

I open the attachment and I scan the list, looking for Brian, Johnny and Leo's names. It turns out they're in the Green group, along with –

'Fock it,' I go.

Honor's like, 'What's wrong?'

'Rob's put the boys in with *the* worst players. Henry Franks, the Bellamy boys and Adam Cotter's son.'

'But they're friends with Charlie Cotter,' Honor tries to go. 'And the Bellamy boys.'

I'm there, 'Rugby's not about making friends,' pointing out the obvious. 'If they're playing with shit players week in, week out, they'll drag them down to their level.'

I stand at the bottom of the stairs and I shout, 'Johnny, Brian, Leo – ice cream!'

Suddenly, the three of them come chorging out of their room and down the stairs like a landslide.

'Where's the focking ice cream?' Johnny goes, looking around the kitchen.

I'm like, 'There's no ice cream. I just said that to get you downstairs,' because I could write the book on parenting. 'Sit down there.'

'You focking dickhead,' Brian goes – five years old, bear in mind! – as they each take a seat at the table.

I'm there, 'Who's that kid at rugby who everyone says is going to play for Ireland one day? He did that skills thing on TikTok that supposedly went *viral*?'

'Hugo Blake-Fox,' Leo goes.

I'm there, 'Hugo! Blake! Fox! God, he already sounds like a Leinster academy player!'

'We focking hate him!' Leo goes. 'He's a knob!'

I'm there, 'Well, hate him or not, you're going to be in the same pod as him,' and I stort scanning the list, looking for his name. 'There he is – on the Blue team.'

I send Rob a message, going, 'Hey Dude, can you move Brian,

Johnny and Leo to Blue? They're already in a pod with one or two kids in it in school,' that last bit being total horseshit.

Rob comes back straight away and goes, 'That's cool, Ross. Would anyone in Blue like to move to another group to accommodate the O' Carroll-Kelly boys?'

Honor's there, 'Dad, I really do think they'd prefer to be with Charlie Cotter and the Bellamys.'

'Charlie Cotter hides from the ball,' I go. 'And Conor Bellamy walks off the pitch crying to his old dear every time he gets tackled.'

'Conor Bellamy is my friend!' Brian goes, like this should somehow *mean* something to me?

My phone storts pinging away then. Mervyn Vesey says he'd be happy to move Gus to the Red group. Rioghnach Riley says she'd like to move Linus to the Yellow group. And Dee Dalton says she'd like to move Clive to the Orange group.

'Okay, that's three,' I go. But then I'm like, 'Fock!' because James Blake-Fox then sends a message saying he'd like to move Hugo to the Black group because he's already in a pod with three of the boys in it in school.

'Let me guess,' Honor goes. 'Hugo moved.'

I'm there, 'I wasn't expecting that. Okay, I'm trying to think strategically here – what's the play?'

Honor's like, 'Why don't you just let them be with their friends?'

'Because they'll hold them back, Honor. Look, I knew players –*good* players – whose parents sent them to the likes of Wesley College and Andrew's. And yes, they grew up to be happy, well-adjusted people with successful careers and stable relationships. But guess what they achieved in rugby?'

'What?'

'Let's just say the words "fock-all" aren't far from this conversation.'

My phone pings again. Angela Bellamy says she'd like to move Conor and Noah to Blue because they're already in a pod with the O' Carroll-Kellys in school. Then Adam Cotter says he'd like to move Charlie to Blue as well, because he's a nervous kid who doesn't make friends easily, and he already knows Brian, Johnny and Leo from their time in Montessori.

I'm thinking Leinster might never win another European Cup again if this is what parents in this port of the world consider a priority.

I type in, 'Dude, on second thoughts, could I move Brian, Johnny and Leo to Black, as I've just realized they're in a pod with a few heads in that group as well.'

Again, I'm just spinning him a line.

'Okay,' Rob goes, 'but we've got thirteen in the Black group now. Would anyone in Black like to move to another group?'

Straight away, Sandrine Nagle says Cian would like to move to Red – which is no real loss. The kid is useless. Luke Lister says Dylan would also like to move to Red because he and Cian are – again, this word keeps cropping up – *friends*? Then Oliver Urch says Sebastian would like to move to Yellow because – get this – his *cousin* is in that group.

I'm there, 'I weep for the future of the game when I see the attitude of some of the parents on here. Still, all's well that ends –'

But that's when my phone pings again. It's James Blake-Fox, saying he wants to move Hugo to Orange – no reason given.

I'm like, 'Hugo's on the move again! What the literally fock?'

Honor's there, 'Have you thought that maybe Hugo's dad is thinking strategically as *well*?'

I'm like, 'What are you talking about, Honor?'

And then she says it – the words that every South Dublin parent dreads. She goes, 'Maybe your kids are rubbish at rugby.'

## 'I specifically moved them into the Blue pod so they could play with Hugo, but you moved Hugo into Black.'
### *The Irish Times, 15 May 2021*

The pork is packed and the air filled with the excited chatter of kids who are just happy to be back playing rugby again. They've all been sorted into, like, pods and they're flinging those Gilberts around like the pandemic never even happened.

All eyes are on Hugo Blake-Fox, who's the most talented kid I've seen with a rugby ball since – let's be honest here – *me*? He's, like, bombing around the pitch, evading tackles, selling dummies and burning off all the other kids with his pace.

'A great little player, isn't he?' Morcus Bellamy – the father of two boys in my children's pod – goes. 'His dad put €1,000 on him at odds of 1,000 to 1 that he'll play for Ireland by the age of twenty-one.'

And I'm like, 'Money in the bank, Morcus. Money – in the bank.'

Meanwhile, I'm looking at my own kids. It's no wonder Hugo's old man didn't want them in his son's pod. Johnny is picking his nose and eating it, Brian is talking to a ladybird that he picked up off the ground and Leo is walking around in circles, singing 'Baby Shork' to himself.

'Okay,' I go, clapping my hands together, 'Brian, let the ladybird go! Johnny, the finger buffet is closed! Let's play some actual rugby!'

'Just before we do,' Morcus goes, 'wearing my Covid Supervisor hat here, can I ask to see your signed confirmation, Ross, that all of the answers you gave in response to the health questionnaire at the stort of the year are still correct as of today?'

I'm there, 'I showed you the screenshot, Morcus.'

'Did you?'

'Er, it was, like, five *minutes* ago? In the actual *cor* pork?'

'I remember you showing me a video of an elephant playing cricket.'

'And then afterwards I showed you the confirmation form.'

'Well, I'd like to see it again.'

And I'm there, 'But I left my phone in the cor,' because there's, like, no pockets in the shorts I'm wearing, which is one of the reasons they're so flattering.

'I'm sorry,' he goes, 'it's for everyone's safety.'

So I end up having no choice but to head back to the cor to grab my phone. As I'm walking back again, I notice Hugo Blake-Fox play this unbelievable no-look, one-handed pass to one of the other kids in his pod. All of the mums and dads watching stort clapping and I'm thinking about how much Brian, Johnny and Leo could benefit from playing with someone of his ability.

When I arrive back, my three sons are rolling around on the ground, thumping the heads off each other. None of the other parents in our pod is saying a word to them. I flash my phone at Morcus, then I go to break up the fight. It's like separating frozen sausages – there's a fair bit of pulling and twisting involved, but I finally manage to get my fingers between them and snap them aport.

'Okay,' Morcus goes, finally satisfied. 'Like Ross said, let's play some rugby. And remember, boys, make sure you pass to everyone – don't leave anyone out.'

I'm like, 'Excuse me?' and I can hear the actual disbelief in my voice. 'What did you just say?'

'It's important,' he goes – and I'm giving you this word for word, 'that all of the boys get to hold the ball for an equal amount of time.'

I'm like, 'It's not pass the porcel, Morcus. It's the first principle of rugby – you get the ball to the flair players and let them do their thing.'

'They never pass the ball to my son,' Susan Franks, mother of Henry, suddenly pipes up.

I'm there, 'Well, he's hordly a flair player, is he? He drops the ball every time someone is dumb enough to give it to him.'

'Calm down, Ross,' Morcus goes, trying to make out that I'm one of those pushy rugby dads you hear about. 'We don't want to discourage them by denying them the ball.'

I'm there, 'Rugby is not just about having the ball. You can have the game of your life without ever touching it.'

'I think it's fairer,' Adam Cotter – one of the other dads – goes, 'if everyone gets to have a little hold.'

'Sorry,' I suddenly hear myself go, 'have any of you ever coached at the highest level?'

The answer in all three cases is an obvious no, but they all just look at each other, mystified as to why that should stop them passing on ideas that could destroy my children's development as players.

I'm there, 'I recently coached Pres Bray to their first Leinster Schools Senior Cup win since 1932 and I also coached at international level with Andorra. I shouldn't have to read out my CV to you people.'

'Well, if you've done all the coaching that you *say* you've done,' Susan Franks goes, 'then you should know that everyone needs to have a go of the ball.'

I hear a cheer behind me and then a round of applause. Hugo is working his magic again. That's it, I think. I turn on my heel and I morch straight over to James Blake-Fox, his old man.

I'm there, 'Would you mind if my boys joined this pod? They're with a bunch of losers over there.'

He goes, 'They're supposed to stick to their appointed groups – health and safety,' and he won't even look at me.

I'm like, 'What's your problem? I specifically moved them into the Blue pod so they could play with Hugo, but you moved Hugo into Black. Then I moved my boys to Black and you moved Hugo to Orange. What, do you think they'll drag his standard down?'

'That had nothing to do with rugby,' he goes.

I'm like, 'So why are you so determined to keep him away from Brian, Johnny and Leo?'

'Because they're the most badly behaved children I've ever met,' he goes.

I notice one or two other dads nodding in agreement.

He's like, 'They swear, they spit, they're violent.'

I look over my shoulder and I notice that the three of them are rolling around on the ground again, killing each other.

'So it has absolutely nothing to do with them being shit at rugby?' I go.

He's like, 'No, it's because they're little thugs.'

'Thank God for that,' I go, a smile breaking out across my face. 'Thank God for that.'

Then – proud dad – I tip back over and try to pull them aport again.

## 'You were, like, four days from the end of your quarantine. Why don't you just agree to go back?' *The Irish Times, 29 May 2021*

I watch the old dear totter into court in her high heels, sunnies perched on top of her head, a scowl of disapproval on her face, like she's ordered a Tom Collins and she can tell from the smell that the borman has stinted on the gin.

It'd be impossible not to feel sorry for the woman.

I'm remembering the night a few years ago when she invited me around to watch the final of *The Big Painting Challenge* and she phoned for a takeaway for, like, *literally* the first time in her life? When I got to the gaff, she had the Deliveroo courier in the kitchen, plating the food, polishing the glasses and recommending an off-dry Alsace Riesling to pair with the chicken Jalfrezi.

She genuinely thought it was some sort of dial-a-waiter crowd. I think she tipped the dude, like, a grand in the end. Then – delighted with the service, if not the way he dressed – she ended up using him for all of her porties for, like, years afterwards, basically paying for his studies to become a sommelier.

The point I'm making is that the woman hasn't a clue what's going on half the time. She shouldn't even be allowed out in the world. Literally, as it happens. I mean, that's why she's *in* court this morning – chorged with unlawfully leaving Mandatory Hotel Quarantine under the Health Act 2021.

'Thank you for coming,' she goes.

I'm there, 'Put your mask on, will you? You're only making things worse for yourself.'

'But I've just had my make-up done.'

'Hey, a mask would hide your five o'clock shadow just as well as the two pounds of foundation you pay them to trowel on your face.'

She thinks about this for a few seconds, then she whips her mask out of her pocket and she puts it on.

I'm there, 'Why does everything have to be a major production with this family?'

She's like, 'What on Earth are you talking about?'

'This,' I go. 'You in court. Sauntering in here like it's the Veuve Clicquot tent in Taste of Dublin.'

'Hennessy thought I should look my best. You know, many, many moons ago, the judge invited me to the UCD Law Ball.'

'And did you go?'

'No, I turned him down. But for years afterwards, he wrote me long letters telling me how much he desired me.'

Seriously, I'm right on the point of spewing here.

'You were, like, four days from the end of your quarantine,' I go. 'Why don't you just agree to go back?'

She's there, 'I would rather spend the next twelve months of my life in prison than endure one more night in a limited services hotel, Ross.'

'You're being used – you know that, don't you?'

'Used? By whom?'

'Er, by the old man and *Hennessy*? They're trying to turn you into a mortyr for their anti-lockdown cause.'

Suddenly, I spot Hennessy glowering at me from, like, ten feet away. He's there, 'I must have missed the bit where you got your Practising Certificate from the Law Society, did I?'

I'm like, 'Excuse me?'

'You're not qualified to give out legal advice. Fionnuala, come with me – and open another button on that blouse.'

It's, like, an hour before the old dear's case is finally called. Then Hennessy gets up and does what Hennessy does.

He's like, 'Judge, this is a very unfortunate case, involving a woman from an excellent background, who returned from a brief trip abroad, only to find herself forced to submit to a form of civil detention. My client intends to sue the state for infringing her right to liberty and freedom of movement.'

'Guaranteed under the Constitution of Ireland!' the old man shouts from the back of the public gallery. 'Nineteen hundred and thirty-seven!'

'That is not a matter for this court,' the judge goes, barely even looking up. 'Your client accepts that she left Mandatory Hotel Quarantine, an offence for which the penalties are clear.'

Hennessy's there, 'Judge, my client was being detained in conditions that would shock even Amnesty International – namely, a so-called no-frills hotel, catering for business people travelling on a tight budget. After ten days of detention, and symptom-free, she exercised her right under the United Nations Declaration of Human Rights to leave. Since then, she has taken a Covid-19 test and has tested negative for the alleged virus. And yet, for reasons of vindictiveness, the state is attempting to force her return to the hotel to face, well, God knows what horrors.'

'Single-ply toilet paper,' the old dear goes.

The judge's head instantly shoots up and he looks at the old dear for the first time.

'Single-ply?' he goes and it's obvious that he suddenly recognizes the woman behind the mask. 'How . . . awful for you.'

'It's not in any way absorbent,' the old dear goes. 'It just sort of spreads the mess around a wider area.'

The dude's like, 'Yes, of course – it would, wouldn't it?'

She's there, 'They only gave us one roll per day too.'

And hearing her voice, it's as if all the years since they last saw each other suddenly fall away.

'It sounds like you've had quite the ordeal,' the dude goes, looking at her all gooey-eyed. 'Been through the proverbial mill – em, Fionnuala.'

She's like, 'There wasn't even a turn-down service, Judge. I shall be having flashbacks for as long as I live.'

'We will be seeking damages for Post-Traumatic Stress Disorder!' Hennessy goes.

The judge is, like, red in the face. I still find it incredible that anyone could find the rubber-faced horse-beast even *remotely* attractive? But there's no accounting for taste, I suppose.

'Mandatory Hotel Quarantine is not a prison sentence,' the dude goes. 'It's a preventative measure aimed at stopping the spread of Covid-19, for which, em, Fionnuala has tested negative. I don't see what public interest is served by sending this woman – clearly a person of exceptional character and, as you say, from an excellent background – back into this fearful budget hotel that has been described in such harrowing terms here today. Neither do I see this as a case in which the penalties provided by the legislation should apply. I'm dismissing this case. Fionnuala, you may leave this court without a stain on your character.'

'A rare voice of reason,' the old man shouts, 'in a country sliding inexorably into Fascism! Exclamation mork, exclamation mork, exclamation mork!'

## 'Everyone has forgotten how to, like, talk to each other?'
### *The Irish Times*, 19 June 2021

'I'm getting the vaccine on Wednesday,' Claire from Bray of all places goes, like this is an achievement, something worthy of a high-five or even a 'Fock, yeah!'

Sophie's like, 'Which one are you getting?'

'Pfizer,' Claire goes – again, inviting us to weigh in with the 'atta-girl's. I say nothing and just switch on the borbecue.

'The woman I do my online PT with ,' Amie with an ie goes, 'was told she was getting AstraZeneca – she showed me the text and it *literally* said AstraZeneca – but when she turned up it ended up being, like, *Moderna*?'

'Are you talking about Líadan?' Chloe goes. 'Because she actually got the *Pfizer* one? Because I remember saying to her, "Oh my God, my sister got the Pfizer one! They could be, like, vaccine buddies!" '

Sorcha sidles up to me. 'Ross,' she goes, out of the corner of her mouth, 'this is a disaster.'

I'm like, 'What is?'

'This,' she goes, meaning presumably the first gathering of her friends since all the madness storted. 'Everyone has forgotten how to, like, *talk* to each other?'

I listen again – except more closely this time.

Claire is like, 'How are your parents coping with the whole thing, Chloe?'

'My *parents*?' Chloe goes.

'Yeah – as in, have they been vaccinated yet?'

'Er, my mom, like, passed away in 2010 and my dad in, like, 2015?'

'Oh my God, I totally forgot!'

'Yeah, no, it's fine.'

'I literally can't believe I asked you that.'

'Honestly, it's cool, Claire.'

'I was actually *at* their funerals. Well, the second one. I had my driving test the morning of your mom's funeral and I just showed my face in Fitzpatrick's afterwards.'

Sorcha looks at me again. She's like, 'See what I mean?'

I'm there, 'The girl's from Bray, Sorcha. If she dropped her kacks and crimped one off in the Caprese salad, no one would be in the least bit surprised.'

'No, I read about this,' she goes. 'There was an orticle in, like, the *New Yorker* – by either a psychiatrist or a psychologist – and they said that after a year of basically not interacting with people outside our immediate family circle, we all need to, like, relearn basic social and *conversational* skills?'

I'm there, 'I still say you're overthinking it, Sorcha.'

'I'm not overthinking it, Ross. We've been here for, like, an hour and no one can talk about anything that isn't, like, *pandemic* related?'

'Okay,' I go, 'I'll tell you what I'm prepared to do. I'll pop into the gaff now and throw on my nudey lady borbecue apron.'

She's there, 'What nudey lady borbecue apron?' because she tends to blank out memories that she finds traumatic.

'Er, the one I wore to that surprise porty we threw for your old pair's fortieth *wedding* anniversary? You took it off me because you said it made Father Glackin feel uncomfortable. And because there were children present.'

She goes, 'You mean the one with the big –'

'The very one, Sorcha. The very one.'

'But how is that going to help?'

'It'll clear the conversational blockage. Trust me on this one.'

Sorcha stares at her friends. I can tell she's conflicted.

Claire goes, 'So do you have *any* elderly relatives who are in, like, the at-risk category?'

'I have, like, a grand-aunt,' Chloe goes. 'She lives in Duleek.'

'Jesus – and has *she* had the vaccine yet?'

'I presume so.'

'Oh my God, that must be such a relief to you.'

'Yeah, no, *such* a relief – even though I've only seen her, like, twice since the Millennium.'

Sorcha looks at me and takes a deep breath. 'It's at the bottom of my underwear drawer,' she goes. 'Be quick, Ross.'

Thirty seconds later, I'm pulling the thing out of Sorcha's – like she said – knicker drawer. I originally bought it as a wedding present for a dude who was on my Sports and Exercise Management Course in UCD, but it made me laugh so much that I ended up keeping it and regifting him one of the three NutriBullets I got for Christmas the previous year.

I put it on over my head, then I tie the straps at the back. I take a look at myself in Sorcha's full-length mirror and I crack up laughing for a good, like, thirty seconds. It really *is* that funny.

I tip downstairs, then out to the back gorden again.

Sophie is going, 'By the way, did I tell you that my mom is looking for a new cleaner?'

'Oh my God,' Amie with an ie goes, 'what happened to Wiktoria?'

'She says she's decided to take some time out for herself. But according to Mom, she can make more money from the PUP than she can for actually *working*?'

'That's a disgrace,' Chloe goes. 'A *total* disgrace?'

I clear my throat to try to get everyone's attention. I'm like, 'Ahem!' except nobody even looks at me.

'Has your mom been vaccinated yet?' Amie with an ie goes.

Sophie's like, 'Yeah, it was *such* a relief.'

'Which one did she get?' Claire from Bray of all places goes.

Sophie's there, 'Moderna.'

'Moderna?' Claire from Bray of all places goes. 'Oh my God, she is *literally* the only person I know who's had the Moderna vaccine.'

'So random,' Chloe agrees. 'So, so random.'

'Is it, like, two shots or one.'

'It's, like, two, but the interval between the two shots is either longer or shorter than the Pfizer one.'

I feel a nudge in my back. Sorcha wants me to say something.

'Anyone fancy a sausage?' I hear myself go.

All eyes suddenly turn to me. And I watch a dozen faces suddenly drop.

'Oh my God,' Sophie goes, 'that is *so* inappropriate!'

Chloe's like, 'How can you think it's okay to wear something like that in the current climate?'

Claire from Bray of all places shakes her head. 'No offence, Sorcha,' she goes, 'but remind me again, *how* did you end up marrying him?'

'By the way,' Chloe goes, 'did I tell you I'm back texting Pete with no neck who played loosehead for Lansdowne's thirds?'

'Oh my God, random!' Sophie goes, the blockage well and truly cleared now.

And Sorcha gives me a look so full of love that I can't even describe it to you. All I will say is that, after pushing on for nearly twenty years of marriage, I hope the rest of you get that lucky.

## 'I have to say, it's a boost to the old ego to see how well I look compared to some of the other yokes here.'
### *The Irish Times*, 26 June 2021

A dude in a fluorescent yellow bib asks me if I have ID.

And I go, 'My face is my ID!' a line I always use in these situations. I don't know why. It's never actually worked.

So I hand him my passport. He opens it, stares at my name and goes, 'Ross O'Carroll . . . *Kenny*, is it?'

'Kelly,' I go. 'You're obviously not a rugby fan.'

'Not really, no.'

'Well, if you'd been in this stadium on Paddy's Day in 1999, you'd know who I was.'

'Why, what happened?'

'Er, I only led Castlerock College to victory in the Leinster Schools Senior Cup. Actually, I got an injection in the stadium that day as well. It's why they took the medal from me.'

The dude hands me back my passport – along with some kind of, like, *information* leaflet? – and tells me to keep moving.

So inside I go and I join the queue for the escalator. I'm looking around me at all the other – yeah, no – forty-one-year-old men, with their grey hair, pot bellies and receding hairlines and I'm thinking how well I look by comparison.

That's when I notice a girl – we're talking five or six people ahead of me in the queue – looking over her shoulder at me. It's a long time since I've caught anyone checking me out, what with the whole mask thing, and it's nice to know that women still find me attractive, even from the nose up and the chin down.

'Asshole!' she goes.

I'm like, 'Excuse me?'

She pulls down her mask to let me see her face. It's Desdemona Lyons. We had one or two scenes together back in my UCD days. The last time I saw her, she was screaming at me that I ruined her life. Which was an exaggeration, of course. I ruined her twenty-first.

I'm like, 'Desdemona, how the hell are you?'

She smiles at me and goes, 'I'm actually amazing. Married to Rob for eight years now. He plays golf off a five handicap. Two gorgeous, gorgeous kids. House in Ranelagh.'

'A five handicap?' I go. 'I'm tempted to say fair focks.'

'How are you?'

'Yeah, no, I'm in top form. I have to say, it's a boost to the old ego to see how well I look compared to some of the other yokes here.'

This line doesn't go down well with the rest of the queue. I don't know why I thought it would.

'You know, looking back,' she goes, as she steps onto the escalator, 'you trying to get off with my mom at my twenty-first was the best thing that ever happened to me. Nice to see you, Ross.'

I'm like, 'Yeah, no, it's been great catching up, Desdemona.'

Fifteen minutes later, I'm still standing in the line as we slow-shuffle our way forwards. The queue snakes this way and that. There's suddenly a girl standing next to me except facing the other way.

'Ross?' she goes.

I'm like, 'Depends who's asking.'

'Joanne Dodd,' she goes.

Someone in the HSE hates me.

'Joanne Dodd?' I try to go. 'No, it's not ringing any bells.'

She's like, 'Holy Child Killiney? We did our Js together?'

People in the queue are actually laughing at this stage.

'In Ocean City,' I go. 'Yeah, no, it's all coming back to me now.'

She's there, 'You said you'd ring me. After we got back. Then I never heard from you again.'

'Jesus, that's, like, twenty years ago, Joanne. You'd want to stort thinking about maybe letting it go.'

The crowd here are really getting full value today.

'I heard you married Sorcha Lalor,' she goes.

I'm like, 'Yeah, no, I did.'

'Poor her. That's all I can say. Poor her.'

We keep shuffling forward until eventually I'm looking out onto the famous hallowed turf, where I did my thing back in the day. I end up getting a bit choked up when I see it. I really was an unbelievable player. It's a pity no one remembers *that* Ross O'Carroll-Kelly? All anyone remembers is the –

'Wanker!'

Oh, no. The news that I'm here has obviously passed up the line because another ghost of girlfriends past has come all the way back to tell me that I'm a –

'Complete and utter wanker!'

I'm like, 'Sorry, have we met?'

'I wouldn't expect you to remember my name, since you couldn't remember it at the time. But I've wanted to say this to you for, like, seven years. You're a piece of –'

'Yeah, no, that seems to be the consensus here today.'

'And by the way, you've massively disimproved with age, like all my friends said you would. The big, fat rugby head on you.'

This draws quite a lot of laughter from the men in the queue, who I suspect are still put out by my earlier comments. Then she turns on her heel and off she focks.

Twenty minutes later, I'm shown into a little cubicle. A dude asks me to confirm my name – again, it means nothing to him and you'd have to wonder how he even got the job – as well as my date of birth, then another dude tells me to roll up my sleeve and jabs me in the upper orm with a syringe.

Five minutes after that, I'm sitting in the recovery room, feeling a bit, I want to say, *nostalgish*? It's a combination of being back here and running into so many faces from my past.

I'm being talked about – and not in a good way. I can hear people going, 'The dude over there in the Leinster jersey – three exes! Can you imagine?'

Statistically, given my history, that's probably not that unusual.

'Ross O'Carroll-Kelly?' I suddenly hear a voice go.

I look up. There's a dude standing over me.

I'm like, 'Don't tell me. I was with your sister. Or your cousin. And I stood her up the night of her debs. Or I proposed to her and she never heard from me again.'

Again, there's a lot of laughter around me.

'I saw you play here,' he goes, 'in 1999.'

I'm like, 'What?'

'The schools cup final. Against Newbridge College. You ran the show. You were incredible.'

'I was incredible,' I go. 'And that's not me being big-headed.'

'Anyway, I just wanted to say it to you.'

Ten minutes later, I'm walking back up Lansdowne Road, with my shoulders back and my chin in the air, eighty per cent protected against Covid, but feeling one hundred per cent . . . invincible!

# Acknowledgements

A huge thank-you to all of my editors at the *Irish Times*, both past and present – Geraldine Kennedy, Kevin O'Sullivan and Paul O'Neill. Thank you to all my colleagues and former colleagues on the newspaper, especially Róisín Ingle, Peter Murtagh, Hugh Linehan, Orna Mulcahy, Rachel Collins, Pat Nugent, Kevin Courtney, Rosita Boland, Declan Conlon, Sheila Wayman, JJ Vernon, Liam Kavanagh and Brian Kilmartin. Thank you, as always, to my editor, Rachel Pierce, for all the hard work and good counsel you offered in choosing this selection. Thank you to Patricia Deevy, Michael McLoughlin, Cliona Lewis, Brian Walker, Carrie Anderson and all of the team at Sandycove, not only for getting behind this book, but for all the support you've given me over the last decade and a half. Enormous thanks to Faith O'Grady, the best agent in the busines. And thank you, as ever – though I'll never tire of saying it – to my family and my wonderful wife, Mary McCarthy.

# He just wanted a decent book to read ...

Not too much to ask, is it? It was in 1935 when Allen Lane, Managing Director of Bodley Head Publishers, stood on a platform at Exeter railway station looking for something good to read on his journey back to London. His choice was limited to popular magazines and poor-quality paperbacks – the same choice faced every day by the vast majority of readers, few of whom could afford hardbacks. Lane's disappointment and subsequent anger at the range of books generally available led him to found a company – and change the world.

*'We believed in the existence in this country of a vast reading public for intelligent books at a low price, and staked everything on it'*
**Sir Allen Lane, 1902–1970, founder of Penguin Books**

The quality paperback had arrived – and not just in bookshops. Lane was adamant that his Penguins should appear in chain stores and tobacconists, and should cost no more than a packet of cigarettes.

Reading habits (and cigarette prices) have changed since 1935, but Penguin still believes in publishing the best books for everybody to enjoy. We still believe that good design costs no more than bad design, and we still believe that quality books published passionately and responsibly make the world a better place.

So wherever you see the little bird – whether it's on a piece of prize-winning literary fiction or a celebrity autobiography, political tour de force or historical masterpiece, a serial-killer thriller, reference book, world classic or a piece of pure escapism – you can bet that it represents the very best that the genre has to offer.

**Whatever you like to read – trust Penguin.**